SWORDS IN THE SHADOWS

• A Swords & Sorcery Horror Anthology •

• Edited by Cullen Bunn •

Published by Outland Entertainment LLC
3119 Gillham Road
Kansas City, MO 64109

Publisher: Jeremy D. Mohler
Editor-in-Chief: Alana Joli Abbott
Chief Creative Officer: Anton Kromoff

ISBN: 978-1-954255-75-3
EBOOK ISBN: 978-1-954255-76-0
Worldwide Rights
Created in the United States of America

Editor: Cullen Bunn
Copyeditor: Scott Colby
Cover Illustration: Ann Marie Cochran
Cover & Interior Design: Jeremy D. Mohler

Printed and bound in the United States of America.

Visit outlandentertainment.com to see more, or follow us on our Facebook Page facebook.com/outlandentertainment/.

CONTENTS

OF SWORDS AND SHADOWS

An Introduction by Cullen Bunn

I'm not going to waste much of your time here. I know, I know. You feel the need to move with barbarian-like focus and efficiency, past the insidious obstacle of my words, to get to the treasure. The treasure, of course, being the stories that await within these pages. Like a cruel sorcerer, I've horded them for too long, kept them to myself, and now you must hack and slash your way to the trove.

If you'll indulge me, though, I thought I'd answer a question.

Why sword and sorcery *and* horror?

The answer is simple enough, I suppose, but let me start at the beginning.

"Let me tell you of the days of high adventure!"

My first excursions into the world of sword and sorcery scared the hell outta me.

At some point in my youth, while paging through a ratty, yellowed, dog-eared paperback (most likely purchased by my parents at a yard sale), I stumbled onto a tale of Conan's escapades. The cover of the book, I'm sure, featured a bronzed warrior, sword in hand, bravely facing down frost giants or apes or skull-faced enemies. The hero of the story! He feared nothing. And, so, neither should I, the reader! What a terrible trap!

I was at least passingly familiar with Conan. I'd read a few comics (also almost certainly purchased in a stack of comics from a yard sale) and I had a Mego Conan action figure (with that wild real hair hairdo). But I had never read one of Robert E. Howard's short stories.

My first, then, was "The Tower of the Elephant." Therein, Conan ventured into a strange and mysterious spire. He transgressed against sorcerers and encountered hideous idols from alien civilizations. He communed with an ageless, monstrous space traveler from eons long past. And that space traveler, this ancient astronaut, begged the square-jawed Cimmerian to carve out its heart.

Star-spanning horrors?

Self-mutilation?

Humanity, as insignificant as dust in the face of timeless entities?

The story terrified me. Deep down in my bones. Not only was it my first experience with sword and sorcery prose, it was my first brush with nihilistic cosmic dread.

I followed that tale with "The God in the Bowl," which also freaked me out with its multiple beheadings and weird, madness-inducing, human-faced serpents.

It was a hell of a double-feature introduction to Conan short stories.

Howard was an accomplished horror writer. His "Pigeons from Hell" is, to my way of thinking, one of the greatest horror yarns of all time. And that gift for frightening his readers comes through in the stories of his most famous creation again and again.

That's how it should be, right?

It's easy to forget, with all the slashing swords and scintillating sorceries, that the "age of high adventure" was not just perilous, not just harrowing. It must have been, even for the bravest of warriors, terrifying.

Fiendish monsters, diablerie most foul, shadow-haunted crypts, the undead, writhing and squirming entities, flesh-devouring ghouls, elder gods. Battle-axe in hand or not, Cullen the Freebooter would have been quaking in his leather sandals.

It wasn't long before I was introduced to the Dungeons and Dragons role-playing game. A friend in elementary school brought one of his older brother's adventure modules to lunch, Together, we poured over that book, fascinated by the art, by the very idea that we could create our own sword and sorcery heroes and send them on wild adventures.

While we sipped chocolate milk and ate sandwiches and Cheetos from our Marvel Superheroes lunchboxes, we became lost in a book full of vile deathtraps; four-armed gargoyles; and awful, jewel-eyed, soul-stealing skulls.

The title of the module was—you guessed it—*Tomb of Horrors*. My mind raced with nightmarish possibilities.

A couple of weeks later, my friend and I were actually playing the game. It's probably worth mentioning that the first module we actually played through was Castle Amber, which was inspired by the fantasy and (you guessed it) horror work of writer Clark Ashton Smith.

So... why sword and sorcery *and* horror?

For me, these genres have always been connected. Not even the mighty Cimmerian himself could hack the two apart.

This book, this anthology of horrific sword and sorcery stories, is the next step, then, in journey I embarked upon long, long ago. Here you will discover a murderer's row of amazingly talented writers who have delivered tales of heroes, anti-heroes, villains, monsters, demons, actin, humor, adventure... And horror.

Oh, the *horror*!

It was a great privilege to bring these stories together. A great honor. More than that, it was pure joy. The only thing better? The privilege and honor of presenting them all to you now.

I've kept them to myself long enough.

-- Cullen Bunn, 2023

The Atoll of Syrash

Wile E. Young

Montston Port, 1695

The sun was high, and it heated the rope around the necks of the doomed. The men of the Crown liked to soak the knots in the seawater here; I'd seen the redcoats at the edge of the ocean, running each hanging line through the surf.

The crows were waiting along with the seabirds, called in by tides and the steady drumbeat. The crowd cheered as the cart carrying the three condemned wheeled through the street. I watched it with my good eye just as I had watched them in the currents of the unseen world.

One of these men did not fear his death; he had fled my grasp and run to the noose. I watched Felton Marth grasp the wooden edge of the cart. I heard his footsteps on the gallows stairs, followed by the sentence of death.

"Felton Marth, Osier Hogan, and Glennie Tack. You have been sentenced to death under the law of his Majesty the King for crimes against the realm and the common good, the most egregious of which shall be read as follows: Piracy, Murder, Theft…"

The royal marine continued the list as I watched my quarry. His flight had not been kind. He wore rags that contrasted with the blue uniform of the soldier. His gaze was fixed on the shore. A sailor spent his whole life heading to Fiddler's

Green. Even when making port you wanted to go back to the ocean's embrace.

That was why the Crown hung the bodies of pirates on the rocks, just out of the tide's reach, a punishment for defiance. It was in my power to save him, but he had declared his resistance to my purpose. Now he would serve a different way. There was no escape in death. Not from me.

The speaker finished. "For these offenses, you are to be hung by the neck until you are dead. May God have mercy on your souls." This was a lie, though the speaker did not know it. God couldn't catch their souls before they fell into my waiting hands.

Felton looked over the crowd as the lever was pulled and he caught my gaze. He made to scream...then he was falling to the tune of breaking bones and jittering limbs.

I watched from the bay as they hung Felton and his companions from a beam on a rock outcropping. The sun baked against my scarred chest as I cast a line and waited for a fish, biding my time until night.

When the sun finally dipped below the horizon, I began to row, feeling the change in the wind. My mind conjured images of a black anchor hauled from the swells, bitter sails catching the wind, and the lighting of candles along a charred hull.

Hundreds of them.

My ship was coming, and I would chain Felton Marth's soul to it.

The waves took me under his body. I pulled my sword and climbed the small sail of my launch until I was face to face with Felton. His right eye had been torn from his skull by a passing gull, bloody, ragged strips of flesh pulled from the socket. His left had rolled up sightless, blind in death. I struck with my sword. The rope split, and Felton's corpse fell. It hit the edge and hung halfway in the sea.

I slid down the line and pulled the body back, watching his distended neck stretch. I leaned in and whispered, "You could not escape, Felton." My words were carried on a hot breeze as the last hints of the evening vanished, and I caught the barest hints of flickering flame on the horizon.

It came in utter silence other than the crash of waves against the hull. Like the remembrance lights that the faithful lit in their chapels, my ship was dotted with hundreds of candles, small motes that warned those on shore who had come this night. The flames flickered across the hull, fueled by magic that not even the water could quench, only ending when the fat that made them was spent.

My crew were waiting, taking Felton's body and stowing the launch. Most of these were hollow souls, little more than practiced hands that had once sailed under the black flag. A ship needed a crew, and at times, I was not discerning.

They bore Felton's body below, where he would wait for me to seize his spirit. I felt the twinge of eagerness, but the lights of Montston Port occupied my mind. I leaned against the railing, feeling the roll of the waves, and listened to the distant shouts of alarm. The warning bells spread through the town like wildfire, and I thought to avenge the man I'd chased across the Atlantic.

Footsteps echoed from the helm, and Serana Omen grabbed the rail, hands mixing into the melting fat from the candles on either side of us. "Orders, Captain?" she asked quietly. It might as well have been a roar in the silence of the dead around us.

I thought of the bodies I'd left hanging. "They killed three of ours. I think we should answer that."

Serana knew what I intended to reap from this place. "Run out the port guns!"

The crew moved to their purpose, heeding my quartermaster's call, as I made my way to the helm. I gripped the ship's wheel and watched. I heard the subtle thuds as the gun ports opened. Cannonballs were taken from barrels filled with blood and viscera, flies still clinging to them as they were loaded, and the whisper passed through the ship. "Ready to fire."

Serana looked to me. "Captain?"

I didn't hesitate, keeping my eye on the harbor. Death should always have a witness of life. "Fire."

The *Tallow* rocked and stormless thunder roared. There was a whistle that sounded like a distant scream, and Montston Port suffered. Stone shattered, roofs caved in, and fire bloomed like a false sunrise.

Another volley, more destruction. A ship at anchor floundered, the sea rushing in. I heard distant wails, like the calls of a gull, and the breeze brought the scent of burning timber and fresh blood.

The cannons resounded one last time, a final payment for the lives this place had seen fit to take. I released the helm and decided that I had waited long enough. Felton and I had a reunion beyond the veil of death.

Serana took my place. "What course, Captain?"

I glanced back at her before making my way below. "Wherever the wind takes us."

She shouted my orders, the crew made for full canvas, and I looked at Montston Port a final time, listening to the cries of the dying and wondering how many more I'd ferry to the other side before I was done.

The *Tallow's* hold was streaked with long crevasses of melted fat and wax. Candles burned in tiny alcoves, fueling the temporary life of the souls who filed past me as they attended the ship. Most of these were silent, averting their eyes. Their flames burned low, and soon they'd be released back to the dark. It didn't matter the prizes we took, the ports we made call in; there was always more flesh to fuel my magics.

I pulled back a curtain in the infirmary where my surgeon, Calder Soames, was keeping watch over Felton's body. He had been an honest sailor once, supposedly a skilled man of healing. Now, he operated as a butcher, carving the bodies I brought to him. He glanced up as I entered. "Taking a personal interest in this one, Captain?"

I divested myself of my sword, my coat, and the brace of pistols I carried. "We sailed under Amaranth, rigging rats both."

Calder washed his hands in a nearby bowl of sullied water. "Hard to imagine Locke Berecraft was ever a rigging rat."

I didn't brook familiarity from many. I thought my name on the tongue of another strange, even if it was from one who served under my sails. I didn't spare a reply to his pondering; darker things now shadowed my mind.

"Let's begin," I said, taking the knife provided to me. I began to work it under the flesh of my old shipmate. Rigor mortis had set in. The blood did not come easily, but what bubbled from the incisions splattered against the deck and into the bowels below.

Calder worked with me, handing the skin to the souls attending us, letting it be ferried away to be used for patches in the sail or binding material for my tomes. Remains did not go to waste on my ship.

The scent of Felton's blood clutched my nostrils, a smell I was long familiar with. The sinews stretched as I pulled them away from the bone. The yellow streaks of fat that I would bind to flame ran. Cauldrons bubbled around us, and I placed the meat into the boiling water. The aroma of the flesh cooking was pungent.

His eyes and tongue were separated from the rest; many things could be done with a man's entrails if you knew how. His heart was taken, a tithe for the fathoms, and the rest would feed the sharks.

"Would you like the bones of this one?" Calder asked, stirring the pot as it separated the fat.

I nodded, watching the last vestige of the man be taken apart. There wouldn't be a grave; there never was for a pirate. Felton would never gaze upon the home I meant to create.

The first line of dawn appeared on the horizon before it was ready. The candle in my hand had solidified quickly; setting the wick had been quicker. I looked to Calder. "I trust you'll clean this before the end of your watch?"

His eyes were fixed on the candle. "That one will burn for some time. Did he anger you when you sailed together?"

I took my accoutrement, answering the good surgeon. "Not when he sailed, Mr. Soames. Only when he tried to run."

Serana was waiting for me in my cabin, stroking the spines of the various manuscripts that adorned the shelves, volumes bound in skin, books of blasphemy. When the tides becalmed us, I would read them to her, and things better left off the maps and charts would listen.

I joined her and looked at the tome that commanded her gaze. "*Book of Af,* a dangerous piece of reading."

Serana smiled and leaned forward, stroking my cheek and pulling me into a kiss. One that I returned.

It ended, and she whispered to me, "That is why I have you to read them."

She looked at the yellow candle I grasped tight. "Is that him?"

"What remains," I replied.

I walked to my desk and the small candelabra at the edge adorned with melted fat, and I placed my creation on it.

Her hand graced my shoulder. "Will he give you what you want?"

I brought the flame close and watched the dim glow blaze to life. "He won't have a choice."

A small column of smoke rose, and features formed, indistinct, like viewing a man through a stained pane of glass. Slowly, Felton's soul was provided ephemeral grey flesh, clad in the same attire he'd worn into death, and when his eyes opened, he took a grateful breath. One that fell away when he realized where he was.

A sigh escaped him, an affectation of memory. Nothing about him required the trappings of life: sleep, hunger, thirst, all of that had been left behind. "How long has it been since..." His hand reached for his throat as he spoke.

A little-known truth in the world was that ignorance was a punishment.

I gave Felton the courtesy of knowledge. "Less than a day. You saw me before the drop. Did you expect me to wait? To mourn? You've far too much to give me."

He shook his head. "I'll be damned before I help you."

I felt the shallow smirk pull at my lips. "You're already damned, old friend." I gestured, and Serana brought the charts I needed, the ones that marked the edges where the reason of the old world was left behind for the unfixed wilds. She spread them across my desk, and I gestured to the burning candle that kept Felton tethered here. "You know what that means for you. You'll be unbound from me when the last burns away. And I have become quite adept in keeping it lit."

I watched the despair flood through him, and the longing that he couldn't deny. There weren't many who would turn away from a near eternity on the sea, unaware of the cost of keeping that candle aflame.

I dangled that penance, then I offered another. "Or...I burn it now. I release you back to the next world." My quill was ready. "So, Felton, where is the atoll?"

His mouth opened, a quick reflex as the spell forced him to answer, then his teeth clenched in a grimace of pain, resisting. But his will wasn't enough. His finger jabbed at my chart. I marked the space and looked back at Felton, who averted his eyes. "It's resting there," he said. "But it will be gone before you can reach it."

I looked to Serana. "Full sail. Take us there."

She nodded and left my old friend and I to our own counsel. The dead pirate watched her go. "A woman, Locke?" He spat the words, held back by his opinions of women and their place. I thought to disillusion him of that.

I reached for the candle. "A woman that will command you if I deem it so."

My fingers pinched the wavering flame, and Felton Marth was carried away like a wisp of smoke in a strong breeze.

The crew worked tirelessly on our heading, a task that I assisted with my magics, entreating the wind to find my sails and for the tides to submit to my will. The sighting was made early on the sixth day. The call came, and I reached for my spyglass. We were adrift in endless white, a fog bank that had come upon. But off our starboard were silhouettes, large masses of dotted and carved stone, twisting obelisks that curved in ways that hurt the eye fate had seen fit to leave me. But the eye I had given myself had no such limitations.

I removed the eyepatch and saw Serana turn away out of the corner of my good eye. The dark pearl that rested in my right socket could show hidden things beyond the sight of men. The sea appeared as a teeming void, and the colors of magic dabbled at the edge of what looked like a vast island, dotted with scattered ruins of past ages, concealing my prize. I could hear it calling to me, a whisper like water from a hidden stream. I lowered the eyepatch, returning my sight to the dull grey of fog and the atoll beyond. I gave my orders. "I'll need thirty; light their candles. Pistols and swords for each. Prepare the boats."

Serana immediately relayed the command. Below, Caulder would do the job of lighting, producing the souls I kept for just this occasion.

There was little time; these candles had burned for some time and were not easy to replace. Men who fought did not usually hang. Then there was the atoll itself; there was no record of how it moved, but move it did, and Felton had warned the island had already lingered for too long.

My crew prepared our longboats, free from fear of the place our oars would take us.

Serana appeared, sword and pistol in hand. "The boats are loaded."

I wished the fog would abate, that the curtain would draw back to show us the way. Serana retained less fear than even me.

"Stay with the ship," I said.

There was no dispute; she kept to the Code and what it entailed. I could spend the souls of the dead much easier than I could spend hers, and if I failed here, she could see the others home.

"If the sun sets, take the ship...and the captaincy," I said, beginning the climb to the boat.

She leaned over the edge and called, "There won't be a need."

I replied with iron in my voice. "No, there won't."

The oars creaked against the silence. I stood at the prow, navigating the rising labyrinth of stone from the sea. Each was carved with ancient etchings I couldn't discern, knowledge that I would return for, should the opportunity rise.

We made shore in a cove of rock smoothed by the tide. I took care with my footing. The bank felt soft, nearly like flesh, and small white crabs scuttled away as my crew made their way through the surf. Other things I couldn't readily identify but for their paleness darted through the shallows before making for deeper waters.

There was a groaning gust of wind, and the ground quaked. The fog parted, revealing passages through labyrinths of ruins. A half-dozen of my men stayed with the boats, taking their posts still as statues, their gazes roving the silent shore.

I began the trek. There was an arch of stone that could have once been a gate. As good a point as any to begin searching.

There were no bird calls, and the crashing surf was swallowed by the paths of stone around us. The arch opened onto a long causeway that once had been a road. Ancient black edifices surrounded us, most bearing weathered images of fearsome beasts. A sickly, pale algae grew on every surface. We passed forks and long straightaways that looked like canyons when compared to the obelisks around us.

Our boots splashed through shallow pools of water as we journeyed through the acropolis. The presence of these pools unnerved me for reasons I couldn't quite fathom. Our passage echoed across the winding paths. If there were things creeping around us, they would make themselves known in time, and receive the portion of death I'd brought for them.

I had seen much over the years with the dark pearl, and

all of it was still fresh, etched in my mind and never fading. Wicked souls with their chains of damnation, sacrileges spit in the eye of God, the fading of life in a womb as it struggled for existence...

To that trove I would add another memory, if I was correct about the man who'd come before me. I took a breath and raised the eyepatch.

There was a marking on one of the decrepit structures across the path, slashed in dark maroon like some beast had been gutted and its entrails spread on the stone, invisible to the naked eye but glowing fresh in the realm of the soul. The marking was two letters: H.A.

Haytham Amaranth, a sorcerer of the brethren, a man who had sailed to every foul, dark, and uncharted place that anchored itself to the sea. My former captain. The pirate who had laid the groundwork for my own mission, who had seen the eddies of what was to come and had strived to accomplish with his own power—before the Crown had rewarded him with a rope.

I shared his purpose. I would establish a throne, see my dream of pirates strong and proud, and watch a great fire consume London as we trampled king and crown under our feet.

I took the path the marking indicated, my ever-loyal men following in my wake. The path curved further upward out of the cyclopean ruins. The country was filled with knife-like rocks, and water ran down the slope as we trudged higher.

We were some distance from the ruins when I saw the first bloom of color. Banks of coral spread across the rocks in green, indigo, red, and yellow. It was alive and vibrant. I half-expected a school of fish to be darting in and out of their brilliant hues.

That didn't disturb me as much as the corpses that seemed to be part of the profane reef. Their hands reached out to mark the way, polyps budded on calcified bones, some that could scarce be said to have ever been men. Their number increased the further we drew into the blistered landscape. It culminated in a tapestry of sea life and dead flesh, surrounding a dark opening built into the rock.

I felt the fear that I tried to deny rake against my soul. I swallowed the lump in my throat and drew my sword, commanding my men. "Wait here."

Alone, I descended, my footfalls echoing around me. Small anemones clung to the ceiling, their tendrils hanging like a forest of wedding veils.

My boots splashed in shallow water as I entered a cavern little bigger than a parlor. The walls glowed as some base sea life responded to my presence, but the meager light illuminated nine objects twinkling under the pool.

The pieces of eight were left for the taking. One alone could see a man wield power beyond their wildest imaginings, and all nine could give a man dominion over the seas. I reached into the water and took the first.

For a moment there was nothing but silence, and I thought myself fortunate. Then I heard a sound like stone splitting. I had retrieved the second coin when it came stumbling from the dark edge of the cavern. In my avarice, I hadn't noticed the corpse fused to the wall, like the others outside. The old skin stretched to reveal empty eye sockets that were now home to coral sprouts.

There was no will here, no consciousness; this body that had been seized by the sea and now only served the spell cast on it: to keep these coins where they lay.

The corpse lashed out with the sword it dragged, little more than a rusted piece of iron. It met my own blade and was cleaved in two. I didn't hesitate, stabbing deep into the dead man's chest. My sword was turned aside by a hard layer of stony coral grown over the ribs, but it bit into a small patch of decaying flesh regardless. No normal weapon could kill this man, but I had forged this blade in the shoals of stranger tides, and the sea came with its bite.

Water began to pour from a ragged hole in the dead man's throat. A drowning blade was the doom of any who drew breath. But this corpse didn't die; it had no life to drown, and its blow sent me sprawling into the pool. The rock split my cheek, seawater immediately stinging the exposed flesh.

The corpse slammed a fist into the water as I dodged, pulling myself to my feet and retrieving a pistol from my brace. I spoke words of power, imploring the lords of the tides, the masters of the wind, and the unseen kings who waited in the reefs. I pulled the trigger, and the shot plunged straight into the thing's forehead. It uttered a rasping cry as the magic that forced it to live unwound. The coral cracked, splashing into the pool. The profane thing took a faltering step before succumbing.

I didn't waste the moment. I could hear the din of battle, my crew fending off the corpses defending the treasure. I pulled the last coin from the water and was immediately thrown to the ground as the world rumbled around me.

There was a roar like a maelstrom's squall, and I realized why the ground was smooth, why these coral reefs growing on the land had not dried out and perished. Why the Atoll of Syrash was never in the same place for long.

I felt the weight of the coins in my pouch as I scrambled up the passage, bits of black rock and barnacle tumbling past me as the land roiled. The grotto rocked, and suddenly I saw the sky.

My hand wrapped around a rock to arrest my fall. A reef man rolled into the cave mouth, grappling with one of my crew.

Both fell past me as I climbed, hauling myself over the cave mouth's edge and emerging into a landscape different than the one I had journeyed through. The reef men crawled like spiders, clinging to the exposed coral and fighting my remaining men.

Most of my crew had fallen away when the land tilted, swallowed by the grey fog. Barely half of those that had come ashore remained, drawing what pain they could from our enemy.

Water fell like a storm around us, and I looked up to see a mass that nearly blotted out the sky. It was long, dark…and it moved, reaching a zenith above us.

A *fin…it's a fin.*

The thought came and drove me to near panic. Profane sorceries and all the iron in a man could save you from many things, but not against a leviathan such as this. I prepared for death, wondering what part of the seafloor my body would come to rest on in the crushing, pitiless dark.

Then the fin began to recede, the great beast beginning to turn, and the ground…no, flesh…quivered. Some leagues distant, I saw the mountains move, and a great shadow blew away the fog.

There were no words to describe the thing that lifted its head from the sea. There was a dread maw that opened wide and a false sun from a glowing yellow eye. Then it plunged its visage back into the sea, roaring waves rising to fill the void left in its passing.

It's diving. The thought had scarcely come before the flesh beneath me shifted. The great fin splashed back into the sea and sent a great wave churning upwards. I slid down the incline, my crew and the reef men falling around me, the lot of us deposited in the remains of the city that had been built on the creature's back.

I felt the pouch, reassured that I hadn't lost it in the fall. Water splashed around me, churning eddies that threatened to sweep me under as the leviathan dove.

Three of my men remained, their wills bound to me, but even dead, I thought I saw the hint of weariness.

I spat water, breathing hard. "Get me back to the ship!" The reef men had regained their footing, making their way toward us, eager to reclaim what I'd taken. More stumbled from the ruins, invigorated by the coin's presence, and my crew did their duty.

I left them there, fighting. The powder in my pistols was wet. No spell or art I had could kill them. I had nothing left but my sword.

A reef man stumbled out, and I swung with all my might. The blade cut through the neck. The head was mostly shell now, and it went splashing into the water as its body flailed.

The current was strong, and the sea churned down the canyon as I struggled against it, clinging to the rocks as I tried to make it to the shore and the boats. The land was sinking; my feet left the ground beneath me.

My ship burned like a beacon. The *Tallow* was clear of the fog, and it rocked on the waves. The cove was gone, the boats were gone, and the men I had left had been swallowed up.

I couldn't make it. The monster's passage would drag me down as solidly as any anchor. Serana couldn't bring the ship to me for the same reason. There was only one way. I had the knowledge; the old charts from my time sailing with Haytham, the ones that could let a man seize the power of a piece of eight.

I pulled myself higher, trying to clear the water, then I reached into the pouch and drew one of the dull pieces, making sure the string was taught as I clutched the coin. I spoke the old words, inciting the gift in my hand to grant me its power. There was a ringing like a bell, and the coin glowed with a dull grey light.

The sea receded from me. It felt like running sand, the unsure depths suddenly gaining purchase, until my still-dripping boots stood on the waves like they were solid ground.

I watched the last of the great mountains that were the thing's spines disappear. The water pulled at my feet, but the power that coursed through the coin in my hand was stronger than Neptune's foundations.

Slowly, I turned and looked to the horizon and my ship. I could hear distant shouts from the deck. Serana would no doubt be wondering if she should follow my last command, hoping against everything that I was still among the living, that she wouldn't have to light a candle for me.

I walked across the waves and heard the calls as I approached. Even the dead would cease their labors to see a man walk the sea. A line was cast to me, and I hauled on the rope, riding it to the deck, feeling the hardened wax and the planks under my boots. Serana was waiting for me, as were the crew that had remained on deck. Many candles were cold, their flames extinguished.

I turned and looked to the calming sea and wondered about the vast thing that swam it, and then I felt the hand on my shoulder. Serana, ever present and loyal. "What course, Captain?"

The coins sang to me, the one in my hand burning, eager to take their place in the hands I'd prepared for them.

"Nassau awaits," I said.

She carried my command to the crew, and I pulled Felton's candle from the folds of my coat. Without a word, I dropped it into the sea.

Red Rose Reign

Glenn Parris

He stood out in the crowds of Savak. Born of a poor, unmarried bar maid, the small town shunned her and the coming of her bastard son—until his birth. Sun-Kissed skin marked the babe as special; if not a son of the gods, at least his father must have hailed from realms south of the southern seas. The shaman named him Siago, God-Known.

The islands boasted artisans and engineers without peer. Sons, native to the isles, burgeoned into soldiers whose naked skin had been witnessed to defy the sharpest blade without bloodshed. Half-heritage unknown, nobles of the four kingdoms coveted such a spawn nonetheless. Every House wanted that seed to bolster their bloodline. Siago grew tall, dark, and strong. Word spread that the blood of gods ran deep in his brawny veins. As every man feared him, every woman, high and lowborn, married or maiden, secretly wanted to bear his sons. Even a cuckold king would welcome a dark heir of the south as his own. Yes, with little effort, Siago could have his pick of women…all but one.

Siago had seen her only once, but she had haunted his thoughts for years. So delicate a creature, this novice priestess pledged to the Order of the Rose lived in his mind like a snowflake, forever on the verge of melting from memory. So graceful a fantasy Fate meant not for his portion. A warrior needed a sturdy mate, one with sound bone and tough sinew.

Siago waded through several women over the passing years,

but he found himself loathe to commit to any of them. Memory of the slight, flaxen-haired maiden, sole apprentice to the Rain Sorceress and student of the arcane arts, consumed him. Though her image seared his heart, he yet knew not her name or the sound of her sweet voice.

When last Siago had seen her, she wore robes of gossamer and slippers of silk. Already a journeyman silversmith by 19, he had begun to share his Uncle Giran's renown as master craftsman of noble armor. Siago had grown broad shoulders stoking kilns that wrought the first arms without the traditional insignia. The blessing of immaculate armor with the inlay of the Rose had declined to hollow ceremony even then.

Always in need of abiding steel, King Pirolin found use for all the skilled craftsman he could muster, but he was not in the business of recruiting smiths to ride in his cavalry. The young artisan soon found a fondness for burnishing the new swords in an effort to impress the maidens. Siago's demonstrated skill with the blades he forged shamed many a foot soldier and even some knights. Witness to one such event, the king granted a rare exception to the darkling smith. If he could not count this spawn of the south among his legions, then by the gods, he'd have him making the finest arms in the realm. And even a smith must know the ways of war, if only to fashion better weapons. Squire training ensued.

Magic had been waning from the Realm for eons, rendering the Order of the Rose inconsequential to the Savakur King and his wars. As a newly inducted squire, Siago had just begun learning the warrior's way. Arduous training consumed the days' hours, both light and dark, and washed the most tenacious man's fancies into the ether at night. Even utter exhaustion could scarcely expunge the plague of dreams embracing the lithe virgin.

Siago…come to me. I've known no man in my life, but your blood calls to me. I'm fading, like the Rose...and she was gone. Like the mist.

Siago woke in a sweat, his chest heaving as if he had run uphill with all the arms of the swordsmith's shop. The following morning, the wispy voice still echoing in his mind, Siago struggled to recall the details of his dream even as his hands and loins sought its substance. He showered under a bucket of fresh rainwater before trudging with his bundle of newly minted blades to the royal castle. The entrance hall stockpiled an assortment of handheld armaments: broad knives, slim daggers, serrated swords, pikes and spears for rapid deployment. Upon a shelf above, accessible only by short ladders, lay a horde of sling bombs, blow guns, long and cross bows in abundance, the trade tools of elite snipers and assassins.

Adjoining chambers warehoused terrible war machines along with sufficient ordinance to make the king's enemies tremble and give his rivals at court pause. Central to the magazine stood an altar with the sacred Red Rose of legend to enrich the deadly cache. After all, was not the reign of the Savakur monarch the ultimate expression of peace? Centuries of battle had left the known world at accord by grace of four mighty empires, subsumed into a single hegemony with the Savaku supreme among them. Ongoing campaigns now focused on consolidating stray tribes and independent city-kingdoms into the Pax Savaku.

Alas, unlike the maiden of his fantasy, the Red Rose of Peace, once a universal symbol of power, had now faded to pink set in its crystal bowl, a symbol of a dying cult.

Or so it would seem.

As a rite of passage, Siago, the newest inductee to the Savakur legions served as messenger. Not a warrior's quest, but an obligation at the command of a practical king. Even Siago dared not refuse—but a soldier's aspiration sometimes came in strange packages: an upstart. One of the city states embarked on a crusade of its own.

Onia swept out of the barren sea beyond the desert to the east. Known as a poor kingdom with fewer than 400 citizens and led by a peasant queen who tilled soil and wove fabric with her maidens, Onia had been a deteriorating subsistence economy for hundreds of years. Rumor had it that Onia's straw-haired queen actually sold her one and only child into servitude for 13 pieces of gold—six pieces less than the price of a single warhorse. But Onia had no warhorses. It had no armory. It hadn't even a sheriff, much less a militia. Now, somehow, surrounding villages had been subjugated and impressed into a workforce capable of building a shining city at the world's edge. Whispers among the local serfs held that Onia's fierce legions, although formidable, had yet to be seen.

Enticed, King Pirolin declared, "Finally, a real fight. Maybe even a challenge!"

By charter, the King was obliged to at least inform the Congress of Generals that he was going into battle. He did not need permission, nor did he need to wait. Swiftly dispatched, Siago delivered the news as herald of Pirolin.

The grumbling council berated Siago in effigy of their king in absentia. They too sought battle. It had become a rare festival in modern times. Savakur armies craved it, but every officer knew what came next: nobles would suit up in their armor. Squires would pack provisions and supplies then, they would embark across the mountains and through the desert to a finished battle and a gloating King Pirolin in time for his vassals to ferry the plunder back to the capital. The mighty Armada Savaku, reduced from proud armies to merchant caravan at the behest of their arrogant liege.

Lo, this king's naïve messenger was not welcomed. After a humiliating hearing before the Congress, Siago was sent on his way with no fresh provisions and only a beggar's meal in his belly. His first duty done, the young warrior was sworn to rejoin the conquering army. Launched by the council to ride his weary mount to the king's side at the front lines with all haste, Siago rode from the capital gates to the horizon at full tilt. He slowed to preserve his horse once out of sight.

Unbidden, memories of the flaxen beauty assailed him once again. He could almost hear her melodic lyric: *Siago...*

More vivid and tactile, too, were his longings, as if her softness caressed him with every gust of the moist mountain zephyr. As he rode into the night, the warm breeze became a biting wind. The youth braced against it, undeterred, as if it too were no more than the first adversary of his quest.

Siago was late. He had permitted sensual reverie to pass time through the lonely mountain road. The desert beyond stretched in the distance and tested his mount's endurance before giving way to his final destination. He crossed the battlefield with rising urgency, advancing on the castle.

That which he begged for lay unwelcomed before his unseasoned eyes. Tarry figures as far as the eye could see, staged a display of horrors amidst the verdant orchard. At closer look, legions of charred Savakur warriors stanchioned at the pitch of combat testified to a victor nowhere to be seen by the light of the last moon. Siago recognized the horrified faces of some of the fiercest warriors he had sold weapons to back home. The peasants' lore seemed eerily divined. From atop his mount, Siago spied massive, blazing footprints stippled through the darkness, the remnant of an unknown legion. Along with the stench of burning flesh, the only evidence of a triumphant foe.

He pressed on. Crossing the field of a disheartening battle, Siago dismounted and walked his steed through open gates at the enemy rampart. At least the burnt corpses were fewer. Waning torch flames burned, untended, along the parapets.

A single pale, pink rose lay near the gate, cleft at mid-stem as if to memorialize the fallen and trivialize the royal symbol of the empire.

A figure still as a monument frozen mid-march smoked in the moonlight. Siago could not tell if it was evening mist or perspiration of battle boiling off a resting hero. He circled the figure in a wide arc so as not to startle him into friendly combat. Siago recognized the facial features as belonging to Nitroel, the king's champion, seared to a crisp. Siago bowed his head in reverence, only to rise in a whiplash motion at the sound of an other-worldly voice, all too familiar to him.

"Siago. Free me. My soul is slave to Her, but she will not have it. I cannot go on, and I cannot go back. Free me!"

Siago broke into a deathly cold sweat and reacted. His sword unsheathed, he swung at the figure with all his might. Dust replaced the likeness, then chased the wind into the night. Siago dropped to his knees and puked a day-old meal seemingly from his toes and testes. He had grown up on Nitroel's training. The man was a legend in warfare who literally wrote the combat manual for Savakur royals and conscripted.

What kind of witch is this dark queen? he fretted. An agonizing howl issued from the tower above. Siago broke into a run at the sight of the fair flower, carrying a gravestone's burden of well-tested sword and armor through the castle halls. Donning the unearned armor of legend en route, Siago's muscles burned by the time he mounted the last flight of stairs reaching up to the towering throne room.

How could she have devastated the entire Savakur army? Siago thought. *No magic is that strong.*

His king wielded the ancient sword, Cyanici. Savakur legend held that Cyanici cut through magic spells and creatures of the netherworld no matter how powerful. Its gleam dispersed all deception. Surely, even if the Hordes of Savak had failed, the

King would have triumphed, single-handedly, against manna so evil.

A path of pink rose petals strewn the last three steps and floor led to the throne room. Siago followed them. They stopped at the chamber entrance. He kicked down the remains of the door, once ten-inch thick oak now no more than cold, insubstantial embers. There, on the steps of the throne, knelt his king, Pirolin, in full battle regalia. Siago dropped to his knees and shrieked in agony.

The Sword of Cyanici had been driven through, not around, the best-reinforced Savaku armor plating. Pirolin's bowed head still bore his battle helmet, now naked of the Savaku crown.

Siago knelt and kissed the still-smoking hand of his king as he noted a crackling sound, followed by rustling then shuffling footfalls. From the faded petal on the stairs emerged fiends, wide-mawed with drooling fangs of fury, undulating torsos bearing elongated limbs from which sprang flaming claws.

Calculating the distance between himself and the sources of the intruding noise, he rose, and even before seeing his intended victims, flung his sword in that direction with extreme prejudice. The blade found its prey. The specter burst into dust at the bite of the spinning steel. Drawing the Sword of Cyanci from his fallen king while still brandishing the weapon of Nitroel, Siago windmilled both swords in defiance of death and challenged the two remaining wraiths to confront the last Savakur warrior.

"Face ME demons, for I am like no Savakur you ever fought. I am Sun-Kissed, born to destroy hell spawn—and I am your doom!" He slashed through the charging phantasm, his swords painting the air between with whirls of soot and ash. A too-gentle breeze cleansed the demon breath from the air as if they had never been. His chest heaving in desperation, Siago wasn't certain that they ever were.

"Haunts of the imagination? Guilt for missing the battle? Were they real or creatures of my mind?" He sheathed both blades.

The following silence was pierced by a sound; a soft sound by any measure, but the first he had heard not generated by the phantoms of his soul or his own egress since entering the castle. Siago drew his swords and crouched at the ready. His best effort at stealth advanced the avenging army-of-one to the parlor beyond the throne room.

As if responding to his assault, the rising sun invaded the room with lances of red and gold at the window. Siago shielded his eyes from the sudden brilliance, then again heard the sound. Just a trill. Soprano, like a child's yawn after the sleep of innocence.

Siago...

At that window, framed in the dawn's light, was she, his nameless priestess. Hair as fine and delicate as corn silk, clad in a gown of gossamer, she stood, conqueror of conquerors. Armed only with the Pink Rose cradled in the jewel-crusted, imperial crown of Savaku, she beckoned Siago to join her.

Her voice was the wind, not the utterance of any mortal. *Finally, you are here. My Siago...*

With each step he took, the wilted rose blushed to fiery life as if a bow of silk steeped in a veritable river of blood. The sanguine rivulets defied the pull of the world, climbing the walls then through the windows of the castle. Creeping along the cracks in the stone floor, the blood dripped upward between delicate fingers to the cradled flower. What amounted to no more than the girl's weight in armor suddenly felt like the weight of his steed as Siago crumpled to a knee, his blade too heavy for his thick muscles to heft.

As he prepared for death at the tip of his own sword, echoing the fate of his liege, Siago felt an incredible lightness of being, almost weightless as the crown of Savak came to rest on his head and the red rose touched it. He looked up, beholden to a new queen. The damsel he somehow had known all his life now clutched the blood red rose to her bosom. For the first time in his life, awake or in dreams, Siago heard her melodious voice echo as she spoke her first vivacious words to him.

"Arise, my king."

The Prince of Dust and Shadows

Jonathan Maberry

A Story of Kagen the Damned

-1-

"If you tell me that we're looking for some kind of gods-damned magic sword, Tuke, so help me I will skin you alive."

Tuke grinned down at Kagen but said nothing. Which said everything.

"Seriously," said Kagen. "Skinned, roasted. Fed to hogs."

"You can always turn around and ride back to that last town."

They sat on their horses at the top of a low rise. Behind them, the Forest of Elgen was darkened to a purple nothingness. Ahead, the road sloped down and snaked through a maze of ancient trees. The sun was a fading rumor and the moon a growing promise.

"Why didn't you tell me that this was another of your stupid fucking quests?" asked Kagen. He was saddle-sore, irritable, and feeling ungracious about everything.

Tuke still smiled. The big Therian was huddled into furs, and his eyes had the merry lights of someone whose well-attended waterskin was filled with wine—and there wasn't much left of it.

"Two things," said Tuke. "No, make it three. First…you're a sour pain in the ass, you know that?"

"Fuck you."

"Second, we are currently on the run from an entire empire. That's not even a joke. Every Hakkian from Behlia to the Cathedral Mountains knows he can get rich and retire if he brings your head and heart to the court of the Witch-king. The force of arms we can bring to bear against that is you—and you're drunk more than you're sober—and me, and I've been so comprehensively slashed and hacked lately that I am composed more of scabs and scars than useful muscle. So…the whole 'magic sword' idea shouldn't be dismissed out of hand."

Kagen glowered but could pick no holes in that. "And the third thing?"

"Third…fuck you."

Kagen sighed. "Yeah," he said. "Fair enough."

They rode on.

-2-

A mile later, just as the eye of the moon began peering over the edge of the world, Kagen said, "What kind of magic sword are we talking?"

Tuke, who'd nodded off in the saddle, snapped awake. "Goat balls."

"What?" asked Kagen.

"What?" said Tuke, blinking away the sleep. "Um…what was it you said?"

"I asked what kind of magic sword?"

Tuke avoided Kagen's eyes. "Oh, a legendary one, to be sure. Storied. There are tavern songs about it. Some ballads, too."

"Really? Sing one."

"What?"

"Sing me one of those songs," said Kagen. "I want to hear about the glories and powers of this mystical sword."

"I...don't know any by heart..."

"Give me a title, then."

Tuke looked everywhere but at him. "The, um, Legend of the, ah, Magic Sword...?"

Kagen stared at him. "You are a terrible liar."

"I'm not lying."

"The Legend of the Magic Sword."

"Yes."

"That's a real song?"

"Yes."

"Swear it."

"What?"

"Swear to it on Dagon," suggested Kagen. "Take that little icon you always carry, hold it in your hand, and swear by the king of your people's gods that there *is* such a song, that there *is* a sword, and that this isn't just another of your tricks to try and sober me up and get me to straighten myself out."

The horses walked a fair way along the road before Tuke answered.

"Okay," he admitted, "that's not the name of the song."

"I'm shocked."

"But there *is* a sword."

"Uh-huh."

"A legend of one."

"There's a legend that there are women on Orgas Tull with four breasts, two of which flow with wine."

Tuke's dark skin turned a shade darker still. "There *is* a legend about the sword," he grumbled.

"What does the legend *actually* say?"

Tuke had to fumble around in his memory for the exact

words, but then he nodded to himself and said, "'*In Hrethlen Wood, beneath the demon tower, is a cave carved by an underground river now dried to dust. There, hidden forever from the eyes of men, is a city of goblins that fell to the hand and blade of Prince Vorlon of Old Shimele. Vorlon brought his army there and did engage in bloody battle with the Goblin King, and slew him upon his own throne of skulls, cleaving the fell beast with a mighty blow of the enchanted sword,* Caladbolg. *Then, having vanquished the lord of the goblins, did Vorlon sit himself upon the throne of skulls to wait until the needs of his people did call him forth once more. Disturb not the rest of the Prince of Dust and Shadows.*"

Kagen studied his friend.

"Now...let me see if I grasp this..." he said slowly. "You've tricked me into looking for a magic sword used to fight and kill the king of the goblins, yes?"

"Yes. It was a great victory."

"Have you ever read about the goblins? In history books, I mean, from before the first Silver Empress outlawed magic across the whole of the world."

"Not...as such..."

"Goblins are not particularly hard to kill."

"There were a lot of them."

"That's not the point. *Killing* them is not much of an act of heroism. But do you remember what happens in every single story about someone killing a goblin?"

"I..."

"Killing a goblin under the best of circumstances incurs bad luck for seven times seven years. Even if you die, the bad luck follows your family until those forty-nine years have passed."

"Well, sure, there's that, but..."

"That's in self-defense," said Kagen sharply. "Attacking them in their own lands incurs bad luck that lasts—and I quote—until the sun and the years have turned the mountains themselves to dust and shadows."

"Poetic license," said Tuke, dismissing it with an airy wave of his hand.

"Or a dire warning."

"It's a metaphor."

"For *what*?"

Tuke waffled. "I mean…it's probably meant to scare off tomb raiders and such."

The road curved again, and soon they were plodding along between the shattered stones of a small city that had clearly fallen many centuries ago.

Kagen took a piece of goat jerky from his pack and chewed thoughtfully, eyeing Tuke all the time. "Are you not seeing how your tale of ancient valor is really a warning for us to stay the hell away?"

"I see it differently."

"Gods of the pit…"

"Besides, Kagen," said Tuke, bristling, "what's it matter? You cannot be cursed. You do know that, right?"

"How the hell do you figure that?"

"Well," said Tuke, "not to put too fine a point on it, but you're actually damned. You saw your own gods—Father Ar and Mother Sah—appear above you and turn their backs on you for what happened in Argentium. They blamed you for the deaths of the Imperial children during the Hakkian invasion. People don't call you Kagen the Damned for nothing."

Kagen's hands knotted to fists around the reins. "Are you making a point here or just trying to piss me off?"

"I told you—you're damned," said Tuke, his smile encouraging. "The damned cannot be cursed by anything mortal, and goblins—despite being ugly little monsters—are mortal. A curse can only be laid on the souls of the ensouled. You're immune."

"Fuck. Is that supposed to be a comfort, you incredible ass?"

"Life's hard, brother," said Tuke. "Your life sucks, I'll grant, but if an advantage presents itself, why not take it? You, because of who and what you are, are immune to any goblin's curse."

They rode on, and Kagen composed several crushing replies but left each unsaid because Tuke made sense. Kagen hated that Tuke made sense, but the big Therian did more often than not. A very hateful trait, the bastard.

"I'm not saying I buy any of this nonsense," said Kagen carefully, "but what powers is this hypothetical sword supposed to possess? I mean, how will it help me kill the Witch-king?"

Tuke tried his best to hide a smug little smile, but his face was too mobile, too expressive.

"The sword Caladbolg can kill anything that uses magic, is created by magic, or is *of* magic." His face grew serious, and now he met Kagen's gaze. "It cannot be thwarted by magic weapons, magic armor, or magic spells."

"You're saying—"

"That the sword can kill the Witch-king and any monsters or demons he conjures against you."

The only sound was the soft clop-clop of the horses' hooves in the loamy dirt.

"Gods of the fiery pit," murmured Kagen.

-3-

It took them the rest of that day and well into the following afternoon before they found the place marked on a map Tuke carried. The map was inked onto a piece of leather so old it might have come from the Dawn Calf out of the creation legends. Or, Kagen mused privately, some old goat whose skin had been cured, boiled in tea, and sold as an artifact. His older brothers, Jheklan and Faulker, had tricked him more than once with such maps.

Yet Tuke, who Kagen privately respected as both learned and wise, believed in it.

Kagen's own doubt cracked and crumbled when Tuke held up the map and pointed to a series of rocks and hills whose contours were close matches.

"Those two hills there," said the Therian, "are all that's left of the Great Gates of the Goblin Kingdom. That hillock there is the mound in which Prince Vorlon buried his own knights along with ten times their number of goblin warriors."

"Looks...similar..." said Kagen diffidently.

"Well, it wouldn't look exactly the same," said Tuke. "The map is over a thousand years old. The landscape's changed."

"Sure," said Kagen. "Whatever."

They rode until they reached the hillock and then dismounted. The sun was drifting toward the western hills, throwing long shadows behind it. There were a couple of hours of daylight left, but that place was deep in a valley and false twilight was nearly upon them. The air was chill and damp, and both men pulled heavy wool cloaks around their shoulders.

"By the icy balls of the god of winter," muttered Tuke, "but it's bitter down here."

"And thanks for bringing me to such a garden spot," said Kagen. He looked around. "There's supposed to be some kind of door into these hills?"

"Yes."

"What's your plan? Find it now or wait until morning?"

Tuke shivered in the cold. "Now."

"Then let's be about it," said Kagen curtly. "I do not like this place and want to be quit of it sooner than later."

They studied the map again and then began their search, though even Tuke's enthusiasm seemed to have dwindled with the failing light and falling temperatures. There was a biting quality to the wind that seemed able to find every opening in cloak and clothes.

Kagen paused in his searching and stood looking at the trees. Tuke came over, following Kagen's gaze.

"What is it?"

"The nightbirds," said Kagen. "They did not follow us here."

Nightbirds was a general term he had given to flocks of birds—crows, grackles, redwing blackbirds, and others—that had been dogging his steps ever since he fled the fall of Argentium. The fact that no ravens were among them had made Kagen believe they were somehow his allies, for the raven was the state bird of Hakkia. He was often annoyed by the inexplicable presence of the hundreds of dark birds, but now that they were gone it made him feel strangely vulnerable and abandoned.

"Maybe they lost interest," suggested Tuke, though from his tone it was clear he did not believe it.

"No," said Kagen. "I think it's this place. I think they're wiser about it than we are."

Tuke began to speak, thought better of it, and loosened his weapons in their sheaths. With one hand he touched the pouch in which he kept his icon of Dagon, and with the other made a warding sign in the air.

They spoke no more as they continued their search.

-4-

It was Kagen who found the entrance.

"Here," he called, and when Tuke came over to join him, they squatted on a rocky lip of a steep slope hidden by overgrown hawthorn bushes and stunted scrub pines. The half-eaten car-cass of a rattlesnake lay at the top of the slope, and all around were the shredded skins and gnawed bones of countless animals. Tuke picked up the femur of a wildcat and studied the bitten end. He turned it over in his hand, showing Kagen the marks of short, sharp teeth and long scratches from savage claws.

"What did that?" asked Kagen, but Tuke could only shake his head. He tossed the bone down the slope, and they listened as it entered a weed-choked hole. The bone rattled and clattered. Beetles and sand mice scuttled out of the way.

Tuke shifted to allow the waning sunlight to spill down onto the opening. He pointed with a long finger. "See there? There were steps here once. And over there? That's part of a wall. You can still see something carved into it. Can you make it out?"

Kagen edged down the slope and looked at the ancient fragment of stone. He spat on his fingers and used them to brush away caked dirt. The image they saw was badly eroded, but as he worked a face emerged, carved in ages past. The face was small and misshapen, with too much brow, not enough chin, and far too many teeth. The eyes were tiny, glaring from pits of fat. The overall impression was that of some unholy mix of pig, ape, and human child.

"Gods," gasped Kagen, recoiling.

Tuke made the warding sign again, and far up the slope the horses suddenly whinnied with fear even though they could not see what the two men saw.

"That's foul, and no mistake," said Tuke, his expression falling into sickness. "A goblin of the old world."

The old tales of those monsters rose up in Kagen's mind. His brothers had used those stories to terrify him as a lad, and those memories returned. He remembered running screaming to the chamber of his elder brother, Herepath—wisest and most learned of the Vale children—hoping to find comfort and even a complete dismissal of all that Jheklan and Faulker told him.

But Herepath had not laughed it off. Instead, he sat all three boys down to tell them what *he* knew.

"They were children once," he said. Herepath was tall, thin, ascetic, and seldom spoke, but when he did, he told truths. Seeking him for comfort had worked against all three boys at different times. "They were stolen from their beds by the *Baobhan sith* and taken deep into the faerie grottos in the deepest woods. In those places they were experimented on, tortured, changed. Why this was done remains a mystery, for who can understand the minds of those ageless creatures? Through darkest magics they forced and twisted nature to their will, blending the innocence of children with the viciousness of swine and the thieving cleverness of weasels and wolverines, apes, and other beasts. No two are alike in form except in that they all share a similar face—the snout of a pig, with the shape of an ape, but the innocent and terrified eyes of human children. To look upon them in the flesh is to have your mind shredded. To encounter them in the dark is to know that doom is upon you, for you will lose your very soul and fall into eternal damnation no matter when or how you die."

Jheklan had laughed at that, while Faulker begged Herepath to say that he was just joking. But Herepath seldom joked, and never about matters involving the old ways of magic and sorcery. The three boys got no sleep that night but instead huddled together in bed, each armed with a knife, and the family hounds clustered close.

Those words came back to Kagen in that moment—precise, exact, and complete—and he recited them to Tuke, who despite the cold—began sweating profusely.

"I...I..." began Tuke, but seemed unable to find anything to say.

"You can't go in there," said Kagen.

"Look, brother," said Tuke, "this is a bad idea and I'm a fool.

Let's just go. There's enough light for us to get a couple of miles back the way we came. There was that grove of young oaks. We can camp there and in the morning head out."

"And go where?"

"Anywhere but here."

Kagen squatted above the black entrance. "You can't go in there," he repeated, "but we both know that I can."

Tuke shook his head. "What if this whole 'damned' thing is wrong? A mistake. You said that you woke up drunk during the invasion and were probably drugged. Then you fought for hours, saw your family butchered and only barely escaped the palace. What you saw in the sky—your gods turning their backs on you? That could have been a dream brought on by heartbreak, exhaustion, and whatever drug was still in your system. Maybe you're *not* damned. I'm a fool for even suggesting this."

He grabbed Kagen's arm and tried to pull him up the hill, but Kagen resisted and pulled his arm free.

"A sword that can defeat magic," murmured Kagen. "A weapon that could slay the Witch-king." He shook his head. "I'm not sure I can go without trying to find it. Everything in my life could turn on this."

"Or you could die and lose your soul for real."

"What does my life mean if I walk away? I have failed in every single thing since Hakkia invaded. In the scheme of things, Tuke, I am worth just a little less than a pile of dog shit. I've spent the last couple of months either drunk or raving like a madman. If you had not found me, I'd no doubt be dead or in chains, being dragged before the Witch-king. Right now, at this minute, I am nothing. If I am not damned, then I am delusional and a fool. If I *am* damned, then what other chance will I ever have to redeem myself? How else can I honor the members of my family the Hakkians slaughtered? How else might I redress the wrongs—the rape and torture and slaughter of the Empress and her children?"

"Kagen, you're rationalizing this beyond sense."

"No, Tuke, you were right to bring me here. This is a chance. This is maybe my only chance to do some measurable good while I still have breath."

"And if you die in there?"

"Then I will have died trying," said Kagen. He shook his head slowly. "That has to matter to the gods, even if it's not enough to restore my soul."

Tuke's face was drawn and filled with agony. "You're mad."

Kagen suddenly smiled. "Kagen the Mad has a ring to it, don't you think?"

With that he rose, slapped the handles of the matched daggers he wore, and nodded. Those daggers had once belonged to his mother, the Poison Rose, feared throughout the empire as the deadliest knife fighter of the age. It had been a terrible bit of dark magic that had brought her down, and now those knives were his.

"Wait for me until morning," he said. "If I am not back by first light, then ride off and never look back."

"Kagen, I implore you. This was a foolish idea and I apologize. Let us be gone."

But Kagen held out his hand. "You are a good man and a good friend. My only friend. I thank you for giving me at least a chance to redeem myself."

Tuke continued to protest, but Kagen turned and slid down the slope into darkness and was gone.

-5-

"Well," he said to himself as the shadows closed around him, "this is insane."

The sound of his voice was uncomfortably loud, and he bit down on other commentary. He also did not like the notes of fear and anxiety he heard in his words. Brave words to Tuke did not grant equal amounts of courage. The truth was that he was terrified.

For a thousand years the Silver Empresses and their armies had maintained the ban on magic in all of its forms. Early in the history of the empire, the first empress had forced all manner of magic out of the world. Vampires and elves, demons and witches, sorcerers and faerie folk all vanished in the space of a single decade. No history book ever said how this was done, and even Herepath did not seem to know—although he threw himself into that field of study in order to understand it. For Kagen, the fact that magic was gone was a comfort, for he had learned to fear it greatly.

Then the Witch-king rose in all of his unnatural power and, as he stretched his dark hand across the length and breadth of the empire, magic had begun to flow back. In great ways, as with the sorcery the Witch-king used to conquer the empire in a single night; and in small ways, like blooming flowers of a color that was so alien it could not be described and could fracture the mind of any who tried to understand it. And countless other ways.

What of goblins, though? he wondered. Most magic still slumbered or was groaning in its process of awakening. There were rumors of a vampire in Argon and a unicorn in Vahlycor. Actually, weird things were being seen everywhere. Kagen had even met a woman who claimed to be a witch and who had spoken prophecy to him.

Madness. Horrors. That's what magic was.

Did the goblins slumber still, down here in this endless dark? Or had the presence of living men stirred them from their sleep and awakened their dreadful hungers?

Kagen patted the wall inside the entrance and found the shaft of an ancient torch, its tarry head wreathed in cobwebs. He sheathed his knives and used flint and steel to strike sparks onto the torch. His relief when the centuries-old pitch caught and blazed was enormous.

And short-lived.

Everywhere he looked—all along the corridor, crowding the walls, hanging from stalactites—were creatures. Pig-snouted, ape-faced, child-eyed. They were ahead of him, on either side of him, and as he turned, they closed ranks behind.

He was surrounded by goblins, and there was no way out.

-6-

"Gods of the pit!" cried Kagen as he spun and crouched, flaming brand in one hand and a dagger in the other.

The goblins hissed at him. Their faces were something out of the deepest nightmares, worse than the description Tuke had given. The blend of pig and ape was horrific, but that alone was endurable; that alone could be accepted by the human mind as merely some new kind of animal. Kagen was not well-traveled, and so there were always new natural wonders.

Those eyes, though. There was nothing natural about them. The fact that they looked so definitely human made them unnatural in the worst possible ways because of what he saw in them. There was a mix of emotions burning in each set of goblin eyes. He saw the hatred, the rapacious hungers of the monster there, but that was not the worst part. Inside those stares he saw something deeper.

He saw the children that each had been before sorcery and corruption. Worse still, he saw their awareness of what they were and what had been done to them. He saw the horror that each of them felt because of what they had become and what they would always be. Children's eyes in monsters' faces, with hope still flickering but forever out of reach. The desperation, the stress, the shame, the pleading that hovered at the precipice of sad acceptance—he saw that in a thousand subtle shades as he looked around.

Monsters who knew that they were monsters, but with the terrible clarity of knowing what they had lost. What had been stolen from them.

And the anger. The frustration that had become rage. The horror that had become malice born of hurt.

Kagen's heart broke for them—for all those stolen children—and yet his fear was a towering thing that threatened to collapse and crush him. He held the torch high but lowered his dagger.

"I am not here to harm you," he said, fighting to keep his fear from his voice. And failing. "I have no fight with you."

"Human…" said one of them, drawing the word out into a snarl, a hiss. "You dare come into our home with bright steel and fire."

The others whispered words in a language he did not know. Ugly words not made for human tongues. Words that sounded painful for them to speak.

"Let me pass," said Kagen. "I am not here for you. I have no wish to fight you or do harm here."

The goblins laughed at that. Their laughter sounded like weeping, and it came close to breaking Kagen's heart.

"You bring us fresh meat and heart's blood," said the goblin. "And we accept this gift."

They shifted, closing in around him though not yet within reach. He saw that their fingers were tipped with black nails that were chipped and broken from scrabbling in that darkness. Many had open sores on their bodies, and the scars from bites old and new. They stank of rotting meat and wormy dirt.

Kagen knew that he had made a terrible mistake by coming

in there. Tuke could not help him, but even if he could, there were so many of the monsters that doom was the only outcome of this fool's adventure.

"We will feast upon your soul, man of the sunlight world."

"No," said Kagen. "You may kill me—though you will earn that at a terrible cost—but my soul is not for you. My soul is forfeit to the Gods of the Garden, who have damned me for all time."

More of the ugly whispering. Uncertainty flickered in their eyes.

"Why have you come here?" demanded the head goblin.

Kagen saw no reason to lie. Things were going to shit anyway.

"I have come for the sword of the Prince of Dust and Shadows."

"Speak not that name in our halls," growled the goblin. "Speak not of the devil who slew our great lord and was damned for it."

"If he is your devil," said Kagen, "then let me take his blade and his bones out of here and you will be free of his shadow."

The goblins let loose with a wail of hatred, despair, and derision—each emotion in equal measures. They slashed at the air with their talons and snapped their porcine jaws in his direction.

"Stay with us," they whispered. "Die with us. Feed us. Haunt our halls and entertain us with cries for pity and release. We will laugh as we eat your flesh. We will crack your bones and suck out the marrow. We will make masks of your skin and wear them as we copulate. Stay with us, O' man of the sunlit world. We will suck the soul from you, and your screams will echo here forever."

Kagen saw a crack in the floor and abruptly drove the end of the torch down into it so that brand stood tall and bright. He quickly drew his second dagger and tapped one blade to the other, creating a single high, sweet, ringing note that floated above them all and rebounded from the stone walls.

"You did not hear my words, you ugly little bastards," he snarled. "I have no soul to take, and any who stand in my way will feel the bite of my knives. I am Kagen of Argon. I am the Son of the Poison Rose. You have no power over me. I have no soul to steal, for I am Kagen the *Damned*."

He spoke these words loudly, with force, and again rang the blades together. The goblins winched and recoiled from the sound.

The chief goblin glowered at him, his eyes feral and his hunger naked.

"You are meat, and you are ours."

Kagen, knowing that this was his death, felt his fear crack and fall away. After all that had happened since Hakkia rose up, this was how he knew his path should end. In darkness. In pain and death and endless nothingness beneath the world. Tuke would not even be able to bury what was left of him.

"So be it," he said. His body shifted into a fighting posture, with his weight shifted onto the balls of his feet, knees bent, body angled, jaw set, and a killer's smile on his lips. "If you want me, you ugly little bastards, then come and take me. Hell will not take me alone."

They stared. They paused.

And then with a mingled, thunderous howl of red delight, they swarmed at him.

Kagen slashed out left and right, his blades meeting the scabrous flesh and tearing through it. The Poison Rose's knives were forged on Tull Heklon by the priestesses of the Sacred Trust. They were finer than the best Bulconian steel, and no blades took a sharper edge or held it longer. He took the chief goblin first, crossing his knives and then whipping them apart so that they bit all the way to the bone. The creature spun away, clutching at a throat that was little more than threads and rags. The force of its heart shot red-black blood out into the faces of a half dozen others. Kagen ignored those for the moment and half turned, kicking out with the flat of his foot to catch a goblin in the stomach, folding it in half and driving it back into the path of others who were surging forward.

He charged into the center of the goblins behind him, parrying the raking claws, making dozens of fast, small cuts to arms and shoulders and thighs, severing muscle and tendon. The wounded goblins screamed and fell away, crashing into their fellows. In the confusion of that crowded tunnel, Kagen fought to wound and maim more than kill. The screams of the injured were one of his weapons, the spurting blood a tool. This was a strategy his mother had taught all of her sons and daughters: to be a storm of blood and pain. Killing mattered less than confusion, sudden agony, crippling injuries, and the pleading of the mangled.

Then he surged forward, using blades and pommels, elbows and knees to bash a hole through the goblins that stood between him and the deeper part of the tunnel. He wanted that godsdamned sword and would have it at any cost. There were but two possible paths out of that moment: victory or death. Retreat was its own defeat, and Kagen was tired of losing.

As he fought, he wondered if his gods were watching. They had brought him to this, and maybe he would shame them for abandoning him so completely.

"You bastards!" he roared, though in that moment he did not know if he cursed the goblins or the gods.

The monsters reeled and stumbled as he charged forward. They had the numbers, but they did not have his skills. They slashed with claws, and he answered with steel. They crowded him, snapping with their pig teeth, but he chopped at them with a savagery that was their match and more.

He slashed and stabbed, chopped and sliced, kicked and even bit when his hands were too busy. His flesh burned from their nails, and his limbs ran with his own hot blood. But Kagen did not care. There was a purity to this kind of mayhem that was satisfying, even healing in some strange way. This fight— beyond the sight of any human eyes—made him remember who and what he was. Son of the Poison Rose was more than a remark; it was a statement.

The goblins ahead rushed him, but his onslaught made them falter, and finally, with howls like children in agony, they scattered, and the way ahead was clear.

Kagen saw this and broke into a flat out run.

The goblins howled and gave chase, and for an unknown time—minutes, hours, or even years, as far as Kagen knew— they all ran. The corridor split into two, and he followed the one that looked most well-traveled, hoping it would lead him to the chamber where the dead prince rested. Though he was aware that it could just as easily have been the one the goblins used. But with no map to guide him, he followed instinct, hoping all the while he was not making a fatal error.

Kagen ran and ran until sweat boiled from his pores, his lungs burned, and he thought his heart would burst in his chest. And then the corridor spilled out into a chamber, and he skidded to a sloppy halt, losing balance and dropping to his knees.

There, as if in mockery of supplication, he beheld the thing that had brought him to that cave. The creature that Tuke had believed in enough to bring them all this way into the wilderness.

He sat there.

Him.

A figure in armor that was so badly pitted and rusted with age that it was more like lace than plate steel. Beneath it was a sur-coat of chainmail that had withered to a red-brown latticework. His face was a sunken and withered mass of wrinkles that had faded to the color of old dust. Spiders had spun webs across his eye-sockets, but those webs drooped now with disuse, and those spiders had long since died. The skeletal hands gripped the arms of a throne-like chair cut from the living rock, but that cold stone held more vitality than anything belonging to this Prince Vorlon of Old Shimele—a kingdom lost so thoroughly in the past that it was referenced on no map Kagen had ever seen. Not even Tuke's map pointed that way. If prince he had truly been, then his princedom was this hole in the ground, and his killers were the ancestors of the goblins who made up the population of this realm of shadows.

Kagen got slowly to his feet and walked over to the foot of the throne.

Across the thighs of the dead prince was a naked blade. If he had expected it to glow with some inner power or to hum with magical potential, Kagen was disappointed. The centuries had not been kind to the steel. It looked like the kind of relics disinterred from burial mounds at the edges of old fields of battle. Or, perhaps, like the fragile weapons dredged up along with shipwrecks.

"Magic sword…?" he said aloud. "Gods damn it all."

He looked into the eyes of the dead.

"It did not save you, did it, my lord?"

A sound made him turn, and he saw that in the mouth of the tunnel the goblins had returned. Scores of them choked the only exit, and many were marked by his daggers or were splashed with the dark blood of their kin. He waited, ready to renew the fight, but none of them entered the chamber.

Kagen sheathed his blades, wondering if that would spark them to enter, but they stayed where they were. His heart was still pounding. The fact that a horde of monsters were afraid of drawing near to a corpse dead more than a thousand years did nothing to ease his fears.

Through sheer force of will he turned away from the monsters and faced the prince. He began to reach for the sword, paused, stopped, and then cleared his throat.

"Look," he began awkwardly, "Your Highness, I don't know how much of the old legends are true. Maybe you're Prince Vorlon and maybe you're just some knight who got lost and had the bad luck to come in here. Why, though? Were you being chased? Had you lost a battle and come here to hide out? Or… hell…maybe you were drawn here with some absurd story of buried treasure. I don't know, and I never will, I'm sure. But listen to me: if there is any part of you still here—ghost or ghoul or whatever—a new power has risen in the south. Magic, outlawed for a thousand years, has returned to the world. It's awakening the monsters and spirits and other things. Dark magic that threatens the entire world of men. We are on the brink and probably going to lose."

He paused, trying not to feel ridiculous and self-conscious talking to old bones.

"The Witch-king of Hakkia has conquered everything west of the Cathedral Mountains. Everything. His power is beyond understanding. I walked through lakes of blood the night the Hakkian Ravens invaded. I know that people like me can't win this war. I'm a man. Not a prince, not a champion, not a hero from some old tale. I have no magic weapons, no impenetrable armor. Nothing like that."

The chamber was utterly silent. Even the goblins were still.

"If you are what the legends say, and if that sword holds some kind of power—hell, *any* kind of power—then I have to take it with me. We need something with which to fight the Witch-king. Can you hear me? Can you understand?"

The eye holes in the skull were black, and the fleshless mouth hung open.

"I will say one thing more," said Kagen. "No…two things."

He licked his lips.

"First, I mean no disrespect by coming here to take your sword. I would do anything, go anywhere, dare it all to stop this evil. If you truly were a prince and hero, then you will understand that."

Silence.

"And second, I offer my thanks to you, Prince Vorlon of Shimele. I hope that by my taking this sword you can rest."

There was a sound that made him turn once more, but it did not come from the goblins. Nor from the corpse. Kagen tried to make sense of what he heard, but it was soft. A sigh or a whisper.

"Only the passage of air," he told himself.

Then he steeled himself to reach out and take the sword. He stretched out one hand but paused, his palm inches above the ornate handle. He saw that there were small gemstones set into the steel of the crossguard and pommel, rubies and sapphires that were dulled by time and dust.

"I will say one more thing," murmured Kagen. "If this weapon is all that the legends say, and I am able to use it to slay the Witch-king, then when he is dead, I will bring it back here and lay it once more across your thighs. I am damned, but I am no thief."

Having made that vow, Kagen closed his hand around the handle of the ancient sword *Caladbolg*.

He braced himself for something nightmarish to happen, for the dead prince to resist him, or to come alive and fight him for ownership of the storied blade.

But nothing at all happened.

The sword was so light, its weight and density lost to time and rust. As he lifted it, the pitted blade trembled, and Kagen steadied it with the fingers of his other hand lest it bend and snap.

He held it upright, trying to sense or feel some kind of power. Kagen had no idea what magic might *feel* like. Maybe like lightning, or something of that kind of intensity.

But again…there was nothing.

"Oh, Tuke, you crazy bastard," said Kagen. "You've sent me to my doom for a piece of rusted junk."

The sighing sound came again, and Kagen turned sharply, knowing with instant terror that it *had* come from the dead prince.

There, on the rocky throne, the figure was trembling.

Moving.

Slowly. So painfully slow.

Kagen stared in total horror as the withered chest of the prince expanded as he took a breath. How, without lungs or flesh, such a thing was even possible, was beyond him. He stumbled backward, hearing the alarmed cries of the goblins but hearing his own sharp yell of terror all the louder.

The helmet rattled against the bones of the skull. The pitted armor juddered as the creature raised its hands, gripped the arms of the chair, and pushed itself erect with painful, impossible slowness.

Kagen moved backward one stumbling step at a time as the prince rose to his full height. Because the throne was on a small dais and the helmet had a spiked crown, it made the thing appear huge, a giant from old stories. Dust puffed from every joint and link of the chainmail. Spiders scrambled from under the seat and cockroaches dropped from under the surcoat.

Kagen tripped and fell, landing hard on his buttocks, the *Caladbolg* out in front of him. Not as a weapon, but as some kind of talisman against this thing.

"By the g-gods…" he stammered, tripping over the words.

Prince Vorlon of Shimele turned his ghastly head toward Kagen and in that moment the empty eye sockets flared with inner light, a red and hellish glow that exuded such heat that Kagen could feel it. The monster raised a hand and pointed a skeletal finger at Kagen. At the sword.

The prince's jaws worked, and Kagen knew that this thing was trying to speak, to condemn the theft or pronounce some deadly curse. Kagen nearly threw the sword at him. It felt heavier than it had before, and when he looked at the blade, he felt his mind toppling. The blade was rebuilding itself—closing pits carved by rust, taking on weight and substance, becoming whole again.

"Magic!" cried Kagen. "By the gods, it's real. This is magic. True magic."

Within moments the weapon he held was whole, the blade long and bright as if newly polished. The edge was like that of a razor, the tip a dagger point.

Kagen looked from the blade to the prince.

He ached to take *Caladbolg* and simply run. With it he could carve a path through the goblins. And yet...

The prince was real, too. Would the sword restore him to life and vigor? Was that the secret here? Not to steal the weapon, but to restore it to its rightful owner? Would that complete some time-forgotten spell? Would it restore this champion of the elder world to life? If so, would this legendary hero choose to stand with Kagen and Tuke against the Witch-king and his forces of darkness? Or was this more evidence of magic returning to the world in the service of the Hakkian usurper?

Kagen was torn. Need said one thing, but honor—even the honor of the damned—said something else.

But he took a chance. He reversed *Caladbolg* in his hand and extended the handle toward the prince's outstretched hand.

"I will not steal from you, O' Prince," he said reverently.

"*Caladbolg* belongs to you, and I offer it once more to your keeping."

The prince stared at him with his flaming eyes. The hilt of the sword was inches from those skeletal fingers. For a moment Kagen thought the prince would take the handle and thereby be restored. That moment stretched and stretched.

And then Prince Vorlon threw back his head and laughed.

It was a crashing, crushing, deafening sound. A peal of laughter boiling up from the very pits of hell. It smashed into Kagen, sending him reeling backward. Cracks whipsawed along the walls, and chunks of stone broke loose from the ceiling as the laugh rose and rose and rose.

"Free!" cried the dead prince. "By the gods of light and thunder, I am free!"

Immediately the skeleton inside the armor began to collapse, bursting into clouds of dust. The armor split apart and fell, disintegrating into metal powder. The skull was the last thing to fall, and, in the moment before it struck the floor, the flaming eyes flared with blinding and painful intensity. Then they abruptly winked out.

Kagen lay there, dazed, covered in dust, the sword heavy in his sweating hand.

On the seat and all around the dais, there was nothing left of the prince but dust.

"G-g-g-gods..." was all Kagen could say.

He stared for a very long time, unsure of what to say or even how to think about this.

Then he was on his feet, heart slamming painfully against the inner walls of his chest. He held the great sword, and now it hummed with power so rich, so potent, that it rippled through his arm and outward to every part of him.

Kagen staggered toward the exit, ready to cleave his way out of this mad place, ready to fill hell with goblin dead, but they saw the sword in his hand, and they screamed as they fled.

He stalked along the corridors, not at all sure he was even going the right way. It was only when he saw the pale flicker of his torch in the black distance that he knew he was on the right path. Kagen broke into a run, aware of the darkness growing thick behind him. Aware of goblin eyes—terrified and hateful—watching from niches and holes in the walls. They hissed at him as he passed. Some wept, and some cried out in their guttural tongue.

He ran and ran.

And then he burst out into the thickening twilight.

Tuke was there, and as Kagen crossed the threshold, his friend grabbed him and pulled him into the cold, clean spill of newly risen moonlight.

"I have it," gasped Kagen. "I have the…"

His words died on his lips.

He and Tuke stared at the sword of Prince Vorlon.

At the pitted, broken, twisted length of time-rotted metal. As they stared, it began to crumble into dust. In the space of a dozen heartbeats, all Kagen held was debris, and when he opened his hand, the night wind blew it away.

Kagen's knees buckled, and he dropped down again. Tuke knelt with him, his body seeming to deflate as the reality of it all struck him.

"Magic sword…" said Kagen, gasping and blinking.

"Magic sword," agreed Tuke, looking stricken.

They turned as a deep rumble thundered beneath them. The mouth of the goblin barrow belched out a cloud of gas and dust, and then that whole section of the landscape shuddered and fell inward. Tuke shot to his feet, caught Kagen under the armpits, and hauled him away. They broke into a fierce and desperate run as the whole world seemed to collapse beneath them. Trees cracked and crashed down. The rumble felt as if it reached down to the halls of hell itself.

They ran half a mile. Their horses, panicked, ran on ahead.

And then the two men collapsed against the rising wall of a slope beyond the field of destruction. There they lay, panting, gasping, bathed in sweat, their minds shocked and filled with horrors.

It was a very long time before either of them could speak.

Tuke said it first, repeating the same words. "Magic sword."

Kagen looked at him and then up at the moon. "Magic sword."

It was Kagen who started laughing first, but Tuke followed close on his heels. They laughed as the moon sailed above them.

They laughed like madmen far into the night.

Wolfen Divine

Hailey Piper

A Story of No Gods for Drowning

At his birth, Mother Wolf sinks her teeth through Mero's membrane, and then his neck, to check the soul in his flesh and be sure it's bound with hers. It is a love-bite, or some call it a soul-bite. Mother Wolf holds the hairy mewling infant down a moment, and when satisfied, she lets him go.

Only decades and betrayals later does Mero learn that all creatures do this, whether they know it or not. The soul-bite is universal. A fawn exiled by a moss-coated doe, a terror bird abandoning her nest of starved hatchlings, a jungle cat devouring fresh cubs, a grim-faced woman plunging her baby's head into the sea and not letting go until the desperate wriggling ends—in every instance, a failure of unity from soul to soul.

All creatures do this. Even the gods.

The castle is a ripe fig tree, and he's come to pluck another fruit before the rest fall and rot against the earth. That is the only eventual fate for the beleaguered crowd filing into the misshapen entrance of mortar and stone.

At their heels, the Holy War breaks mountains into mist and swaps bone marrow and skin around skeletons, wrongful miracles turning stone and human alike inside out.

Mero has seen his share of horrific miracles. He was born one. These clustering folk should pray thanks they'll never know his life. Even when death takes them, reincarnation will likely find their soul a creature untainted by divine curiosity. The Holy Psychopomp Tree loves the grateful.

This castle—what a miserable place. High and mighty when it housed a minor temple, but better a humbly built home from the start than this crumbling display of former grandeur.

And yet, in pour the refugees from across southeastern Aeg. They pack themselves behind stone walls like hares in a too-small den. Their watchful eyes peer over parapets as if they could do a damn thing should some monstrous god bring the Holy War to their gates.

The sky blooms crimson, and clouds burn with furious eyes. The gods have rent the world asunder in such spectacle that these frightful hares only look out for grand figures.

Never for man-sized shadows slipping into the empress's home.

While others posture, or cower, or cover their faces and cry, he looks as disaffected as the unchanging moon. Guards armed with poleaxes and barbed swords watch for trouble-makers, and at the corner of Mero's sight he catches a tricorn hat tucked over a curious figure in a pulled-up coat, but he doesn't worry. To them he looks like any other man. They would never guess his wolf-wombed birth or the touch of divine darkness bristling beneath his skin.

Lineage beyond Mother Wolf was a mystery for the longest time. He didn't even know he could change into a boy until the end of his second year, and then he stalked villages with both feet and paws, learned of gods and their mortal children, and found the marble temple of his forebears. At least, he guesses they're his forebears. He's never spoken to them, only eavesdropped on Father Ornich, God of the Night, and the white-faced visage of Carimeldra, Grandmother Death.

I am not death incarnate, she once said, but not to her secretive grandson, hidden between mighty columns and hunched faithful. *Death is my friend and ally and purpose.*

Gods speak in riddles, but they perform in blood. Mero is hated enough for his strangeness—how much worse would he be hated if anyone knew he was a descendant of those who started the Holy War? Carimeldra, her godly children and grandchildren, her half-brother Savvas and the progeny birthed from his divine womb, all feeding on humanity to carve out a new function of death's domain.

Never mind that one mortal mistake has slipped through the cracks. Always Mero is that shadow, sliding through paths unseen. Unwanted.

Underestimated.

He passes beneath the overbite of the castle's iron portcullis, where clustered refugees spread through the courtyard, circle one of the wells, or slip inside, where the empress and her bride offer shelter and food.

Mero joins the last of these, but he does not eat the hearty black bread or orchard-grown fruit. His eyes feign bleariness as he watches the guards, their weapons, the hatted stranger, and fellow refugees. Every moment needs care. Were he to die here, who would take up his cause?

He can only act the part of frail man and keep the wolf tucked deep in his belly until the sky hangs dark as his innards. That's when he'll get his chance.

Here comes the dusk, and the night, where a full moon glowers like a god's eye from above. Those watchful guards might stare into it, expecting it to blink, too busy watching the sky to keep an eye on their castle full of refugees.

By the time they notice anything's wrong, Mero will be on his way home. Back to his cause.

To Liza's chamber.

"Boy?" The first word Liza said to him, what she called him before they pieced together a name. Any other villager this stretch of Aeg would have shouted him away, but she was all silver-eyed curiosity.

Even when he began to change in a panic. She should have screamed and ran for help, but instead she was enchanted. Bemused. Welcoming.

As if somehow, even all those years ago, she already loved him.

Firelit sconces play shadow games in a music-free dance. The only rhythm is the cacophonous breathing within the gloomy castle corridors, where Mero huddles with the refugees beneath woolen blankets. Overwarm and itchy, he tolerates it through crawling moments, waiting for the empress and her bride to retire to the castle's core, with their best-armed guards too distant to catch him.

When all is still, he rises in careful inches up the stone wall. His torso wobbles on firm legs, a pantomime for grogginess as he feigns searching for a latrine, though he would never relieve himself here. Regardless of his chosen shape, his piss will stink of wolf, panicking messenger starlings and stable horses. The stagger is only another disguise should anyone stop him as he searches for a straggler.

Here—a corridor ends where the ox-hair rug runs out. Most sleepers have clustered on its soft surface or packed themselves into nearby chambers, but a gangly young man has curled into a ball alone, choosing the privacy of the cold stone floor.

Or maybe when he was small, a parent sank teeth into him for that post-birth soul-bite and found they could not love him. An unwanted child, grown to an unwanted man. Maybe what comes next will be a mercy.

The grapevine tells that on the continent's western shore, great Logoi murders a dozen a day to power her fight against Grandmother Death. Godly cleverness in that Goddess of Reason, she tells any who'll listen that life has purpose, never mind the thousand corpses draping her temple steps. It must sting even her immortal flesh to know that, hearing of these deaths, Carimeldra grins a skull-faced grin.

Against that mountain of sacrifice, Mero's need to steal away a body every few days is a raindrop in the Merciless Sea. Logoi herself might call it reasonable to tend his ceaseless cause.

"With me, you are wanted," Mero whispers to his prize. "For Liza."

He hunches beside the gangly young man, cups the jaw in one hand, the scalp in the other, and lets the wolf spill through limbs to break the man's neck.

No one stirs at the wet crack. Mero has to kill this way; a god's mortal child will drink blood through the skin, and he can't risk a cut. He hurries out of his pilfered rags and ties them into knots that bind the young man's body over his back. The makeshift rope is loose. Mero needs the give for what he's about to become.

Some say the gods can change their shape, and Mero believes it. Either Father Ornich blessed Mother Wolf with a divine fragment, or he chose a wolf's form and created a child the usual way.

Mero is no unkillable god, but he changes shape in his own slick transmogrification. He wonders if it hurt his father to change like this.

It hurts Mero every time.

Claws drive through his fingernails and toenails, and they drag his limbs stretching behind them. His back curves, and his mouth twists snout-like, and flat teeth melt into sharpened points. Some of the changes come like a miracle, rewriting what is real. Others slide through flesh, bringing speed and strength through agony.

He swallows every scream until black hair coats his form, and then he races like a demon wind over sleeping forms, past sconce-held fires, back the way he first came into the castle. The portcullis is shut hard against earth now, but the outer walls have narrow breaches, and he is a hairy shadow. Good at slipping in and out. Gone before anyone notices him or the dead refugee bobbing on his back.

A new fire dances ahead. Strange, he doesn't remember a wall there, and he knows paths too well to have forgotten one.

Someone stands in his way.

Flames lick at a splayed palm and fingers. They should eat through skin and muscle, leave the burning figure screaming, but the crystalizing shadow stands resolute. Respected by fire. Cloaked in a thick coat, the figure keeps a collar raised over the lower half of their face and a tricorn hat dipped low. A firelit eye glares through the crack between, curious and inquisitive.

What are you? Mero would ask, but his wolf-mouth can't speak.

Fire slides through this stranger's fingers as if they're cupping water, and they splash flame against air and stone. Other shadows stalk from the corridor, carrying swords and spears.

"Miss Aspa?" one of them asks. "It's—what do we do?"

Mero forces a growl up his throat. How did this happen?

His thoughts turn to ash when Aspa races at him. Flame-laced fingers seize his fur, and their light catches in the sorceress's left eye, a glare of fury ready to burn through the castle's half-wolf intruder. He tenses, expecting raw screaming pain.

Except the burning never comes. The fire doesn't catch.

Aspa's eye widens, mirroring Mero's surprise. Of course—the fire is her gift, same as transmogrification is his. She's another descendant, and divinity can't hurt divinity. Whose child is this? Avgi, Goddess of Fire? Diadres, Goddess of Light?

Whichever branch of godly family tree she's from, Aspa stands in Mero's way, only one more disappointment spawned by some god or another.

Mero raises an arm and slams a firm fist into Aspa's gut. He bunches her coat collar in his clawed fist and lifts her against the wall, to his snout, higher, ready to drive tooth and claw when the sorcerer's hat tips against the stone and falls away.

"Miss Aspa!" a voice barks, and now the corridor rouses with mumbling and gasps.

But Aspa doesn't cry out. Remnants of ancient burns coat her lips. Her right cheek and eye are patterned in a lightning storm of scars. Ordinary mortal blood should have healed these wounds when they were fresh, same as blood does for Mero, but the scars tell a story of ignorance and isolation.

No godly parent stayed to raise her. Pregnancy, abandonment, a child staggering into adulthood with no idea what she was or what she could do until she found out for herself.

We're the same, Mero wants to tell her. He understands; he *knows.*

In times of plenty, the gods' mortal descendants are respected, but these are times of a god-made war, and descendants are the only parts of the divine that can be hurt. That can be killed. Miss Aspa—investigator, sorceress, descendant—has made herself indispensable, binding her gift to the empress's will. What choice did she have? Become an outcast, like Mero?

There is no god of mercy, but Mero thrashes his arm, tossing the sorceress into the group of nearby swordsmen. They tumble in a heap, and he breaks for the outgoing halls.

Another guard stands in his way, spear aimed forward. Others stand beyond him.

Enough of this. Mero's spent all the mercy he can afford tonight, and he won't be driven from his cause by an overconfident man who thinks a leather jerkin and wooden shaft can stop the child of a god.

Claws carve through leather, skin, and bone. Ribs crack around Mero's fingers, and before the spear can plunge into his belly, wolfen teeth snap forward, close around the guard's cheeks, nose, now-soppy eyeball, and tear his face from his skull. He might resemble Grandmother Death were his facial bones not red and glistening.

The sudden blood pours tingling joy through Mero's muscles. Hunger and exhaustion fade as his flesh sponges up liquid power, and he launches over the screaming mangled man to make his escape.

This is a descendant's gift, Aspa, Mero thinks. *Healing and power in blood.*

Something strikes him from behind, but he keeps running. Only when he's about to make a turn in the dark corridors, spilling over once-sleeping refugees, does he glance back at Aspa.

A brutish short sword juts from one hand. Red rain drips from the blade.

Mero will tend his own wounds later. He rushes along the castle's main hall, through another man's soft body, which he paints across the gate and pillars before bounding into the courtyard. Screams chase him toward outer stone walls, but he soon finds a breach and wriggles through with his dead man of a prize.

His feet and claws fly over field. Over bridge. Into thick green darkness and toward home.

Only when he's nearly reached the toad-like mound of stone does he realize why his energy feels limitless, why Aspa didn't need to chase. She didn't even need to hurt him.

She only needed to ruin his task by cutting open the body at his back.

That gangly young man's belly has been split open. Organs grease Mero's flank and hindlegs, and blood has splashed stone and grass and seeped inside him.

Only a husk bobs at his back. Nothing remains for his cause. His skin drank it all without meaning to, without knowing he was doing it, as greedy a creature as when he first met Liza at her village's outskirts, gulping well water. That was the dry season, years ago. She would have been within her right to call other villagers with water so scarce, but she chose otherwise.

His cause began with that small mercy.

He stares at the forest canopy, where branches and broad leaves form black silhouettes against the bone-white moon. The night has been for nothing. And worse, he'll have to risk it all again.

For the blood.

A noise disturbs him just as he's falling asleep. Leathery boot soles crunch the rodent bones he's scattered within his runt of a temple.

Someone is here. Come for him. They'll end him, his cause, find Liza's chamber, and what then?

No, he won't suffer them. These interlopers want to make of him like the cramp-burrowed hares he's made of their kind, but if any descendant can build a place of power, this is his. The wide entrance deceives all comers. Piled flat stones form slender tunnels, narrow and dark, forking and circling and treacherous.

It is a place unsuited for anyone but his hairy shadow. They bring their scent, and he chases it beneath sloped ceilings.

Intrusive firelight breaches the inner black, where unfamiliar eyes try to understand the little world he's built. He creeps closer, gets a sense for the light, the figure holding it. A tricorn hat. Coat collar raised to guard a face. The fire taking the shape of a hand.

That inquisitive sorceress, Aspa.

A slick cunning works through his mind as he pieces the night together. He was expected at the empress's castle. A trap sprung, a body bled, Aspa's half-wolf prey tracked to his lair. Before tonight, she must have known he could look like a man, an understanding gained from his past raids. She must have expected the murderer to slide in with the refugees, but she didn't know which haggard face hid her enemy until Mero showed her the wolf.

He can show her the wolf again. They are siblings in sweet neglect, discarded by divine parents, but he will see her throat torn by wolfen tooth or man's fingernails before he lets her destroy his world.

You don't know my cause.

Mero watches Aspa curl and uncurl fingers, giving commands by firelit hand. Two shapes walk behind her, and they can read her signs while Mero can't, their plan as unknowable as their thoughts.

Fine, they can have their signals and ideas. They can't have Mero's home. Their light thickens the darkness beyond them, and as death is his grandmother's ally, shadows are his.

He circles behind the small party of interlopers. Aspa's fire is a forever beacon, giving away her location, gleaming in steel, telling Mero where to sneak, to rush, to catch one swordswoman and make quick work of her throat.

Mero leaves her gurgling and sputtering at an intersection

of paths. She's too far gone to help, but noisy enough to bring another guard running. A sword clangs against rippled stone floor where this sweet ally sinks to one knee, meaning to check a wound, say a prayer, hold a hand.

The invader hardly has time to look up as Mero howls from the darkness. He sinks harsh teeth into a bicep and twists, snapping the bone, and then he goes for the neck. The man's gore soon smears Mero's snout.

Moments before fire takes the world. Aspa springs at him, swiping her short sword through empty air where Mero recoils from her steel and grins. Her mistake was leading only two allies into his temple, as if that would be enough.

Always underestimating him.

She slashes again, driving every blow in silence, like she isn't tired, like she's drained blood from her fellows. Mero can do the same. Her divine-imbued blood is useless, but she's helped his cause in bringing these bodies full of sweet crimson nectar. All he has to do now is kill her. Keep her from Liza's chamber.

He bites Aspa's arm and tenses to break it, but a palm flares in his eyes, and he slips back in blinded panic. Aspa's descendant-fueled flame can't hurt him, but light is light, and he's used to the dark. She drives close again, and he ducks toward another corridor. He should turn, run, circle around. Never let her know from which side the killing bite will come until he pops her head from her neck.

A tiny-boned crunching pricks his ears. Music for his mistake—the assumption that Aspa only brought two allies to help her.

A short blade jabs Mero's flank, and he whirls around to claw through skin and muscle. The figure is already retreating, and now a god's child bleeds thanks to ordinary weapons.

What now? Pray to Father Ornich? Grandmother Carimeldra? Aunts, cousins, half-siblings? The Goddess of Death unites the family in war, but the dregs like Mero prowl in darkness alone. When Liza's cause came to him, he begged help from Aeda, the once-generous Goddess of Birth, painting her winding sign of the umbilical cord, but she is only a distant cousin. No answers, no miracles.

If there's any god for this darkness, he doesn't know them. He can only hope the lack of light continues to love him like his family never could.

Come then, all of them! Take him on with their steel teeth built by hammer and anvil, with their soft bellies full of bread and fish, never knowing the sweet fullness of ripe red meat.

A blade clangs against stone behind his left hindleg. He whirls around again, ready to chew through Aspa's wrist and rip her hand away. He'll fade back to man's shape and drive her own blade through her heart.

He's halfway turned, halfway changed, when he finds emptiness at his left side. When he realizes the feint.

The sword catches between his ribs, and he ducks back, screaming. A clawed hand clutches blood-soaked hair and skin. He scuttles deeper into the temple, thoughtless, hopeless. Fire swells in his face, and he readies for Aspa again. Her step comes from the left, and this time she means it. A brutish blade drives deep into his belly, and Aspa lets it go, lets it float back with him into the dark.

He doesn't mean to stumble into Liza's chamber or crash to the floor. No hiding his cause now. No way out.

"I'm keeping this because I want to," Liza said, smirking. "You're staying because it's your fault. You're the one who followed me to bed."

She had such fire in her silver eyes, dark hair flaring in the forest wind, hand on her swollen belly. Mero looked the wolf that day, but his teeth shined with a smile. Liza wanted him to stay. And he wanted to stay with her, raise their child.

He wanted to be a better father than his ever had.

Mero claws at a floor coated in human bones, desperate for rejuvenating blood to soak his hands and heal him. It's his god-descended right.

He finds only husks. His cause has drained them already.

"Wait," he whispers, his face shriveling to that of a man.

Aspa looms, hand blazing, sword gleaming. The same fire that lights her skin flashes in her left eye, peeking between hat and collar. Blood stains her coat. She has the look of someone used to that. She might even be used to what Mero will show her, what he's shown no one else since his cause came into his life.

Tucked into a corner away from the kidnapped husks and beside a pile of stolen clothes and blankets, there lies another, older husk.

Liza's head lolls to one side, arms curled over her torn abdomen. Between spread legs, Mero has built a linen nest, where a gasping infant struggles to breathe.

She has the foot of baby girl, and another of a wolf cub. One paw lies beside her, while a human hand curls against her chest. Both eyes are squeezed shut, one rounded by hairless flesh, the other by gray fur. Part of a snout stretches from one side of her head. There is no other mouth or nose, and her disconnected throat sprouts from a cavity where no stomach has ever formed.

Can Aspa see in this dim light? Can she understand this infant girl is trapped midway through a change she can't control?

"She can't eat," Mero says, half-speaking, half-moaning.

He doesn't have the power to tell how he bathes his daughter in victims' blood. That there's no other way to keep her alive. That this is the flip side of the soul-bite. Mero bit into his daughter, same as Mother Wolf bit into him. A child might be turned away by the parent, but when the bond is true from soul to soul, the parent will do anything for that little one. Even die. Even kill.

Aspa's last swordsman leans beside her. "He's taken a little one," he says, approaching the nest where a nameless daughter struggles to breathe.

Aspa raises a warning hand and speaks with firelit fingers.

"Descendant gift?" The swordsman looks again. "Gods' sakes, she's a baby. She needs care."

Were the swordsman to lean over the makeshift nest, Mero would tear open his throat and rain sustenance over his daughter. Or try to.

But Aspa holds the man back. Her gleaming eye studies the room, probing it for answers. She doesn't know Liza's name, but she can infer a dead mother when she sees torn belly and frail infant. Does Aspa guess that Liza bled inside, where the little one began to drain her own mother before birth? Can she infer that Mero tore his daughter free before she drowned inside a corpse?

Can she tell the child might live to grow strong, learn to control her changes, and then she wouldn't need human sacrifice to survive? Does Aspa have children herself? Is she familiar with the soul-bite's bond?

Aspa's eye twitches in Mero's direction one last time before she slides back into the temple's darkness. A fiery hand flickers new signs to the swordsman, and then they disappear.

Mero can only hope, even pray they won't come back. There is no god of mercy, but maybe someone divine should take up the mantle. The world could use a little mercy.

Collapsing stones shatter his optimistic reverie. He grunts to half-standing, sword still buried in his gut, and staggers toward the chamber's entrance, where a thick scent and rumbling sound have overtaken the air.

He only makes it five steps before he finds interlocking stones. The temple was hard to build, but scrape one wall loose, and a chamber can collapse into a tomb, where a father and daughter might be buried like common god-betraying witches. Like nothing.

This new darkness is not Mero's friend. It chokes the air and makes the child's shallow breaths a little more desperate. He staggers toward Liza's corner and drops to the floor beside the baby's nest.

"Change, my girl," he says, almost begging. "Whichever shape you take, I'll love you the same. Finish the change, one way or the other, so you can live."

Had he brought her to his father's temple, would Ornich have helped? Would he have bled priests to feed his granddaughter, for days and months and years? Or would he have ended her then and there, and ended his unwanted son, too?

Mero pools wolfen strength into his arms and draws his daughter close. He would bleed for her, if it would matter. He would die to give her life. Descendant blood can't feed descendants, same as their gifts can't harm each other.

But he can grant another gift.

Sometimes, a parent kills the young when the soul-bite reveals a stranger. Exiled fawns, abandoned hatchlings, devoured cubs, drowned infants.

But sometimes, death comes from love. Maybe that's why Grandmother Carimeldra wages her Holy War, in a vicious act of love toward every creature in Aeg. Maybe that's why death exists at all.

Mero cannot let his daughter starve and writhe in an empty tomb at his passing.

He clutches her close, warming her with his fur and breath.

He tells her of love, and reincarnation, and what fragmented hopes and dreams he can manage as steely pain sucks at his gut.

And then he sinks his teeth in. The darkness becomes his friend again, hiding this moment from his eyes.

When his daughter's gone still, and he's finished crying, he leans against the stone wall and goes on cradling her, and he wonders if Aspa foresaw this end. He wonders what kind of creature he'll become when this pain sees him into his reincarnated life. And he wonders whether the next parent's soul-bite will find him wanting.

Or if he'll be loved.

The Seventh Queen

Heath Amodio

I am the seventh queen to stand at the side of the peaceful King Phillip IV. The previous six women have all died, four in the very same tower I find myself locked in now. It is said that all six killed themselves. I am not in the least bit suicidal. Still, I have an eerie feeling that I won't survive the night.

The tower faces east. It allows for stunning sunrises but darkens quickly once the sun passes midday. Candles are required several hours before Bethany, my lady-in-waiting, arrives to gather me for dinner. There are two windows, and they both face east. Two more windows on the western side were filled with stone after queens three and five fell to their deaths. The people say they leapt, but I've chosen to reserve judgment for now.

When looking out from the remaining windows, one can see the courtyard below, where princes of various ages practice their swordplay. Of my predecessors, only three lived long enough to bear children. All five children are boys.

Beyond the courtyard stands the castle wall. It towers over the nearby trees like a boy looms over an ant, and yet my tower dwarfs the wall in comparison. Further out, after a mile or so of woodland, lay the ocean. It glitters like glass beneath a thousand candles when the sun rises from behind it. The shimmer blinds me for a moment, even from such a great distance.

My dungeon, as I've come to call it, would be pleasant if it didn't feel like such a prison at times. Between the quickly fading light and the locked door, one can imagine how the other queens fell into despair. I am allowed out of the tower four times a day: breakfast, lunch, followed by a brief respite in the courtyard, dinner, and to fornicate when the king finds himself wanting. A proper wife would describe the latter as making love, but I barely know my husband. I cannot say that I love him.

Phillip is an attractive man by all measures. Tall, with dark hair and light eyes. His jaw, much like the muscles that make up his physique, is carved from stone. Everyone is infatuated with him and loves him for the peace he's maintained across his vast kingdom for several decades. But love for accomplishments does not equate to the all-encompassing love between a husband and wife. While a wife's duty may give justification to call the shallow surface connection love, I refuse to cater to such trivial definitions. If I am to love Phillip, he will have to earn it.

A timid knock at my dungeon's heavy wooden door announces Bethany's arrival. It must be dinner time.

"Enter," I say.

Bethany enters. She stares at her feet as she always does, a habit I've tried to break her from to no avail. It wasn't out of fear for me, but rather pity for my circumstance. She, a servant girl, was free to move about the castle. I was not. One could assume the guilt she must have felt.

"The King awaits your presence in the dining room, Your Grace."

"Must you be so formal all the time, Bethany? I've told you countless times that you're my only friend, my only source to everything beyond that door. You must have some great gossip. Perhaps the story of a love affair in the kitchen? Some secret festivity in the village, perhaps?"

"I'm sorry, Your Grace. I know nothing of lovers or parties. I mostly sleep or tend to my father when I'm not at your service."

"Your life mirrors the misery of thine own, dear girl. I suggest you find yourself some mischief. If only to save both of our sanities from dreadful boredom. I need someone through which to live vicariously."

"Yes, Your Grace. I'll do my best. The King—"

"Yes. Yes. I know. What's the main course tonight?"

"Lamb, Your Grace."

"Splendid. I'll be chewing the damn meat long into the night."

I make my way past Bethany. She closes the dungeon door behind me and descends the stairs at my heels. I picture her clipping the back of my ankle with her wooden shoes. I wonder if I'd tumble the entire way down. I could count the steps until my neck broke. That would give Bethany a grand story to tell.

We enter the dining hall to find Phillip flanked at our obnoxious table by his five boys. The six of them sit clustered at one end like shy children at a Yule ball. The room itself is comfortable considering how vast it is. A fireplace takes up the entirety of the wall behind the king. A healthy fire crackles and pops there. The sounds always comfort me. Burgundy tapestries, the color of my husband's family's crest, hang from the ceiling in each corner. The beautifully crafted velvet comes to a rest just above the smooth stone floor. The floor itself is polished marble, white with specks of gray.

Bethany leads me to my seat at the other end of the table. Opposite of the rest of my family. Her wooden shoes click clack on the stone.

"Must I sit so far away, Phillip?" I ask.

My husband frowns at my informal use of his name. He believes in tradition. I believe our marriage vows grant me the right to call my husband by his name—something I made crystalline to him on day one.

"It's where the Queen sits, My Lady. As they always have," says Phillip.

"Are we expecting a dance, or perhaps even a jousting match to take place between us? There's certainly enough room," I say.

Bethany stifles a laugh behind me. I fight the urge to join her.

"Can the knights joust for us, Father?" asks the King's youngest son, Paul. He's five and easily excitable.

"Don't be absurd, son. The Queen speaks in jest," says Phillip as he glares at me.

"Only a little," I say before I bypass my assigned seat and make my way over to where my second eldest stepson sits.

He's a handsome boy, blessed with the crystal blue eyes of his dead mother. His cheeks burn red as I pull the empty seat beside him back from the table. The feet of the chair squeak as they scrape across the floor. The high-pitched sound echoes around the room. I pull the seat back far more than is required, just to drag out the sound a little longer. One must find fun whenever possible in my position.

"Do you mind, William?" I ask him.

"I don't. I mean to say, I—"

"It's fine," says Phillip, stepping in to save his son from further harassment at my hands. "The Queen may sit on the floor if she so desires. That is her right."

"Does that apply to after dinner as well?" I ask—and immediately regret it. Sometimes I hate my own candor.

"Leave us!" says the King.

Bethany leaves at once. Her head is down. Her shoes scuffle across the stone.

"But our dinner, Father?" asks Phillip V, my husband's eldest son.

"You'll be served in your rooms. Go. Now. I'll not tell you again."

"I was only kidding about the knights, Father," says Paul with a quick glance in my direction.

"Let's go, Paul," says Phillip V as he takes the younger boy's hand.

The King waits for the boys' footfalls to fade away before he downs his entire goblet of wine and hurls it across the room. The metal cup strikes the stone wall and clatters to the floor. The collisions are deafening in the cavernous room.

"Why must you vex me, woman?"

"It was not my intent to—"

"Horseshit! It is always your intent. Ever since I put that damnable ring on your finger, you've done nothing but test my resolve."

"You've left me with nothing else, Phillip."

"You'll refer to me as Your Majesty when I'm this angry with you, woman."

"And you'll refer to me as Queen. I'm no mere woman. You'll do well to remember it."

Phillip stands and strides over to my side. He grips my chin between his thumb and forefinger, and forces me to look him in the eyes.

"I'll not deal with your insolence. You'll not embarrass me in front of my children."

"Are they not our children, my love?" I say with a bite in my tone.

"You've not earned that right yet, my Queen."

The last word drips with contempt.

"How can I earn anything from a prison cell?"

"Is that how you see it?"

"I see it as it is. Nothing more. Nothing less."

He releases my chin and melts into the chair beside me. His anger is gone with his next exhale.

"Is that the cause of your blatant childishness? Do you truly misconceive why you're in that tower?"

"You barely speak to me. You explain nothing. I'm forced to leap to my own conclusions."

"Do you mock the deaths of my wives with such painful puns?"

"God no! I swear, that was not my intent. Do you believe I'm capable of such cruelty?"

"I don't know. As you've alluded, we're complete strangers."

"We have time to rectify that, Your Majesty."

"Phillip. Please. You make tradition sound like wind from a bull's ass."

I could not help but burst out in loud ugly laughter. The sort where one snorts like a pig at dinner time. He joins in despite himself.

"You have an infectious laugh," he says.

"You mean it makes you ill? Like the Black Death?"

"Quite the opposite."

The smile on his beautiful face emboldens me.

"Can I stay in your bed tonight? Lay with you as a wife should? Rise beside you in the morning like the sun over the sea?"

His smile fades at once.

"I'm sorry. I can't allow it."

"Then at least tell me why. Without explanation, I must assume you detest me, and are disgusted by my mere presence."

"You assume to the point of absurdity."

"As I said, my thoughts are all that I have."

He takes a deep breath and then speaks with a softness that takes me aback.

"You know what I've gone through. The fate of the six queens before you."

"Of course."

"Then how can you question the fact I'm only trying to keep you safe?"

"By locking me in the same tower others have died in? That makes no sense, Phillip."

"After my first two wives died, I locked the next two away to keep them safe. When they died, I locked the next two away to protect myself. I thought I could protect them too, of course, but I kept them at a distance because I couldn't handle any more loss. I did not love them. The pain was still unbearable when they passed, though nothing like the ones before."

"Do you prefer I remain a stranger? To protect yourself?"

"No. I prefer you live to a ripe old age, and we have an enduring love that strengthens over time."

"In four-hour intervals."

"If it keeps you safe? Yes."

"And if I don't want to live that way?"

"Then I will find myself with an eighth wife. I'm sorry to be so callous, but the kingdom needs a queen. It needs heirs. The peace I've worked so hard for depends on it if I want it to continue. I know I may be cursed for some mistake I've made in the past. I'm sorry that I've brought you into it."

I stand and turn my back to him.

"Will you require my company tonight?"

He stands and places one of his hands on my shoulder.

"I was speaking truthfully with all of my heart that I wish for us to endure a long-lasting love, my Queen."

"Will you send for me or not, Your Majesty?"

His hand falls from my shoulder.

"No. I don't think either one of us would be much company tonight."

"Very well then. Bethany?"

The loyal girl steps into the room with her eyes locked on her own feet.

"Yes, Your Grace?"

"I'll be returning to my dungeon. Please bring dinner to me. Leave the lamb. Bring the wine. All of it."

I walk out of the room without looking back. For a moment, I consider telling my husband about my sense of dread, but the fear of what he'd do under the guise of protecting me stills my tongue. Phillip did what I asked of him. He was honest with me, and I hate him for it.

Back in my tower, Bethany brings my dinner to me with two bottles of red wine. Bless the poor girl. She attempts to spark a conversation for the first time, and my heart breaks when I tell her...

"That's all for tonight, Bethany. I'll see you on the morrow."

"Yes, Your Grace," she says as she turns to the door.

She steps to the fire and pulls a fistful of something from the front pocket of her apron. Then she bends before the hearth, opens her hand, reveals a pile of dust and dried flowers, and blows it all into the flames. The fire burns a bright blue for several heartbeats before returning to its usual orangish red. The smell from the fire is intoxicating. Sweet and dizzying.

"What was that, Bethany?"

"A flower called Angel's Wing, Your Grace. It grows wild along the shore of the sea. It calms my father's fits. Lets him sleep in peace."

"I appreciate you sharing it with me. It has a lovely aroma."

"Yes, Your Grace."

With that said, Bethany heads for the door once more. She turns back and looks me in my face with strong, determined eyes.

"Do not despair. Please. I couldn't bear to lose another."

And with that she rushes from the room. Then she closes and locks the door behind her. That's when it hits me: the King and his sons weren't the only ones to lose all of the queens that came before me. Bethany did too. I make a resolution to be kinder to the girl moving forward. My first act would be to replace her dreadful wooden shoes.

Several glasses of wine later, I feel my eyelids grow heavy. Between the fireplace, abundance of candles, and sweet red drink, perspiration begins to coat my flesh. I let my clothes fall to the floor and climb in beneath the smooth cold sheets of my bed. Mere minutes pass and I'm asleep. Dead to the world.

I have no idea how many hours have passed when I wake from a sudden, body-rocking chill. The flame in the hearth has expired. The room is cold enough to see my breath float in the air in front of me.

"Bloody hell," I say. I don't want to climb out of bed, but I have little choice.

"I can light the fire, Your Grace."

The sudden voice from the shadows grips me in fear. I dare not move or even breathe. No one. Not even Phillip, my husband, my King, would dare enter my room in the middle of the night unannounced.

"If you make me a promise," says the voice.

I open my mouth to yell. To demand they leave my chamber at once. All that comes are more clouds of breath. My eyes are slits as I focus on something deep in the shadows of my room. It stands with the stillness and terrible foreboding presence of the stone gargoyles that loom on the ledge beneath my windows. The damnable things have given me countless nightmares since my first night, but they pale in comparison to the horror I feel clutching at my chest.

My unwelcome guest is nothing but shadow cast upon

shadow until it opens its eyes. They are golden, as if touched by Midas himself. Streaks of glittering crimson cut across the gold irises like a spider web spun from the finest rubies. The eyes are the most beautiful and most horrific things I've ever seen. They're far larger than the eyes of a man. Shaped like almonds, they continue on around the sides of the thing's head. I could fit five of my hands in the shadows between them, where the thing's nose should be.

"You assault me with your silence. Are you a queen without common courtesies?"

The insult helps me find my voice.

"Who are you? You're not permitted in my dungeon. Leave at once, and perhaps the King will spare your life."

"Dear Queen, who do you think invited me in?"

Its words were like echoes of my own dark thoughts. Was there truly something there with me, or was it a mixture of the wine and my own paranoia? Has my mistrust in my husband manifested into some wretched, foul demon?

"You're lying," I say.

"I think you know I am not," it replied.

"If you're real, ignite the fire, let me see you," I say, even though it's the last thing I want.

A burst of fire erupts across the room and engulfs the hearth in flames. I avert my eyes. I don't want to see the thing. Even if it's a figment of my imagination, I don't think I could handle the sight of it.

"Look at me, Your Grace. I am your end. Your demise."

"Why would the King sacrifice my life to you?"

"I'll tell you our tale once you meet my gaze. Not a moment before."

Every fiber of my being screamed for me to keep my eyes shut, but I needed answers. My curiosity supersedes my fear. I open my eyes and turn my head towards the corner of the room. A breath catches painfully in my chest. My lungs refuse to expand as I meet eyes with the dragon.

It grins and reveals a mouth full of endless blades of teeth. Rows upon rows of knives with one purpose, to tear through flesh. The fire shimmers across its dark green scales. The beast is a behemoth. More than half of its massive body remains outside the window. The tips of its wings scrape each wall to my right and left. Its long snake-like neck raises its giant head towards the cathedral style ceiling.

"Are you real? I still feel like you're a nightmare that's escaped from the darkest recess of my mind."

"Do you feel the heat from the flame?"

"I do."

The dragon lowers its head to within inches of my bed.

"Shall I rip an arm from your shoulder to prove my substance?"

"The feel of your armored skin would be proof enough."

"Then caress my flesh, dear Queen. I welcome your soft touch."

I raise my hand. It shakes. I'm unable to tame it. For some reason, I expect the dragon's rough skin to feel moist,. Aas if the green of its scales consisted of damp moss or algae. My fingers press against its flesh, and find it dry, cracked. It's warm, almost hot to the touch, as if the beast spent all of its time beneath a sweltering sun.

"Am I real enough?"

My hand falls to my side as it raises its head towards the ceiling.

"Yes, you're real. Tell me, dragon, why do you want me dead? Why have you killed all the queens that came before me?"

"Because your King killed my beloved."

"Then shouldn't you kill the King?"

"If only I could. Those are not the rules."

"Rules? Rules for what?"

"When one kills a dragon, they're granted a single wish from the dragon's surviving lover. Your husband wished for peace across his kingdom. I made it so. But each wish comes with a caveat, a cost the widowed dragon may levy upon the wish, that the dragon slayer cannot contest."

"The lives of his queens."

"And every queen his heirs dare to marry for the rest of my extensive life. He slayed my lover as we slept. His cowardice earned him his peaceful reign, but the cost of my lover's life will be the lives of anyone he or his sons marry."

"But we've done nothing wrong. We're as innocent as your murdered lover. Why not claim his son's?"

"Because my pain is something he and his should endure for generations. That's why I allowed some of his queens to survive long enough to bear children."

"There's a flaw in your grand scheme, dragon. The King no longer loves his wives. You've made that impossible. Our deaths cause him nothing more than inconvenience. He simply replaces us, and the cycle continues. Kings seldom marry for love. They do it out of duty, and to ensure their lineage continues. The loss of his sons will break him, and he'll always need to make more."

"What would you have me do? The terms have been set. I can not change my caveat."

"What if I killed them for you?"

"You'd kill your own sons?"

"As you know, they're not mine. The king married me knowing that it would forfeit my life. I have no love for him or his children. If I spill their blood, will you spare my life?"

"Aren't you delaying the inevitable? I'll return for you next year. And the year after. And so on. You'll run out of princes to kill. The king will kill you himself if you fail to birth him an heir. Eventually, it'll come down to your life or the life of your true born son. What will you do then?"

"You misunderstand me. I'll give you the lives of all of his sons. In return, you'll let me flee this kingdom. I won't stay with a man that doomed me to death by dragon."

"Your heart is as black as his. You deserve each other."

"I simply value my life over the lives of strangers."

"Children."

"Of the man that killed your beloved. Do we have an accord?"

"Yes. If you fail, I'll take your life without hesitation."

"Then I'd best not fail."

"You may have done just that before you've even begun, unless you've magically procured the key to your door."

The dragon's words almost floor me. How could I forget about the door? The damn thing has been locked every minute that I've been alone since I first set foot in the tower. I made a deal with a dragon, and I was mere seconds away from failing.

I reach for the door's knob. The air around me shifts as the dragon lowers its head. Its hot breath blows my hair away from the back of my neck. An uncomfortable shiver rocks through my body. The beast rests its heavy chin on my shoulder. I see the glint of its teeth in the corner of my eye. If I fail, if it's locked, I won't live long enough to regret my promise.

Grasping for the knob, I go to turn it, and find it unlocked. A long exhale escapes from between my lips. A calm washes over me. The dragon's head lifts off of my shoulder, but I still feel its breath on my neck.

"Now it's real, dear Queen. Do you truly have the stomach for it?"

"I'll deliver your sacrifices. Then I'll grow old beyond the sea."

I step through the door and descend the stairs. My feet are

bare, but I still feel like each step echoes throughout the castle. Will they hear me coming?

A plan starts to unfold in my mind. Where do I start? Who should be the first to die? The elder princes pose the most danger. If one should wake during my attack, they could overpower me. They're far more skilled at combat than I. I should start with them. Their deaths will make it easier to slay the younger ones. My hands will already be stained with blood. What's a little more?

Maneuvering through the castle's dark halls is difficult. I've never seen them so late at night. Torches hang from mounts along the walls, but they're so far apart that they do little to illuminate the floor in front of me. I keep one hand on the stone wall to my right as a guide. It scrapes and stabs at my fingertips. A small price to pay for what I'm about to do. Each dark corner fills me with terror of discovery, but I picture the dragon's gold and red eyes. Their fiery glare drives me forward.

Should I stop in the kitchens and gather my weapon of choice? No. I wouldn't even know where the kitchen is, or how to find it by candlelight. Thankfully, the boys love their daggers and short swords. There will be weapons aplenty in their chambers.

I manage to reach the room without incident. Strange, I'd imagined more guards in the halls, but there were none. Maybe they're all outside the king's room? Turning the knob, I push open the door to Phillip's room. It creaks. The sound echoes down the hall behind me. I consider running but stay. Failing is not an option.

The room is pitch black as I enter. Thanks to the shadows of the hall, it doesn't take long for my eyes to fully adjust to the blackness that surrounds me. Phillip's bed is to my left. The boy is fast asleep beneath his heavy wolf pelt blankets. His long, deep breaths are the only sound.

It takes a mere moment to find his sword. It leans against the end of his bed. The tip of the blade cuts through a thick rug and rests between the cracks of the stones that make up his floor. He must've been practicing just before turning in for the night. Lucky for me.

I grip the handle of the sword, and hate the feel of it. I abhor violence in all of its many variations. It makes what I'm about to do all that much more ironic.

Lifting the sword, the weight of it nearly topples me. I wrap a second hand around the hilt and step to the side of young Phillip's bed. Pondering how best to proceed, I freeze as the boy turns onto his side to face me. His eyes flutter open. He looks at me with confused sleet eyes.

"Step-mother?"

"No. Don't call me that. Not here. Not like this. Go back to sleep, Phillip."

"What do you mean? Why are you in my room?"

He sits up, and panic fills my throat with bile. Then he wipes sleep from his eyes. Another moment and he'll be awake. A strong young man, trained in the art of combat, he'll rise from his bed, and rip his sword from my grasp.

Strike! Strike now, or stab yourself through the heart. Your end will come either way if you don't strike him down now!

I thank the lord that my throat is too dry to allow for the scream I unleash to make it past my lips as I swing the blade with all of my strength. It slices into Phillip's throat, but stops when it meets the bone. I'm not strong enough to decapitate him.

He looks up at me with horror in his eyes. Blood runs from his mouth in thick streams. An inaudible scream drowns amidst the blood. Phillip reaches up to touch where the blade has cut halfway across his throat. He attempts to grip the blade in his bare hands, but it slices deep into his palms. Tears stream down his face, and his eyes scream one word into my head over and over again. *Why?*

Phillip V lays back down with the sword still protruding from his neck. Our eyes never break their heart-wrenching gaze as the last remnants of life drain from his. He reaches out for me. I take his hand in both of mine without hesitation. His palm is wet with blood. It warms my shaking hands.

"I'm sorry, Phillip. I wish there was time to explain. I had no choice."

His mouth moves in reply but there's no sound. Only a cold exhale of breath. Seconds later, he's dead. The last bit of blood oozes from his neck. It covers the bed in a dark pool. The deed is done. Only four more princes to go.

I attempt to draw the blade from Phillip the V's throat, but it doesn't budge. The sword is embedded in the boy's neck, and there it will have to stay. I'll find another in William's room.

The second eldest prince's room is across the hall from Phillip the V's. I find no sword, but a long dagger lays on a table near his bed. He too stirs as I hold the dagger over his chest. Its tip, so similar to the dragon's teeth, hangs inches from his bare skin. I hesitate. Do I want him to wake? Am I enjoying this?

As if in response to my own questions, I jab the blade down. It pierces his flesh without resistance. His eyes burst open, but they never turn their gaze in my direction. Shock fills his face as he stares up at the ceiling. Pushing the dagger deeper, I feel the steel jerk as it nicks the boy's ribs. I continue to shove the blade further until the hilt rests against his chest. It pierces more flesh deep within him, and I assume it's his heart because he dies.

"Rest in peace, sweet boy. This is your father's doing," I say out of guilt more than sorrow.

Drawing the blade from William's chest feels worse than killing him. The sound of the steel as I withdraw it from his dead muscle and flesh will haunt me. Now, onto the next.

The deaths of princes three and four are as uneventful and forgettable as the boys themselves. I scarcely remember their names. It's the murder of young Paul that gives me pause.

He's the boy I've grown most fond of. His excitement and joyous nature are infectious. The days that I'm able to spend time with him are always enjoyable. I've had scarce good days since a crown was placed upon my head, but the few that I recall were because of this boy. I wish to see his effervescent smile one last time before he dies, but the painful wail of a grown man somewhere off in the darkness forces my hand. The King has found one of his princes.

I don't have long. Bringing the knife down, I stab young Paul in his stomach. Yank and stab. Yank and stab. I repeat the process again and again until—-

"No!"

Phillip IV grabs the back of my nightgown and hurls me backwards. I slam hard into the wall behind me. The back of my head thuds against the stone, and I'm dazed. The room spins, and I lose focus. Phillip is a blur as he cradles his dead son a few feet away.

"Why?! What have you done?!"

Words build on my tongue and die there. I want to tell him that I won. That I'm the one that survives his curse, but there isn't time. I have to get to the dragon before the king pulls himself together. If he's able to push past his grief, he'll kill me, and the blood I've spilled will be for naught.

My knees buckle, but I don't go down. I manage to push myself to the door, and use the frame to steady myself.

"Stay where you are, murderer!"

Taking a deep breath, I shake the cobwebs from my head, and stumble into the hall. Reaching for the nearest wall, I lean my weight against it for balance. The hall expands and contracts all around me like it's breathing. My hand leaves a trail of fresh blood behind me.

"Stop where you are!"

Phillip the IV shuffles into the hall. I run as fast as my scattered brain will allow, slamming into stone walls as I round dark corners. The King's footfalls come faster and faster. His seething fury fills the halls. If he catches me, there will be no trial. He will behead me, and the dragon will drown in the blood of all its sacrifices.

Somehow, I find myself at the stairs to my tower. I spread my arms wide as I ascend, allowing my palms to push off from each wall as I struggle against my own imbalance. I'm halfway up the steps before I hear the King enter the tower's staircase. I thank the Lord for making my husband bigger than he is fast. As long as I don't fall, I'll beat him to the dungeon. The dragon can whisk me away, and I can leave all of this tragedy in the past.

"I'll kill you with my son's blade!"

I hear the sound of metal running across bedrock as the king fills the tower with the echoes of my impending demise. The sound ascends in both volume and distance as if building to an inevitable crescendo. Looking back, I see sparks of flame amidst the shadows as sword slices stone. It feels as if Phillip is on my heels, that I am moments from death. Then I see the door to my dungeon.

With one last burst of strength, I rush for my door, throw it open, and hurry inside. I slam the door shut and slide across the bolt that's mounted to the inside of the door. It's the first time I've ever had a use for it.

The fire still crackles in the hearth. I round, expecting to see the dragon where I'd left it, but I find only Bethany there instead.

"Bethany? What're you doing here? Where's the dragon?"

"Dragon, Your Grace? There are no such things."

"Don't you dare say that to me. I've just met one. It was in this very tower. The widow of the dragon my husband cut down."

"I know of no such dragon, Your Grace."

I open my mouth to protest, but the sound of my husband slamming against the door draws my attention.

"Open this door, woman! So I may have my justice!"

"What've you done, Your Grace? I've never seen the King so angry."

"The dragon gave me a choice."

SLAM!

"My life for the lives of Phillip's sons."

SLAM!

"And you chose to murder children?"

SLAM!

"Their demise rests at their father's feet. It's his sin that put them in harm's way. He owed the dragon a debt. One I'm not willing to pay."

My husband stops slamming his body against the door and unleashes his son's sword on the thick wood.

"But there are no dragons, Your Grace. There never were."

HACK!

I run to the window behind my Lady-in-Waiting.

"I'm not mad, girl."

"I said no such thing."

HACK!

I lean far out of the window, searching the night sky for the dragon.

"I didn't mean to leave the door unlocked."

"I know that. So will the King."

HACK!

Splinters from the door fly across the room behind us as I continue to search the sky.

"The smoke from the mushrooms always drove the queens to harm themselves. Never another."

"What're you talking about, girl?"

HACK! CRACK!

The door breaks, and I know I'm seconds away from death. Where is the damn dragon? What is Bethany talking about? Mushrooms driving my predecessors to madness? I've never heard of such folly. But didn't that make more sense than a dragon?

"I only wanted him to notice me. Maybe now, now that he's truly alone, he'll see me right in front of him."

I round on the young girl, my eyes wide with the discovery of the truth. Rage fills my head and heart at her betrayal. My husband struggles to reach for the bolted lock from outside the door.

"It was you. You've killed them all."

"No, Your Grace. They killed themselves. I've only killed you."

And with that, Bethany shoves me hard in the chest. I stumble backwards. The backs of my legs crash hard into the windowsill, and I tumble out of the window. I slam into one of the gargoyles and feel a crunch in my side. Breath is knocked from my lungs as I reach out for the hideous stone demon. My fingers grip it around one of the wings, but it's a fragile grasp at best. My eyes meet Bethany's, and the sick girl smiles at me. Then she turns from the window, and I hear the click- clack of her wooden shoes as she walks away.

Those damnable wooden shoes, I think just as my fingers slip.

The Shadow in the Swamp

Brian Keene

A Tale of the Wasteworld

In hindsight, splitting up had been a bad idea, and since he'd been the one to suggest it, Kilmar's mood worsened. He trudged along through calf-high mud, forcing his way through a thicket of reeds, and cursed himself for the decision. It had made tactical sense at the time. Nemesis and Sorghum had been taken captive the previous night. The purpose of their kidnapping was uncertain, although there was a dreadful possibility that they were being transported to the nefarious city-state farther south, a place spoken of only in hushed tones: the Kingdom of the Mouse. After selecting a rally point on their map, he, Cabal, Uronymus, and Best Western had each gone in a different direction, hoping to find tracks or some other sign of the abductors more quickly. Instead, not only had his search proven fruitless, but now he was lost as well, here in this vast swamp that the local denizens called Murk.

Kilmar wore a simple tunic, trousers, and boots, all of which were now caked with mud and soaked from the terrain. They stank. He stank. This entire blasted landscape stank. His progress was impeded with every step. The ground squelched underfoot, sucking at his feet. He picked his way around seemingly endless pools of stagnant water, many of which were often covered with scum, algae, or a sheen of oily toxins. The mud had a consistency somewhere between clay and feces. Several times he'd lost his footing and landed face first in the muck. As a result, he discovered that it tasted like both. Welts and insect bites covered his exposed skin. His long, uneven bangs hung plastered to his forehead, and sweat stung his eyes.

He'd attempted several times now to retrace his steps, but the oozing landscape seemed to be maliciously erasing signs of his passage. This also made finding signs of his friends, or of the group who had abducted Nemesis and Sorghum, nearly impossible.

Kilmar realized that his anger stemmed from a deep fear as to Nemesis's fate. He was worried about Sorghum, too, of course, but the farmer–like Best Western–had joined them only recently. Nemesis had grown up in Yurk with him, Cabal, and Uronymus. He'd known her since they were children. They had traveled half the world together in the last few years. He knew that Nemesis was a formidable warrior, and that her captors would rue taking her, but he couldn't help but still picture her as that little girl he'd played ball with. He remembered a game of hide and seek in Old Tuck's grainfield, and how she'd squealed and giggled when he'd expressed his frustration with the length of the game upon finally locating her among the golden fronds.

"I didn't think you'd ever find me," she'd said.

"I didn't think I would either," he'd replied.

"I'll find you." The swamp seemed to have a dampening effect on his words. They felt muted and plodding. "I promise. I'll find you, just as soon as I find my way out of here."

As the day turned to evening, a thick mist began to fill the air, seeping through his clothes and making him even wetter. Worse, it obstructed his vision, obscuring anything beyond a few feet in front of him. Tree stumps, swamp grass, and rocks took on twisted, sinister shapes in the gloom. Kilmar plodded on with stubborn determination, but as the landscape darkened and the fog deepened, he finally relented, deciding to make camp for the night.

Finding a broad, blackened tree stump jutting out of a relatively dry patch of ground, Kilmar sat down with a heavy sigh and leaned his back against it. He had no need for a fire. The night air was warm, even with the disappearance of the sun, and he had plenty of dry rations in his pack, as well as two bruised but still edible apples. He sipped from his canteen, mindful that fresh water seemed scarce amidst all this stagnation, and then rummaged through his pack, producing an orange-skinned apple. He chewed this slowly and thoughtfully and tried not to worry about his friends.

As darkness fully enveloped Murk, he considered using his sword. The weapon had been in his family for many generations, but it was far older than his family line. It had first been found by his great-great-great grandfather, who–unlike the rest of Kilmar's family–had been said to have journeyed far from home. He'd recovered the sword in a city of the Ancients, located deep beneath the earth. It had been passed down from parent to child since then. Kilmar's mother had given it to him when he and his friends first ventured forth from Yurk.

He leaned his head back against the wet stump and closed his eyes, trying to remember his mother's face or the sound of her voice. He opened his eyes again when he found that he couldn't.

He tossed the apple core as far from camp as possible and heard a quiet splash. Then he rummaged around in his pack again and withdrew the weapon. It appeared to be a simple, bladeless hilt, but when he pressed a small button inset on the shaft, a magic beam of light erupted from it, extending nearly the length of his arm. The light was dazzling in hue and beautiful to look at, but composed of sorcerous energy that destroyed anything it came in contact with. Steel and wood. Flesh and bone. Kilmar had cleaved through all of these and more during their journey. He would have been dead many times over if not for the heirloom. And with his friends now missing, it was his sole remaining connection to home.

No, he decided. Better to not have light in this gloom. No doubt there were things about whose attention he'd be better off avoiding.

Sighing again, Kilmar stowed the weapon back in his pack again. Then he settled back as best he could against the stump. He tried to recall a time he'd felt this low, but he was certain that he never had. Loneliness and oppression clung to him like the mist. He stared up at the two broken fragments of the moon. Other than the sun, they'd been the only constant on this journey. But the moon's halves were a muted silver, barely visible through the haze.

He was weary down to his bones, but sleep eluded him. The darkness was full of bothersome insects and sounds both familiar and strange—night birds, the whisper of the wind in the reeds, incessantly croaking frogs, but also odd creaking and groans, and the occasional gaseous belch of swamp gas bubbling to the surface. At one point, he thought he heard voices from far away, and the distinct sound of Cabal's weapons—which also possessed the sorcerous designs of the Ancients. But when he leaped to his feet and scanned the surroundings, he saw nothing. The worst moment was when a monstrous shape lumbered past on four massive legs. The mist hid its true form, but judging by how the pools splashed and the mud shifted as it strode overhead, it must have been very large indeed. The creature—whatever it was—made no sound, save for a ragged, gruff breathing that sounded loud as a storm. He considered drawing his sword, but worried that the sudden movement or the light from the weapon might invite an attack. Instead, Kilmar cowered against the stump, expecting to be stomped flat, but the beast passed on, either unaware or uncaring of his presence.

Eventually, despite all of this, he slept, albeit fitfully.

When he awoke, the first thing he became aware of was the chill in the air.

Then he noticed that the birds, insects, and frogs had all grown quiet.

He sat up slowly, listening.

In the darkness, something moved–a shadow, blacker than the rest of his surroundings. It loomed over him, arms out-stretched, and before Kilmar could react with anything other than a frightened squawk, it lashed out. He fell backward, dodging the strike, but felt the air around him shift as the inky appendage zipped past. A chill ran through him. It was as if the thing was lowering the temperature between them.

Kilmar scurried backward through the mud and then sprang to his feet. Now that he was fully alert, he had a better sense of his opponent. It was human-shaped, possessing two arms, two legs, and a head. Its height was equal to his own. But it had no discernable features. No eyes, mouth, or nose. No hair or scars. No clothing or jewelry. Nor did it have dimensions. When the creature turned, he was shocked by how thin it was. Kilmar recalled his childhood again in that second, and how Nemesis used to make little figures out of leaves. She'd cut the leaves into human shapes and then play with them, but they deteriorated quickly due to their thinness. This thing reminded him of those figures—just a flat black shape, darker than the darkness around it. Indeed, it had all the attributes of a shadow, but he saw nothing that could be casting it, nor was he sure how something could even have a shadow in this dim light.

Maybe it's invisible, he thought.

The shadow stood over his pack and watched him, as if waiting for Kilmar to make the next move.

Frowning, Kilmar weighed his options. His sword was inside the pack. If he leapt for it, that would put him in striking distance again. But without it, he was defenseless. He decided to try Nemesis's method of conflict resolution instead.

"What do you want?"

The shadow remained motionless. Although Kilmar couldn't be sure, he had a sense that it was staring at him.

"If I am trespassing, or have offended you in some way, it wasn't intentional."

The thing didn't react.

Kilmar pointed. "Those are my belongings. I'd like them back now."

The creature stayed still.

Kilmar took a cautious step forward and felt a rock beneath his foot. Without taking his eyes off the entity, he stopped down and dug through the muck. Clutching the projectile in his fist, he stood back up again.

"Look… maybe you don't understand my words." He motioned with his free hand, indicating the pack and the ground. "I need that back. You can return it, or I can take it."

There was still no response.

"Okay, then, I have no choice but to…" He reared back quickly and flung the rock overhand. It hit the shadow in its center mass and sailed right through it, splashing in a puddle behind the thing.

"Oh for…" Kilmar's frown deepened. If the creature was intangible, then how was it clutching his pack?

The shadow turned away and began to stride across the marsh, seeming to glide over the swampy surface. It left no tracks in its wake.

"Hey!"

Kilmar raced after it. The shadow sped up, racing ahead, but then stopped again, as if waiting for him to catch up. When he did, it took off again.

"Is this a game for you? I don't think you'll like playing with me!"

Ignoring him, the shadow continued on its way, with Kilmar's belongings in tow. Yelling in frustration, he gave chase, pursuing it across the Murk, splashing through puddles and sloshing through mud. At times Kilmar thought he'd lost it, but then the thing appeared again, waiting for him.

Eventually, they emerged through a particularly dense thicket of reeds and the ground began to slope uphill, growing dryer and more solid. The vegetation changed, as well. Grasses and shrubs grew here, albeit stunted and sickly-looking. He saw the remnants of what had once been an orchard, but it had been ages since anyone had tended the trees, and they were now choked with vines and tangles amongst their dying limbs.

"Where are we going?" Kilmar panted. "What do you hope to gain from this?"

The shadow made no reply, but its pace slowed. It led him forward, and there, nestled between the trees, sagged the ruins of a small shack. The roof had long since collapsed, and the wall timbers bent and bowed. The door hung off its hinges, and the yard around it was an overgrown thicket. The shadow flitted inside the structure. Kilmar had no choice but to follow.

He hesitated at the open doorway, expecting a trap. Glancing around, he found a length of half-rotten wood with a nail sticking out of it. He snatched this up and wielded it, testing its weight. The makeshift weapon would probably disintegrate the moment he struck anything with it, but having it in his hand made him feel more confident. Taking a deep breath, he strode inside the ruin.

The interior of the shack matched the exterior. The floor was covered in old leaves, fragments of broken pottery and other detritus. The only thing of note was a pile of bones against one leaning wall. The shadow stood over these, holding Kilmar's pack high. He approached slowly, leading with his club. The shadow slinked backward, flattening itself along the wall. Only the arm still clutching his belongings stood out.

"Nowhere left for you to run," Kilmar said. "Now…give me my stuff!"

Bewilderingly, the creature shook Kilmar's pack up and down, as if taunting him.

He lashed out with the club, striking the shadow in its mid-section. As expected, the wood exploded into rotten fragments. The thrust of the attack carried Kilmar's arm forward. His fist went through the creature and struck the back wall. Immediately, Kilmar stiffened. Air hissed through his teeth. The thing was frigid–far colder than anything he'd ever felt before. His teeth chattered and his body shook. His hand felt as if it was burning. He had never experienced coldness like this, not even during their time in the Mines of the Dark Elf, in the vast polar wastes at what Best Western had insisted was the top of the world. He yanked his fist free and staggered backward.

The shadow held out his pack and dangled it above the bones.

Wincing in pain and cradling his hand in the other, Kilmar stepped forward and studied the remains. The skeleton was no longer intact, but it had been human, judging by the skull and other bones. Scraps of faded cloth still clung to the fragments. He stared at the pile, and then gazed back up at the thing. The shadow stood still.

"I understand. Anywhere in particular?"

The shadow didn't respond.

"Okay, then. The orchard is as good a place as any."

He hunted through the debris until he found a tarnished brass serving platter that could act as a shovel. Then he spent an hour digging up the earth. His progress was slowed by roots and stones. The shadow watched from the tree line. Then, Kilmar wearily but carefully transported the remains to the new resting place. He filled in the grave and then spent another hour stacking rocks overtop it. By the time he'd finished, he was too exhausted to move. He simply sagged to the ground, leaning his head upon the cairn.

"There," he gasped. "Now please…"

The shadow swept over him, but he was too tired to do more than close his eyes as the cold embraced him.

When he awoke, it was daylight again, or at least what passed for daylight in the Murk. The shadow was gone, and his pack sat atop the cairn. Kilmar grabbed it and hurriedly rummaged through its contents, verifying that all his belongings were still there. Satisfied, he stood up and shivered.

He made a fire to warm himself, and spent an hour hunched beside it. He ate and drank and plotted his next move. Eventually, he extinguished the fire and marched off again in search of his friends. The loneliness he'd felt the day before had lessened somewhat, although it was many weeks before he felt truly warm again.

The 19ᵗʰ Legion

Josh Roberts

The shroud of mist covering the forest this morning is so thick that the trees themselves look like frozen ghosts, waiting for a spring thaw that never comes. There is no sound, no birds or beasts, no movement of leaves or buckling of bark and limb coming from the trees.

It is as silent as a grave.

Baldric, the tribal elder, appears at the edge of a round clearing like an apparition and shambles to a stone altar in the middle. His robes are black and mud-caked, tattered and threadbare as if he has worn them for ages. His long, thin, grey hair is matted with the morning dew, and his beard, equally as grey and scraggly, clings to his neck with the dampness of the nigh-impenetrable mist from the forest.

At his side is Uwe, his young apprentice. Uwe was born a farmer's son but was given to Baldric at a young age when he showed no interest in farming but rather an ability for the sorcery, and depravity, practiced by the elder. Uwe's labored gait is accentuated by the blood-soaked bandages that cover half of his face, both of his hands, and his splinted left leg. The rest of his brown cloak and robe are as tattered and mud stained as his master's. He looks gaunt and ashen, as if death were creeping into his bones with every step. His face holds little to no expression, and his movements disguise the excruciating pain of his injuries.

Baldric motions for Uwe to stop just short of the altar as he places his hands on the cold, wet stone. "You have done your part in this deception, Uwe. Now I must do mine. If I had known how savage these butchers were, I would never have sent you. I shall return the savagery to them a thousand-fold."

He pauses for a moment, then begins to chant in a low, guttural voice. The words are foreign, even to Uwe, but they are rhythmic and grow in volume slowly as he repeats them.

As his voice grows loud enough to echo in the clearing, the trees begin to groan, the sound of bark snapping echoes above the chanting, and the ground begins to roil and heave around the trees. The mist is still so thick that it goes unseen, but Baldric continues to chant until his voice is a scream, loud enough to wake the dead.

He stops abruptly and sinks to his knees in exhaustion, which causes Uwe to rush to his side.

"It is done. Our ancestors will save us now."

In the mist-shrouded forest, the ground buckles and heaves as countless warriors, long dead and buried, begin to break free from the twisted soil and roots of the ancient wood, beckoned to defend their homeland from another foreign invader.

On the other end of the forest, the encampment of the 19th Legion of Rome wakes, bewildered by the thickness of the morning fog.

Felix stirs from an uneasy sleep. His dreams were haunted by shambling figures and death. The dense fog is a bad omen, in his opinion. It only furthers his belief that this war is wrong.

The Romans have been fighting the tribes of Germania for years now, with very little success until recently. It has taken so long to gain even the smallest foothold in the area that it seems like this campaign may be endless. The 17th Legion was the first to enter the fray, but the war of attrition made it necessary for the 18th Legion to join them. The 19th Legion was sent to reinforce them four years ago. The legions of Rome do not retreat or surrender, nor do they *ever* give up.

Felix hates being a soldier. He was born and raised on a farm in the hills outside of Rome, content to raise goats, tend crops, and live a calm, solitary life with his mother and father. He often dreams of returning to the rolling hills of golden grain, the sunlit days and cool, starlit nights of his homeland.

He was conscripted into military service in the fourth year of the campaign to conquer Germania, when the leaders of Rome realized that their army was being chipped away at a pace greater than their ability to gain ground on what they thought were loosely assembled tribes. This is now year eight, and Felix feels like the great army of Rome is treading water at best in this gods forsaken land. He fears he will never see his home again.

Commander Varus shouts orders from the middle of the encampment, snapping Felix from his meandering thoughts.

"Today, the 19th Legion marches to victory! We are less than four leagues from what our interrogators have learned is the main encampment of these savages. The only thing between us and a glorious victory for Rome is this forest and this damnable fog."

The interrogators had become quite fond of torturing women and children that were captured to get any information about where the men were camped, or what plans they had for attacking the Roman legion. The information gained from these poor innocents had proven more accurate than any information captured soldiers had given during the agony they endured.

This bit of information was taken from a young farm boy who had been sheltered in said camp. They flayed the flesh from his hands and gouged out his left eye even though he told them what they wanted to know without hesitation. Then they broke his leg just to show their cruelty and had every intention of torturing the young boy until he died.

Felix had accidently stumbled upon the interrogators as they were inflicting this punishment upon the farm boy. His stomach turned sour, feeling an instant kinship to this poor young lad. It was his encouragement that convinced the torturers to let the boy go, seeing how he was no threat to them and would most likely be eaten by wolves long before making it back to warn anyone of where the Roman legion was camped. They reluctantly agreed and abandoned the boy to the elements. Felix felt that he had at least done a small deed of good amid this tragedy of wrong.

The 19th Legion form ranks, Felix among them, and begin to march into the thick, dark shroud of the forest, their objective clear, their resolve solidified. Maybe, once they defeat this main camp, the rest of the tribes would pay tribute, and they could go home. Maybe.

The first mile into the march is uneventful. Felix immediately notices the absolute silence in the forest.

"No birds, no wind, no movement in the trees. Something isn't right."

The rest of his phalanx are silent as well, focused on the impending task a mere four leagues away.

As suddenly as the words are uttered, an overwhelming stench of rot and decay envelopes the legion. The smell is a foul, nostril-burning mix of old, dank, rotting earth and maggot-ridden offal left in the heat and humidity to fester for days. It is so powerful that many of the soldiers stop dead in their march, retching as the putrid smell fills their mouths and prevents them from getting breaths of clean air. The commander stops as well, looking around to try to find the source.

His search is short, as a wall of men charge from the left flank and crash into the Roman army like a tidal wave.

The 19th Legion is taken by surprise, not just by the imperceptible movement of the enemy, but by the gut-wrenching smell of rot that assails their senses as the tribesmen slam into the ranks.

"Phalanx! Form up on the left!"

It is then that Felix realizes the true horror of the situation. This German army is comprised of skeletal men in rotting armor, clothes and flesh dripping off them. They ooze blood and ichor, their bones bare in many places. Some are draped in rotting tunics, stained with old, dried blood and putrescence; some are adorned in rusty armor from ages past, dripping with the remains of their long dead flesh. The corpses are a conglomeration of warriors from all ages Germania has occupied this land.

They descend upon the 19th Legion, slashing and rending his brethren with reckless abandon. Their teeth sink into the first line of soldiers as their rusted and chipped swords flail and pierce whatever they find, whether it is Roman or German. The phalanx is broken before it can even form, as terror fills the men closest to the conflict. The wave of the dead crashes again and again into the Romans, scattering them to the ground where they are enveloped by multiple foes, ripping and tearing flesh and shattering bone as the screams turn to gurgles and then are silenced.

Many of the Romans try to flee but are set upon by the unrelenting mass of rotting barbarians and their tireless attack.

Felix, shock turning his legs to stone, stands transfixed as the legion is literally torn to shreds.

He comes to his senses just in time to raise his sword, impaling a charging enemy in the chest. The enemy does not stop, however, and continues to swing its sword at Felix, causing him to lose his footing as they crash to the ground. The rotting German, clad in rusted armor and scraps of cloth covered in blood and gore, whose sword is now firmly planted in the wet ground, gnashes its teeth as he slides down the blade of Felix's sword, eager to bite the face that holds the hilt. Felix rolls out of the way at the last second, leaving his sword impaled in his adversary as it thrashes and bucks, trying to free itself and continue its attack. He looks around in a panic and seeing a large stone, picks it up and smashes it down on the head of the German soldier. The first crack causes the gore-soaked enemy to pause, the second crushes the already rotten skull and brings his thrashing movements to an end.

Felix looks around to see total chaos. Romans are running in all directions. Some are fighting, some are fleeing. Many of those fleeing are overwhelmed by the sheer number of assailants. All that fight are meeting gruesome, horrific ends. The dead army is seemingly limitless and undaunted in their attack. He watches in disbelief as Commander Varus, chopping and swinging his sword in all directions, is pulled from his horse. The horse is torn to pieces, blood and organs spewing and flying in all directions. Commander Varus meets a similar fate as multiple barbarians rip his flesh from his bones, gouge his eyes with their bone-shard fingers, and disembowel him as he screams in agony.

Coming to his senses again, Felix runs. He runs in the opposite direction from the screams and anguished cries. He runs without looking back. He runs until he no longer hears anything, and the forest is silent again. Then he slumps down, his back to a large tree, and weeps.

Felix wakes with a start to the sound of approaching footsteps. He is terrified at the thought of how long he was asleep. Having left his sword behind, his only weapon is a knife used to gut and clean game. He quietly draws it from its scabbard and presses his back hard against the tree. The footsteps approach from his right side. He steels himself for what comes next.

A Roman soldier stumbles as he passes the edge of the tree Felix is pressed against. Felix relaxes slightly as he sees it is friend, not foe. He whispers to the soldier.

"Legionnaire, are you alright?"

The soldier jumps with fright, landing on his backside as he faces Felix.

"Oh gods, I thought I was the last one alive."

Felix stands and offers his hand to help the soldier to his feet.

"We may be the only two that remain. I haven't seen anyone else this direction. What is your name?"

The soldier stammers a bit, then answers.

"M…my name is Qu…Quintus. I'm just a b…blacksmith. I'm not a soldier."

Felix nods.

"I'm a farmer, Quintus. I understand. My name is Felix. We should keep going this direction. I haven't seen or heard anything."

Quintus nods, and they continue in silence.

They march in stunned silence through the eerie stillness of the forest. The fog has never lifted, so the visibility is only a few feet, causing the pair to move very slowly and deliberately. Hours seemingly pass before they begin to hear a commotion in the approaching distance.

Quintus suggests they turn another way and avoid it, but Felix can vaguely hear speech, making him think it could be more surviving brethren. There is no stench of decay and rot either, which Felix remembers from the first attack. He convinces Quintus that they should investigate.

As they get closer to the noise, it is obvious that a group of men is up ahead, Roman men. Felix calls to them in a hushed but audible voice.

"Legionnaires, are you alright?"

The sound of swords being drawn echoes in the forest, even though the men are still not in view.

"Announce yourself!" comes from the parting mist.

Felix responds.

"We are Felix and Quintus of the 19th Legion."

The pair cautiously step forward as the men come into view. Five more Roman soldiers have found shelter by a rock outcropping. The rocks provide cover on all sides but one, which is the direction Felix and Quintus are coming from.

The men are battered and bloodied. Each has crude and hasty bandages covering multiple slash and tear wounds on their arms, legs, and faces. They each have a look of shock but stand with swords ready. Realizing they are seeing friends, not foes, they lower their swords and welcome them.

"I am Gaius. I am in command. Are you injured?"

Quintus stammers a response.

"N…not physically…b…but I cannot say for what m…my eyes have seen."

Gaius nods as Felix and Quintus join the men. He introduces them to Silvanus, Lucius, Caius, and Titus, all veteran soldiers. They are welcomed with fresh water and a place to sit.

Gaius asks the two stragglers, "Are you soldiers or conscripts?"

Felix, head held low, responds first. "We are both conscripts. I am a farmer; Quintus is a blacksmith."

Gaius looks around the camp at the other men.

"We are soldiers. Born to it. Raised for it. The glory of Rome is our purpose in life."

Gaius leans down near the faces of Felix and Quintus. "How did you escape what happened earlier? Neither of you have wounds that need to be treated."

Neither Felix nor Quintus are quick to answer.

Gaius, disgustedly, answers for them. "You ran. You left your countrymen to die. I can see it on your cowardly faces."

Felix tries to explain. "I'm not a soldier like you. My purpose is to feed Rome, not fight for it."

Gaius's expression turns to anger. "Your purpose is whatever Rome requires, whenever Rome requires it!"

Felix, ashamed of his actions, looks away from Gaius. "How do we get out of this forest?"

Gaius, sullen and serious, glances at the other soldiers.

"We don't. I believe this place is cursed, and all that have set foot upon it are cursed as well. I don't believe we will ever leave this forest."

Before Felix can voice his rebuttal, the thick, dank smell of rot and decay fills his nostrils. Another solider beckons them to be quiet as the stench nearly overwhelms them. A faint sound of metal clanking and clattering can be heard in the distance. As they listen, it grows louder with each passing second.

The realization strikes Gaius like a hammer. "The dead are coming. We must go *now*!"

The seven frantically grab their gear and turn to run from the increasing din, but it is too late. The shambling mass of dead Germans is within sight and moving with supernatural speed now that they have seen their prey.

Felix turns to Quintus. "Gods help us. Run!!"

Gaius, fully aware of his impending doom, turns towards the wave of dead and points his sword defiantly. "Come and feast, you worthless bastards!"

He swings his sword, striking the most advanced skeleton across the jaw, sending shattered fragments of bone and rotten flesh flying in a cloud of gore. As he recovers to swing again, he is slammed into the nearest tree by a wave of the dead, smashing his head so hard that his skull splits in two, brains and blood dripping from the trunk of the ageless timber. The unrelenting mass tears him limb from limb as the air quietly hisses out of his opened chest.

The four remaining centurions advance, swords raised, into the mass of chaos as Quintus and Felix flee the opposite direction. The bravery of these soldiers makes Felix weep as he runs with all his muster to escape their fate. The army of the dead plows through the last of the 19th Legion like the grinding wheel does to grain, crushing them into bloody pulp as their screams echo through the once silent forest.

Quintus and Felix duck and dodge tree limbs and downed timber as they attempt to outdistance the mob of rotting corpses that follow.

Quintus, not quite as fleet of foot as Felix, turns to see how close their oppressors are and trips over the roots of a large tree. He falls, face down, into the soft earth of the forest floor. As he recovers his bearing, he looks up just as the broken, rusted axe blade of one of his pursuers comes crashing down upon his forehead. It is impaled in his skull as his eyes cross slightly and blood pours from the misshapen gash. He stammers his last words.

"F…Felix! Felix, h…help me!"

The mob envelops him, and Felix hears his muted screams as flesh-stripped hands pull and rend his armor and tunic, then bury their knife-sharp digits into his soft exposed flesh, pulling and slashing as blood and entrails are ripped with abandon from his steaming chest and guts. His words turn to labored gurgles and then stop as his throat is bitten and chewed while his face is flayed and punctured by the relentless wave of rotting soldiers.

Felix doesn't look back. His only thought is home. If he can get out of the woods, maybe he can make it home. This thought consumes him as he runs through the ever-thickening forest. Soon, the trees are so close together that he must turn sideways to get between them. Fear rises in his guts as he realizes that his pace has slowed enough for the dead to catch him.

What he doesn't realize is that the massive wave of dead that pursues him is also being hampered by the density of the forest. Dead soldiers impale themselves on broken, low-hanging tree limbs as they run with reckless abandon after the Roman. The once mist-covered forest begins to turn red with the clouds of blood sprayed into the air by the rending and tearing of the rotted dead as they slam their way through trees and underbrush.

Up ahead, Felix sees the mist beginning to lift as he notices a clearly defined tree line. He pushes his body even more in hopes of reaching the end of this cursed forest.

As he bursts through the last barrier of underbrush and trees, he finds himself in a round clearing with a large stone altar in the middle.

He runs to the altar and ducks down on the opposite side, glancing around it to see if the dead are still in pursuit. To his shock and relief, they stop at the edge of the forest, but don't follow him into the clearing. They continue to appear at the edge of the clearing, filling every gap between every tree until almost half of the circular clearing is ringed with the skeletal remains of the warriors of Germania, all of them watching Felix, but not moving.

Felix looks around and sees Baldric standing at the edge of the clearing on the opposite side of the dead army. Their eyes meet, and Felix can see the anger and hate that Baldric projects.

"I'm so sorry. I never wanted to be here. I just want to go home!"

A bolt of blue lightning strikes the altar, hurling Felix from the base of the stone. His clothes give off wisps of smoke as he tries to regain his senses.

"You come to our home. You desecrate our land. You poison our water. You enslave us. You torture our children."

Another bolt of lighting strikes the ground between Felix's ankles. He screams in pain as he scrambles to his feet. A gale force gust of wind knocks him back to the ground as Baldric conjures the very elements to his cause.

Felix slowly rises to his feet again and, seeing Baldric's hand movements and gestures, realizes that this old man is somehow controlling the wind and lightning.

Twigs, leaves, and dirt fly from the ground around Baldric, striking Felix with enough force to tear exposed flesh and knock him back to his knees.

Another bolt strikes the ground mere feet in front of him, the flash so bright it blinds him momentarily.

Felix, his clothes shredded and blood-soaked, his hands and face sliced with countless twigs and stones, staggers toward Baldric as his vision returns.

As the wind swirls around him as if to blow him back once more, Felix realizes he is closer to the old man than before, so he ducks his head and runs headlong toward Baldric.

Baldric was not expecting this maneuver. He steps back in surprise but, being frail from his constant conjuring and not sure-footed, stumbles and falls to one knee.

Felix reaches the sorcerer just as he is recovering his balance. Once again, their eyes meet.

Baldric's anger turns to shock as Felix hurls himself into the old man, and they both tumble into the forest, striking a tree several feet from the clearing opening.

Felix recovers quickly and, seeing that Baldric is still stunned, picks up a stone lying nearby. He raises it over his head and brings it down with all his fear and anger in one decisive blow, crushing the face of Baldric. He then lifts the stone and brings it down again, spraying Baldric's blood and brains all over his face, the forest floor, and the tree that stopped their fall.

The dripping blood on his face brings him back from his berserker rage. Seeing what he has done to the old wizard, he drops the rock and falls to the ground. Tears now mix with the blood that streams down his cheeks.

Moments pass, and Felix regains his composure. He sits up on his knees to survey his situation. Baldric is dead. He turns to look across the clearing to see if the dead still stand at the edge. To his amazement, they are gone. Fear wells within him again.

"Are they coming this way?"

He frantically sniffs the air for any sign of stench and decay, then listens intently for the clank and clamor of their rusted and rotting armor. Nothing. Still on his knees, he turns to look at Baldric again, and standing in front of him is Uwe.

Felix's heart sinks. "You're the farm boy that the interrogators tortured, aren't you?"

Uwe plunges Felix's hunting knife, which had fallen to the forest floor when he tackled Baldric, into Felix's stomach. Uwe says nothing, but the flame of hate burns so brightly in his one eye that Felix knows the answer. As Uwe twists and slides the knife up Felix's torso, there is no expression on his face but seething hatred.

As his guts spill out onto the ground, steam rising from the flow of blood and entrails, Felix's final thought is of home.

Piper At the Gates of Dawn

Allison Pang

A Fox & Willow Story

Author's Note: *This story takes place between* **Blinded By The Light** *and* **The Better To See You With**.

A soft whimper emerged from the pile of rocks filling the entrance of the cave, a small white hand wriggling in desperation, nails torn and jagged as they scrabbled against the stone. Josef couldn't hear it, the way he couldn't hear anything, anything at all.

He stared at the bloodstained fingers, the blue woven bracelet around the wrist half torn away. Marie, he thought. Marie.

But she had just been beside him, laughing, dancing; the Piper in his frock of ever-changing hue had stood at the front of the line, children trailing behind him, singing a secret song only they understood.

The Piper smiled broadly, nodding and gesturing onward, leading the merry band of his friends. One hundred in total, all the children in the village. Stella, Cynthia, John and Tomas and all the rest. The older children carried the younger, even Marie, clutching a red-cheeked infant who shrieked with delight.

Ribbons, nosegays, butterflies, fireflies, soft illuminations, and brilliant colors to light up the forest path that grew ever deeper, ever darker. And Josef, poor deaf Josef, trailing along at the end, swept up in the odd thrumming he could feel from the bottom of his naked feet up to his chest, making his arms and legs jerk this way and that in a pale imitation of what the others were doing.

But he could hear nothing of the song itself, and if he smiled, it was only because he wanted Marie to think he was having fun too. After all, the Piper had said it was a secret, just for children, just for them, promising them a delightful tea party at the end, full of balloons and toys and any number of delicious treats.

But Josef couldn't help but notice the way the Piper's smile grew tighter and more brittle the deeper they went. He'd been to the forest a few times before, of course. They nearly all had. But never so far, and never so dark.

The sunlight waned further and further along, the small shafts of gold seeming to struggle past the thick green shadows of the fir trees, the old and creaking oaks, flanked by pale and slender birch.

He grasped Marie's shoulder so as not to upset the baby, signing a worried gesture at her. But Marie's eyes were glassy and sightless, and she just giggled and turned around, her feet dancing her up the path just as easily as before.

He marveled at how well she did it, her brown shoes skipping over stones and logs with ease, even as he stumbled along, a sharp rock painful against his sole. But then, sweet Marie had always been so graceful.

The Piper led them to a clearing; on the far side framed the entryway to a cave. Josef hesitated as the Piper smiled and laughed and played, striding up to the cave and knocking on a ramshackle door that barred the entrance.

The door opened, flooding the clearing with golden light, the promise of a thousand summer days, the scent of green grass and wildflowers, the tickling whisper of trees to be climbed, and stones to be skipped, warm jam, cold milk.

Marie turned and tugged at Josef's hand, pleading with him to come along as she merrily followed the others through the door. And Josef let out a clumsy laugh that seemed to cut through the music. Her eyes darkened for a moment, widening as though they truly saw him.

But the others slipped through the doorway, and Marie followed right along with them, swept up like a fish caught in the currents. Josef's vision flickered, the sudden warmth of the clearing slipping away, an icy chill running down his neck to take root in his spine.

He shivered, glancing up at the Piper who was gently pushing Marie in with the others. The Piper paused when Josef hesitated, giving him a friendly wave. But when Josef stood rooted to the spot, the Piper shrugged and closed the door.

Josef lurched toward the man, but the Piper had stopped playing, and the ground shook like a bucking horse as the mountain growled. Josef tumbled to the ground. The Piper smiled, but this time his mouth widened and widened and widened, full of glittering, pointed teeth.

And then he was gone, leaving Josef crying alone in the clearing, Marie's hand growing cold and still.

"Move over, Princess. I can't see past your backside." Gideon shoved his way past Willow to peer over the edge of the cliff from where she was crouched. Willow gritted her teeth in long-suffering fashion, shifting her weight to make space for the fox.

"There's nothing to see," she groused.

"Speak for yourself," he said smugly. "There's a town down there. If we hurry along, we might make it in time to get a room. I'm sure there's at least one inn." He sniffed. "You're getting a bit ripe, you know."

Willow wrinkled her nose. The fox spirit wasn't wrong, though he could have phrased it a little more nicely. But then, he wouldn't be Gideon if he'd done that. "Fine." She stood up to brush the dirt from her legs and picked up the traveler's harp in its leather case to rest it on her hip. "Lead on then, o sharp-seeing one."

He huffed out a *ke ke ke ke* sound and trotted in front of her, his white-tipped tail waving back and forth like a lantern. From this angle, it was nearly impossible to see the red collar about his neck, but visible or not, it lingered in her mind, constantly. The curse that had been laid upon it was slowly and surely killing him. If it remained unbroken, there would only be a fox in that body and whatever magics made up Gideon would be gone forever.

Her mouth pressed grimly. Her own issues could wait, as tied up as they were with his destiny. But that was neither here or nor there, and the sudden rumbling in her belly only made her realize how much she longed to get off the road for a night or two.

If nothing else, maybe she could trade a few songs for a warm supper.

The town was more of a village, she realized as they drew closer. Not exactly a hub of commerce, but it would do for tonight. Two watchmen eyed her suspiciously as she walked through the gates, their grim gazes sliding past her to Gideon, who was trotting at her ankles like some sort of trained dog.

Sometimes she felt as though a leash for appearances might be prudent, but the proud fox spirit would never stoop to such a thing. The collar was bad enough.

"Well, at least they've got an inn," Gideon observed, stepping over the muddy cobblestones. And indeed, the one inn that they came across was a good size, its sign creaking in the breeze. The Feathered Rat. A soft, golden luminescence illuminated the windows, but no sound of merriment or music slipped past the crack of the slightly ajar door.

Willow frowned. Rare to have an inn be so quiet this early in the evening. For that matter, the whole town seemed to have an unpleasant pall upon it that she couldn't quite place. The few patrons inside were clustered by themselves in one of the corners, their heads down low. One man appeared to be weeping, his shoulders shaking as the others watched him sadly.

A serving girl emerged from the kitchens and gestured at Willow to take an empty table near the fireplace.

Grateful for the crackling warmth, Willow did so, placing her harp case on the floor next to her. The serving girl brought her a trencher of bread, filled with what might have been stew in a former life, coupled with a mug of ale. Willow ordered a second bowl for Gideon, who nipped at her ankle until she acquiesced.

The serving girl pointed at the harp after setting down the bowl. "There's no music allowed in here."

Willow blinked, her hopes of trading a night of song for a meal dashed almost immediately. "Are you sure? I can make it merry or soft…whatever you prefer."

The conversation in the corner stopped completely, and Willow froze. "There's no music allowed anywhere in Hamelin," one gruff old man spoke up.

"My apologies," Willow bowed. "I meant no offense."

"Indeed. You aren't from around here, clearly." He drained the remainder of his ale, staring at the table with an empty expression. Willow returned to her meal, suddenly wishing to get out of the common room as quickly as she might.

After a bit of bargaining with the innkeeper, a stooped man with graying hair and a quiet smile, she managed to get a room. They hastily made their way up the stairs and into what was nothing more than a glorified storage closet. But it had a bed and a small window, and for the two travelers that was more than enough.

"Seems, odd, doesn't it?" Gideon said sharply as Willow closed the door. "No music?"

"Maybe it's a religious thing," Willow mused, unbraiding her long, dark hair to run a comb through it. "Or perhaps only local musicians are allowed?" She felt around in her bag for her coin purse. "I've still got some money from the pearls I exchanged in Tamiris, so I think we should be fine."

The fox spirit stared out their little window. "I've got a bad feeling about this place. Best be on our way in the morning."

"Maybe we can find ourselves a traveling merchant," Willow mused in agreement. "Save our legs the trouble. Besides, the further north we go, the more likely we'll get stuck in the mountains from snow, and I don't think we really have time for that."

"Don't rub it in." His tail twitched like a cat's, the red collar around his neck a blatant reminder of how little time they had. Willow murmured an apology, knowing he was sore about the whole thing, but who wouldn't be, really?

Quickly undressing for bed, she slipped into the warmth of the wool blankets on the creaky mattress. The blankets were itchy, but exhaustion won out in the end and she drifted off to the sound of rain on the windows, Gideon curled up against the inner curve of her knees.

"Master Flik is probably who you want to talk to," the inn-keeper said, polishing the glasses above the bar, when Willow inquired about merchants in the area the next morning. "He usually arrives this time of year to trade furs before heading north."

Relief surged through Willow. As long as she managed to keep her head down, they'd be on their way in a matter of days and this odd little town would be nothing more than a faded memory.

"Will you be going out today?" the innkeeper asked. "I would reconsider the harp if I were you. People will think you're in league with the Piper."

"The who?" Willow's brow furrowed as she set her spoon down, her porridge finished. "And I tend to carry it with me wherever I go."

"Suit yourself," the innkeeper said. "But I'd suggest you be on your way as soon as you can." He grimaced at the harp before returning to polishing the glasswork. "Bad for business, you know."

"Indeed." An uneasy feeling twisted Willow's guts into ribbons. Leaving the inn to wander about the village didn't improve matters, the mud spattering her shoes as she maneu-vered around the larger puddles.

After the rollicking crowds of Tamiris, Hamelin felt almost like a morgue in its washed-out quiet. Tamiris had been full of merchants, travelers, children scampering underfoot...

Willow paused, shaking her head as she searched the streets and storefronts. "Children," she breathed suddenly.

"Oi?" Gideon said, his ears pricked at her, the earring in his left ear jingling.

"There's no children," she said. "Can you hear any?"

"Maybe they're all in school, aye? Working the fields? What-ever it is backwater children do in backwater towns," he mut-tered, clearly not interested.

"Even so, there would be at least a babe or two with their mothers, wouldn't there?" Willow chewed on her lower lip thoughtfully. "A mystery."

"And not one you need to be concerned about." Gideon flattened his ears. "Let's get some provisions."

He beelined for the supply store and Willow followed, looking for goods that were lightweight and easy to transport. Before long she had a basket full of dried fruit and jerky, enough to last them another week or so.

They moved onto the local bakery, the scent of the fresh baked bread making her mouth water, but as she squatted to get a closer look at the confections lined behind the glass, she noticed a small, golden-haired figure beneath the baker's workbench, clearly immersed in a book.

"See?" Gideon's tail curled smugly. "Children. Nothing to worry about."

"Hello there. Would you mind getting me a loaf of the brown?" Willow pointed at one of the brown loaves, a dust-ing of flour on top like snow. When the boy didn't react, she tapped on the glass. "Hello?"

He yawned and shifted away, ignoring her completely. She frowned.

"We don't have all day," Gideon said, popping over the case to the other side.

"Gideon—don't," Willow hissed, pinching the bridge of her nose.

The fox spirit ignored her utterly, nosing about the table until the boy looked up, his mouth dropping in surprise.

Gideon rewarded him with a fox grin and returned to Wil-low's side. The boy paled, peering up at Willow with a great deal more fear than she would have thought to be awarded to a possible customer.

"This is Gideon," Willow said, squatting down to his level as he came out from behind the counter. He seemed a sturdy enough lad, maybe ten or eleven, but his face had the sort of sadness one might expect from some sort of tragic event, as though an old man resided within.

He stroked her harp case with a light touch of his fingers. "That's my harp. Do you like music?" He tapped it again and gestured at the clasps. Ah. He wanted her to open it.

She hesitated, but he seemed so insistent, and in the end she undid the case, giving him a peek at the rosewood harp inside.

"Josef's's deaf," the baker snapped, emerging from behind a curtain, her hands dusted in flour. "So you can dispense with all of that nonsense." Her face darkened when she saw Gideon, and she snatched the boy by the wrist to drag him away from the front of the store.

"What do you want?"

"A loaf of the brown, please," Willow said, making her purchase in quick order.

"Best you move on from here, aye?" The baker said, thrusting the loaf of bread into a paper sachet. "We don't take to strangers around here, particularly ones that poke their noses into business that isn't theirs." She pointed at Gideon. "And keep your filthy animal out of my establishment."

"He travels with me wherever I go," Willow said by way of apology, though she bit down the words she really wanted to say. She and Gideon left quickly and retreated to the inn as the rain fell harder, driving a chill down her spine. With any luck, Master Flik would arrive sooner than scheduled and they could be out of this place for good.

Willow sopped up the last of her soup with a bit of bread. Quietly desperate or not, at least the inn at least served a decent supper. The evening had grown sharp, and with her mind inclined to wander, she busied herself at one of the tables in the great room, scratching notes on a bit of paper she'd found tucked away in her purchases.

Josef aside, she still hadn't seen any children, but the mystery of the empty village was less important than trying to figure out the route to the north. Gideon's foster-father, Master Chen, had mentioned a mysterious sorceress who might be able to help the fox spirit break his curse, so for now, she focused on the logistics. Transportation, money, supplies. What they might need to travel into the mountains. At least Gideon had a fur coat, most of the time.

When the serving maid swung by to refill her ale mug, Willow cleared her throat. "Excuse me, but who or what is the Piper? The innkeeper said people might think I was…working with him?"

The serving maid flinched, eyeing the handful of other pat-rons nervously. "Hush." She nervously lowered her head closer to Willow's ear. "It started with the rats, aye? We were overrun with them months ago. Our crops were being destroyed, couldn't bake our bread, finding them in our ale barrels…" She shuddered. "Nasty things. But then some wandering minstrel showed up and offered to get rid of them for a pretty penny. The village elders agreed to it, and he played his magic flute, and next thing we knew the rats were gone."

Willow exchanged a look with Gideon. "Seems like awfully convenient timing. And then what?"

The woman let out a soft bark of humorless laughter. "Skin-flints is what this town is made of. They didn't pay. All that grain saved, the crops…all they had to do was pay the miserable fee and we'd have been fine." A ragged breath escaped her. "But when they didn't…he took the children instead."

"As payment?" Horror clamped down on Willow's chest. "What did he do with them?"

"No one knows. They went the same way as the rats, I suspect, but no one knows what happened to them either." The serving maid's mouth grew grim.

"And no one went after them?" Willow's frown grew even deeper, unable to comprehend any of these villagers simply standing there as their children waltzed away.

"We couldn't hear the music. Not a one of us. Only the children. By the time we realized it, they…" "My little Marie is gone too." The serving maid's mouth trembled, her grief so thick Willow could have wrapped it about her like a blanket. "Only Josef returned–and we've not gotten two words out of the poor boy about any of it."

"I'm so sorry," Willow murmured, unsure of what else to say. In the romance stories, she might have boldly proclaimed she would rescue the children like some kind of hero. But sometimes there was no justice at all.

The door to the common room flew open, slamming hard against the wall to reveal the baker, her hair still dusted with flour and her face red with fury as she strode over to Willow's table. "He's gone! My Josef is gone! This is all your fault! I saw you open that harp case and show it to my boy."

Willow blinked beneath the onslaught. The tavern room of the inn had grown so quiet, a mouse could have waltzed across the mantel and everyone would have heard its footsteps. "He asked to see it. I was only there to buy bread, and I left right after."

"Don't you play innocent with us!" The old man in the corner said, getting to his feet. "You…you…music is the devil's work. Come to tempt us, come to make promises, only to take our children as payment! I'm off to get the constable."

The baker crossed her arms. "Now we'll see what's what." She pointed at the other patrons of the inn. "Get her! Keep her here!"

"Oh, no. I don't think so." Gideon finally spoke up from his place on the floor, the baker's mouth dropping open in horror as the fox spoke.

"Gideon…" Willow's heart dropped. Any chance of getting out of this unscathed was growing smaller and smaller by the moment.

"Well, say what you will, I've no intention of becoming a scapegoat." Gideon shivered, the fur melting away as he stood upon his hind legs, finally revealing himself as a pale-skinned man with the ears and tail of a fox, naked from head to toe, save for the red collar still fastened about his neck.

"A demon!" screamed the baker, fleeing the inn. The rest of the patrons hesitated for the span of two breaths, staring at the naked fox spirit before following suit, crying out in panicked horror.

"Indeed," Gideon said mildly, taking Willow by the hand as they scrambled through the kitchens and into the courtyard behind the inn. In the streets, torches and accusations of witchcraft scattered through the night air like fireflies.

Willow swallowed, holding her harp close as she tried to peer around the edge of the inn. The villagers were buzzing about the town, their voices taut and angry, but Gideon could smell the sharp scent of fear riding through it all, like a needle and thread sewing them together.

"She needs to burn! What kind of woman travels alone? And with an instrument! And that…animal of hers! It became a demon!" The baker, nearly in hysterics, circled about the mob. "There can be no doubt she's in league with…with the Piper!"

A great wail rose up when she said the name, fingers pointing and jaws clacking with wild accusations. None of it meant anything good, of that he was certain.

Gideon took Willow's harp from her, giving her a sly wink. "Let's get out of here, aye?"

Not that Willow had any experience with escaping angry mobs, but Gideon loped along beside her bearing a foxy grin that spoke volumes. Although not an athlete by any stretch, months of hard living on the road had made her far less soft than her princess status would normally have indicated, and she took full advantage of that to put Hamelin as far behind her as she might.

With any luck it would take the villagers a little time to realize she was gone.

"Where are we going?" She gasped.

"The forest. Over past those fields," Gideon said. "We should get off the road."

Panting, she nodded, regret at having left her other belongings behind. If they were going to be stuck roughing it in the forest for a few days, the jerky would have come in handy.

Gideon dodged around a log, leading her down an incline and toward a rivulet that grew by measures until it was a raging river.

"We'll crack our skulls in here, if we're not careful," Willow said, narrowly avoiding a sharp rock. Her palms were scratched from prickers, small stinging cuts that made her want to plunge her hands into the cooling waters. "I can't see in the dark like you can."

The fox spirit paused to glance behind them, his ears flicking back and forth. "No torches chasing us yet, anyway."

"Small favors." Willow sagged against a tree with relief, taking advantage of the moment to catch her breath. Her fingers brushed something soft caught on the bark and she pulled her hand away, a piece of cloth stuck to her palm.

She peered in the dim light, trying to make out what it was. Gideon took it from her and sniffed it. "Josef," he said. "He went this way."

"Are you sure?" Willow frowned. "If we find him, maybe that will prove our innocence."

"Don't be so naïve," he retorted. "Even if you somehow produce him, they'll assume you were just trying to save your own skin, never mind they think I'm a demon."

"Let's just focus on finding him first," she said, irritation making her bite her lower lip. "We can figure out what to do then."

Magic skittered over his skin as he shifted into a fox. He could track far better with this nose anyway. It was getting harder and harder to move between these shapes, as though he were somehow trying to walk through a wall of spider webs, the old form clinging to him. One of these days he wouldn't be able to complete the change, but that didn't bear thinking about.

Willow gathered up the harp and followed along behind him as he led her through the forest. A slick scent of magic rode the breeze, making him uneasy. It was oily. Rotten.

He didn't voice this to Willow yet—no sense in worrying her until he knew for sure what it was. In the safety of the woods, he only found traces of the occasional rabbit or deer. A sleepy bear fattening himself up for winter, and the thin brush of that rotting magic, sickly sweet, like a bouquet of decaying flowers.

It had an element of coaxing to it, a bit of a siren song. *This way, this way...*

The faint traces grew stronger as he followed along, avoiding snares and other distractions, winding further up and around the mountain, coming to a dead end at what appeared to be a cave-in, a pile of boulders blocking the entrance to what might have been a mine shaft or perhaps a tunnel.

Gideon's hackles rose, the magic here far more malevolent

than before. A small hole on the side of the cave-in remained open. He hesitated, his tail lashing nervously.

Willow only caught a glimpse of a pale hand reaching through the rubble, focusing instead on the stout figure of Josef, his golden hair a dandelion wilderness. His entire body shook, tears running down his trembling chin as he sobbed.

She knelt beside him, staring at the tiny hand clutching a bouquet of wilted flowers. He startled, and she reached out to squeeze his arm. "Are you alright?"

Josef fell into her arms and wept, as though the secret of what had happened burst through the dam of his reserve, regret and horror rippling through him in a wash of tears. Gideon sniffed at the hand, a breath of decay emanating from the gnarled fingers.

"Gideon, what if all the children ended up in there?" She gestured at the hole, her eyes brimming with tears as she clutched the sobbing boy. "What if some are still alive?"

He hesitated, his ears twitching. He could detect no movement from beneath the rocks, but one look at Josef's tear-streaked face and he swallowed down the negative answer. What harm would it do to check? He sighed and wriggled on his belly through the hole.

The magic felt stale inside, like it had been somehow trying to devour itself. It latched onto him as he worked his way through the tightness of the opening, his sides scraping against the rocks.

Nostrils flaring, the scent of death grew stronger when he emerged into the cave proper, revulsion making his mouth dry. A growing sense of something foul and desperate clung to his fur like oil as he stumbled upon a rustic altar. A desiccated rat was splayed out atop it, a splash of dried blood staining the pale limestone beneath it.

Gideon's nose twitched, wondering at the obvious sacrifice. What was the connection to the Piper?

The thought tumbled round and round, a flea on a high wire until he stepped on something soft. He jerked his paw away, half expecting another rat. When he finally saw the empty faces staring up at him, framed by filthy sweaters and scuffed shoes, he let out a whine.

Not a just a cave, then. A tomb.

Willow watched the place Gideon had disappeared into, her stomach nervous. In an effort to distract Josef, she pulled out her harp, plucking the first few idle notes of a lullaby. "Did you want to see it?" She tapped Josef on the shoulder and showed him the open harp case. He wiped away at his tears for a closer look and then froze.

A harlequin shadow emerged from the trees, a flute in its hands, pointed teeth and black fur and an elegant tail...rat-like, but not a rat exactly. Josef gestured anxiously, and the rat man laughed, a hideous wet guttering that made Willow want to vomit up everything she'd ever eaten.

"An audience," it hissed at Willow. "Lovely playing, my dear. With a little magic, you'd be quite formidable."

Willow's upper lip curled as she swallowed her fear. Beside her, Gideon suddenly emerged from the hole. His ears flattened as he crouched beside her.

Josef pointed again at the rockslide.

"Stubborn boy," the Piper snapped. "Only the one who awakened me can ask a boon. Your mother already did that. Ah, and here she is."

Willow blinked. "The baker?"

"Knew I'd find you here, you devil woman," the baker woman snarled, limping into the clearing, a bruise blooming on her right cheek. "And you're lying."

"I never lie," said the creature. "Lying undoes magic, you

know. You found my altar, woke me with your sacrifice. You said rats were ruining your grain stores and destroying your ability to bake, correct? I removed the rats, as we agreed on, but your village did not pay, so I collected the debt personally."

It glanced at Josef slyly. "It's a very simple contract. One hundred gold coins or one hundred souls, though one soul remains outstanding. Yours or his, either will do."

A shadow crept over the baker's face, as though she were caught in a trap with no way out but to gnaw off her own own foot. "Take him," she shrieked, shoving Josef at the creature. "Just leave me be!"

Josef stumbled forward, off-balance, his mouth opening in fear as he scraped his shin on one of the rocks. The entity smiled.

"Done." And then it launched itself at him.

Willow stumbled toward the boy without hesitation. "No!" Her fingers grasped his torn coat, tumbling the two of them away from the Piper.

Fury erupted over the Piper's face. "No interfering with my bargain, human!" He raised the flute to his reddened lips, the first hollow notes dripping from the instrument like oily snowflakes.

Willow froze, a seashell shiver radiating through her body as her limbs stiffened. She snarled, fighting the clumsy movements as she stepped forward, her fingers clutching Josef's arms like talons.

Gideon crept up from the side, leaping to snatch the pipe from the creature's elegant hands, his teeth closing on the infernal instrument with a metallic click. The Piper snarled, struggling with the fox spirit, Gideon rabbit kicking the creature in the face. He twisted like a cat in midair, the pipe tight between his jaws as he ran toward Willow.

"No!" The Piper staggered, a dark fury emanating off him in waves. "It's useless. No mortal can destroy my flute."

"Not a mortal. Not exactly," Gideon gasped, changing his shape again with a groan. This time his animal form unfolded from him slowly, like a peeling grape, his fox muzzle lingering far longer than it ever had before, but he shook it away, standing up to break the pipe over his knee.

The Piper let out a howling roar, his skin sluicing away like an unbuttoned coat, leaving behind a shapeless shadow, small and dark and ugly, bristling with pointed teeth. It cackled as it shrank away into the cave.

Willow dry heaved at the scent of the rotting flesh, her hand covering her mouth as a cluster of wriggling…things rolled around in the leaves. Gideon rubbed his hands on the rocks, as though trying to wipe away the corruption, his mouth curling in disgust.

A cluster of rats, all tied together by their tails, lay twitching nearby. "Rat king," he muttered, nudging it with his foot.

"Is it…is it dead?" Willow hesitated. "The Piper?"

Gideon shook his head. "Whatever form it took is gone, yes. But that was…some sort of local forest god. A spirit. The baker woman must have rekindled his power through her sacrifices of the rats, hence this form. I'm sure he's only retreated, but perhaps the price was met, after all."

He pointed to where the baker lay still, blood pooling from where she'd lost her balance, her skull cracked open like a nut. Josef buried his head in Willow's arms and wept as she hugged him.

"What should we do?" she asked finally. "We can't just leave him here. And his…mother. Those children…"

Gideon's expression softened as he watched her comfort the boy. "She was no mother," he murmured. "The children were all dead inside the cave. There's nothing to be done for them now–and with that spirit lurking around, perhaps it would be best not to disturb them further."

Willow let out a ragged breath and got to her feet. "It would be cruel to deny the townsfolk their grief. They must be told."

"Not in person." Gideon picked up Josef to carry him. "The best we can do is return him to the town entrance. We certainly can't take him where we're going."

"No." She sighed, shouldering her harp. "I suppose not."

The wagon creaked beneath the weight of the hay, the scent of snow riding the breeze. Willow let her legs hang loose, Gideon curled up at her side as she strummed her harp idly. "It was good fortune we met you on the road, Master Flik," she called to the driver, a well-meaning sort with a pleasant face and kind demeanor. "Thank you for allowing us to travel with you."

Flik tipped his hat at her. "The pleasure is all mine, Mistress Willow. Especially given your circumstances–it was just as well I avoided Hamelin, seeing as half the town burned down to the ground nearly overnight." He shook his head. "Damn shame, that. Sounds like they were looking for a witch or a cunning woman or some such, and the wind took the sparks of a torch and lit the damn place up like a tinder box."

Willow and Gideon exchanged a glance. They'd dropped Josef off at the smoking ruin of the gates, watching as he'd run straight for the arms of his innkeeper's serving girl, a map to the cave scrawled on a piece of parchment in his pocket. Whatever Fate allowed him, he'd have to find it on his own, the same as them.

"Ah well, let's not think on it too hard," Master Flik said cheerfully. "How about a song?"

Dobrogost

Jonathan Janz

"Apprentice Halsey," Elder Lyndon murmured, "would you please check on the family?"

Halsey nodded and moved briskly away. As grim a task as it was, he'd gladly check on the family. Anything, even speaking to the parents who'd lost their only daughter, would be preferable to gazing upon that mud-rimmed hole in the ground.

But when Halsey knocked and the haunted face of Alvina Morgan peered out of the darkness at him, he realized how foolish he'd been to crave this duty. Though not yet thirty and quite fetching, Alvina had been ravaged by Fern's death. Her eyes were sunken-in pits of brow and cheekbone. The poor woman hadn't eaten or slept since her daughter died. Halsey suspected she hadn't bathed either. Her sculpted features were smudged with grime, her hair as tangled as a rook's nest.

Halsey's gorge rose at the yeasty odor wafting out of the Morgans' meager hut. He stood on the pointed toes of his leather poulaines and spotted a grubby urchin, a lad of four named Speck, sitting crosslegged and fiddling with some wooden toy.

There was no sign of Wyot Morgan. Nor his deceased daughter.

"Yes?" Alvina said.

"Apologies. Elder Lyndon bade me retrieve you." When Alvina merely stared at him, Halsey added, "It is time."

The anguish in her bloodshot eyes nearly forced him to avert his gaze, but he reminded himself to play the man and perform his duty. Elder Lyndon and the others were waiting.

Alvina hesitated. "May I leave Speck here?"

Halsey pursed his lips. "Dying is but another chapter in the story of our earthly existence, Mrs. Morgan. We can't shield our loved ones from any part of that narrative, even the tribulations."

Alvina lowered her head.

"We'll expect you in five minutes," Halsey murmured, and with that, he turned on his heels and started down the gloomy path.

Such a sad business. Death was never a cheerful affair, particularly when the deceased was a little one. Fern Morgan had not yet reached her eleventh birthday when the accident befell her. A shame.

Halsey navigated the squelchy earth and thanked the stars that young Fern's misfortune had occurred in October, before the lands hardened like flint and made digging a burden. The deadhouse near the parsonage was ghastly enough in the best of times, but the thought of little Fern's body resting there until the thaw would have rendered his winter nights unbearable. Halsey shivered.

Coming around a bend, he heard voices, Elder Lyndon's restrained, others making no attempt at decorum. Most prominent among them was Lord Redgrave, the mayor of Caldea, his once-virile frame sagging, the shoulders broad enough but his muscles withering like November crops. A slender black mustache traced a filigree over Redgrave's nearly nonexistent lips, and a touch of rouge showed on his sunken cheeks.

Attending Redgrave was Aldermen Bede, a pink-faced, sweaty stump of a man whose fog of cologne couldn't mask an odor that always put Halsey in mind of overaged cheese. The alderman was gripping a stein of foamy ale and chuckling at something Redgrave had said. In truth, Halsey couldn't recall a time when Redgrave had uttered anything even mildly amusing, but of course Halsey would chuckle right along with the others. Here and there scurried servants of the noblemen, primarily girls ranging from early adolescence to the cusp of womanhood. The young women serving Lord Redgrave, Halsey noted without surprise, were in full bloom. Halsey chuckled inwardly. Given Lord Redgrave's appetites, it was no wonder he'd selected such buxom specimens.

"Pastor Halsey!" Alderman Bede called. "Tell us you were able to rouse that indolent woodcarver. I'll catch my death of cold if I remain out here shivering in the dark."

Lord Redgrave favored Bede with a droll look. "It is a good forty minutes before nightfall, and I'll wager you've imbibed so much you no longer feel much of anything."

A servant girl threw back her head and crowed. Bede laughed too, but livid spots showed on his cheeks.

Redgrave turned to Elder Lyndon. "I do think we've idled out here long enough. My supper awaits."

Elder Lyndon was peering through his spectacles at the *Book of Truth*, but now he regarded Lord Redgrave patiently. "We will begin soon, old friend. The woodcutter's family will collect themselves, and—ah, here they are now."

Halsey looked up in time to see Alvina and Speck Morgan emerging from their hovel. A hush fell over the assembly. Alvina said nothing, her face bereft of emotion, her body a perambulating husk from whom all vitality has been leeched. Her son was similarly expressionless, and as woman and boy drifted closer to the open grave, Halsey distinguished the scar under Speck's left eye, an inch long and so deep it cast a mote of shadow on the child's unkempt face.

Feral country children, Halsey thought. The boy had nearly lost an eye fiddling with one his father's gouges. Fern, too, had suffered from Wyot Morgan's negligence. When only six, the child had mishandled a chisel and, inflicted a deep cut in her left index finger, and the resulting infection had necessitated amputation. In a home with such lax rules as this, Halsey mused, was it any wonder Fern died of an accident?

A hand clapped Halsey on the shoulder, startling him from his reverie.

It was Bede. "Must we wait on the woodcarver? At this rate we'll be here past midnight."

"It isn't just the woodcarver for whom we must wait." Halsey indicated the open grave. "The work isn't yet finished."

Bede grunted. "If we wait for Danes, we'll grow roots. He's hardly lifted a spadeful since the woodcarver's wife appeared."

Halsey saw it was as Alderman Bede said. Danes wasn't old, but drink and other vices had rotted his teeth and latticed his nose with scarlet skeins. He was feigning work but accomplishing very little, his energy devoted to furtive glances at Alvina Morgan.

At Halsey's ear, Bede murmured, "I find Alvina's bosom as beguiling as the next man, so's it's not as I blame Danes, but my God, Halsey, the temperature's plummeting out here, and I have my own itch to satisfy." Bede tipped a nod at one of his serving girls. She was no older than fourteen.

Halsey sighed. "I shall speak to Danes."

Bede grasped Halsey's shoulders and gave him a squeeze. "Good boy. I knew you'd move things along."

Halsey suppressed a sneer. *Boy*? Good *boy*? Just because he was an apprentice? *Damn it all*, he thought. Until he proved himself, that's all he would remain to most of the village. To Redgrave and Bede he was no better than the serving girls. As he neared the grave, Halsey drew himself up. He would simply have to prove he was more than they believed.

"Mr. Danes," he said.

The sexton kept digging, seemingly heedless of Halsey's presence. Halsey drew in breath and spoke more loudly. "I need a word, Mr. Danes."

A mirthless chuckle, Danes's spade never ceasing. "He needs a word. How 'bout I trade you a word for a hand. Like stabbing at iron, this is."

"It's growing late," Halsey remarked. "Need we dig so deep?"

Danes dumped another spadeful of dirt over the lip of the grave and leaned on the handle. "Do I tell you how to do your business, young man?"

Halsey gritted his teeth but kept his voice level. "The alderman is getting restless. Lord *Redgrave* is getting restless."

"Drunk, you mean," Danes corrected. "Listen, Halsey. I've done my part. You do yours."

Halsey raised his eyebrows. "And what is that?"

Danes's mouth drew into a slit. He jabbed his shovel at the noblemen. "Making those ghouls show some respect."

"Do your job, sir."

"I'm making sure poor Fern isn't dug up by wolves." He gazed meaningfully at Halsey. "You need to give this poor child a decent ceremony. Don't you think you owe her that?"

Halsey opened his mouth but could find no retort. Blushing, he fled the graveside, and by the time he'd returned to Elder Lyndon, he'd only partially recovered.

"Speak some sense to the sexton, did you?" Elder Lyndon said without looking up from the *Book of Truth*.

"I merely reminded him of our purpose here tonight."

Elder Lyndon peered at him over his spectacles. "And what is that?"

The knowing cast of his mentor's gaze robbed Halsey of speech. He gestured feebly. "We're here to ensure this child the respect she deserves. That is to say, the solace she—her parents, rather—need in their time of…"

But Elder Lyndon was no longer listening. He was peering at something beyond the open grave. A figure was distinguishable some distance back in the yew trees.

"Who's there?" Lord Redgrave demanded.

The figure remained where it was, a dark silhouette on a sable background. Halsey glanced at Elder Lyndon uneasily.

Then little Speck wandered forward and squinted into the veil of forest. "Papa?"

The figure finally moved, and Speck dashed forward to greet Wyot Morgan.

Halsey found it possible to breathe again.

Speck tossed his arms around his father's leg and said something Halsey couldn't make out. The woodcarver reached down and patted his son's back, but even in the thickening gloom Halsey could see something was wrong with Wyot. The woodcarver was garbed in habiliments better-suited for manual labor than a funeral service. The open-throated rag that passed for a tunic was filthy. In wretched condition also were the mud-stained breeches and soil-caked shoes, the latter so smeared with muck that the goatskin was scarcely visible.

As Wyot approached, his urchin still grafted to his thigh, Elder Lyndon folded his arms. "Have you forgotten the occasion, woodcarver, or is it your intention to attend your daughter's funeral thusly arrayed?"

Wyot scraped a calloused palm over his chin whiskers and muttered something Halsey couldn't make out.

Redgrave stepped forward. "See here, Morgan, we've dallied out here in the wilds long enough. It's time we bury your daughter, or else this frost will put more of us in the ground."

Alvina strode forward to meet her husband. The couple embraced, their foreheads pressed together.

"Looks as if someone's not touched by this familial devotion," Lord Redgrave murmured, and when Halsey tracked

Redgrave's gaze he discovered Danes scowling at the family from over the lip of the hole.

"Jealous, he is," Bede agreed. "Had a thing for Alvina back when they were kids."

Redgrave slurped his ale. "Bet he wishes the woodcarver would've broken his neck rather than the daughter."

Elder Lyndon winced, but he quickly recovered. Lyndon murmured to Lord Redgrave, "If your people will tend to the flambeaux, we'll prepare for the rites."

Redgrave barked orders to the grooms and underlings, and they set about immediately hammering stakes into the half-frozen earth. How many hours Danes had been out here toiling Halsey had no idea. The depth would not reach five feet, but a shallower grave was preferable to a winter in the deadhouse.

At thought of poor Fern piled in some corner, her innocent flesh defiled by rats, Halsey shuddered. He slid the *Book of Truth* from his cassock and wandered away from the group. Elder Lyndon would be officiating, of course, but his trust in Halsey was growing, and Halsey must needs be ready to assist. He'd lain awake the night before imagining Elder Lyndon turning his benevolent face toward him in the middle of Fern's service and inviting Halsey to read.

Now Halsey crowded into a deep-green stand of laurels and thumbed through his scripture until he happened upon a much-loved passage:

> "Fear not the chaos of the past, for the divine
> wisdom gifted to seers shall bathe us in the
> light of order."

Halsey smiled. A most affirming sentiment. To the woodcarver's family, Fern's passing must've seemed cruel. An affront, even. Yet the *Book of Truth* and the power it vested in good men like Elder Lyndon provided assurance. Halsey pored over the passage again, weighing the words and experimenting with the cadence. Should Elder Lyndon grant him the opportunity, and should Halsey perform capably, rumor of it would reach every ear in the village. Perhaps even the surrounding areas.

Halsey pursed his lips. So many benighted hamlets in this part of the country. If Providence willed it, Halsey might impart his wisdom to one of those unenlightened places, hone his craft, and eventually return to Caldea a master orator. He imagined Elder Lyndon, his hair gone from steel-gray to white, grasping him by the shoulder and declaring it was time for Halsey to succeed him. There would be a ceremony in the church, a coronation of sorts. Halsey would stand before the populace, smile benevolently, and—

"Get them under control, damn you," a voice growled.

Halsey whirled with a gasp and fumbled the *Book of Truth*. It was Danes who'd spoken, Danes whose rough-hewn features were twisted in rage. Halsey made to back away, but the laurel branches forbade it.

"I need to speak with Elder Lyndon," Halsey managed.

"*Need to speak with Elder Lyndon,*" Danes mimicked. "What you need is to behave with some decency."

Halsey blinked at him. "I hardly know what—"

"*Listen* to them, man."

Halsey shook his head.

Danes stalked closer, the toe of a muddy workboot kicking the *Book of Truth*. "That family," he jabbed a grubby finger at the Morgans, "is about to bury their little girl." He turned sideways so Redgrave and Bede were visible to Halsey. "And those goblins are carrying on like this is the Midsummer Festival. I mean, look at them, for pity's sake."

Halsey did. They ogled the serving girls and slurped their

steins, the foam that didn't slosh over their knuckles glistening on their chins.

Halsey bent to retrieve the *Book of Truth*. "You covet Wyot's wife. Why should you be so unmanned at the loss of Wyot's daughter?"

Danes snagged Halsey's arm, his grip like forging tongs. "How dare you make light of Fern's death?"

Halsey considered crying out for help, but if he allowed this lowly gravedigger to best him, he would surrender all authority. He arranged his features into an expression of disdain. "The *Book of Truth* warns against lusting after another man's wife."

For a moment he was certain Danes would strike him. Then the man's viselike fingers relinquished their grip, and Danes averted his eyes. "I'll not deny tender thoughts toward Alvina. Wyot Morgan's no friend of mine, and he never will be."

Halsey smiled a slow smile.

Danes fixed him with a look so penetrating Halsey felt his smile fade. "But that don't mean what's happening here is proper. The children know what occurred that day. My own boy told me."

Halsey tightened. "I have no idea—"

"The children *saw*, damn you. You know it to be true." Danes brought his face so near that Halsey could smell the man's rank breath. "Where were you when Fern fell, Halsey?"

Halsey lurched away from Danes, his heart thumping like a doe brought to bay. He was sure the gravedigger would follow him, but the wretch evidently thought better of it, for when Halsey pulled up next to Elder Lyndon, he discovered the gravedigger trudging toward the grave.

Elder Lyndon placed a hand on his shoulder. "Are you unwell, Apprentice Halsey? You're lathered with sweat."

Halsey mopped his brow. "Just my reading, Elder Lyndon." He flourished the *Book of Truth*. "You know how it affects me."

Lyndon's grin broadened, a knowing grin that rather caught the twilight shadows. "You've not been indulging in a draught of ale?"

Halsey looked blankly at his mentor. "Sir?"

Lyndon squeezed his shoulder almost sensuously. "There is nothing shameful in the occasional indulgence. No man is entirely free of wickedness, Halsey."

And so deep was the darkness cloaking his mentor's features and so spectrally did the newly-lit flambeaux gleam within Lyndon's pupils, that Halsey had to fight an urge to shrink away.

Lyndon released him and sniffed. "Let us proceed, Apprentice Halsey. We have a duty to perform."

He nodded, but as the holy man moved toward the grave, Halsey couldn't escape the impression that Elder Lyndon had just appointed himself Halsey's confessor.

"Good evening, Beloved Brethren," Elder Lyndon began in his deep, resonant voice. "Though darkness is wrapping the countryside in its inky embrace, the glow of our faith will serve as a beacon for all who are lost."

Halsey glanced about at the flickering torches, the makeshift flambeaux intended to reproduce the sterling-silver tapers in the church sanctuary but giving instead the impression of a pagan ritual, some blasphemous ceremony meant to mock the deceased girl rather than honor her.

"The forces of darkness," Elder Lyndon continued, "seek to extinguish the nourishing light of truth. But the time of chaos has past. We have triumphed over destruction, over death, over an existence spent cowering in shadows in the hope that the demons would not find us."

Gooseflesh prickled on Halsey's forearms. Sweat peppered his forehead despite the night breeze. Allusions to the dark times were expected in ceremonies such as these, yet they never failed to chill Halsey's marrow.

"The powers of good—of *truth*—are present tonight," Elder Lyndon declared. He turned and addressed the family. "Wyot Morgan, Alvina Morgan." A warm smile. "And dear Speck. You have lost a beloved daughter. A sister. A source of joy."

Firelight flickered over the Morgans' faces. Speck peered at the open grave. Alvina leaned against her husband, her careworn but still-pretty face cushioned by the woodcarver's chest. Wyot's gaze remained on the forest.

Halsey frowned. Dignitaries like Elder Lyndon and Lord Redgrave were under no obligation to traipse out here into the wildlands during inclement weather. The least the woodcarver could do was show some gratitude.

Ah, but that's why people need guidance, Halsey reminded himself. Heathens like the Morgans must be shown the way, lest they squander their lives in a shroud of ignorance.

"Yet we must not fret, Beloved Brethren," Lyndon went on, "for the *Book of Truth* teaches us that fear is the bastion of dark forces. Of sinful things."

As Halsey surrendered himself to Elder Lyndon's rhythms, it was the child Speck to whom Halsey's gaze was drawn, the boy evidently unmindful of the dire occasion, all his attention fixed on the toy in his hand, no doubt fashioned by his father. It was a crude thing, though Halsey could see why it appealed to the child. Winged and taloned, it featured a sinuous neck that tapered to an inverted triangular face. Halsey squinted to better discern the toy's features. The intermittent firelight precluded confirmation, but it appeared to Halsey that the woodcarver had whittled gaping jaws and razor-sharp teeth. The closer Halsey looked…yes, even the eyes were skillfully rendered, vast and leering. A revolting effect. Halsey had to admit that as ill-suited as the toy was to…well, *any* occasion… Wyot Morgan did possess some measure of skill.

"Gods damn thee, girl!" a voice exclaimed, and all heads

swiveled toward Lord Redgrave, whose leather tunic glistened with ale. "How do you expect to be a wife when you aren't even capable of operating a decanter?"

"Ever so sorry," the girl whimpered. Ginger-haired and freckled, Halsey recognized her as one of Bede's servants, perhaps the youngest present at tonight's ceremony. She fluttered about Redgrave, who cursed her and dabbed at his tunic with a handkerchief. The girl's ministrations were clumsy, and as everyone looked on, she jostled Redgrave's drink once more, this time splashing ale over his beaver-pelt poulaines. Redgrave roared and shoved her away. The ginger-haired girl sprawled in the piled grave dirt.

His plump face taut, Alderman Bede rushed forward and seized her by the wrist. "Get your foolish tail up and cease degrading me." He jerked her to her feet and dragged her toward the Morgans' hut. They disappeared around the thatched corner of the dwelling, but Bede's voice rang out clearly: "You'll receive no wages for a month, you blithering whelp!" The crack of an open palm striking flesh. "If you embarrass me again, you'll wish you were in the ground rather than that Morgan brat."

At this Alvina let out a little whimper, and Speck peered up at his mother. No one seemed quite sure what to say. Even Elder Lyndon appeared nonplussed.

So it was that the gravedigger shuffled over to the Morgan family. Danes knelt before the boy and nodded at the wooden monstrosity dangling at his side. "What you got there, lad? An eagle, mayhap?"

Speck responded in a clear, high voice: "Dobrogost."

Halsey froze. Everyone froze. Lord Redgrave glowered down at the child, his jowls darkening to a deep shade of crimson. "How...*dare* you utter that accursed name? Mr. and Mrs. Morgan, have you no control over your offspring?"

Alvina gazed at Redgrave mildly. "It is not control we seek, Lord Redgrave. It is spirit."

"Spirit?" Redgrave scoffed. "Foolish talk from a foolish wench."

Elder Lyndon half-raised a palm. "Let us grant each other grace. This is a difficult time."

"Difficult time or no," Redgrave countered, "there are words one does not utter." He hooked his thumbs over his stamped leather belt. "I demand an apology."

Alderman Bede rejoined the group, but his servant was nowhere to be seen. By way of explanation, he murmured to Redgrave, "Forgive my girl her impertinence."

Redgrave nodded and fixed Alvina with a stern look. "A child is never too young to learn respect. Perhaps if Fern had received stricter tutelage, she mightn't have wandered from the schoolyard."

Halsey felt as if he'd been punched in the belly.

Alvina glowered at Redgrave. "What did you say?"

Elder Lyndon sighed. "Mrs. Morgan, I must agree with Lord Redgrave. There are words that must never be spoken." An apologetic smile. "Please correct your son."

A tiny muscle beside Alvina's left eye twitched. "He's not the one who needs correction."

She and Elder Lyndon stared at one another a long moment, the clearing utterly silent. Something new seemed to pervade Elder Lyndon's face. He removed his spectacles.

"Let's finish this business and go home," Lord Redgrave muttered.

"No," Elder Lyndon said, his eyes blazing at Alvina with preternatural intensity.

Halsey took a step toward him. "Elder Lyndon?"

Lyndon ignored him. "Where did your son hear that name?"

"Perhaps the village children," Alvina suggested.

"He did not hear it from the *children*," Elder Lyndon said, his words clipped. He loomed over Alvina. "Try again now, with a more rigorous attempt at candor."

A flinty smile touched Alvina's lips. "Perhaps your grip on the children isn't as tight as you fancy."

Someone gasped, but Lyndon's smile was as sleety as Alvina's. "Tell your whelp to apologize."

"I will not. And Speck is a good boy."

Lyndon's shoulders seemed to expand, and for a wild instant Halsey was certain his mentor would strike Alvina in full sight of the onlookers. But instead, Lyndon brought a forefinger to his lips and appeared to consider. "Do you know the meaning of the word your son uttered, Mrs. Morgan?"

Alvina held Lyndon's gaze. "Aye."

"Not only the stories told about the creature, mind you, but the derivation of its name?"

Alvina did not answer.

Elder Lyndon began to pace in a slow circle about her, the firelight glittering in his dark eyes. "Dobrogost The Beast's name is not mentioned in the *Book of Truth*. There is reason for that." He skewered Alvina with his profound eyes. "It means 'falsehood.' It has also been translated as 'darkness.'"

Alvina smiled up at Elder Lyndon. "What's wrong with darkness?"

"I've heard enough of this," Redgrave snapped. "Bring out the corpse so we can dispose of it."

Movement from the gravesite drew Halsey's gaze. It was Danes, who gripped his shovel with both hands, looking for all the world like he might bludgeon Redgrave with it.

Elder Lyndon nodded. "Perhaps you're right, Lord Redgrave. One cannot help those who choose to dwell in shadow." He snapped the *Book of Truth* shut and ventured closer to the woodcarver. "It is time, Wyot. Please retrieve your daughter's body."

Wyot murmured something Halsey couldn't make out.

Alderman Bede cackled. "The woodcarver's sotted."

Redgrave stalked toward Wyot. "Speak up, man. This is your daughter's funeral."

The woodcarver murmured something under his breath.

Bede asked, "What's he babbling about, Elder Lyndon?"

Lyndon favored Wyot with an appraising glance. "He says the body is not here."

Redgrave made a scoffing sound. Bede stepped closer and gestured with his stein. "Not here? Then where by the gods is she? Still at the foot of that goddamned tree?"

Halsey's breath caught in his throat. No one in the clearing spoke. No one moved.

Then, slowly, Wyot turned his countenance toward Lyndon. "I've already buried her."

Lyndon's mouth dropped open.

Halsey moved to Lyndon's side. "You're telling us that this man," a nod at Danes, "has spent the entire day digging...that all of us have wasted an entire evening shivering in the woods... when you've already interred your daughter's corpse?"

Wyot's expression sent the hackles at the back of Halsey's neck bristling. "There's another meaning," the woodcutter said.

"Another meaning to what?" Halsey demanded.

"Dobrogost."

Redgrave shook a fist at him. "You were told to stop—"

"It means 'good,'" Wyot interrupted.

Lyndon's mouth curled in a sneer. "*Good*? Tell me, woodcarver, is darkness good? Is murder?"

"Depends on whose murder," Alvina answered.

Bede jabbed a finger at her. "Heresy! She's speaking heresy!"

"I quite fancy the darkness," Wyot said.

Lyndon seemed about to respond when there came a deep groaning from the forest, as though a mighty oak were being uprooted.

"What was that?" Bede whispered.

Wyot stepped closer to Elder Lyndon, and to Halsey it appeared that the woodcarver had grown in stature. "If you deigned to read something other than this," he tapped the *Book of Truth*, "you'd know things weren't always this way."

Lyndon jerked the *Book of Truth* away. "Don't lecture me about history, woodcarver."

"You'd care more of history," Alvina said, "if your present circumstances weren't so prosperous."

"Ah," Elder Lyndon replied, "but riches aren't always ill-gotten, and the meek sometimes deserve their misfortune."

Wyot ventured into the noblemen's midst. "When it benefits them, powerful men have always lied for one another."

Bede poked the woodcarver in the chest. "You have forgotten your place."

Wyot's arms shot out, and the plump alderman went soaring backward. Bede landed in the ice-flecked mud and gawked up at Wyot.

Standing over Bede, the woodcarver roared, *"My place is with my daughter!"*

Bede climbed to his feet and took a backward step. "It's time I return to the village."

But Danes barred his way. Bede stumbled as he collided with the gravedigger.

"You will hear him," Danes said.

Bede blinked up at him as if Danes had spoken in some extinct tongue.

Halsey licked his lips. His fingers slipped into his cassock and grasped the blessed tome.

Redgrave scowled about the clearing. "What is this? Have you all gone mad?"

Wyot said, "Dobrogost was the last of his kind."

"Monsters," Elder Lyndon snarled. "Devils."

"Protectors," Wyot corrected. "Gentle creatures, hunted to extinction by men who feared their justice."

Halsey couldn't contain himself any longer. He brandished the *Book of Truth* at Wyot. "Do you care nothing for the word?" He tapped the worn leather cover. "It's all inside. How the demons plunged this land into nightmare. How they devoured the flesh of good men and reveled in their suffering."

"They were not demons," Alvina said. "They spared the innocent."

"I'm sorry," Lyndon said, smiling sadly. "But you are deceived."

On his last word the ground beneath their feet seemed to vibrate.

"You see?" Alvina whispered.

The ground trembled again, and this time Halsey couldn't pretend it was imagination.

"Come, gentlemen," Lyndon said. "We did not venture out here to be insulted."

Underfoot, the ground shuddered.

"What *is* that?" Redgrave demanded.

Alvina strode toward Redgrave. "The people came to you for help. They told you what goes on in that church. What happens in those woods."

Wyot spoke into Lyndon's face. "Had I known what went on in that forest, I never would've allowed my Fern within a mile of you."

Lyndon laughed softly. "Whatever it is you think you know, woodcarver, I can assure you—"

"You watch them," Wyot said.

Halsey's extremities went numb.

Lyndon opened his mouth, but Wyot seized him by the frock and shook him. "You force them to bathe in the forest pool, and you *watch* them."

Halsey hardly knew that he was backpedaling until Alvina called, "You can't flee, Halsey. Nowhere will be safe for you."

Halsey stopped, and it was just as well, for the ground shook harder, and another groan sounded from the forest.

Lyndon's eyes were overlarge. "I will not be accused. I am a beacon—"

"You are a *scourge!*" Wyot roared. His eyes strafed the noblemen. "All of you!"

Alvina advanced on Elder Lyndon: "That day in the forest…you were showing your apprentice what you do to the children."

Lyndon reddened. "Who was your witness?"

"A dream," Alvina answered.

Lyndon laughed incredulously. "A *dream*? You have a dream, and suddenly every good man in the village is a fiend?"

"Not my dream," Alvina said. "My son's."

Lyndon threw back his head and bellowed laughter. "Alvina Morgan, you've fallen prey to hysteria."

"She's saner than you," Wyot said. "It was her idea to tell Dobrogost."

The mirth bled from Lyndon's face. "I told you not to utter that name."

A deep creak echoed from the forest, and the ground lurched so violently that Halsey found himself on his knees. The sounds of tree boles cracking filled the night.

Lyndon stared at the woodcarver with wide eyes. "What did you do?"

Wyot's grin was terrible. "The old tales are true. The ones Fern loved hearing me to read to her."

"The dark times," Lyndon said, eyes darting about the clearing edge.

"There's more truth in fairy tales than there are in your damnable book," Alvina said.

"Blasphemy!" Bede cried.

The earth split open at the timberline, hawthorns and laurels toppling. The fissure zigzagged toward them until it reached the grave.

The servant girls cowered, but Alvina rushed over to them. "Run," she urged. "Run to the village and keep your families safe." When they only watched her uncertainly, she shouted, "*Go!*"

All but a few serving girls fled. Danes chucked his shovel aside and followed them down the village path.

"Witchery," Elder Lyndon whispered. He began to backpedal.

Halsey's heart was thundering. A scrim of sweat ringed his brow. Alvina stepped toward him. "How many times did you join Lyndon in the forest? How many times did he touch the children in your presence?"

Halsey swallowed. He retreated a pace. "I'm not sure what—"

"Fern begged you to stop him!" she shouted. "She *begged* you."

Halsey shook his head, the accusation in the woman's eyes more damning than the words.

Thunder shook the clearing. The woods split apart, and a massive shadow burst through the treetops.

"Dear God," Lyndon murmured.

The dragon's tenebrous wings were broader than the sails of some enormous maritime vessel, the gusts they produced fierce enough to knock the men back. Iridescent scales armored the beast's body and glinted like emeralds and beaten copper in the firelight. The throat quivered with muscles, the chest three men across, the legs as stout as walnut trees. Halsey felt his bladder let go within his woolen breeches.

"The devil," Bede murmured. "The devil lives."

Bede retreated as the dragon beat its veiny wings and hovered before them, thirty feet above the forest's roof.

Dobrogost gave out a bellow. Halsey, Redgrave, and Lyndon fell to the ground, but Bede broke for the trees. He shoved a servant girl out of the way, the lass too transfixed to flee. Bede's stubby limbs propelled him past the Morgans' hut, beyond the last of the flambeaux, and into the dense forest. An ear-bruising whipcrack sounded as Dobrogost shot after him. Halsey watched awestruck as the dragon whooshed overhead, his tailwind rolling over the clearing, chilling the air and flinging aside the flambeaux like matchsticks.

One second Dobrogost was diving toward the forest, the next the dragon was surging heavenward with something clutched in its muscular hindlegs. It looped back toward the clearing, and even before Halsey identified the flailing-limbed figure clutched in the beast's hind talons, he distinguished Bede's screaming amidst the deep throb of the dragon's wings.

Dobrogost reared up and landed almost gently in the clearing. As soon as his feet encountered soil again, Bede attempted to scramble away, but one of Dobrogost's forepaws shot out and pinned him face down on the earth.

"*Help me please oh please,*" Bede gibbered.

Halsey glanced at Elder Lyndon, but the holy man appeared as terrified as the rest of them. Light flickered to Halsey's right; an upended flambeau had landed against the Morgans' hovel. The flames licked at the base of the dwelling, the woven thatch igniting like dry tinder.

Halsey turned back to the dragon and felt his innards liquefy.

Dobrogost's head was as massive as the church belfry, and while the face was not as triangular as Speck's wooden toy, it was infinitely more sinister. Scaly creases tapered upward, creating horned protrusions sharp enough to impale a man. The great jaw unhinged to reveal hooked, sword-like teeth.

"Have mercy on me," Bede moaned, but when Halsey beheld the dragon's expression it was clear there would be no mercy tonight. Dobrogost's eyes glowed a phantasmal orange, the vertically-slitted pupils as black as pitch. In those eyes Halsey discerned nothing but sadism, a hunger for suffering and fear.

As deft as the woodcarver's own hands, the dragon's fore-paws manipulated Bede into a sitting position before the dumb-struck group. The talons closed over Bede's soft chest like an iron maiden, and Bede thrashed his head to be free.

"Do something, gods damn you!" Bede shouted. *"Lyndon! Red-grave! Stop this before—"*

But Bede never finished. The dragon slid its jaws over Bede's head and slowly sank its awl-sharp teeth into his eyes. Bede let out a high, razoring shriek, and blood frothed over his lips. Bede spasmed, his limbs jagging as if in holy ecstasy.

Redgrave tottered to his feet and broke into a tiptoeing jog, as though he might sneak away in full view of the beast.

Dobrogost took two thundering strides, seized Redgrave by the back of his coat, and hoisted him into the air. For a moment Halsey was certain the beast would decapitate Caldea's leader with its razor-sharp teeth, but instead it swung Redgrave toward the Morgans' hovel, which blazed like a harvest bonfire.

"Please!" Redgrave wailed. *"Please have mercy!"*

The dragon lowered him toward the seething roof.

"I'm sorry!" Redgrave shrieked. *"I never meant to..."* His words devolved into a shrilling wail. His beaver-pelt poulaines caught fire immediately, and his legs pumped as though he were sprinting over solid earth. The flames raced up his thighs and girdled his midsection, and just when Halsey could weather

Redgrave's howls no longer, the dragon dropped his body into the raging conflagration.

Dobrogost shifted its gaze toward group. Halsey crawled closer to Elder Lyndon, who knelt in awe. As Halsey studied his mentor in hopes of finding strength, a thick string of drool leaked over Lyndon's bottom lip.

Whimpering, Halsey returned his attention to the dragon.

But Dobrogost was not stalking toward the holy men. Instead, it approached the Morgans. The woodcarver had hefted Speck onto his hip. Alvina joined them. The family evinced no terror as the dragon lumbered nearer.

Dobrogost halted before the Morgans and performed a little bow.

The family fell on the dragon and embraced its pestilent body like some much-loved relation.

"It was an accident," Elder Lyndon murmured.

Wyot's jaw went firm. A hand resting on Dobrogost's scaly cheek, he glowered down at Lyndon.

"I didn't mean for her to get hurt," Lyndon explained. "She was running from me." His eyes flicked to Halsey. "From us."

Halsey's airway thinned.

"She climbed that cursed tree," Lyndon hurried on. "Little Fern...she wouldn't listen. We called out to her, but she...she..."

"She knew what you'd done to the other children," Alvina said, spitting each word.

But Wyot seemed not to hear his wife. He actually kissed the side of the dragon's snout and whispered, "You know what to do, girl."

Girl? Halsey thought. *Girl?*

Then he saw it. As Dobrogost's shadow fell over Lyndon, the dragon's left forepaw came into view. One of its talons was missing.

Like an amputated forefinger.

"You can't blame me," Lyndon cried.

Dobrogost seized the holy man by the foot. Lyndon wept and importuned the heavens, but the dragon raised him upside down into the air and grasped his other foot.

"I didn't mean for you to die," Lyndon cried.

A sick crunch rang out as Dobrogost wishboned the holy man's legs. Halsey watched in horror as the crotch of Lyndon's breeches split open and blood splurted through the torn fabric. Yet rather than flinging aside Lyndon's maimed body, Dobrogost continued to pull. Lyndon gibbered and flapped his arms as his hipbone popped and a leg ripped free. Blood vomited through the ragged pantleg, and the worst part was the way Lyndon's mindless wailing went on, even as Dobrogost laid him on the earth next to Halsey.

"Oh my God," Halsey moaned.

Lyndon's eyes rolled and came to rest on Halsey.

"Elder Lyndon?" he whispered. "Elder Lyndon?"

Lyndon coughed, and viscous gout splattered Halsey's face. Gagging, Halsey scrambled away, but the ground disappeared beneath him. He tumbled into slimy darkness. Halsey looked around, his breath hitching, and only when he peered up at the oblong of deepening night sky did he realize where he was.

Fern's grave.

Speck's face was the first to appear above him. Then his mother. Finally, Wyot joined them in gazing down at Halsey.

"I never touched her!" Halsey cried. "For pity's sake, I'm only an apprentice!"

The Morgans showed no emotion. Halsey could bear their impassive faces no longer. He closed his eyes. He heard the ragged huff of the dragon above him.

"Look upon her," Wyot said.

Halsey refused. If he kept his eyes closed, this nightmare would surely end. He'd done nothing wrong. It was Lyndon.

Halsey slipped the *Book of Truth* from his coat pocket and clutched it to his chest.

"*Look upon my Fern!*" the woodcarver commanded.

With a whimper, Halsey obeyed.

Dobrogost straddled the open grave, the dragon's eyes blazing in triumph. The massive chest seethed a hellish orange.

Halsey lay paralyzed. Only his lips moved, though no prayer escaped them.

Dobrogost drew in a deep growling breath, and as Halsey watched, transfixed, the fireball swelled in its throat, the heat shimmering the very air. Halsey finally found his voice, but a furnace blast of heat consumed his shriek, his book, his body.

The Suture Kings

Mary SanGiovanni

In the realm of dreams, it was said that no one had ever encountered the Suture Kings and lived. Its myriad of inhabitants, most as familiar with horror and terror as with beauty, strangeness, awe, and wonder, did not speak of such ancient beings if they could hush the talk or change the subject. When they could not, they spoke in whispers, for the Nightmare races were said to fear them, and what even Nightmares feared, one best avoided altogether.

The Suture Kings were said to dwell in Outer Arc, where the Nightmares held dominion, somewhere on the island of Baku Mora in the South Komatos Sea. Tales of their casual savagery frightened children in their beds and men in their cups. Old sailors used to tell tales of moaning heard from the island caves, back when trade routes took them close to the shoreline. In a tavern in the town of Liderca, an old Ereborian man, a half-blind pirate with a scarred face and neck and a missing leg, once asserted that the Suture Kings had taken both his left eye and that absent appendage, and that he could still feel both. His manner did not invite further question or conversation about it, nor much of anything else.

That was back when a third of the ships that sailed to Baku Mora never returned. The Nightmare villages that dotted the coast simply gave them up for lost, determined that nothing so absurd as rescue efforts should draw further attention from the Suture Kings. No one who lived in those villages could be induced, for riches or blood, to ferry the occasional naive stranger across the water to the island; any business there was a fool's errand, and any who assisted with such an errand, perhaps an even bigger fool.

Of the appearance of the Suture Kings, few could speak first-hand. They were said to be very old, though–perhaps ancient when even the immortal, shapeshifting Ilanilia were new. Tall, gaunt, needle-fingered, and eternally placid of expression, the eyes of the Suture Kings, black as the Oblivion Cliffs, gathered all the unhinged hate within them to swirl within the glassy orbs. Their faces were mannequin masks of bone-white, delicate of feature and mostly immobile; it was said that when they spoke, their lipless mouths never moved, though few would have understood so antediluvian a language as theirs, anyway. The tops of their hairless heads slanted backward like a large spade with scythe blades that arced to either earless side. They wore long robes of white silk and satin with ruby-red and gold trim, the hems of the garments barely brushing the ground as the creatures hovered above it. It was, in fact, the soft rustling of the robes that provided the only auditory herald of their approach.

It was not their eerie appearance, though, nor their strange, high-strung language which frightened the people of the Dream Arcs, as the realm was populated with many strange beings of varying shapes, hues, and visual aspects, as well as numerous mother tongues. Rather, it was the barbaric pastime of the old ones which was, for so many varied races, an inconceivable fate. The Suture Kings were notorious for their tendency to separate limbs and/or head from an often ambushed source. This unfortunate victim retained all feeling in both the main body and the limbs, and continued to live, despite the disarticulation. The Suture Kings then applied the deftness and artistry for which they were named in resewing an assortment of other appendages to the main body, which became part of a new monstrous, lumbering, confused, and utterly agonizing whole. These new creations were then kept by the Suture Kings, sometimes as pets, sometimes as slaves. Sometimes, if the artist was not pleased with the work, the subject would be destroyed, or recombined into something new. The caves of the Suture Kings were said to be filled with the wailing of the never-quite-dying, those who could feel the limbs they'd lost and the limbs they'd gained in equal measure, and could sometimes guess the full extent of the monstrous things they had become.

It came to pass one night, in the Waxing Gibbous era, which was the Second Age of the Fourth Archaia, that a young Ereborian man, an accomplished Rider of the Circadian Plains and a decorated warrior, lost a great love to these beasts, or so the legend goes. Turquoise-skinned and soft-spoken, with gentle ridges just above the temples to either side of his smooth head, the warrior stood over seven feet tall and was tightly muscled, with eyes the color of the darkest ocean. He moved gracefully and with purpose on the front pads of large, bare, two-toed feet. Bare-chested, as was common with his people, he wore the simple armor of the Ereborian warrior: dark pants of a thin but nearly impenetrable material that came to the knee, a cape of black, bracers on his forearms, and a heavy belt which held the scabbard of a great sword. To his people, the warrior had been known for three things: his extensive skill in riding and on the battlefield, his cool, even-tempered demeanor, and his love for the maiden who had been taken from him.

In the castle in the capital city of Saturniel, the gathered elder tribesmen warned him that his maiden may well already be lost. The Suture Kings were not known for keeping victims intact for long, and the journey to Baku Mora was far. Even with time such as it was in the dream realm — sometimes faster and sometimes slower—the islands were the distance of several weeks' travel even on the swiftest-footed of the purple schylla beasts. Surely, argued the elders to their best warrior, the maiden would no longer be as he had known her, and it would only break his heart further to see what she had become.

Still, the warrior, whose name was Ezieri, insisted that he had to try. Should the girl still be alive by some amazing boon of fate, he would rescue her. Should the Suture Kings have "made art" with her by then, he would see to it that no living part of her remained tormented.

"And what of you?" asked the *inil*, the king. "What if they apply their art to you? What shall become of you—and of us, your people who rely on you?"

"Great *inil*," said Ezieri with a deferential fist to his chest, between his two hearts, "I must see to it that she is at peace, either alive and whole by my side or in death, given proper passage to the Reverie beyond. I beg that you let me make the journey, and I swear I will return to you."

After much argument from both king and council, Ezieri said, "I implore you to consider this final point. A man injured in battle must have those injuries mended, to prevent death from getting into the wounds, festering, and taking hold of him. It is not noble to die such a death; rather, it strips the warrior, piece by piece, of the armor of life, reducing his faculties over time until he is a shade of his former self. No warrior wants the prolonged and painful death of battle-rot. Does he who suffers from internal injury not fade away until at last he succumbs to despair? Is he who bears the burden of a broken heart not in similar a situation? I assure you, respected councilmen, that this is my fate, should you deny me leave. Only in seeing for myself what has become of my beloved can I put the pain in my heart to rest and continue to serve this dominion, this council, and my king as I have in the past."

The king leaned back in his velvet-seated marble throne, seeming to consider the warrior's words. His eyes, much older, seemed to be searching for something. Ezieri held fast, his expression even. It seemed the king found what he was looking for and spoke.

"You are indeed a warrior of great valor, whose loyalty and service to this dominion is unquestionable. For all the reasons my Great Council has laid before you—and more—it would pain me to let you go."

The warrior continued to meet his gaze unflinchingly, although inside him, his hearts thudded.

"However," he said, "I can see the merit in your arguments. Further, I see that you are determined to undertake this quest. I would grant you permission –" he held up a hand to stave off the protests of the counsel "—to settle this matter quickly and return to us. Do not make me regret this decision."

With great thanks, the warrior bowed low and took his leave of the king and his council. Before he left, one of the council, an oldin by the name of Grevorrah who had not spoken during the meeting, pulled him aside in the hall.

"If you insist on going," said he, "I would advise you."

"I welcome and appreciate any wisdom you have to give," the warrior replied.

The old one nodded, his gnarled hand resting on Ezieri's shoulder. "I would not waste your time with mundane warnings of thieves and pirates. Rather, let me tell you what little I have managed to uncover regarding the Suture Kings and how to defeat them." He glanced around, as if to make sure none were listening.

"You will need provisions," Grevorrah said. "The markets of Dab Tsog are amply stocked, and you would do well to acquire three things. The first, of course, is an Undorian *ishiri*—that is a magic boat which can fit into a pocket when not in use. No one in the city will take you to Baku Mora; if you insist on going, then this will be your only means to get there and back. Second, you will need, if you can find it, Orian restoration salve. Should you have to...disassemble and then reassemble your woman, the salve of the healers of Oria may just keep her alive long enough to heal. Third," and the old one looked at the sword hanging in the scabbard at Ezieri's side, "choose another weapon. Those which cut or cleave have little to no effect on them. Find a vial of venom from the stinger of a Scorpiari. Only this, I am told, can damage the Suture Kings, and then, seek only to injure their hands; that should be enough. A Suture King who cannot use his hands to take apart and put together is far from harmless, but much less deadly. My sources across the Arcs tell me that with these items, you may have a chance at success. Be prepared, however—they will cost you dearly. Nothing in Dab Tsog is done out of kindness or sympathy."

"I am indebted to you, wise one, and will heed your advice. But if I may be so bold as to ask," Ezieri added, "what moved you to come by this knowledge?"

The old one's expression clouded over, and pain flashed in his dark blue eyes. "Once," he said, "I had a brother. In our youth, he left home to sail on ships rather than ride the plains. The Suture Kings took his eye and his leg during a pirate raid of the island long, long ago. I could not help him." His exhale carried the weight of horror gone cold with time. "It was not the loss of those things which drove him to drown himself in the sea years later. It was the use of that leg which was lost to him, but which he could still feel, and the horrors he still saw through his stolen eye."

The following moonrise, Ezieri traveled from the capital city of Saturniel to the first city of Erebor, skirting the Somnia

Mountains and following the hidden paths through the Lucidia Range. Through much of his travel through Olan lands in Mid-Arc, the people welcomed him, fed him and his schylla mount, Igra, and gave him warm blankets and a place to lay his head. The Olan, to Ezieri, looked much like those who passed between the dreamgates of Portal Henge. Those travelers, who called themselves *humans* and only came during periods they called sleep, seemed nearly indistinguishable to Ezieri from the Olan, who also had varied skin colors (though none were shades of blue like the Ereborians), white in their eyes, all manner of hair growing from their heads, and multiple fingers and toes. They wore leather coverings over their feet. They were small, the tallest of them still a head shorter than Ezieri, and their dress was elaborate, particularly that of their women. He found they ate odd things like meat, which was culled from dead animals. To the Ereborian, they were strange, but he was in their land, and to them, he was even stranger.

The Olan of Bekhetek, where Dab Tsog Port lay, were not as friendly as those in Reticula. The country was ruled by an Olan family called Algol. Set Algol had wrested much of the eastern land away from the Chimerians centuries before, and now few sentient non-Olan beings lived there. Those who did were Nightmare people and drew other Nightmare people to their lands. Their cities were crowded, noisy, and dangerous. Their countrysides were wild with beasts like the night terrors, the vargkvinna who had the head, arms, and torso of a woman and the lower body of a wolf, and the fire giants. Ezieri saw the the phantoms that haunted the ruins of Ara Altar and the harpies of Tartarus Hills. His adventures in the Nightmare countries of Khyadamri, Naraka, and Bakhetek, battling its monsters with sword, tooth, and nail, are recounted in the tome *Dangers of the Outer Arc*, penned by the historian Glavibor. But this story is of Ezieri's encounter with the Suture Kings.

Ezieri and Igra arrived in the port city at moonset, just as the dancers and drinkers and brothel patrons were emerging from their stone homes for the next phase of business. The shoppers on the market streets haggled for last-minute deals on exotic fruits, vegetables, meats, bolts of fabric, glass, wood-carvings, tools, and weapons. In other, more tucked-away corners, others sought magic.

It took some time wandering these less-lighted areas before Ezieri found the market stall of an *ishiri* salesman, a short, squat Mardrom man with hands trisected to his wrists, each segment featuring two fingers. He had one very large eye which seemed both suspicious and watchful, and a thin slit of mouth above it which barked single-word sentences in the common language of trade.

Ezieri produced from Igra's saddle bag some Ereborian silks that had once been his grandmother's, and the merchant eyed them greedily, his lipless mouth moving up and down in delight. He agreed to trade the silks for the magic Undorian boat, which he shoved into Ezieri's hand in the form of a nut. He managed to roughly bark out the instructions, which were to throw it into the water, where it would expand and take the form of a boat.

Ezieri was skeptical, but he thanked the man and pocketed the *ishiri*. Then he made his way to a tent whose merchant was hawking potions and salves. For a vial of his own blood, drawn with his own sword from his bicep by the deft little hands of a shriveled old woman inside the tent, he was able to purchase the Orian salve. He suppressed the nagging doubts regarding what kind of magic the old woman intended with his blood and the strength she claimed was infused in it and moved on through the streets.

The Scorpiari venom he bought at the end of a shadowed alley just before the docks, from an Olan man with a scar trailing from the corner of his mouth. The man sat on an overturned box, with vials fanned out on the ground before him. He asked for one of Igra's head-tines and for the luck-pendant carved with Ereborian runes which hung around Ezieri's neck. The warrior gave him both.

When the third moon was high in the sky, Ezieri and Igra went to the docks, and the warrior tossed the nut into the water. For a moment, it sank, and with it, Ezieri's hopes of reclaiming his beloved. Then it bobbed back up to the surface and expanded into a boat just big enough for the warrior and his mount. It took some coaxing to get Igra into the boat—the schylla are land animals, and not comfortable on unstable surfaces like boats and water—but the bond between rider and animal eventually prevailed. Ezieri was able to convince the creature that the uncertainty of the sea was preferrable to the near-certain harvesting of its meat by unscrupulous hunters in the city.

One full cycle of the moons passed on the water, with the magic ship sailing itself through the dark waves. The sea was quiet, its waves almost suspicious, watching, lapping at the sides of the boat with curious aggression. The two passengers saw no other living creatures, not even birds winging their way across the water. They heard no siren-song. Still, they did not rest.

As the third moon crossed the sky and the first moon came round again, Ezieri spotted land. The main island of Baku Mora rose like a massive, dark head of a great beast from the water. As the boat got closer, Ezieri could see the sandy shoreline, pale gray in the moonlight, and beyond, steep limestone cliffs topped with thick jungle foliage. As the boat came to a near-silent stop where the ocean met the land, Ezieri spied a series of dark-mouthed caves about one hundred and fifty feet ahead. Strange shells and bits of smooth stones glittered here and there in the sand.

Ezieri frowned. Disappointment and frustration coagulated in his chest. There were no footprints, no torches, no signs of life. He had always heard that the Suture Kings lived all along the coastline of the main island. It had not occurred to him that this far north, there might only be abandoned cavern settlements. He had expected at the least to see firelight, to hear the moans of the Suture Kings' creations, but for all he could detect, there was no one there.

He stepped off the boat. Beside him, Igra whimpered, and Ezieri took his lead and led him onto the sand. He dragged the boat onto the beach, where it immediately shrank to a nut again. He pocketed the nut.

Igra lifted his head and sniffed the night air, then lowered it and growled. His head tines rose, and the tendrils which formed a kind of mane whipped the air above him anxiously, their tips sparking with tiny electric flashes. Igra sensed something, and Ezieri knew enough to pay attention.

Perhaps this part of the island was not so empty after all.

The two crept up the gentle slope of sand toward the caves. No sound of birds or bats came from the jungle above. No remnants of campfires, no banners, no tools, no barrels—there weren't even docks along the length of coastline, as far as the Ereborian's eyes could see. There were no footprints on the sand other than those of the warrior and the schylla. The air, which should have been warm, grew colder as they neared the yawning black of the cave mouths.

Igra tensed, and so did Ezieri. There, on the breeze—a faint, ghostly keening had come from inside the cave ahead of them. And was that a pinpoint of firelight, deep within?

Could she be in there? He allowed himself a flicker of hope that she was still alive. He wanted to plunge headlong into the cave to find her, but Igra held back, tugging on his lead.

"What is it?" he whispered to the creature, who returned

a grunt and a few quick puffs of air. The schylla was wary. Something wasn't right.

"I have to see," the warrior whispered into the creature's ear. "I have to know."

Igra nudged his master's cheek with his muzzle. He would follow, but they both had to be on guard.

All creatures in the dream realms have excellent vision in the dark, but the caves of Baku Mora were painted with a different kind of darkness. There, the lightless interior suggested things... shapes moving, close and silent, flashes of light that left impressions of distorted faces on the backs of eyelids. Sometimes, the sounds of footfalls and shallow breaths were swallowed up. Other times, moans and soft sighs came from close by, while low sobs echoed all around, making it impossible to determine the direction of the source.

Deeper and deeper into the cave they went, feeling their way against the uneven stone of the passage, stumbling when the path dipped downward, until at length the way straightened out and the dark began to dissipate. Ezieri could make out the rough-hewn walls of the passage and could see an opening ahead into what looked like a massive cavern of faintly glowing stone. The temperature dropped sharply. Behind him, Igra tensed, his tendrils giving off tiny sparks.

"Easy," Ezieri said, pausing to pat the creature's nose. "Easy now."

Soft sounds of sobbing drifted to them from the cavern. There were many voices now, whimpering and crying, moaning, occasionally shouting, shuffling and stumbling. It had to be the creations, the victims of the Suture Kings in there. His chest tightened at the thought of what he would find.

Then, as if rising just above the sounds of suffering, came a frenetic murmuring whose tone and cadence chilled his bones.

The wretched, refashioned things within were not alone.

By instinct, Ezieri reached for his sword. Then, remembering Grevorrah's words, his hand moved instead to the vial of venom on his belt, checking to make sure it was still there. He had no solid plan for what to do next, other than to assess the situation, find a way to save Ollaria, and protect Igra as best he could. His chest felt tight, his dual hearts beating so thunderously that he was sure the Suture Kings in the cavern beyond could hear them.

He crept to the opening, sticking to shadows on his side, and assessed the sight before him in horror.

The cavern was enormous. Long stalactites hung from above like stony swords, dripping a pearlescence onto the stone floor below. Outcroppings of crystals grew outward from the walls, glowing faintly blue, then orange, then red, then purple, illuminating the space.

In the center of the floor, long, broad stone slabs more than four feet tall had been arranged in a wide circle. Each slab had an elevated step on one end, where silver tools of varying sizes were laid out in rows. Bodies—torsos, mostly, with various limbs in array around them—lay on each slab. Ezieri recognized features specific to animals like night terrors, harpies, and vagkvinnas, as well as sentient beings like Olan, Orian, Undorian, Wanderer, Trifoyle, giant, Incubari, Scorpiari, and Spinnari, as well as some whose disembodiment made them impossible to discern. Decapitated heads with glazed eyes moaned and blinked. Tails whipped back and forth like snakes. Wings flapped and fell back onto the slabs. Hands clenched and unclenched. Exposed hearts in dismembered torsos beat feverishly. Spines, skulls, and rib bones had been stripped of flesh, and piles of meat had been stretched, tanned, tightened, cut, bunched, and sewn into flower-shapes, bows, ribbons, and assorted bits of trim. No single slab held a body in its entirety, either whole or in parts; rather, the grisly items on the slabs were a collection of various portions from multiple bodies.

Moving between the slabs to sew wing to hand, head to stomach, and talon to thigh were three Suture Kings. Their needle-fingers dripped with the thread-secretions they used to weave together their hideous constructions. While they worked, crossing each other's paths, trading projects, they murmured in their strange, ancient language. Perhaps the words, if indeed they were words, were incantations or spells, or perhaps they sang while they worked. The sound, Ezieri thought, sliced beneath the flesh and dragged across the soul.

The Suture Kings seemed oblivious to the clutching of shaking hands, the shuddering of limbs, the half-articulated pleas for death that arose from their materials. They calmly pierced flesh with new bones, and broke bones sheathed in flesh to refit them into new shapes. Ezieri saw one of them scoop and lift an eye from one head, and drop it into the socket of another. Both heads wept.

Then Ezieri noticed the far wall, where the ostensibly finished creations hung from chains like grotesque puppets. These tortured figures slumped against the rock, occasionally finding just enough strength to rattle the chains. Their sutures, it seemed, were still fresh, oozing blood and death-rot as well as the clear substance of the threads which held their segmented bodies together. There, Ezieri reasoned, they were likely kept until the parts took to each other and the whole grew cohesive enough to serve its new masters. Anxiously, he scanned the wall for any part he could recognize as belonging to Ollaria, but he saw no Ereborian parts at all. This both relieved him and ignited a new anxiety. Where was his woman? How many caves like this existed on the island?

Then he saw her. His hearts soared.

Long, narrow recesses had been carved out of the rock wall

above the finished creations. These were nearly all empty, except for two. In one, half of a skeleton sprawled, its arm, leg, and partial head hanging over the side. In the other lay Ollaria. It was hard to tell from the other side of the cavern, but she appeared to be sleeping.

Ezieri signaled to Igra to stay unless he was summoned, and the mount reluctantly soft-snorted his agreement.

The warrior crept into the cavern, skirting the slabs stealthily around the perimeter. He moved slowly out of caution and an unacknowledged dread of the beasts whose savage work wreaked of death and decay, but he was impatient. He had had not allowed himself the luxury of allowing hope nor the weakness of entertaining doubt. To see her, with her chest rising and falling softly, unmolested by her captors, was more than he'd dared to even secretly imagine. Each second that passed heightened his anxiety that she might be taken from him. Each foot closer raised those stakes higher. He couldn't lose her, not now.

Finally, he reached her. The alcove where the recesses had been carved was shadowed, and he was fairly certain he could retrieve her before they spotted him. He rose silently, and with a glance over his shoulder—they hadn't noticed him yet—he slipped his hands into the recess to claim her.

Gently, he took her in his arms and removed her from the recess. She was light, so light, *too* light, but she was in his arms and his heart soared and he looked down at her to tell her—

Only half of her face was there; only one blue eye looked up at him. One arm clung to his neck, half a chest heaved and shuddered, and one leg dangled from his grasp. The left half of her was gone. She had been bisected down the middle. The thud of pain, the gutting void in his two hearts, crushed the breath in his lungs. The partial skeleton...that skeleton in the other recess...He glanced at it, and saw it reaching for him as well.

"My love," the half of her in his arms said in Ereborian,. The words were mangled by what remained of her lips. "My love." Her one-eyed gaze flickered over his shoulder, and she wailed.

Gently, gently, he laid her on the ground at his feet and turned around.

All three Suture Kings stood before him, watching him with their dark, hate-storm eyes.

Instant rage, lightning hot, surged through him. Forgetting for a moment the vial in his belt, he drew his sword and ran it through the gut of the Suture King to the left. The monster looked down at the blade, then back up at Ezieri, but otherwise remained still, its face placid, its body unmoved by steel.

He pulled his sword free and found no blood, no clinging flesh on the blade, and so he sheathed it. The punctured Suture King waved its needle-fingers, and Ezieri's right hand began to tingle. Then, all feeling in it drained away. He tried to clench his fist and found he could not. He sank to one knee. The paralysis spread up his arm to his elbow before he had gotten the vial of venom free from his belt and worked the cork out of the top with the fingers of his left hand.

As the Suture King reached for him, he splashed some of the venom onto the back of the monster's palm. The venom, a dark green, sizzled across the stark white flesh, eating black into it as it bubbled and dissolved its way toward bone.

The Suture King did not cry out, but it did yank its hand back, clawing at the spreading decay with the fingers of its other hand. Its eyes stormed in their sockets, its murmured speech high and thin. Ezieri took advantage of the creature's shock to stand, and then splashed more of the venom onto its chest. The fabric of the robe it wore dissolved immediately, but the pallid flesh beneath remained unmarred. The hands, then—they were its only vulnerability.

The pain in his heart was subsumed by rage, and the rage by the finely honed instincts of the battle-forged. He grabbed the free wrist of the Suture King and doused its good hand with venom, then delivered a powerful kick to its bare chest, sending it flying backward. Ezieri turned to the other two. The closer one was waving its fingers now, and Ezieri felt his chest grow cold and tight. In moments, his head grew light and it was hard to breathe. He staggered forward, stumbling to one knee. He managed to croak out a command as he toppled to the ground, his sword clattering beside him. The edges of his vision grew dark.

A moment later, there was an electric crackle in the air and Igra's tendrils had wrapped around the needle fingers of the closer one, restricting movement. Some of the pressure on Ezieri's lungs and hearts diminished.

Murmuring angrily, the third Suture King turned on the schylla, plunging two of those sharp fingers from each hand into the flesh of his flank. Igra roared, snapping at the creature.

The Suture King that had attacked Ezieri struggled to free itself from the schylla's tendrils. It must have been distracted, because whatever had been crushing Ezieri from the inside finally relinquished its grasp. Ezieri sprang to his feet, pouring more venom on the jerking, tendril-bound hands. The monster howled and dropped to the floor, cradling its melting hands, once Igra's tendrils let go.

Then Ezieri turned sharply on the last Suture King. The monster had dragged its fingers from the wound in Igra's flank down its side. Igra had managed to keep the monster at bay by snapping his tail at it, but the Suture King seemed to move out of time and jabbed its own warning at the schylla.

The poor animal's wounds were beginning to turn gray and brittle around the edges—the death-rot that those foul fingers had wrought against their enemy. Ezieri felt a new pain in his heart. He had, for all intents and purposes, lost one beloved friend. He would not accept losing another.

He bellowed in pain along with his schylla friend and lunged at the last Suture King. In the struggle, the vial of venom slipped to the floor and broke. Driven to frenzied heights of hatred, Ezieri clamped down like iron on the Suture King's hands. He squeezed tightly, funneling all his strength into his own hands until he heard the crunch of bones and felt the jagged lumps in his palms. Only then did he let go, and the last Suture King dropped. Ezieri leaped onto its back, clamping onto the monster's wrists again, and wrestled with the Suture King. He dragged the creature's mangled hands to the broken glass and venom puddle and forced them into it. Some of the substance splashed onto his own hands, and he could feel pinprick burns burrowing into his skin.

The Suture Kings did not die. They crouched on the ground, muttering in their strange language and holding their ruined hands close to their chests. Ezieri didn't have much time. He glanced from Igra to Ollaria, the salve in his hand. He couldn't save his beloved—no amount of salve could reflesh and reconnect bone. And still....

"End this," Ollaria's voice said from behind him. He turned, crouching down to her. Her remaining hand squeezed his forearm, but the grip was weak. When she saw the pain in his eyes, she said, "I love you. I always will, and some day, we will be rejoined in the Reverie. Until then, you need him." She nodded at Igra. "Save him. And...end this for me. Please. If you love me, do this for me."

He hesitated a moment longer, but the pleading in her eye moved him. He nodded once and moved to Igra, then spread the salve on his wounds. Immediately, color returned to the flesh and the punctures and slashes knitted together. Where the salve touched his own venom-burns, the pain evaporated and the skin healed.

Replacing the salve jar in his belt, he swooped and picked up his sword. The Suture Kings, from their places on the stone floor, watched with hatred as he ran the edges of his sword in the venom still on the ground. The steel of his sword sizzled, but when Ezieri swung the blade, it did its work.

It cut through the flesh and bone of each Suture King's wrists.

Then—only then—did the Suture Kings look afraid. They backed away from him, huddling together in the center of their slabs, and watched without interfering.

Clutching one of the hands in his own, he crouched beside his beloved, said a quick prayer to the Allcreator, and lovingly kissed Ollaria's forehead. She nodded at him, then closed her eye.

He plunged the needle-fingers of the Suture King's severed hand into her remaining heart, and Ollaria and her skeleton stopped moving. He wrapped her remains in the single remaining silk of his grandmother and lay them over Igra's back. Then he packed up the hands of the Suture Kings in a saddle bag and guided Igra back through the cave to the beach, where he launched the nut-boat into the water and sailed into the rising moon.

Songs of history tell of his lone victory over the Suture Kings, but those who knew him remember him for his bravery, his loyalty, and his love. It is said that Ezieri made a gift of two pairs of hands to his king, and those hands became a symbol of power and prestige for the *inil* throughout the courts of Middle Arc. The last pair he gifted to Grevorrah, in honor of the old one's fallen brother.

The remains of the Lady Ollaria were interred in the cemetery on the grounds of the small keep given to Ezieri as reward for his accomplishment. He never married, nor did he leave the

Circadian Plains again. He served his king and country until he was an old man, and when he died, he was laid to rest beside his beloved.

The Castle Cauchemar

L.C. Mortimer

Once you walk into a castle filled with bloody footprints and whispering walls, there's really no going back.

Elizabeth stood at the entrance to the crumbling castle and questioned whether she was right to come here at all.

It had taken her three days of trekking through the Forest of Cauchemar through the mud and rain and storms. It was strange that the rest of the kingdom surrounding the woods had been enjoying the sunniest, prettiest weather they'd had in centuries, but Cauchemar always seemed to have a perpetual raincloud hovering over it.

Today was no exception.

Her clothing was soaked. Her dress and cloak had been wet since she'd embarked on her journey, and now even her leather boots squished with each step. The icy water made her toes curl.

Or maybe it was the fact that she was finally here.

Maybe the legends are true, she thought, staring up at the once-beautiful castle.

It wasn't beautiful anymore.

The stone walls were barely standing, and although some of the windows still held their original glass panes, most of them had been broken over the years. A few glass shards were piled outside of one of the front windows. She peered through the pouring rain and spotted a dark crimson hue on them.

Blood?

She shook her head.

Couldn't be.

The Castle Cauchemar was a place filled with legend and longing, but it was also a place that was impossible to find. Adventurers set out regularly in search of the place, but the forest surrounding the castle was full of traps and dangers. If you weren't prepared with a clear plan for finding the castle, you wouldn't make it far.

She'd been searching for the space for nearly a year, pouring over maps and letters in the king's library, when she'd finally found a note slipped between the pages of a history book that had clearly scripted instructions for finding the castle.

And now she'd found it.

Elizabeth rushed to the wooden door of the castle and paused for just a moment before pushing it open and stepping inside out of the rain. She slammed the door closed and leaned against it for just a moment. Fishing around in her satchel, she tugged out a few of her supplies. Despite the dampness, she was able to light a miniature torch that lit up the space around the entrance of the castle.

Dust particles floated, and she waved her torch around until she found a lantern sitting conveniently by the door. Relieved, she lit it and held it up, giving herself a clear view of the grand hall. Cauchemar looked much like the castle Elizabeth was a maid at, and she was intimately familiar with the layout of such places.

Putting out her tiny torch and returning it to her satchel, she took the lantern and started walking forward.

She was here, and there was no turning back now.

The Castle Cauchemar had once been a beautiful place

located just beyond the Kingdom of Rêve, but it had been lost to time. It was unfortunate, really, because it held incredible treasures that many wealth-seekers had tried to claim as their own. Over the last decade alone, more than thirty-seven men had attempted to find the castle and claim the enchanted sword that rested here as their own.

But Elizabeth was the first woman to try to do so.

She wouldn't fail.

She slipped off her wet boots, leaving them by the front entrance of the castle. When she came back with the sword, her boots would be dry enough for her to embark on the next part of her journey, which would be returning home with the weapon. Her king had offered anyone who dared find it a handsome reward, and Elizabeth planned to use that money to leave the king's employ and go off as an adventurer. Her brother had left Rêve years ago to be a pirate.

She could do that, too.

Stepping deeper into the castle, she ignored the cold that seemed to wrap around her. It was more than just her damp clothes, she knew, and she was quite sure she could hear whispering in the walls.

She paused, straining to hear. "Hello?"

Elizabeth stood still. She was imagining things, she knew. The walls were playing tricks on her. Still, she closed her eyes and listened at the whispers calling out to her.

Leave now.

Go back before it's too late.

You will not find what greatness you seek.

Her eyes flew open, and she frowned, glaring at the walls. Moving closer, she pressed her hand to the stone next to her. Instantly, her hand flew back. The stones were hot. They were *so* hot that they had burned her, scorching her palm, and she looked down at the blistering skin of her hand.

That was going to make retrieving the sword a bit more complicated, wasn't it?

"How could the walls be hot?"

The stone floor beneath her bare feet was cold, almost icy. It didn't make sense that the walls would be nearly on fire, but Elizabeth knew that there was a reason people were scared of this castle.

"*It's haunted,*" one of the other castle maids, Angelica, had told her.

Elizabeth hadn't believed her.

Angelica had been a silly girl who was scared to ever do anything new. She'd always worked as a king's maid, and she would always be working as a king's maid. Not Elizabeth. She was going to be something else. Something better.

She kept walking.

Aside from broken furniture and the occasional glass shards on the floor, the main level of the castle was innocuous and boring. The whispers continued, but Elizabeth pushed them out of her mind, dismissing them as silly, childish nightmares.

She'd always had bad dreams. Everyone in Rêve did. Angelica said the nightmares had started years ago when the Castle Cauchemar had fallen, but Elizabeth knew the truth. It was something in the water. There was no such thing as ghosts. There were no truly haunted castles. The king had an idea that the Sword of Cauchemar was enchanted, but that was just a silly story.

Still, Elizabeth could deal with a silly story if it meant getting the money that she needed to leave the kingdom once and for all.

Finally, she reached a narrow staircase.

Do not go up the stairs.

Run now.

Go back.

The whispers in the walls were now desperate, anxious shouts. Elizabeth's hand was aching with pain, and now her ears were, too. She was going crazy, she knew. She was going properly mad, but she'd spent months trying to find the location of the castle, and she wasn't going to give up now.

"Leave me alone!" Elizabeth cried out, and the voices in the walls fell silent.

Good.

She could have a little bit of peace.

For now.

The stairs creaked as she made her way up the wooden planks. Her feet began to ache, but it was no longer from the cold. Elizabeth glanced back to see that her footprints were no longer wet, but bloody.

Had she stepped in glass?

She stopped, sitting down on one of the steps to more carefully examine the soles of her feet. They were nearly black from the dust of the castle floor, but despite the pain, there was no blood on her feet.

She glanced back at the footsteps.

They aren't mine, she realized. There was something else in the castle. Maybe *someone* else. She closed her eyes for a moment as her body begged her to flee the castle. Maybe there was a logical reason behind the bloody footsteps.

"They've probably been here for years," she whispered out loud. "Maybe I've disturbed the dust, revealing the prints." She reached down to the step beneath her and pressed her finger into the blood, expecting it to be dry and stale, but her finger came back warm and red and wet.

No, the blood hadn't been here for years.

It was fresh.

Elizabeth stood up and turned, continuing up the staircase.

She wouldn't let something like a stupid ghost keep her from finding the sword. It had to be here somewhere. The king had assured all of the treasure-seekers in the land that the sword was not only here, but obtainable.

He claimed that none of the treasure-seekers in the past had gone the right way to the castle, that anyone who didn't return had simply chosen to leave the kingdom of their own free will.

Only, Elizabeth knew the truth.

She was the one who cleaned the king's chambers. She was the one responsible for cleaning his desk. Most of the other girls simply cleaned and left the room, but not Elizabeth.

She knew how to read.

And she did read.

She read all of his correspondence over the last few years. She knew that the king was worried that the sword was going to grow in power. He believed it had been cursed by a witch long ago, and that was what had led to the Castle of Cauchemar's downfall.

The damn sword.

Her feet continued aching, and the pain was growing sharper, but she didn't stop until she reached the second floor of the castle. There she collapsed on the ground and looked at her feet once more.

Still, there was no blood, but the footprints continued to follow her.

She was going crazy, trapped in a nightmare no one could pull her from, but she was close. She had to be close.

She paused where she was, looking back down at the bloody footprints. She watched as they continued past her, moving forward on the wooden floorboards of the castle's second floor.

"Is someone there?" Elizabeth whispered, taking a chance that if there was a ghost, for real, that it might talk to her.

Only, the walls had suddenly fallen silent, and the footsteps continued moving away from her.

Jumping to her feet and cringing at the pain, she hurried after the footsteps. They led her from the staircase down one narrow hall, around a corner, and finally into a large study.

They'll lead me to the sword.

That was her only goal.

She *had* to get to the sword. Had to find the weapon and get it back to the king. Only, Elizabeth was already starting to realize that this quest hadn't been what she was expecting. She'd assumed it would be a simple endeavor: get in, get out.

It was *not* proving to be quite so simple.

And then she saw the fireplace.

She dropped the lantern she'd been carrying, ignoring the sound of it clattering to the ground because her eyes were on the fireplace in the center of the room. The fire was burning brightly, filling the room with greater warmth than she'd felt in days.

Elizabeth rushed to the fireplace, dropped to her knees, and held her good hand out to allow the heat of the fireplace to warm her. The injured hand stayed balled in a fist resting on her knees. She wouldn't move it until she had to, but even without checking it again, she could tell that she would have scars.

That was okay.

Every good pirate had scars.

Didn't they?

"Are you enjoying the castle?"

Elizabeth shrieked at the voice and spun around on the ground. A tall man stood in the doorway behind her. He was dressed in silks and a royal robe. He was a king, to be sure, but he didn't wear a crown. He smiled at her agitation and waited for her screams to subside. Then he spoke again.

"I asked if you were enjoying the castle."

There was something there, something terrifyingly cold in his voice. His words were warm and friendly, but his tone was...wrong. It was as though he'd *read* about what you were supposed to say to a guest in your home, but he'd never actually done it before.

Who was this man?

How was he here?

The castle appeared completely run-down from the outside. There had been no sign of life at all, and it had taken her days to make the journey to the dilapidated structure, yet here stood a man who seemed to think that he lived here.

And why was there a fire in only a single room of the castle?

"I am not enjoying the castle," Elizabeth whispered. She wasn't quite sure that this wasn't a hallucination of some kind. She hadn't eaten much on her journey. Her rain-soaked bag had ensured the total destruction of her food, which meant that it was quite possible she was imagining this person in front of her.

She *wasn't* imagining the warmth of the fire, though. For the first time in days, she could feel her clothing starting to dry, and her long hair was no longer matted to her neck.

He stared at her, cocking his head as he considered this answer. A shiver shot through Elizabeth that had nothing to do with the coldness of her journey, and she realized suddenly that this man was a dangerous person.

If he was real, which she was still unsure about, then he wasn't someone she could trust.

"May I offer you food?"

She stared at the man.

Oh, she *really* couldn't trust this person. No reasonable person, especially a king, would allow a stranger to enter their home, drip water and bloody footprints all over it, and then offer them a meal.

"I'm really not hungry," she told him.

Her stomach chose that moment to growl, giving her away.

The man nodded and turned, leaving the room, and Elizabeth turned back to the fire. She pulled her legs up to her chest, holding them close. Her injured hand wasn't going to do her any favors once she got the sword, and having this man here certainly complicated things.

Did the sword belong to him?

Did he know where it was?

Would she have to fight him in order to take it back to her kingdom and her own king?

A moment later, the man returned with a tray of cakes and beef and stew. There was fruit and cheese and a goblet of wine.

Only one goblet.

It was red wine.

It's blood, she thought, thinking of the footprints she'd seen on her way to this floor. There was something seriously wrong with the castle, but she'd come too far to turn back now.

The man set the tray down on the floor beside the fireplace.

"Eat," he commanded, but Elizabeth shook her head.

"Thank you, but I'm really not hungry."

The man smiled at her. His teeth seemed too sharp, too bright. They reminded her of her old dog Henry's teeth.

"Eat," he repeated, and even though Elizabeth didn't want to, she found her injured hand stretching out toward the food and bringing a small cube of cheese to her lips. Her eyes latched onto the man's, and she couldn't seem to look away as she continued eating.

Stop, she silently begged herself, but her hands were no longer under her own control.

Was he a warlock of some kind?

A wizard?

He was making her do this and she didn't want to.

Be strong, Elizabeth, she told herself. *You're here for the sword, and then you'll leave.*

Only, she wasn't going to be able to get the sword if she couldn't stop eating all of the food in front of her.

"Please," she said to the man. Maybe being polite would convince him to stop whatever it was he was doing to her. Elizabeth's injured hand ached with each touch of the food. One of the blisters that had formed popped, dropping puss onto a piece of fruit that she brought to her lips. She gagged as she ate it, yet she still devoured the entire thing. "Please stop this," she said.

"I'm not doing anything to you, Elizabeth," the man said.

"How do you know my name?"

"I know a lot of things," he smiled. "I know you're from the Kingdom of Rêve, for example."

There was no way he could know that if he was an illusion, she thought. She hadn't told him where she'd come from, and there was nothing on her sack or her cloak to give away her location. She'd worn a dull old brown cloak instead of her country's tell-tale bright blue and gold. She'd been careful in case someone in the forest caught her during her journey.

Yet this man seemed to know where she was from.

A cold chill slipped through her.

Did he know what she was looking for?

"I don't know what you mean," Elizabeth said. She hadn't shoved any food in her mouth since he'd started talking. Whatever he was using to force her actions, perhaps he couldn't do that while speaking to her at the same time.

She rifled through her memories, trying to remember if she'd read anything about warlocks or magic users in the king's study. When she'd discovered the directions to the Castle Cauchemar, it had been in a book about legends, but it hadn't said anything about magic.

Had it?

"Oh, Elizabeth," the man said. "Haven't you figured it out yet?"

She stared at him, waiting to find out what the twist was, what his real purpose was.

"I'm the one who sent the king the book," he smiled. "I'm the one who chose you."

It had been happenstance, she'd thought, that the book had simply fallen into her hands. Now she knew the truth: that it had been planted in the king's quarters.

"What do you mean?" Elizabeth whispered. She was shaking now, but not from the cold. From fear. For the very first time, she was starting to think that perhaps coming to Cauchemar hadn't been such a good idea after all.

And perhaps she would not be leaving the castle in one piece as she'd expected.

The man sneered at her, and Elizabeth's stomach twisted. She thought she might be sick. Then she grabbed her stomach. Yes, she was quite certain she would be sick.

Poison.

He must have poisoned her. Only, it wasn't fair! She hadn't been able to resist the food. He'd put some sort of hex on her, some sort of spell.

She needed to get away from him and find the sword.

Once she found the enchanted weapon, she could kill this man and return to her kingdom. She could pawn the sword off on her own king and be free to go.

She would be *free* from everything.

He said nothing, just cocked his head and looked at her, watching her as she clutched her stomach. She stumbled to her feet and turned, leaving the room. Her feet ached as she made her way to the hallway. He stayed close behind her, following as she silently went from room to room.

The bloody footprints continued behind her once more, no longer offering any sort of guidance as to where she should go. Soon she paused, out of breath, and leaned against the wall.

This one didn't burn her.

This one chilled her.

She leapt away, once more falling. Landing on her side, she rolled to her back.

The man stared over her.

"Where are you going?"

Four simple words that she would never answer. If he had, in fact, sent the note, and he had, in fact, lured her here, then he must have something he needed from her. She just had to figure out what that was.

Elizabeth was a simple person. A woman. A maid. A servant. She spent her life ensuring that the king had everything he needed even though it wasn't very fair.

A man like the king didn't need people fawning over him, yet that was what he had.

So, what did *Elizabeth* have that the magician wanted?

She had cold, wet clothes. She had a lantern. Well, she'd had one. She'd left it by the fire, she realized, yet somehow, she could see quite clearly. It must have been the wizard man. He'd done something to the space to brighten it. She closed her eyes for a moment and opened them again.

Yes, the room seemed lighter.

It was him, she realized. He was almost glowing.

She didn't have anything else on her. She'd brought only the directions she'd found in the book and now...

Now it was all going to end if she didn't find the sword.

"Do you make a habit of luring women to your castle only

to poison them?" Elizabeth spat out, once more getting to her feet.

He silently followed her room-to-room until she reached what appeared to be a once-beautiful library. She paused in the entrance to the room, and he came up behind her. He didn't touch her, but she could feel his presence behind her like a shadow.

Elizabeth stared at the dusty rows of bookshelves. Each of them was filled to the brim with the same book. She squinted, trying to see the title, but then she realized it was the same book she'd found in the king's library.

It was the same book she'd found with the note.

"What is this place?"

The man chuckled.

"Haven't you figured it out yet?"

She hadn't.

He lowered his voice, speaking in a tone that was obviously designed to make her uncomfortable.

"This place is cursed."

"Cursed?"

She turned, looking over her shoulder at the strange man with the magical powers. He resembled her king a little. At first, she'd assumed it was simply the way royals carried themselves, but it was something else, wasn't it?

They had the same nose and the same eyes. They also had the same curve of their jaw.

"You're brothers," she realized, whispering.

How had she not noticed this before?

"Very good," the man said sarcastically.

"And you send out the books to lure people here."

Another nod.

"Why?"

She still hadn't figured that part out just yet. She knew he wanted people coming here, but there was no sign anyone else had been here in decades. Maybe longer.

And that still didn't explain why *her* king wanted the sword so badly, or why he wouldn't just tell people where the Castle Cauchemar was.

"I was cursed a long time ago, dear. My darling brother knows this. He's after my sword." The man cocked his head. "You aren't here for that, are you?"

"No," she lied easily. "I'm here because the king said there was treasure in this place."

A lie.

They both knew it.

She *was* after the sword.

"Why bother luring people if you're brothers with the king?" Elizabeth wanted to know.

"My brother has something I want. I have something he wants. Neither one of us can reach the other's castle. I'm cursed to stay here, never to leave. He's cursed never to come here, yet always to long for it."

"Who cursed you?"

She wasn't sure that she believed in magic. There was probably a likely explanation for everything she'd encountered–the bloody footprints, the walls with the strange hot-and-cold sensations, and even the whispering in the walls.

Elizabeth had been taught that magic, that witchcraft, was just pretend. Those were legends and stories made up to convince children to behave so they wouldn't upset their nannies or mothers.

Those things weren't real.

"Our mother," the man told her. "She was an enchantress who believed her magical abilities were better than they were. Either that or she hated us more deeply than we'll ever know."

"And now you and your brother are fighting over a sword," she said. Elizabeth wanted to know something else. The man seemed talkative. Anxious. Ready. He didn't seem afraid of her because he didn't think she'd be able to beat him.

Either that, or he didn't think she'd be able to find his sword.

She'd already spotted it, though, leaning against the wall by the fireplace in the library. There was a velvet armchair next to the fireplace, as well. She imagined sitting in that chair and holding the sword while watching the fire. It was the kind of thing people in books would do.

Elizabeth eyed the library. She still had to get the sword. If this man had really lured her here, then she had to kill him before it was too late.

Nobody had been here in years. Decades. Maybe longer, judging by the looks of the space. It still didn't explain how they could be brothers. Elizabeth's king was very much alive and healthy, and probably almost in his 60s. This man before her couldn't be older than 30.

She stepped into the room, and instantly, it seemed to spring to life. The dust on the bookshelves vanished. The fireplace roared to life, and the sword seemed to sing to her.

Then the walls started whispering again.

Run.

Leave the sword.

Leave while you still can, lass.

She ignored them. She was imagining things again, and she tried to rush directly toward the sword. The man behind her laughed.

Only a few more steps.

With each step, her feet hurt more. She looked down to see that the bloody footprints following her were now smeared on the floor. She raised one of her feet and saw that it was now actively bleeding. Somehow, the magic of the space had caught up with her, but it was almost over.

She reached for the sword, gripping its hilt, and spun around slowly to face the King of Cauchemar.

"It's time for you to die," she said, and she lunged forward, slipping the sword just beneath his ribs.

She expected him to fight back.

She thought he would try to step away from the weapon or that, at the very least, he would fall to the ground, dead.

He did neither of those things.

Instead, he looked down at the space where she'd stabbed him.

Then he stepped forward.

That was when she realized he wasn't a person at all. He was a ghost. He looked real. He could touch things, but he didn't have a real, solid body. He couldn't die because he was already dead.

"What are you?"

"Someone who is very grateful you located the sword and chose to pick it up," he smiled at her. "Go ahead. Try to put it down."

That was when Elizabeth realized she couldn't. She was clinging to the hilt of the weapon, but she couldn't release it. Couldn't let go. Couldn't drop the blade to the ground.

Why couldn't she let go?

And that was when Elizabeth felt herself start to die.

It was slow at first, and painful, but soon her spirit left her body, and she hovered above her corpse, which was lying on the library floor. The man stepped forward, knelt down, and placed his hands on her body. The air around them seemed to swirl as Elizabeth's physical body disappeared and the man began to change.

He looked younger, brighter. Stronger.

He looked up at ghost-Elizabeth and smiled.

"Thanks to your sacrifice, I'm one step closer to being able to leave this place and kill my brother," he said.

He was tied to the sword, she realized. As long as this king had the sword, he'd live as an immortal. Her own king must have known that. That was why he'd been sending hunters to find the sword.

He wanted to destroy the weapon, and his brother along with it.

She wanted to speak. She opened her mouth to try, but nothing came out.

There was no sound.

Only silence.

"Yes," the man nodded. "It takes the ghosts some time to learn how to warn the visitors. It doesn't matter, though. A few more sacrifices, and I'll be strong enough to leave. My brother thinks if he can get the sword away from Cauchemar that I'll die and be gone for good, but that will never happen. Once I've consumed enough bodies, I'll be able to leave. The curse will be broken, and I'll be free."

How long had he been doing this?

Had it really been as long as she'd thought?

Or did the castle appear to be in such disrepair because of the curse?

"It's been nearly a decade since I've been free," the man said, answering her. "And in another year, maybe two, I'll be free once more."

He set the sword back, leaning it against the fireplace, and Elizabeth stayed where she was. He turned, leaving the room, and as the vibrancy dissipated and the dust returned to the library, she realized she wasn't alone.

A dozen other spirits floated there with her, staring at her.

"Run," one of them whispered. "You should have run."

It was a rainy day at Cauchemar when the castle door creaked opened.

"We found it," a voice called. "I can't believe we actually found it."

"It took longer than I thought," said someone else.

There were two visitors. Explorers. Two people who were going to try to claim the King of Cauchemar's sword. Two souls who would be captured by the king and forced to stay until he was strong enough to leave.

"Where do you think the sword is?"

"Probably upstairs. It might be hidden, but we have plenty of time. You have your torch?"

"I've got it."

Elizabeth and the other ghosts slipped quietly down to the first floor to see the two peasant boys standing in the front hall.

She opened her mouth, desperate to warn them away.

"Run."

She'd been practicing all year, but it was the most she was able to say in her spirit body. She wasn't even sure if she was able to say it loudly enough that they could truly understand her.

"Say," one of the boys said, turning to his friend. "Did you hear something?"

"No," the companion said. "It's probably just the wind."

The Beast of Bel'Hamin

Mike Oliveri

"Are we certain this is the way, brother?" Eivor shouted over the wind howling into their faces.

"No!" Rasmus shouted back, then laughed.

"We've lost the moon. Surely it's late, and if we don't find the witch or shelter soon, he'll be upon us!"

Rasmus grabbed Eivor by the arm and pulled him in close. "Then we fight in the snow! Would you have us turn back? We wouldn't make it to the bottom of the trail, either!"

"Fair enough. We keep walking."

Eivor pulled his arm free and trudged on through the calf-deep snow. Between the darkness and the flurries, he could just make out the pines lining either side of the trail. In winters back home, this would have been nothing more than a leisurely walk to the alehouse. Unfortunately home, and proper winter dress, were three hundred leagues northward. The stitching in these leather boots couldn't hold back the damp like a good pair of beaver pelts, and the furs they'd stolen from a merchant in Kathar Pass let the wind rip through every seam. They were clothes for a dandy to be seen in, not for proper living in the Frostlands.

Thirty-eight days of fighting this cursed creature had also left them exhausted and hungry as they climbed in search of the witch's home. Every night this…this ghost? This demon?

This *thing* appeared at midnight, and every night they fought and killed him. They beheaded him, they burned him, they buried him, they hacked him to pieces, and the next night he reappeared, a silent assassin bent on their destruction. He had left them bruised and scarred, driven from every lodging and struggling to earn enough coin for a decent meal.

A twinge of pain shot through Eivor's left knee with every step, a remnant of the seventh night when the thing had kicked his leg out from under him. He'd wrapped his leg in a long strip of cotton from thigh to calf to reinforce it for the climb, but the knot had worked itself loose halfway up the mountain and the wrap piled up around the top of his boot where it pinched and chafed his flesh. They couldn't find this damned witch soon enough.

He remembered her from the tavern, sitting opposite him near the fireplace, just a pale face staring out from beneath a brown, hooded cloak. She had gaunt, matronly features, framed by wispy blonde hair. She stood out not for her looks, but because she sat quietly while the rest of the patrons shouted and cheered, trading bets and guzzling ale. They made eye contact for just a moment, then the crowd obscured her.

It wasn't until they returned to the tavern that the locals labeled her a witch. They spoke to the barman, to some patrons and some locals, and had almost given up before a serving maid admitted to remembering her. After a little coercion and a threat or two, a few of them finally directed the brothers up the trail to the witch's home. They'd started climbing right away, weather be damned.

Something hard and heavy struck Eivor's right side, knocking him to the ground. He cried out as a sharp pain lanced through his right upper arm. The object thudded into the snow in front of him, and he saw it was a rock, easily twice the size of his head.

"He's here!" Rasmus's sword sang from its sheath.

Eivor's arm wouldn't cooperate, and fresh pain stabbed at him when he planted it against the ground. He scrambled to his feet and reached across his hip with his left hand to unhook his axe from his belt.

"Do you see him?"

"No. Blast this snow!"

"He's broken my damned arm."

Rasmus glanced at his brother's dangling arm. "Can you fight?"

"I'm still breathing, aren't I?"

"*There!*"

The hulking brute rushed at them from uphill, holding a tree limb as long as a man is tall over his head. He plowed through the snow as if it wasn't even there and swung the limb in a downward cut like a sword. Eivor stepped back several paces, while Rasmus dove to one side and rolled. The limb struck directly between Ras's footprints with a loud crack.

The brute's head snapped toward Eivor. He had been a man once, a traveler and a fighter called Javed Mehr. He stood a full head taller than both Eivor and Rasmus, his shoulders were half again as broad, and his frame was packed with slabs of muscle. He had laughed raucously that night Rasmus challenged him to a fight.

Now his eyes were black pits beneath a furrowed brow. His tanned flesh had turned ashen, his cheeks hollow. Bits of snow clung to his black hair and naked shoulders, but he seemed oblivious to the cold. He snarled, and while Eivor puffed out cloud after cloud with every panicked breath, no mist escaped Javed's lips. He had been known as the Beast of Bel'Hamin in life, but never before had it been so fitting.

Rasmus leapt forward and thrust his sword at the Beast's neck, but the Beast parried with the back of its right hand, then kicked Rasmus in the chest and sent him sprawling to his back.

He started to raise his makeshift club, and Eivor swung his axe down in a wide arc. The blade cleaved the Beast's left hand at the wrist and bit deep into the wooden limb. The Beast gave no cry of pain, and there was no spurt of blood. He hurled the limb to one side, wrenching Eivor's axe from his hand with it, then smashed Eivor across the side of the head with his raw stump.

Eivor's teeth crashed together, and his ear rang. He tasted blood as he stumbled back, and the Beast turned on him. Rasmus pushed himself up to a seated position with one hand and held his sword in a guard position with the other as he struggled to regain his breath.

The Beast advanced on Eivor. They had found he could be killed like a living man, but he was much hardier. He showed no pain and shrugged off most wounds. Impale his heart, separate his head, or cleave his skull and he'd stay down, but most other attacks had little effect.

Eivor drew his dagger in a reverse grip. He also knew the Beast's muscles still worked like any living man's, and he wondered, did the same apply to his eyes? Eivor sucked blood and spit—and one shattered tooth—to the middle of his mouth.

The Beast lunged for him. Eivor spat in his face. Blood spattered his eyes and the tooth bounced off his forehead. Eivor sidestepped. The Beast's right hand closed on nothingness, and Eivor lunged low and slashed. His blade cut a long furrow to the outside of the Beast's left knee. As he rose on the other side he spun, pulling the dagger back across the base of the Beast's hamstring. The dagger's sharp point sliced through cloth and flesh alike, and the Beast collapsed to one knee.

Rasmus regained his feet, and Eivor retreated to his side. The Beast wiped the blood from his eyes and turned on his ruined knee to face them.

"Are you alright?" Eivor asked.

"He may have broken my rib. You?"

The Beast moved toward them, dragging his ruined leg. They stepped back out of his reach.

"He's cost me another tooth," Eivor said.

"Then we best finish this while you can still chew your steak."

"Aye. I'll fetch my axe."

The brothers separated, moving in a wide circle around the Beast. Rasmus waved his sword point up and down while Eivor went to the tree limb. He stepped on it, grabbed the handle of his axe, and pulled it free.

"Ready?" Rasmus asked.

"Do it."

The brothers roared and rushed the Beast, blades swinging. The Beast tried to shield himself, tried to grab at them, but they kept out of reach, cutting again and again without pause. Flesh hung from the Beast's arms in tatters. His remaining fingers flew through the air. Eivor cleaved his shoulder, Rasmus slashed his cheek, and still he thrashed and flailed and reached for them. Rasmus slashed again, cutting through the Beast's nose and right eye. The Beast lunged and hooked the remains of his right hand around Rasmus's ankle.

Eivor circled behind the Beast, stomped on his back, and swung his axe hard. The curved head split the back of the Beast's head, and his body went rigid. Rasmus turned his sword point down and drove it with both hands straight through the base of the Beast's skull.

They waited, their breaths lost in the howl of the wind.

"It's done."

Eivor stepped on the Beast's head and removed his axe. He examined the axe head. Bloodless, as always.

"Done for now," he said. "Let's find the witch before we freeze to death."

Rasmus sheathed his sword. After their first encounters with the Beast, the fight exhilarated him. He would taunt their fallen foe or let fly with a cry of triumph. He had always enjoyed the hot-blooded rush of combat, whether in the playful wrestling matches of their childhood or the mad rage on the battlefield.

Now Eivor watched him heave a deep sigh, pull his fur jacket tighter around his shoulders, and continue up the trail.

The falling snow dwindled to a light flurry, and dim, gray light spilled across the land by the time the brothers found the cabin. Firelight flickered behind its glass windows, and pale smoke rose from the stone chimney. It looked solid, built from stacked logs with a steeply sloped roof to prevent the snow from piling up. A small path forked from the main trail, curving gently through the trees and to the front stoop. If the heavy snow were still falling, they may well have missed it.

They stood near one tree, taking in the scene. The snow along the trail was pristine. The wind whispered through the pines, but they saw no sign of movement around or inside the cabin. An owl hooted from somewhere down the main trail.

Rasmus hurried forward.

"Ras, wait!" Eivor limped after him. The pain in his knee had worsened since the fight, and he winced as his broken arm slapped against his side.

Rasmus leapt onto the stoop and pounded the heavy wooden door.

"Open up, witch!"

"Easy, brother!" Eivor called after him. "A little finesse may be called for if she's truly a witch!"

"My damned toes are too frozen for finesse." Rasmus pounded the door harder. "Open this door or we'll kick it down, woman!"

Eivor watched the windows as he approached the stoop, worried his brother had acted in haste. The witch—or indeed anyone—could be beyond that door, greeting them with a sword or crossbow. Maybe the people of the valley had done them wrong and set them on the wrong path.

"I'll not ask again!" Rasmus shouted.

At last, a metallic clunk sounded through the door, and it swung open several inches. Orange and yellow light shone through familiar, wispy brown hair.

"Who are you?" The woman's voice was smooth and silken.

"Don't claim you don't recognize us, witch!" Rasmus drew his swords six inches. "I'll just remove your head now and spare the trouble of an argument!"

"Mm. You'd best come inside so I can get a better look at you, then." She withdrew into her cabin.

Rasmus nudged the door open with his foot. It groaned softly on its hinges, revealing a single room with a large wooden table toward one side. Colorful tapestries hung over shelves all along the wall to the right, and glassware and small boxes and chests adorned a long countertop beneath them.

Rasmus pushed the door open the rest of the way and stepped across the threshold, with Eivor close behind. The heat from the fire felt wonderful, and now Eivor could smell cooked meat and spice wafting from a stewpot hanging from a hook beside the fire. A long knife rested near a half loaf of bread and a small pile of carrots and turnips on the table. A tall cabinet stood against the far wall. Eivor glanced up and saw another window built into the roof and a high, vaulted ceiling marred by patches of soot. Chains and ropes hung from some of the beams, and a circular iron chandelier hung above the center of the room. Unlit candles of varying lengths stood in its sconces.

The woman stood near the fireplace. She was short, and she held a thick blue blanket around her shoulders, clutched tight in front and revealing only a few inches of tan pants and a pair of brown, furry slippers. Metallic trinkets adorned the mantle beside her, some of them gold and silver. Beyond her, a purple curtain filled a narrow doorway.

Eivor closed the door behind them. The clack of the latch echoed around the vaulted ceiling.

"I see you now," she said, "but I know you no better."

"I am Rasmus, and this is Eivor. We are the sons of Sten Stormhammer."

"Northlanders, then. I hear Sten Stormhammer was slain by his own cousin."

"We don't speak the usurper's name!" Eivor said. "We seek our fortune to raise an army and retake our lands."

She looked them up and down, and her eyes lingered on Eivor's limp arm. She smirked. "It appears you have a long way to go."

"No thanks to you, witch!" Rasmus shouted. "We were doing fine before you set that demon upon us!"

"Again you call me witch. I fear you've been misled."

"Do you deny you were at the tavern in the valley below a month ago?"

"It seems likely. I'm a frequent visitor there."

"You try my patience, witch!"

"Show a little skill with herbs and medicines, and possess half a mind for knowledge of the world, and they call you 'witch.' I simply make my own living tending to the needs of locals and travelers alike for pay. As for you, Northlander, you are no more familiar to me than my own intestines. I've never seen them, but I know they're there, and I know they're full of shit."

"Then perhaps I'll introduce you to them!"

Rasmus lunged toward her, but Eivor grabbed his shoulder and pulled him back. "Enough!" Eivor barked. "Please, my brother and I are exhausted and impatient, and I am injured. Forgive our temper; we merely seek answers. Be true with us, and if you're not who we seek, we'll be on our way."

The woman's eyes narrowed. Eivor noted she did not so much as flinch when Rasmus threatened her, and even now she regarded them with a steely calm. Whether witch or healer, that was not the end of her talents.

"Your arm," she said at last. "Is it broken?"

"Yes."

"Put your weapons by the door and I will set the bone for you. Then we can discuss your questions."

"No," Rasmus said.

"Do it, Ras." Eivor pulled his axe off his belt and set it next to the door, head down. "We'll not make progress with threats with this one."

Rasmus did not move.

"I'll even throw in a hot meal." The woman inclined her head toward her stewpot.

Silence.

"Ras—"

"Alright! I'll do it." He slammed his sword home, then unbuckled his sword belt. "I'll be watching you closely, witch."

She watched Ras set his belt and scabbard beside Eivor's axe, then move to the other side of the table, opposite her. He crossed his arms.

"Remove your coat and help me clear the table." She let her blanket fall open, revealing a polished short sword. Rasmus's eyes went wide as she set it on the mantle.

Eivor chuckled.

"What are you laughing at?"

"Nothing, brother. Help me with my coat."

Eivor wiped sweat from his face. His jaw and head hurt from biting back the pain. His arm still hurt, but it faded from a lancing heat to a throbbing ache. He sat up on the table, then eased himself into the chair beside it. His right arm, held by the sling, stayed secure against his side as he moved.

"Thank you," Eivor said. "This is much better."

"You're fortunate the break did not go all the way through the bone. It should heal well if you take care of it," Audra said. She had given them her name while she worked but offered little else.

Rasmus had watched her close while she worked. He had removed his coat, and he leaned against the long counter with his arms crossed in front of his chest. Audra approached the counter to his right and sorted through the vials and containers on top of it.

"What are you doing?" Rasmus asked.

"Making something for the pain."

"Mm. What do we owe you for your service tonight?" His tone had softened.

"Do you have anything to offer?"

The brothers looked at each other, shrugged.

"Then call it humanity." Audra opened the cabinet and removed a jug and some wooden cups. "Would either of you care for some mead?"

"Please!" Rasmus said.

Audra poured out three cups and set the jug on the table. Eivor sipped it, finding its sweet taste remarkably similar to the mead back home. He took a larger glug while Audra returned to the cabinet for bowls and spoons.

"So tell me, what has the sons of Sten Stormhammer hunting witches on my mountain in the middle of a snowstorm?"

"We saw you at the tavern," Eivor said. "It was the night my brother fought a man named Javed Mehr."

"Killed, you mean," she said.

"Aye, killed."

"So you admit you *were* there?" Rasmus asked.

"Yes, I was there. And I saw the money changing hands. Now that you tell me your purpose, I see the stakes were greater than I guessed. Is that why you drew your dagger, Rasmus?"

He said nothing, but helped himself to more mead.

"We picked the largest man in the room," Eivor said. "We stood to make the most money. It wasn't until the fight started that I heard another man call Mehr the 'Beast.' We've taken on larger men, but this Beast, he fought differently. And yes, we stood to lose a lot of money."

"A sore loser, then?"

"It's not that simple," Rasmus snapped. "One doesn't raise an army showing weakness."

It was mostly the truth. Eivor recalled his brother being knocked to the floor at his feet, with blood in his teeth but a gleam in his eye. He pulled the dagger, showed it to Eivor, and as the Beast seized his shoulders and pulled him around, Rasmus spun and thrust it right between his ribs. The Beast gasped once, looked down at the dagger, and collapsed to the floor. Placating the bettors had taken the better part of an hour, and Eivor counted them lucky to have left with their skins intact.

"And what does his death have to do with me?" Audra asked.

"You were seen talking to him after the fight," Eivor said. "After his death."

"Did he speak back to me?"

The brothers exchanged a glance.

"No. But his ghost has been hunting us ever since. He appears nightly, and we've killed him repeatedly, but he won't stay down."

She raised an eyebrow.

"Last night, he broke my arm not long before we found your cabin. If you were the last to speak to him, and you really were a witch, then perhaps you're the one who set him upon us."

She laughed, but the brothers only looked at her.

"If only I did have such power," Audra said. "Perhaps I'd have a better home than this chilly mountain. But yes, I spoke to him. It was words of sympathy and a final prayer, nothing more, as I tended to the body. The Beast was a warrior priest of Bel'Hamin. He earned his name fighting in the pits, always in honor of his god. The fights in his homeland are part of their rituals. I can't say why he traveled in the valley, or why he agreed to fight you. Maybe it was for sport, or even for money, but you dishonored him when you drew your weapon. You shamed him before his god, and maybe it's his curse you need to break."

"Impossible," Rasmus muttered.

"Oh? But a simple mountain woman setting him upon you is more plausible?"

"Tell me, then, 'simple mountain woman,' how you know so much about his gods and their magic? Tell me how we stop this demon from hunting us!"

"I think you already know."

"Death," Eivor said.

"What!?"

"Death," Eivor repeated. He looked at Audra. "Blood for blood. Vengeance."

"I'm sorry," Audra said.

"No!" Rasmus hurled his mug against the wall. This time, Audra did flinch. "How do we know you're telling the truth? What use was climbing this damned mountain if you can't help us? Maybe we should just kill *you* and find out if he dies with *your* magic!"

"Stop, brother."

"Why? What have we to lose? Three different people saw her with the corpse!"

"Enough!" Eivor pounded the table with his good hand.

"She's set my arm and given us warmth. She's said her piece. Calm down and let's think this through together, see if she has a solution."

Rasmus muttered under this breath and crossed his arms again.

"Yes, pout like a child. That will help."

"Don't push me, brother!"

"Or what?"

"Or I'll—"

"Stop it! Both of you!" Audra snapped. "You're giving me a headache. Here, eat something. Maybe full stomachs will clear your heads. Or at the very least you'll be quiet for a moment."

She had brought the stewpot to the table as they spoke, and now she ladled the thick, brown stew into their bowls. Steam rose from the surface as Eivor pushed his spoon through the meat and vegetables inside. He took a bite of the meat. Rabbit, perhaps. The broth was savory and peppery, and it warmed his belly.

"Please, have some bread with it." Audra brought the bread back to the table and handed a slice to Rasmus, who had already finished most of his stew. He swiped the bread around the edge of the bowl and took a healthy bite of it.

Eivor cut himself a slice, took a bite. It was hard and coarse, but tasty, almost sweet. A good balance to the peppery stew.

Rasmus coughed. He looked up at Eivor, his eyes wide.

"What is it?"

"I can't feel my hands." Then his eyes rolled into the back of his head. He fell sideways and crashed to the floor.

Rasmus looked at Audra, saw two of her. He blinked hard, and her two selves merely swam around one another before him.

"What have you done?" he barely managed to whisper before everything went black.

"Wake up, Eivor!"

He snapped awake, still sitting at the table. The cabin was dim and cold. The fire had faded to a few embers, and there was no sign of Audra.

"The witch has taken our weapons. You should have let me gut her on the spot!"

Eivor stood and looked down at his cold, bare feet. "She took our boots?"

"Our coats are gone, too!"

They took a few frantic moments looking around the cabin, but their weapons and furs were nowhere to be found. They found her bed empty and cool, and a small larder mostly picked clean.

Eivor walked out to the stoop. It wasn't daybreak, but night-fall, and the moon had just cleared the horizon. They found her tracks leading away from the cabin, mingled with their own from their arrival, but the way they'd partially filled in suggested she had a long head start on them, and if she made it to the village, it would be impossible to say what tales she'd tell about what happened in her cabin.

Eivor's left hand touched his belt and found he at least still had his dagger. If they caught up with her, maybe he'd gut her himself this time.

"Now what?" Rasmus asked.

"We deal with the Beast, then we deal with the witch. But first, we start a fire."

The brothers warmed themselves as the moon climbed higher in the sky. They spoke little. Rasmus dug through the larder and put a small meal together. Eivor was not hungry. He instead rummaged through the herbs and powders on the counter, but none of it looked familiar or useful. As the time grew near, they overturned the table and pushed it against the door, then sat in the chairs to wait.

BOOM.

Something heavy struck the door.

BOOM!

Eivor would swear it was a battering ram. The top door hinge hung loose from the jamb.

BOOM! The door brace crashed to the floor and the planks cracked apart. The Beast's head flashed past the opening.

Eivor clutched his dagger, and Rasmus wielded the fireplace poker. Better those than the witch's forks and bread knife.

One more crash and the table slid away from the door, the Beast right behind it. He sprang over the table and rushed them. Eivor stabbed for his heart, but the Beast deflected his dagger and punched Rasmus while he swung the poker. Ras recovered and swung again, but the Beast absorbed the blow on his shoulder and kicked Rasmus in the gut. Ras flew back against the wall.

Eivor slashed, putting a deep, bloodless gash in the Beast's forearm. The Beast countered with a hard punch to Eivor's right arm. White hot pain shot up through his shoulder and neck, and he screamed. The Beast pushed his chest and swept his legs out from under him, and he crashed to the floor, landing on his arm and sending a fresh wave of pain through him.

The Beast raised its boot over Eivor's head, but Rasmus leapt upon him and rained down blows with the poker, shouting all the while. The Beast backhanded him and spun straight into another punch square in the face, then grabbed the poker, ripped it from Ras's grip, and threw it across the room. Rasmus landed several punches, but the Beast was unmoved and shoved him to the wall.

Eivor struggled to his feet. He picked up his dagger, lunged, and drove it deep behind the Beast's shoulder blade. The Beast straightened. Eivor pulled the dagger out to stab him again, and the Beast threw an elbow back, striking his temple. The cabin spun. Eivor stumbled, leaned onto the table, and steadied himself.

The Beast hammered Rasmus over and over with his fists, then hurled him toward Eivor. He crashed into the edge of the table headfirst and collapsed. The Beast grinned. Rasmus grabbed the edge of the table and pulled himself up. Blood trickled from the crown of his head, down his forehead, and into his left eye.

Eivor could barely keep his eyes open. He let go of the table, and his legs felt wobbly as he bent to pick up his dagger. The witch had doomed them.

No. *Rasmus* had doomed them. His temper with the Beast, his temper with the witch, *that's* what got them here. If the Beast wanted death, then maybe that's what it deserved.

Rasmus put up his fists and approached the Beast, but Eivor loomed behind him. He thrust his dagger forward, straight into his brother's back.

Rasmus staggered toward the Beast, clutching at the dagger. He turned slowly.

"Ei...Eivor?" He dropped to his knees.

Tears filled Rasmus's eyes. "I'm sorry."

Rasmus fell forward onto his face. Eivor knelt beside him, weeping, apologizing. He draped himself across his brother's back.

The Beast stepped over Rasmus's legs. He walked around the table and out the door.

"No!" Eivor shouted. "You don't get to leave it like this!" He chased the Beast out the door, but there was no sign of him in the darkness. Eivor found his footsteps. He followed them in the moonlight for six paces. Seven.

Then nothing.

Eivor built a pyre for his brother with half the witch's firewood and set it alight as the first rays of sunrise spilled across the mountainside. He watched it burn well into the morning, then went into the cabin and propped the table against the shattered door to keep out the cold.

He tended to the fireplace, but he didn't much feel like eating. His arm hurt, and he worried the bone would need to be set again. He found some clothing and furs he could lash together to get down the mountain, but for the moment he just sat and stared at the fire. He found a whetstone in the cabinet, and he set it on his lap. He worked his dagger up and down, up and down, as he waited.

Tonight, the Beast would return, or it would not. Or the witch would return, perhaps with a posse to flush him out of her home. If he had to fight again, so be it. If it was over, he would trek down to the valley and start over.

After a time, he fell asleep.

"Wake up!"

A woman's voice, echoing through the cabin. His head snapped around one way, then the other. The cabin was dark, empty, the fire low. He stood and the whetstone thumped to the floor beside his dagger. He crouched to pick up the blade, then went to the window.

The night was still, quiet, and dark.

Boom.

Eivor leapt away from the door and flipped his dagger into a reverse grip.

Boom! The remains of the door rattled, and the table slid several inches.

"I knew you'd return, demon! Let's finish this!"

A bare foot crashed through the door and kicked the table

away. Pale fingers curled around the jamb and pulled a pale visage through. Rasmus bared his teeth, his eyes black and empty, his flesh ashen, his hair matted with black blood.

Eivor lowered his dagger and wept.

Shades of Ruin

Scott Schmidt

The journeyman stopped his stride at the edge of a stoney ridge. He looked down, then drank deeply from his water pouch, the last drops spilling down his raven beard. The canyon below stretched far into the earth with a river grazing peacefully along the bottom.

With the sun sweating his traveling leathers through, he spent the rest of the day blazing trail down into the gorge with sword and axe.

That night he made camp on a sandbar and slept lightly next to a fire of driftwood, the rustling river awash in the light of a silver moon.

Once in the night he awoke to what he thought were shouts of battle. He lay alert for some time, but drifted off after hearing no more.

He broke camp just before sunrise, setting off down the valley as the sun stoked the earthly chamber until it blazed the red of a blacksmith's forge. He tramped the river bottom for half a day more before it fell off into a shadowy cavern that began to jut and veer like the branches of a gnarled oak.

His awe was audible when he reached the river's point of termination at a waterfall that gushed into a vast crater. At the center of the immeasurable expanse stood a great structure hewn from bedrock. It resembled a great colosseum, a remnant from another age.

He searched for a path but could find only one way down as he peered over the rim at the pool far below. It bubbled and churned from the falls, making any judgment of its depth uncertain.

But the journeyman saw no other way.

He untied his foot leathers and secured his sword and axe to his pack with the laces. Then, with his only belongings in this world held tightly to his chest, a chest that beat wildly with the thunder of his heart, he sprang into a run and dove over the water's edge.

A moment later, he pulled himself from the crashing pool. He sat upon the rocky shore to catch his breath and wrung the cold water from his long hair.

The colosseum loomed before him, its infinite columns and archways pitching deep pockets of darkness and shadow.

He scanned the canyon floor but found no other trace of civilization. This was no lost city struck by calamity and strife, just a single arena, silent and solitary.

He recalled the sounds from the night before, and a shiver rippled beneath his bronzed flesh.

But, with no other path before him, he dressed and set out toward the ruins, eyes agaze like a hawk perched over a field.

The journeyman circled the colosseum for an hour or more before coming to the dilapidated skeleton of an iron gate, rusted and bent beyond purpose. He wasn't the first one in or out of this arena.

He stepped gingerly through the ancient arch, careful to restrict his sound upon the sand, but even his quiet step sent an echo out into the vast stone stadium. He halted and searched the interior for an acknowledgement of his presence. None forthcoming, he continued across the main stage of the grand theater.

Littering the colosseum's floor was a myriad of bones, weapons, and armor, remnants of glories past. Several paces ahead, he spied a curious skull and made toward it, for he had never seen its like. Before he could get close to inspect it, he heard a crunch of sand underfoot that wasn't his own.

He whirled with lifted sword but was struck with a blinding blow that laid him flat upon the ground.

He awoke shortly to the dull roar of a cheering crowd.

A groan issued from the journeyman's throat. His thoughts were muddled as the unmistakable sound of people in this abandoned place left him confused.

His eyes fluttered against a glare of light passing through the iron bars that surrounded him. As his hand passed over the swollen knot on his forehead, he noticed the heavy manacles at his wrists.

He was a prisoner.

The crowd roared once more, but this time screams of agony rose above them. And then something deep and guttural.

Something bestial.

Words spoken from beyond the confines of his cell startled him further.

"Would have been better off had they killed you outright, barbarian," croaked a withered voice.

"Call me that again and I'll run you through," the journeyman said, rising to his feet.

"Aye? With what?" the voice cackled, then sputtered into a wheezing cough.

It was a fair point. He had been stripped of his weapons, left with only his leather breeches. Whatever his captors' intent, they didn't plan for him to be well prepared for it.

"Sounds like I won't have to, old man. That cough tells me you haven't long anyway."

"Oh, I'll outlast you, warrior. They'll be along for you shortly."

The journeyman gripped the iron bars and peered into the gloom of the dungeon to find the old man, but all he could see was a withered arm, barely more than bone, hanging loose between the bars of a cell like his own.

"Who will be along?" shouted the journeyman. "What is this place?"

The old man spoke no more.

"Answer me!" he cursed, slamming his chains against the cell.

In response, the arm curled back into the shadows as if it was never there.

The journeyman heard then the heavy clang of a thrown latch, followed by feet marching toward him.

He was thrust beyond the gate by spearpoint. The harsh light of day blinded him and washed the chill from his bare skin as he climbed the ramp leading to the arena floor.

All along the march from his cell, the noise of the crowd swelled. Now it boomed as he stepped out upon the ancient battlefield in full view of those gathered.

He turned full circle, an expression of bewilderment on his face. He hadn't seen a soul since passing through the lonely mountain fort at the edge of the western mountains. He knew the stains of civilization when he saw them, and this land had been cleansed of them long ago. This colosseum was but bones in a wasteland.

Yet, here were thousands of people lining the stadium, laughing and shouting, drinking and dancing. And now their attention became fixed on him.

From their mouths spilled strange words the journeyman had never heard spoken. He had seen it written on dusty scrolls, but never uttered. This was a dead language.

But while he didn't know the words, their intent was obvious. He was their sport, their entertainment, and after a survey of the area, littered with the detritus of battle, he knew the nature of the performance expected of him.

He cursed the chain at his wrists as he began scampering across the field in search of a weapon he could wield despite his bonds. He came to a stiff corpse and turned it over in search of a blade or bludgeon. The dead man's garb was of a tribe the journeyman recognized, but he knew not the weapon that had made the gaping wound in his chest.

With nothing of worth about, he turned to another corpse. This one bore the markings of a soldier in the emperor's army. That was the only aspect of the body he could make out as the man's frame was crushed as if trampled in a cavalry charge.

The glint of steel caught his eye beneath the mangled corpse, and he dug an ivory-handled short blade from beneath the blood-caked dirt. He recognized it as the sword of the empire, a dreaded weapon that had sent more people to hell than even the gods. He swung the blade with his manacled hands, gauging his reach and power despite the restraints.

Then, his blood froze and his breath ceased as a primal roar cut through the stadium's deafening din.

The crowd erupted into a unified cheer, for they knew what was coming.

The journeyman crouched low and skirted to the edge of

the arena, an inevitable fear welling up inside him. He heard the slam of a gate nearby and knew that something had been unleashed.

Suddenly, the ground began to stir with the force of a stampede, and he witnessed an unfathomable beast thunder into the arena from below.

It was dark as starless night with the brutish features of a bovine. It bore a wicked pair of black horns that caught the shine of the intermittent sun. Its four giant hooves, large as tree trunks, pummeled the earth to dust.

And then the mighty creature pulled its gallop up short and rose to stand on two legs. The journeyman looked on in horror as he saw that it had the torso of a man. When the demon locked its gaze upon him, he feared it had the soul of one as well.

The beast bound into a mad charge toward him, bellowing a sound like that of an ancient war horn.

He had been charged by animals before, but never one so large as this bullman. In any case, his only course was to dive at the last second to clear the beast's ruinous path. He realized then the fate of the soldier whose blade he wielded.

The journeyman crouched and stood firm despite the trembling earth. His sword tip pointed out toward his foe, ready to stab at the eyes and neck of the beast, but he knew if the monster came that near, it would be his doom.

With the sound of the crowd swallowed by the clack of the bullman's thundering hooves, the journeyman held as still as he could hope. Then, when the beast took up nearly all his vision, he sprang with the grace of an elk.

But this was no lumbering prairie animal he faced. This was a monster, bred in the blackest pit of hell to kill, maim, and wreak vengeance upon the land.

At the last moment, the bullman shifted its weight and caught the journeyman's body with its rippling shoulder.

As he bounced across the sand from the blow, he tumbled through the rotted wreckage of a sunken chariot. He came to one knee amidst its shattered remains, gasping for air in the billowing dust.

The beast roared and the crowd cheered. It was coming for him once more, and he knew he had no hope of escaping its terrible charge.

A shape caught his eye amongst the wreck, and he darted for it, his fingers seeking the metal edge of a battered bronze shield. He could hear the bullman's heavy snorts growing closer as he wrenched it from the debris.

In one fluid motion, the journeyman freed the shield and let it fly at his adversary. The heavy disc sailed true and smashed into the bullman's snout, spit and blood gushing from the impact. It reared and howled, and the crowd groaned.

The bullman staggered like a drunk, shaking its massive head to clear away the pain, then found its rage once more as its prey came into view.

The journeyman thought of the mountain bears of the far north, tall as trees, killers at the apex, as the bullman stalked toward him on two hooves. He had caused it harm, and it respected him now, which made it even more dangerous.

As the beast stomped in, the journeyman saw the sword he had lost. He thought to circle around but knew he couldn't expect to evade the giant for long. He thought no more and bolted for the weapon.

The bullman huffed and rushed forward, but not in time to stop the man from grasping the blade. Close enough to smell the beast, he dove under its towering legs. He had visions of his impalement upon both horns, pinned to the floor of the arena, another victim of this doom lair.

But the bullman struck only the hard crust of earth. The journeyman was clear of the beast's fury.

In the seconds he had left to act, he fixed upon one monstrous leg and stabbed upward into the meaty thigh, then dashed away.

When he looked back, the bullman had fallen to a knee, blood spurting from the sword bite. It rose despite the wound and came after him, but he could see it was hindered.

He gave the beast a wide berth, and the two danced in this manner for several minutes, the journeyman batting at the tips of its horns as it swung them in his direction.

He kept his movement to the left, forcing it to lead with its wounded leg. Several times he was able to weave through its defense and strike. After a time, the beast was covered in shallow stab wounds, blood trickling out to wet its black coat.

By now, the crowd had grown tepid and the sun waned, the shadows of the colosseum casting long and dark. The beast before him was not the same one that had thundered out a short time ago. It staggered from blood loss and huddled in defense instead of striking out at him.

The sword had taught it fear.

The journeyman could finish the beast, but he knew it would need coaxing. Though gravely wounded, its hatred for him was so great that after a clever feint, the bullman lurched out with a wild swing of its horns.

The journeyman felt the twin points slice the air as he leaned out of reach. As the bullman stumbled past, he leapt onto its back. The beast reared to toss the man, but he had already clambered onto its shoulders and raised the sword to strike.

He drove the blade to the hilt, down into the bullman's neck, and felt the beast go slack as he rode it down, dead before it hit the floor. He gathered himself slowly as blood pooled beneath it.

He looked to the crowd then, deathly silent. Some stared in disbelief while others rose to leave. Then, he watched them fade and disappear, vanishing into the twilight one by one until the arena was again empty and hollow, a carapace of its former glory.

He looked to the bullman and saw not the slain corpse of the beast but only a monstrous, sun-bleached skull, sunken in the sand. His sword rusted before his eyes, and the chains at his wrists crumpled to dust.

The journeyman forwent contemplation of what had just befallen him and moved to escape the haunted place. He tossed the sword to the ground and found his way to the gates. A chill rippled down his spine as he found his belongings in the corridor leading out, but he retrieved them nonetheless.

Then, as day fell to night, he shouldered his pack and journeyed on.

Bones and All

JimmyZ Johnston

It's not just the color of a bleached skull reflecting back at her, it is Rie'ma's skull. Laid bare for all to see. Her long white hair that used to flow below her shoulders is gone. The blue eyes her mother told her were a portal to the sea—and every time she looked into them she could tell how water was going to be pivotal in her child's life—those too were gone. She had no idea how it was possible she could still see without them.

Slashing the water with the fleshless bony talons of her hand she cursed. Shattering the reflection as her hand broke the surface of the river, but just as quickly the water regained the calm flow and she found the empty sockets where her eyes should be staring back at her.

Slowly she stood. Bones grinding against bones without soft tissue between them to soften the connection, without muscles and tendons to guide them. The memory of them seemingly enough to make not just her legs work, but all of her. Her fingers curled curiously around the hilt of the sword she held. Flexed her wrist and the sword sung through the air in a well practiced strike. A flick here. A twist there. All the moves and motions of an experienced swordswoman.

She looked to the north, seeing the landscape around her even though her eyes were no longer in place. She saw with a clarity she never had in life. Not that her vision was bad before, but now, standing quietly she watched across the river as a hawk dove from the sky, plucking an unsuspecting mouse from the grass.

Food. It had been seven sunrises since she escaped from the slavers who had been forcing her to work. In all that time she had not thought about eating, nor during her time in their pits. She had teeth to gnaw and gnash, and could easily chew meat and fruits, but what would become of it. There was no belly needing to be filled. There was no hunger needing to be sated. There was no flesh beneath the jaw to hold the food and no tongue to help push it down the throat which too was no longer.

Every thought simply leading to questions. Questions without answers she could conceive. A single name came to mind. Ni'ell. They had been close as children, until Ni had been forced to leave the care of her father to go learn from her sorcerer mother. A mother Ni'ell hadn't seen since a few months after her birth. And Rie'ma had never met.

Sword in hand, Rie'ma was ready to resume her trek. The sword no longer gleamed in the sunlight. Dried blood clung to the steel. She sliced it into the water before turning back to her journey. Crimson droplets fell from the blade as she walked. Slowly the blade regained its shine.

For now.

The passage of time no longer mattered to Rie'ma. With no muscles to tire, no hunger to sate, no thirst to quench. She simply kept marching to the north.

On the tenth day of her march, she was approached by a pack of hungry wolves. Seven in all. Their fur a combination of black and grey. The better to hide in the shadows and sneak up on unsuspecting prey. She took up a defensive position, but the wolves didn't attack.

One by one the smaller wolves crept close to her, sniffed, and then retreated.

Rie'ma didn't let down her guard, but she was confused by their actions.

The alpha wolf slowly padded across the grass. Circling around and smelling. Rie'ma pivoting as it circled, never allowing it to be in a flanking position. Instinctively the alpha lowered its nose to her foot to sniff, yet never taking its eyes off the sword being held steadily in striking distance.

Slowly raising his snout, the nose twitched repeatedly as it tracked deliberately up along her leg. Rie'ma noticed for the first time the large unnatural protrusion on her shin, where she had broken it as a child playing with Ni'ell. A springtime pain that went away, yet hounded her whenever bad weather approached for the rest of her life. For a moment she wondered whether it would still affect her when the weather changed, but that thought was rapidly pushed from her mind as she recalled the threat surrounding her.

After another tense minute, the Alpha turned its back to Rie'ma and trotted away. The pack slinking after.

Realization dawned on her in the aftermath of the encounter. No flesh. No meat. The only concern for the Alpha and his packmates is survival. Finding food. A lone skeleton was of no interest to them, and luckily her patience and discipline prevented it from turning into a meaningless fight.

She doubted that her journey would continue without any confrontation. Animals may see no use in challenging her, but surely humanity would not simply allow her to walk away as easily.

The sun had barely travelled more than a few hours across the cloudy sky before she realized how right she was.

A wooden bridge appeared in the distance crossing the river. She saw no traffic moving on it or toward it, so kept on.

Within twenty feet of the road, a voice startled her, causing her to pause.

"What the hell do we have here? Let's have ourselves a bit of fun."

Tracking towards the voice, she saw a group of three obvious brigands standing at the edge of the treeline waiting to waylay unprotected travellers.

"Gareth, take that monstrosity down," continued the presumed leader. He stood with one hand resting casually on his sword handle.

The man presumably known as Gareth stepped forward with a long bow in hand, nocked an arrow, and drew back the bow string. Seconds later Rie'ma saw the arrow flying towards her. The suddenness of the attack kept her standing still as the arrow struck her in the chest. Or rather didn't. It passed through her rib cage unobstructed by the flesh and organs it would have lodged in.

A bellow of laughter rang out from the leader.

"Come now Gareth, surely you can do better than that," he taunted.

Gareth stepped closer and launched another arrow her direction.

The results identical.

She began moving towards him as he continued to advance on her.

Another arrow passed through her just above her pelvic bone.

"Try something more solid. You need a larger target. Go for the head."

Gareth planted himself and with a look of concentration on his face, once again took aim.

Now barely a dozen feet away from her as the arrow took

flight. This one struck her forcefully directly between the eyes. The wooden shaft splintered on impact as the steel tip embedded itself into her skull. The impact snapping her head back, redirecting her gaze to the billowing clouds passing overhead, carried by winds that only soared high in the sky.

"It broke mah bloody arrow," Gareth whined, glancing back towards his two idle companions.

"You still have your misses out in the field to go pick up," the leader laughed. "Knock that dead thing over as you go to retrieve them."

Rie'ma slowly lowered her head just as Gareth got to within five feet of her. As he stepped towards her to shove her to the ground, she raised her sword and plunged the sharp steel into his belly with an upward thrust. Through the stomach, slicing through a lung and piercing into Gareth's heart. Like him, she missed the protective rib bones.

Surprise registered in his eyes as blood traveled up his throat and spilled from between his lips. A wet squelching sound broke the silence of the moment as she pulled the sword out. Gareth's legs supported him for less than a second before buckling beneath his weaght. He fell to the ground. Dead.

Lowering her head to look at the now lifeless body beneath her, the arrowhead and broken shaft dislodged from her skull. Twisting in the air with the weight of the steel so it landed point first in Gareth's thigh.

"Brother," cried out the other brigand as he ran towards the fallen body, withdrawing a long heavy club from beneath his cloak.

Rie'ma stepped back with her right foot, adopting a defensive stance and waiting as the brigand ran at her.

He swung wildly, missing her as she sidestepped his attack. As he passed by, her blade swung easily at his exposed back. A glancing strike, but still drawing blood.

He turned. Rage in his eyes, but a calm now in the rest of his face.

"Abomination. You are an unholy abomination. You took my brother from me, but I will make sure it was the last thing you ever did."

Stepping in to her reach, he swung the club. It connected hard with rib bones.

She felt the bones break. No. She saw them break. She heard them break. But there were no nerves to feel pain. The club missed her spine but sent a spray of bone shards across the grass. Her sword sang through the air in a responsive attack that she knew so well her muscles performed it automatically. Except she no longer had muscles. The memory of long gone muscles kept working even in this after life she was experiencing.

The cut she just made in his leg bled profusely, but didn't slow him down. It was a lethal blow, she knew. Even if he didn't realize it yet. He swung again, this time aiming for her sword arm. And connecting.

She watched as her arm snapped in half. Bone dust filling the air as her now detached arm fled from her body taking her hand and sword with it.

"Bill, ya damn fool," yelled the leader. "That cut on your leg..."

It was the last thing she heard him say as the club smashed into her head, knocking her to the ground. A pyrhhic victory though as Bill tumbled to the ground alongside her.

A grin spread across her face. Or would have. She didn't know what a grinning skull would look like, but she knew she had killed him the second her sword penetrated his leg.

Darkness overtook her vision.

And then the darkness returned to her vision.

No longer the darkness of death. The pinpricks in the night sky offered a pittance of light for her.

Where her skull had been crushed, she could feel it was whole once again. Raising her hands, she gently felt the shape of her head. Fingertips probing into the smooth recesses designed for her eyes, brushing briefly past the awkward and ugly feeling hole where her nose should be, scratching against teeth as her jaw bone dropped slightly. Pulling her hands away, she saw that both hands were part of her again. The damage done by the brigand's club had somehow healed itself. A most unnatural magic it was that kept her together and apparently stitched her back together when she fell apart. All the more reason to reach Ni'ell to try and figure out what happened to her.

She laid her head back looking at the night sky above.

The two lifelong friends would often lie in the grass at night watching as the lights above would appear and begin to shine. That's what they were doing the last night. Her last night. The final hours before Ni'ell would turn to her sixteenth year and be leaving to join her mother.

The two girls were lying on their backs in the short grass. Most of the fields in Nu'ma still had grass so high that they wouldn't be able to see each other, but that morning Ge'ray had driven his cows to this field to graze. Leaving patches that were perfect for them to lie next to each other. Normally they would alternate between gazing at the night sky and each other. Tonight though they both found it harder to look at one other.

"I shall miss this," Ni'ell said quietly.

"Childhood's End... It comes for us all. You get yours first though," Rie'ma replied.

"Only by a few days. Don't play the 'You're so old' bit with me. Not tonight."

"It's not like you haven't played the 'You're so young' bit with me in the past. Fairly often actually."

They both laughed. It was not the easy laughter they had a lifetime of. It felt forced in a way it never before had. And ended quickly.

"Not tonight..." Ni'ell whispered.

Silence hung between them, only broken when the wind changed. Bringing with it the heavy stench of fresh cow dung. It had only taken one time not checking the grass for dung. One time of Ni'ell falling heavily into the grass and landing in the rather fragrant recent droppings from a cow.

"When must you leave?"

"Rie, you know already. Father will have me on the road before the sun rises. We have to reach Mother before the sun sets on my sixteenth."

"It's the ritual," they both said quietly and simultaneously.

"I am not even supposed to be here now. He will be cross with me, but he also knew there was no way he could have prevented me from being here one last time. Seeing you one last time."

"One last time..."

"And you will soon be busy with your training with your father. A woman of the watch! You will hardly even notice I'm gone," Ni'ell said, trying to convince herself.

"It's not like I don't already train with him every day. It will be the same for me. I will still be here. Sleeping in the same bed, eating the same food, wearing the same clothes. Always practical clothes as father insists. I don't get to wear the pretty and fun dresses like you," Rie'ma said trying to hold back tears and failing.

"You will. I can't take them with me. I left them outside behind your home. You can wear them in your room before slumber. And always remember me..."

"Ni, you know I could never forget you. You have been my life."

———————————————

Rie'ma couldn't remember how that night ended. Still looking upwards at the night sky, she silently wept for her friend. No tears came, as none could. Another thing taken from her in the monstrous state she now existed in. The harsh blackness of the night was losing its edge. As the sun began to rise, Ri'ema decided she would go into the darkness and cover of the woods and continue her journey through the daytime. Keeping an eye out not just for the seedier elements like brigands, but anyone who might be inclined to confront the monster she had become.

Standing, she surveyed the area around her. Two bodies remained on the ground at her feet. The brigand leader must have stripped all value from his companions. Or at least as much as he could carry. The bow and her sword were gone. The boots from both men, and the pants from the archer. Perhaps the damage she had done to the club wielding brigand was too much to try and repair.

Rie'ma bent and retrieved the club. Nowhere near as fine a weapon as the sword she had been using, but best not to be unarmed. And a lesson learned the hard way. Be wary. Avoid contact with others.

Perhaps traveling in the night would be best to keep her hidden.

She knew the bridge though. It was two days south from the village she lived in. The bridge that went to the larger town of Highvell. A place her father went to trade every tenth nightfall. She traveled with him on one occasion. And quickly learned that she preferred her home and village she was born in. Nu'ma may not be as big as Highvell, but to her that made it much better.

Edging towards the treeline, she resumed her journey north.

She held on to hope though. If anyone could help it would be Ni'ell. When Ni'ell turned sixteen her father sent her off to train with her mother. Rie'ma only knew that Ni'ell's mother was some sorcerer.

Uncertainty now the constant companion for her. What would happen when she found Ni'ell?

Journeying through the woods was a much better choice. Very few people ventured too deep into the woods, so she managed to travel without stopping for two days unaccosted. She knew that she was deep in the woods to the East of Nu'ma. She was no longer certain of where she was heading, only that she felt like she was going the right direction.

The dense forest she had been in lightened a bit as she reached a place that felt familiar. Ahead she could see the outline of a rather large building. The size of a decent inn, but no inn could thrive so far from a road. With no second level, it definitely wasn't an inn of any sort. Solid walls all around, not even shutters on the side to allow light and air in. There were signs of a few trails used on occasion, but no road.

Rie'ma cautiously approached the building. Just as she was about to leave the cover of the trees, she saw a figure angrily approach the front door from the opposite side of the building. Unaware he was being observed, he barely paused as he forcefully opened the front door.

"Necromancer, " he bellowed as he crossed the threshold.

Rie'ma instantly recognized the voice. The third of the brigands that tried to kill her. After he disappeared from view, she closed the distance between her and the open door.

"What is it you want Salo? You come empty-handed and

angry," a disembodied voice responded. A woman's voice Rie'ma thought she recognized. She leaned her back against the wall next to the door and eavesdropped on the conversation.

"Empty handed? You have no idea how true that is. I am more than empty handed, I am down two men!"

"How are your men my concern?"

"One of your abominations killed them!"

"Absurd. They leave here with one purpose, which you are well aware of."

"Never the less... Me and two of my men came across one at the bridge to Highvell."

"And it killed your men."

"Aye, it did. Wielding a sword, it cut them both down with hardly any effort."

"Salo," the female voice responded rising in anger as she did. "We have a purely transactional relationship. You bring me bodies and I pay you. There is nothing more to it. I have no care for the troubles you claim to have outside of my door. If you have nothing to offer me today, then I suggest you take your leave."

Rie'ma tightened her grip on the club she held. Anger rising in her. Had she eyes, they would have been narrowed. Had she lips, they would have been tight in a grimace. But she did have teeth, and they were grinding hard enough to threaten cracking a molar.

Bursting through the open doorway, Rie'ma let out a silent scream as she swung the club at Salo. Her friend Ni'ell looked in quiet wonder as the club slammed into Salo's shoulder. Striking with such force that the humerus bone broke free from its home in the shoulder blade and his clavicle ruptured through both skin and shirt pointing straight up into his ear. Blood splattered from the impact as Salo was spun around. His right arm useless, not just in this fight, but forever more.

Angry, Rie'ma pointed the club accusingly at Ni'ell and then back at Salo.

Salo fumbled, trying to draw his sword wrong-handed and only succeeding in dropping it to the floor.

Rie'ma turned her attention fully back to Salo. Swinging the club at his head, he raised his left arm instinctively protecting his face. The club broke three fingers on his hand along with a dozen other bones in the hand and wrist, all while pushing his own hand into his nose.

Ni'ell calmly retreated and grabbed some components from a shelf. Mixing a powder as she chanted.

Rie'ma swung into Salo's face. The crack of his skull fracturing momentarily drowning out Ni'ell's quiet casting. One of Salo's eyes popped out and dangled close enough to his lips that he could have licked it. The light of life had gone out in his other eye. He still stood, but that was just a temporary defiance of gravity. Corrected instantly with one last swing from the club into his skull.

Rie'ma turned towards Ni'ell, bright crimson blood spattered all over the stark white of her bones. Blood dripped from the club to the floor as Rie'ma took slow steps forward.

Scooping the powder she had haphazardly mixed into her hand, and speaking a final word, Ni'ell blew the dust into Rie'ma's face.

A fine blue cloud obscured her vision and Rie'ma began choking and coughing. Within seconds, the cloud had dispersed completely.

"Aref be damned…What was that?" Rie'ma asked between coughs.

Startled at the sound of her words, she took a step back from Ni'ell.

"I have placed a spell upon you to let you simulate speaking.

It isn't as good as the natural voice you were born with, and sounds rather stiff."

"I…. can talk?"

"Yes you can. And I'm sure you have many questions. As do I," Ni'ell said soothingly.

"How…" the question hung in the air between them. Rie'ma didn't know how to ask all the things racing through her mind right now.

"It is a long story, and I am truly sorry you are having to hear it ever. Much less like this. I discovered when I went to learn from my mother that she dealt not just with arcane energies, but specifically with reanimating the dead. Giving them the ability to walk again, and engage in simple tasks. Many regions employ her services to gain a slave labor force that needs never be fed or paid and can work without rest."

"You did this? To me?"

"I did. The man you just killed is one of many who bring freshly dead to us for processing. He brought you to us one day. I broke down and cried when I saw you. My mother dismissed me and began the process. Removing the flesh from the dead. I couldn't bring myself to help. It is a gruesome and foul aspect at the best of times. A simple spell does the work of removing the flesh. But processing it afterwards and selling it. Let's just say I shall never again eat anything which I have not seen caught and killed with my own eyes."

"Why?"

Ni'ell began crying as she continued. "You were already dead when they brought you here. There was nothing we could do to help you. I was able to add some to the spells giving you an afterlife. The memories that we shared together until I left. Extra protection to keep you from harm."

"To live like this. He called me an abomination."

"That is not what you are. You are my best friend. You were my life."

"No," screamed Rie'ma.

The club still in hand, she lashed out towards Ni'ell. Missing her friend by inches.

Ni'ell fell to the ground sobbing.

"I couldn't live in a world knowing you were dead. It was the only way," Ni'ell managed between sobs.

Rie'ma stooped down to where the dead brigand fell in a pool of blood. Dipping her stark white skeletal fingers into the blood and lifting the dripping fluid into the air, she turned towards Ni'ell.

"This, " she began while caressing her bloody fingers across Ni'ell's face, "is not the mark of a friend."

Ni'ell looked up from her knees, a drop of blood balancing dangerously on her quivering lower lip. Tears streaking through the blood on her cheeks. "Forgive me."

Without another word, Rie'ma turned and left.

The Dog in the Corner

Stephen Graham Jones

Lorn liked to imagine daylight as wave after wave of granular softness sifting down over the forest, the village, his master's roof. Himself. He liked to believe that when he breathed in through his nose in that concentrated, tasting way, he could actually smell this "sun" he had never seen, had only felt on the skin of his back, and in the heat it left on tools, and the packed dirt of the trail.

Lorn had been born in a darkened hut, and the master had scooped his eyes out with a spoon fresh from the fire, so it would cauterize the holes. Because babies shouldn't bleed from the face that much at birth. Not if they're going to be their master's best dog.

The reason for taking Lorn's eyes so early was so he could learn to navigate the world by scent alone. Which real, actual dogs could do just fine, without having to lose their sight.

But people, the master explained after training, people need scent to be their eyes, if it has any hope of becoming sensitive enough to be used. What Lorn's master was doing was shaping a dog that also had language. Teaching a boy to follow a trail with his nose was far easier than teaching a dog to speak—though, on his own, Lorn had sniffed out those experiments as well.

How they were different was that, unlike Lorn, they'd originally been dogs. But, unlike Lorn, they'd been banished from the master's fire for being failures. Because his incantations and his staff kept them from ever crossing his threshold again, they lived out past the trees, spitting human words that were meaningless to them.

The dogs the master had shaped with his muttered incantations and the whispering staff that kept him alive far longer than he should be, they now lived out in the woods, where he had banished them for being failures. Furtive creatures, who instead of barking or growling would spit words in warning, but those words were meaningless.

One night after dark, Lorn had crept outside while his master was captivated with another of his ancient tomes, and he had followed his nose to one of these dogs. She had just whelped, so the scent was a beacon. She curled her lips at Lorn but backed off when he nosed in, to identify each of these pups such that he would know them for as long as they lived. It was his duty to keep track of everything out here, that might someday threaten his master.

Three days after that, just checking the perimeter, relishing the freedom his master allowed him, Lorn had keyed on blood, and found a large man sitting against a tree, his breath fast and shallow. The man swung his great, foul-smelling sword when he realized he wasn't alone, but Lorn stayed out of its reach easily.

The oil and sweat on the man's skin was a story of strife and battle, and there was a seething infection wafting out from the man's midsection, both harsh and tangy. It curled Lorn's nose but also made his drool run.

Lorn stood unsteadily on two feet by his master's workbench and waited for him to look up, ready for Lorn's report.

They went out to the dying man together, the master walking with his staff, wearing his dusty robe, Lorn padding ahead on all fours so any scents he needed to read would be closer.

"Chexyzma," the master said, about the man.

His name, Lorn presumed. In his head, he placed the name alongside the man's scent, now that he had both of them together.

"What is that...*thing*?" this dying man asked, and when he pointed to Lorn, Lorn recognized the gesture by the way the desperate pungency under the dying man billowed out like a shout.

"Worry not about Lorn," the master said, lowering his palm to the crown of Lorn's head.

Lorn pushed his head up, into the master's hand.

"And what is that you have there?" the master asked, squatting to the man's sitting height.

Lorn heard the man's great, bitter-smelling sword drag around to his other side, to keep it from the master's grasp.

"You don't even know, do you?" the master asked, and how Lorn knew the master was grinning was that some more of his sweet breath escaped.

"It's not for you," the dying man said. "It's mine. I found it."

"And you're studied in how to wield an instrument of the old metal?"

"Like this," the dying man said, and Lorn heard the sword slice through the air.

The master chuckled about this, then instructed Lorn to stay here for the night, and alert him when the time was right.

Lorn padded just out of reach of the dying's man sword, but well within his scent.

In this way Lorn came to know the village, which he had only ever heard from a distance, at night, its smell so cacophonous it was almost meaningless.

"So he gave up on the bears, then, did he?" the dying man said to Lorn.

Lorn didn't answer, knew he wasn't to talk to this dying man.

There were bears in the woods, yes. Lorn had inhaled deeply

from their tracks, and knew from the scent of blood between their great clawed toes the violence they could do.

"I would say you'll—bring him a nice bag of coin," the dying man said between spasms of pain. "Except for how you—look."

Lorn stopped pacing and, considered this. Not how he looked—his wasn't a world built around sight— but the bag of coin.

"Oh, he hasn't told you, has he?" the dying man said with a grunt, the injury in his gut festering with the most interesting tastes. Was there a trace of saliva in that wound? Lorn waited for it to connect to a scent in his head, but it was refusing.

Lorn stood to his full height and inhaled deeper, insisting that if he drew this taste on the air in deeply enough, it would register.

The man went on: "I think your master...does it for his own purposes, just to see if he has any limits, if he can...best nature again. But when the right buyer comes through, with the right gold, well...there's always another pup, another babe, another—whatever."

The man coughed, and Lorn both heard the blood spatter onto his chest and tasted it on the air, fresh and warm, swirling with history.

The man didn't say anything after that. It took him almost until dawn to die, at which point Lorn fetched the master.

"Well, well, well," the master said about the dead man, and stepped in, unplanted the sword from the ground by the tree. The upturned soil was loamy and rich to Lorn's nose, and the great plunging blade had bisected a worm, and that lone worm's bared insides were a scent Lorn wanted to live in. It made him gulp.

"You can have the rest, Lorn," the master said, and turned with the sword, leaving Lorn to bury his face in the dead man's gut, reel the slimy slick intestines out and bite through them for the man's last meal, which, surprisingly, didn't taste of the village, but somewhere further away, that Lorn couldn't even imagine.

For the next three days, the master worked on the sword at his workbench, and when he broke into the magic of the old metal at last, the smell on the air was bright blackness. Lorn cowered in the corner, mewling.

"Ah, yes, *yes*," the master said, holding the fizzing magic core up, probably to inspect it.

Lorn ceased breathing. He didn't want this scent inside him, as it might latch on, spread out, and consume him.

The master hammered the magic into some of his specially pure silver, muttering his incantations the whole while, the staff by the door whispering as well, and at the end of it, the master had...Lorn wasn't sure what. But it was smaller than the sword had been. A spike, of sorts?

"It's for the *ear*," the master explained, as if Lorn had asked. "That's what this twist here is for, see?"

Lorn cocked his head over now, for more.

The master chuckled, and when he did, Lorn caught the scent of the corruption in the head of the staff opening to listen, to taste, to... . . . Lorn had never been sure. The staff was older than him, older than the master, but the thing in the head of the staff was older than the wood it resided in, perhaps older than "wood" itself.

"To activate the senses beyond what we're born with," the master expounded grandly, "you have to scoop out the *eyes*, cut off the *tongue*, drive *this* into the ear and another up into the nose, and probably burn off the fingertips, wouldn't you think?"

Lorn just sat there in his corner and tried to imagine being a just-born infant, all your senses being ripped away from you, in hope of another one opening up.

"But first we need the right candidate, don't we?" the master said, and from the pressing silence, Lorn knew this was an order, a command.

"A babe," Lorn creaked.

"Yes," the master said, and so Lorn was off to skirt the road, move around downwind of the village, and read each of its inhabitants by the scent trailing off them.

On the second day, he smelled her. She had a life pulsing within her. A life about to emerge.

Lorn scampered back and stood by the master's chair until the master lifted his hand, giving Lorn permission to deliver his wonderful news.

When he did, the master nodded as if he'd known it all along—Lorn could hear his great beard rasping against his chest—and then, granting the only reward Lorn needed, he lowered his palm to Lorn's head again and, held it there in satisfaction.

Two days later, he left with his pack for the village.

After he was gone, Lorn woke in a startle, aware a new scent had invaded the home: the banished dogs. In the master's absence, they were inspecting the walls of the house. Lorn wanted to burst through the door and scream at them, but the latch slowed him down, as it always did. By the time he stepped out, immediately dropping to all fours, the dogs were gone. But they'd left their taste on the air. Two of them shared a scent with the newborn pups he'd nosed—must be from a previous litter. Lorn followed them as easily as if there were a string tied from them to him. In the mud just shy of the creek, he delicately placed his hand into one of their pawprints, and they matched perfectly. This was something his nose had been unable to tell him: that this litter of pups had human hands. The master's magics were strong indeed.

Being careful, moving slow, he followed them up to the rocks and the cliffs, and then to the mouth of a cave. It smelled cool and musty, and somehow fertile.

Lorn stood to taste it all better, really get it to set, and that was when he realized the mustiness was from an animal who never felt that soft, granular sunlight.

A bear.

"Lorn, is it?" the bear asked in its grumbly voice, and it was as if the cave itself were speaking, at first.

Lorn shrank away, arm raised to fend off the blow he knew had to be coming.

All around him now, he could smell the dogs, padding around on their human hands.

The bear didn't attack, though it did draw close enough to hook its great head under Lorn's chest and lift, propping him up on two feet so he could smell the armpits, the crotch.

"Do you come to live with us at last?" the bear asked.

The circling dogs muttered.

Lorn shook his head no, expelling the bear's taste from his nose to signal the insult this was, which was when he realized: the bear's fur hadn't scraped him, had it? Instead of fur, there'd been just a wrinkled, dry smoothness, not at all like the normal bears he'd encountered down the mountain.

"I'm sorry about your eyes," the bear said.

In response, Lorn inhaled deeply: *this* was the gift the master had bestowed upon him.

"You ate of the man who came for us," the bear said. "He wanted our pelt, to sell, but he found our claws instead." As punctuation, the bear galloped its claws on the stone apron they were standing on, and what Lorn smelled from that wasn't some version of his own nails, like he expected, but the old metal.

The master had built it into the bears, then. Their claws, probably their teeth.

"*Our* pelt?" Lorn asked, his voice creaky.

He had only ever spoken to his master.

"Come," the bear said, and then all at once Lorn smelled the rest of the bears rising from the fetid cave, his mind trying desperately to catalog each of them. Their scent was harsh and comforting at the same time, and the muscled parts of their hind legs rubbed against the sides of their bellies, the scent there so rich as to be overwhelming.

"Oh!" one of them, a female by her scent, said about Lorn.

"The old man's onto his own kind now," the first bear said.

They were talking about the burned caverns that should have been Lorn's eyes, he knew. He stopped breathing. He didn't want to be in this moment anymore.

"He returns," the bear said. His breath tasted of rotting meat and, yes, the old metal.

"Master?" Lorn asked.

"He's using the creature to light his way," the bear said, and Lorn hissed, hating how much farther eyes could see than noses could. But, once something's gone from sight, it's not gone from smell.

Lorn raised his nose, took a reading, and realized the bear was right: the leathery thing in the head of the staff had swelled, the cracks in its skin releasing some of its redolent power. It smelled of starshine, of a vastness that always left Lorn reeling.

"Go home now," the bear said, and when Lorn turned to pad away, the dogs parted for him and then followed him to the creek. No, they were *escorting* him, weren't they? Because he belonged in the world of men, not in the forest with the talking bears and the dogs with human hands for feet.

One of them said words to Lorn across the water. The words were meaningless, but still Lorn listened. There was something pleading to the tone, but at the end, he was pretty sure that was supposed to be a warning.

Lorn was waiting in his corner when his master opened the door.

In his scratchy rucksack was the scent of a struggling babe, still slathered in its own birthing. Lorn dutifully lodged the scent in his head, so he could track it forever.

The master extracted his new spike from the pouch at his belt and set it by the fire, and Lorn turned his face to that heat. He could feel it warming the back of the caverns that should hold his eyes, and for the first time, maybe because of the magic from the core of the sword, he sort of saw something: himself as an infant, a struggling pup, being extracted from his mother in a hut by the river down at the village, and the master stepping forward from his wall of shadows with a blunt spoon held low down by his thigh, everyone around the thatched bed slumping over asleep from a cascade of words the master was uttering, hissing to a part of them they didn't know they had anymore.

The Lorn in this vision looked up to the master's face like he had in life a thousand times and more, and, like every time, the master's face was swirling, indistinct. Smell can give you location, it can give you history, it can divulge intentions, but it can't map planes, it can't draw lines, it can't inhale the shape of a thing. Of a face. A person. A master.

All the same, Lorn inhaled deeply, and what was thick in the air was the terror the babe he had been was exuding. It was on his breath, it was wafting from his skin, it was dripping to the floor, and it was in his lungs, coming out and coming out.

Beyond the babe Lorn had been, the mother was reaching, she was rising, the master's uttered commands meaningless in the face of her need to be with Lorn, such that the master had to direct his staff at her to amplify his words, get them to lodge as he needed them to.

After that, first one small eyeball fell to the dirt floor, its bloody stalk keeping it from rolling, the individual motes of dust from the floor adhering to the sticky white, and then the other eyeball fell just the same, and with it all the colors of the world, which Lorn knew indirectly were a thing, but he could never imagine what they were, exactly. Was it like the differentiation between the scent of one field mouse and another? Was it the earth before the rain, and then after? Was it the way dry wood drank in smoke from the cookfire and held it, as if awaiting its turn under the pot? And then, when the master stepped in to pick the babe Lorn had been up, cradling him in his arm, the calloused heel of his bare foot—his order measured devotion in callouses—had inadvertently, carelessly come down onto that second eyeball, such that the dark, striated coin in it bulged and bulged, and then popped, spewing a clear jelly into the dirt.

A smell Lorn would taste again, he knew, when the master untied the top of this sack and, lifted this writhing babe up over the workbench, to scoop its eyes out just the same, to plunder its ears, to sear its tongue through at the base, and hold its delicate small fingers to the cooking pot long enough for the cooking flesh to release tendrils of smoke Lorn knew would make his mouth water.

And so would this child never see the sun, never hear the grass, never taste the creek water, never feel the rasp of the stone wall. Instead, it would be locked in its own head, reaching out and reaching out, either with the lost sense the master thought he could summon up, or with his grub of a mind, never knowing what it itself was, or what the world around it was, or why this had been done to it. It would be—Lorn clutched the wall to either side of his corner—it would become a minor version of the thing in the head of the master's staff, wouldn't it? Something that had to reach out in a way nothing else could, its intentions always dim and dull, but inexorable, too.

There wouldn't be a bag big enough for all the coin such a prize would bring.

Lorn shook his head no.

For his whole life, he had been thankful to the master for gifting him this nose, this ability to taste the world on the air. And he still was thankful. But that bulging tumor trapped in the head of that staff—that was another thing altogether, wasn't it?

Lorn walked his fingertips up his face and ran them gingerly into where his eyes should be, and his wrist grew wet against his mouth, because he was slavering for the treat he knew the master would allow him, momentarily: those two newborn eyeballs, let fall to the floor. And then, if Lorn was lucky, the master would even let him lick that spike, the bitter magic fizzing against his tongue in the best way, the protuberance in the staff holding quiet, to soak this moment in better.

Lorn hated himself for anticipating this.

He stood to his full height in the corner, and the master caught the movement. "Not now, boy!" he hissed.

But it had to be now.

Lorn twitched forward, dropping to all fours again, and for a moment he hesitated, lost in the mass of scents coming off the master's robes and feet, his hair and beard: the village. He had walked through it, his staff held high, everyone to either side falling asleep, to remember none of this.

Lorn could smell their bowels and bladders relaxing.

And he could smell the babe's fear, in that sack.

It was emitting an oily scent on the air for the mother—for her to rise, to come save it.

But that mother was just waking in her hut, Lorn knew. Just waking with no memory of having delivered this babe, never mind the blood and mess, the strain on her body, the ache in her muscles, the new emptiness inside her.

The master had been using the villagers in this way for

generations, now. Ever since he found the ageless thing in the staff at the base of a tree, and squatted down to inspect it, then looked up to see where it might have fallen from—a story he still told Lorn in the quiet of the night, proud of his discovery, and of the ingenuity it took to know to build a staff to hold this tumor from the stars.

One of Lorn's standing orders was that, on his patrols, if he ever found a formless leathery thing at the base of another tree, or in the creek, he was to run directly home and inform the master at once.

Would he, though?

Before, yes, without question.

Now, though...Lorn wasn't sure anymore.

What he did know, though he didn't want to, was that the floor of this corner he called his held the scents of previous versions of himself. He wasn't the first to crouch here in fear, wanting only to serve.

And now, with this babe the master had come back with, Lorn knew that neither would he be the last to crouch here. He was but one in a series.

"Down, Lorn!" the master called, pulling his leather glove on to extract the spike from the edge of the cook fire, and, while the master was looking, Lorn cowed in submission, but the moment the master leaned forward for that spike, Lorn surged across the room on his hands and feet.

He took the mouth of the rucksack in his teeth, hit the metal door with his shoulder, and—

It was latched.

Lorn reeled back, vaguely aware of the master shouting behind him, crossing the room for his staff, which, if he reached it, then this was the end.

Lorn wasn't a dog, though.

He had been born to stand on two feet.

He did, the rucksack still in his mouth, and fumbled the latch with his man hands until it popped open.

He turned back to the master, the top of the staff beginning to swell, the malignancy buried in that wood exposing itself to the air with a scent so harsh it made Lorn cringe, but he was already falling through the doorway, into the night.

On all fours he dashed away, scrambling through the pens.

He wasn't going anywhere, just "away," but when the sweet, crisp scent of the creek came to him, he heard other feet running alongside his own.

Other feet, and other hands.

The pack was running with him, mewling and shouting their incomprehensible words.

Behind them, the master was coming just as fast, his staff scorching the trees and grass at Lorn's heels.

He ran faster, holding his chin high to keep the bag from dragging, and when he splashed through the creek, he lost his footing and, fell and the master would have been upon him then, except the pack, as one, turned.

Lorn loped off, holding the rucksack in his arms now. He was unsteady on two feet, and half-blind, this far from the trail, this far from the ground and all its scents. But he ran all the same. Because the wind was behind him, he got the unwanted taste of the pack's blood, mixing with the creek water, because even dogs with human hands for feet were no match for the master when he was angry.

But they snarled and fought and hurled their meaningless words all the same.

Lorn had to drop back to all fours when he came to the rocks. He swung the rucksack over his shoulder and gathered the open end in his teeth, his head turned to the side for this awkward climb.

For this, he had to think, *last* climb.

Already he could hear the master's calloused feet on the rocks close behind him.

There was no going back, though.

There was only this.

Lorn pulled, climbed, slid, ran—and then he smelled it: the pulsing thing in the master's staff, whispering its corruption, its foul influence oozing out through the night. A moment later, the master was only a handbreadth behind. Less, less.

A finger hooked in the rucksack and Lorn pulled ahead, tumbling onto a flat, stony apron, one already swirling with Lorn's own scent, for he had stood here just the night previous.

"No more, Lorn!" the master boomed, his voice filling the night completely.

Lorn pulled the rucksack around to his chest, clutching it to him, and kicked back, back, and that was when he smelled it: the fetid, sweet stench of rotten meat, mixed with the old metal.

And the dried saliva on the skin of a bear that had never had fur.

"*You*," the first bear grumbled.

"You?" the master said back, slowing his advance, and then, for the first time in all his years, Lorn caught a scent wafting from the master he'd never expected to taste: fear.

It was oily and fast, desperate and wrong.

But it was so right, too.

Lorn opened his mouth, leaned forward, and screamed to the master about his lost eyes, screamed that he was a *person*, a man, that he had a mother before all this, that she should still have him, and then a great clawed paw came over his shoulder and pulled him back into the coolness of the cave, still clutching that rucksack. Outside, had Lorn had eyes to see, he would have seen the night becoming as day with this battle.

But he could *hear* it. The tumor from the stars bulging and writhing, the bear's metal claws and metal teeth carving and snapping, the folds and wrinkles in its furless skin opening and closing like little mouths breathing ancient scents out into the world.

When the master's insides finally spilled, and then spilled again, Lorn *smelled* it, them, and heard them splashing down on the stone. Unsure what might come next, he curled himself more tightly over that rucksack and opened it with his teeth, breathing in the scent of this newborn babe, breathing back his own taste, and he laughed the littlest bit, then, for the first time in years and years.

Not because he had any sense what tomorrow might hold, but because it wouldn't be the same as yesterday.

Not anymore.

Osanobua's Garden

Justin C. Key

The 9,483rd year under Osanobua, God of All Life

In their youth, long before thoughts of Europeans, slavery, or treason, Omoba Jalen of the Uhuri Empire and his twin, Omoba Jacquin, competed. Archery, swordplay, spirit hunting, anything that pitted one against the other. Jalen's natural talent and encouragement from their father lit a competitive fire in Jacquin that soon burned hotter than her brother's. As the years rolled on and their youth fell away, Jalen found he worried less about games and more about his role as Uhuri's Omoba and, eventually, its Oba.

After a long, far-from-routine day of spiritual training with the Uhuri army Jalen would one day lead, he returned to his room defeated, confused, and more filled with fear than he'd ever admit. Nikia, his lifelong lioness companion, purred against his leg as he climbed the stairs of the castle. Jalen's hope for a moment of rest died at the sight of his dear sister waiting in his room.

"I am tired," Jalen said.

"As am I." Jacquin gestured to the table. A chessboard centered the space, its pieces elegantly carved of Sanain stone. Their favorite game.

Jalen sat. Nikia circled and lay at his feet, her strong tail thumping against the table leg. Despite the day's fatigue, Jalen missed competing with his sister, the simplicity of it. It was, as his father might say, an inconsequential battle. While incompetence in being the spiritual leader of the Uhuri could lead to their nation's ruin, a childhood game of chess wounded only a brother or a sister's ego. Above all else, his sister was a worthy opponent.

His room overlooked the city. The busy merchants, flashing their latest crafts of bronze and ivory, the hopeful night hunters, crossing paths with their daytime counterparts, praying for Osanobua's blessings, the tap, clink, crack of their kingdom's army sparring into the dusk. These were once marvels of wonder and possibilities for a boy set to be Oba. Now, Jalen felt only the fear of responsibility when gazing upon his father's land. How could he rule this?

"You look spooked, brother," Jacquin said as she took one of his pieces. She bit the head of the captured rook and smiled, showing the pearly-whites father always complimented her on. She knew the gesture annoyed him. "Is the training too much for his highness?"

"Nothing you would understand," he said. "Oba things."

"Residing over the trials? A silly use of an Oba's time."

How little she knew. Jalen still had the screams of the day's defendant in his head. As the Trial's spiritual master, he lost control over the eran igbe. The undead beasts ripped the man to shreds, long past the point of usual mercy. Iliana, one of the general's daughters and a close friend, tried to comfort him with talks of unrest in the spiritual world. Jalen's father made no excuses. A marred Trial could very well send an innocent man to wait another year in Ogiuwu's Limbo before his next chance.

"The Trials keep the spirit of Uhuri together."

"It is an old way, having animals decide the fate of prisoners. They can be used for more than spiritual fodder."

Jalen looked at his sister, surprised at his own shock. "You speak of trade with the Portuguese? The Uhuri would never."

Jacquin smirked. "You still have a boy's mind. A good Oba is more than a spiritual leader. We need a strong will to deal with our visitors from across the water."

"They wish only to trade in human flesh."

"Trade is trade. How much longer can we survive by offering only tea?"

"I thought you had taken interest in brewing," Jalen said, hoping to shift the discussion away from bondage. "You spend so much time with the herbs. Perhaps tempted by the shadow gods?"

"Talk of necessary things makes you queasy. I understand. As for my alchemy studies, they are for our own Uhuri strength and knowledge. Which I have always had a better eye for. Your move."

"Trade is trade. But I understand how such things make you queasy. Your move," Jacquin held up her prize. "I've taken your olori."

"You overvalue her," Jalen said after surveying the board. He hadn't known if his sister would fall for the simple trap he'd learned from Niambe, his father's top general; Jalen had never been bold enough to use it himself. He moved the elephant piece to flank his sister's Oba. "That's game."

Her smile withered; he felt his own curl. Her ocean-colored eyes chilled to an icy blue when her mood soured, a doubly unique feature that didn't go unnoticed in the palace. She began to reset the pieces.

"Again," she said.

"Not today, sister."

"Afraid you can't beat me without cheap tricks?"

"I'm more afraid to waste a future Oba's time."

Jacquin erupted; the table and the pieces flew. Nikia sprang up, the hairs between her shoulder blades standing at full attention, her fangs barred in a confused growl. Shoulder to shoulder most of their childhood, Jacquin had sprouted a half head above Jalen in the last year. Her face was as tight as her many bantu knots. "Again! That's a challenge!"

Her lion, Dado, roared as he rose from a lazy rest against the far wall. The great lion's white-streaked mane was near maturity. Nikia, divinely gifted to Jalen as a child, was a shock to the kingdom. That his sister paired with a male lion was as equally baffling. The lion siblings' love and hate for each other mirrored the relationship of their human companions.

"That behavior is not of an omoba," their father said from the doorway. His voice was stern, but his eyes were worn. The tension between royal siblings and eran igbe alike dissipated as he crossed the room, kissed Jacquin on the forehead, and turned to his son. "What did you notice today during the Trial?"

"I was weak and unprepared. I will not let it happen again."

"That you were, but that alone cannot explain their fervor. I wasn't sure before but now have word. Something is hunting our spirit brethren in Osanobua's Garden. We leave at dawn."

"But that's through the Mad Lands."

"I'm aware of the geography," his Oba said.

"Coward," Jacquin threw at Jalen. She turned to their father. "Bring me. I won't let you down."

"And I will?" Jalen said.

"One shouldn't ask questions with unbearable answers," his sister said.

The Oba sighed. "I do not have time for this, Jacky."

"I am Jacquin, Omoba of the Uhuri Empire and firstborn of Oba Ehengbua. I'm the oldest. And the strongest."

"You will marry Omoba Obinna of Sanai and our cities will be one. The best Sanain sculptors will line up to raise monuments in honor of your beauty. You will learn their song and be revered as a healer of all people. As Olori, the people will love you for your generosity and your grace. Obas are despised. Oloris are loved."

"The only thing I want to sing is my blade," Jacquin said. "Bring me. I have the courage you hoped for in a son."

"Enough. The woes of an Oba are not your burden to carry. Be grateful of this." He touched his fox skin with the edge of his fingers, as if to remind himself of the weight on his shoulders. His hand then went to his quickly graying stubble of a beard, long unshaven for an Oba.

He picked up the game board and began to reassemble the pieces. "Play again, sweet children. Remember the roles and you may surprise yourselves."

They left before dawn while the stars of the Nine Gods still gave sight to the night sky. Nikia stepped with caution that her own father, Benwe, didn't share. Oba's legendary companion knew only confidence. Both beast and man alike seemed to shrink in Benwe's presence. Nikia, in contrast, was still small in her youth but more senior than the other lionesses paired with the Uhuri warriors. Her unease around their army reflected Jalen's own. He'd spent the night in and out of dreams, wondering what unknown horrors the fabled Mad Lands and Osanobua's Garden might bring. The Uhuri people regularly entered the spiritual realm, but only through either the Citadel for Trials or through seances for communion with the dead. Never in the flesh.

Twelve of their best Uhuri Warriors waited at the gates. Some tended to their life-bonded feline eran igbe while others stared off into the distance. The earth's dust billowed off the lionesses as the warriors stood at attention at Ehengbua's and Jalen's approach. Their Oba waved them at ease.

"My Oba," Niambe said. Jalen had memories of the kingdom's eldest general since he was a small child. With thick hands the size of skillets, Niambe was a friendly man who loved to laugh and take Jalen on walks through the royal market. Since becoming Jalen's trainer, however, he was cold and unforgiving. Oba touched Niambe's neck; the general bowed slightly to receive the welcome.

Tunde stood quietly beside him. The old mage was as thin as he was tall. He'd taught Jalen only a few times, all in the context of the Trials. His own lioness has a pink tuft of fur halfway down her spine.

"This is more than I asked for," Jalen's father said. He ran his hand over the caravan, feeling its size and checking its cargo. Wrapped meats and produce, corded wood for the fire, cloth wraps and crushed herbs to tend to wounds, enough for a week's expedition. And, of course, the weapons. As Oba shifted the purple curtain, Jalen glimpsed stained-tipped spears, longswords, bunches of arrows, and glittering daggers.

"And less than we need," Niambe said.

"It would be a greater tragedy to leave our kingdom unprotected. We must always consider the possibility of failure."

"Which begs the question..." The general's eyes flicked to Jalen. "Are you sure—?"

"You question your Oba?"

Niambe tittered. The Oba was a merciful ruler, but firm. Ehengbua broke into a smile. "An issue of the eran igbe is an issue of the Uhuri. If he is to lead, he must be as loyal to them. If this were something hunting our men, would you question his presence?"

"No, my Oba. But if you were both to perish—"

Oba held up a hand. "I value your council, especially when sought. Not exclusively, but especially." The Oba half turned to his son. "Jalen, I trust you are apt. Would you rather stay?"

Nikia didn't like the question. Jalen patted her belly. "I go where my Oba asks me to go."

Unrest filled Nikia's feline eyes as Jalen prepped her for riding. Jalen reached back into his satchel and unwrapped a pound of dried gazelle shank. She jerked her head away from his offer and let out a low purr that rumbled through Jalen's thighs.

Oba and Omoba greeted all twelve warriors personally before setting off their expedition. They stuck to the edge of the kingdom so as not to raise alarm to any farmers tending to their crops before the sun made the day's heat unbearable. Their step was slow and somber.

"Jalen, come walk beside me."

Benwe dwarfed Nikia as they fell in step with each other.

"Why are you here?" Oba said.

His father's questions left so much unsaid. Often they were puzzles within themselves. Jalen had learned young that asking for clarification meant he hadn't thought hard enough.

Excitement welled. "The coming of age trial."

There was a great sorrow in his father's eyes. "Possibly. The Uhuri aren't ready to receive you as their warrior. But you will need to force them to accept you."

"They favor my sister."

"Jacquin is ambitious. She will make a great Olori one day."

"Do you think she will settle for that?" Jalen said.

"If she were your brother, the choice would be clear. But that does not mean it would be right. I would not be able to stop a male Jacquin. I have learned over the years what things deserve fear. Your sister is one of them."

The following silence between them was marked by the morning's first sunlight. Jalen chewed on his father's words as they left the main farmland and entered a countryside thick with trees and birdsong. As much as it pained him to admit it, he'd had similar thoughts. Osanobua had not only blessed

Jacquin with the mentality of a warrior and a leader, he had also chosen her spiritually, marked by her eran igbe pairing. The Oba's overriding of this was controversial but complete. The gravity was not lost on Jalen. Any weakness, any misstep, and his leadership would come into serious question.

Jalen had a question on his tongue, one he'd chewed on all morning. He'd also learned that his father judged a man by the questions he asked.

"Does what's going on in the Garden have to do with the Portuguese?"

The silence was so deep and long that Jalen feared he'd made some grave mistake in his inquiry. Finally, his father spoke. The seriousness in his voice brought the opposite of relief.

"Before this is over, you may see me differently. What I have done—it's for our survival. You may not understand the decisions I've had to make until you are Oba."

"You will be there to guide me, right, Oba?"

His father stared forward, his jawline tight beneath his beard.

"Look, we come upon the Mad Lands."

Jalen and his father stayed near the middle of the procession as the forbidden wasteland wrapped around them. Everything peeled back. Lush, full trees fell away to sparse ferns. There was no vegetation. The sounds of a healthy forest gave way to cautious silence. There were no animals except for vultures that waited for death amongst the dead. The soft soil turned to ash underfoot: steam lifted off the ground, causing the horizon to twist and turn as if under a terrible curse. Even the clouds, which had supplied a soft cover from the midday sun, curled away from the sky as if even the thought of rain was forbidden. The place between physical and spiritual realms was not meant for habitation. Everything about it warned the traveler of the wrong way.

And then, there was the smell.

Jalen didn't cover his nose. The Uhuri soldiers already saw him as small, weak, and a likely ineffective successor. Even as the acrid stench of their own puke and bile touched the air, their eyes were on him. He couldn't let their humanity give him a pass to show his own.

Nikia mewled, a low hum that wasn't quite a growl.

"What's wrong, girl?" Jalen said, welcoming the distraction. It was always easier to worry over another. "She doesn't like it here."

"Of course she doesn't. The smell of death welcomes no animal." Oba Ehengbua pulled up beside him on Benwe. The elder beast's jaw hung slack. Drool coated his grayed fur. Jalen's father draped his headdress over his nose, not out of discomfort or weakness, but of recognition of the state they passed. "What does it do to you? The stench?"

"Nothing," Jalen said.

Oba's open palm rocked his chest. Nikia tensed. Benwe reared his head and roared.

"Don't give me lies."

"It makes me want to run." Jalen turned away from the light to hide the water in his eyes. He hadn't prepared for the blow as well as he'd thought. The man, gentle as a father, fair but flawed as an Oba, was solid as a warrior.

Oba nodded. "It is protective. The Mad Lands are the last stop before our maker's Garden. That smell is to keep mortals like you and me away. It will not kill you, though. Offering yourself to the spirit world, now that can be fatal. The warning is a mercy."

"But we are Uhuri. Our eran igbe bow to us."

"They bow out of respect, not necessity. We will find great allies and welcome and praise on the other side of these lands," Oba said. "But we are vulnerable to the magic that protects us. There is a reason we monitor the Trials detached from our corporeal bodies. We are vulnerable in the Garden. And even the greatest of allies will be tempted by vulnerability."

Jalen offered Nikia another slab of rolled lamb. She turned her nose. Jalen insisted. Finally, she took the meat, quick and rude even for a lioness. But when he reached to scratch her chin, she let him.

"We enter," Tunde said. He gestured skyward. A cold breeze cleaned the air. The cracks in the desiccated land thinned and congealed. First bushes sprang up around them, then strips of greenery

"Finally," said Ochuko, the youngest besides Jalen.

"Don't be too eager," Tunde said. "Osanobua's Garden has more to it than beauty."

Soon they were surrounded by forest thick with exotic colors, blooming flowers the size of small huts, waterfalls starting and emptying midair, and a soil alive with an essential cycle. The path they walked, overrun by mischievous roots and even more imposing hanging vines, narrowed around them. Soon they were almost single file.

"Stay focused, my Uhuri," their Oba said. He paused briefly after the first word, as his voice seemed to come not only from him, but from every creature in the forest. "We will head straight for the Citadel to set up camp. We should be safe there."

As if in answer, a low-pitched growl rose from the front of their pack. The rest of the lions quickly took up the roar. Nikia tensed under Jalen. Even Benwe, chronically unbothered, lifted his head and bared aged, experienced teeth.

A warrior's yell lifted above the fray. Jalen and Nikia tensed as the Uhuri ahead of them scattered and toppled off their eran igbe. Nikia herself bucked underneath Jalen. She threw her head back; her jaw smashed into Jalen's shoulder. A low growl began in her throat and rumbled through her body.

Benwe reared up as a wide-eyed lioness—Ochuko's foot

caught in her harness as his upper body dragged along the forest floor—tried to run through them. The Oba's lion slammed the lioness down with one giant paw. Ochuko finally fell from his entanglement. The lioness nipped at Benwe. The pack leader twisted his paw into her chest. Red bloomed across her fur.

"Easy," Ehengbua said. Benwe grunted but let up just enough for Ochuko's companion to squirm out. She ran away, tail tucked, howling towards the heavens.

The Uhuri huddled around their fallen comrade. But Ochuko seemed less concerned with his own injuries. He jumped up and turned back towards the front of their procession, as if what he'd seen might be coming their way.

The Oba pulled ahead. Jalen urged Nikia to follow.

An elephant lay across the path. A black gash parted its belly from front to back legs. Entrails leaked out, a sloppy, unfinished feast. One tusk curled into the air while the other had been snapped in two near the base. Instead of a foot, the front leg was a mangled mess of blood and bone. What was left kicked sporadically.

The elephant's chest rose in shallow breaths. "It still lives," Jalen whispered. Oba frowned and motioned him forward.

"This is fresh," Oba said, pulling up beside Niambe. "Whatever attacked this animal may be close."

"Is it what we came to hunt?"

"No normal beast did this," Tunde said. His voice was soft with a nasal wheeze toward the end. Blood trickled from a gash on the mage's temple. "I fear the realm itself is sick. Our eran igbe feel it."

"Ready our weapons," Oba said. Niambe nodded, turned, and got his men into formation.

The Oba leaned forward to whisper something in Benwe's ear as he stroked the lion's grayed mane. The lion calmed, partly.

"It's okay, Nikia, we are safe." Jalen wasn't as adept at calming his own companion.

"Tend to her later," his father said. "You cannot ask an animal to walk toward death. Come, Jalen. Let us see what we are up against."

But you can ask an Omoba. Jalen shrugged off the thought.

The smell of death surrounded the wounded animal. Not one of decay, as the elephant's spirit had not yet left the flesh, but of sour disease and danger. A vibrating fear lay over the dying elephant, unlike anything Jalen had experienced. He had seen many mortally wounded animals during royal hunts or after a roughly decided trial. Death created a uniform serenity. He saw no sign of that now. This animal feared something a lot less natural.

"Notice the claw marks on her hide?" Oba said. "How many?"

Jalen counted quickly, his mind split by the fervor around him. The Uhuri wasted no time arming themselves with longswords and daggers. The eran igbe became increasingly agitated. The air vibrated with a visceral energy.

"Four," Jalen said.

"Slow. The world will be the world. An Oba must see the things others cannot see. Count again, my son."

Jalen did. Still four. One, two, three, four. One, two, three, four. He dragged his mind to the calm reflection his father introduced to him as a boy. There, to the right, angled, almost lost in the ruin of the belly, a cut not as deep as the others. Easily missed.

"You see," Oba said. "What leaves such a mark?"

"I don't know."

His Oba spread his fingers and held his hand up, slightly tilted. The wind caught in Jalen's chest as his father's hand fit the outline of the wound.

"Neither do I." Oba touched the dying animal. It heaved in response. "Steady. Steady, my eran igbe. We will provide safe passage."

Jalen was still thinking of the way his father's hand synced with the marks as the Oba traced his fingers up the elephant's hide and to the neck. The Oba paused. The click of metal had come clearly from the animal. Had it swallowed something? Was an unseen knife lodged in its throat?

Jalen looked around. Birds watched silently from overhanging branches. Eyes peaked out at them from the brush. Flowers bloomed and curled to rot and then bloomed again, a fervent wave that was like a colorful ocean. More clinking. His father's fingers maneuvered something heard and not seen.

Oba brought Jalen's hand to join his. "Here. Feel this."

Instead of warm, rough leather, Jalen felt cold, circular bands of metal.

"Chains," Oba said. "Feel where they link, here?"

Jalen did. "What does that mean?"

"Tunde!" His father traced the chain across the neck. He called for his mage again. When Tunde came over, half his face was covered in sweat.

"My Oba..." Tunde whispered as he felt the chains. "This poor eran igbe has been claimed. This is old magic."

"That's not possible," Oba said.

"With due respect, nothing is impossible. Not here in the Garden. Whatever spirit did this is tainted. And restless. But most of all, crafty. The physical marks are of a beast, but the method is sinister and meant to incite."

"How will we hunt it?"

"We will need to tap into the full power of the Garden." The mage's eyes went all white.

"We spoke of this," Oba said. "To invoke Osanobua's power is to also invite its wraith."

"I fear we already have that exposure," Tunde said, "with none of the protection."

Their Oba broke away suddenly, grabbed his longsword from the caravan, and, without hesitation and in stride, plunged his sword into the elephant's neck, straight through. He pulled toward him with all his strength until the blade was free of flesh. The elephant did not struggle with the last of its life but rather took in a full, rattling breath and settled into death.

The Oba turned to face his men. "We have come for danger, and it has found us. We will push toward the Citadel and attempt to commune with our eran igba brethren. We must not waste daylight."

As they passed, the Uhuri warriors bowed to the now-dead elephant and sent up a silent prayer to Osanobua for his mercy. The lion pride gave their own condolences with hooting mewls. Any hunger for the carcass did not show.

They walked in silence into dusk. The forest, thick around them, glowed with living florescence. A thousand questions tormented Jalen's head. None were formed enough to convey his inner affliction.

A guttural scream cut the night. The air vibrated with collective fear. What started shrill and inhuman, otherworldly, soon showed itself to be that of a man. Jalen's heart filled with terror. He sought out his father and quickly fell in line behind him.

The chaos parted for Oba, who walked with calm purpose up to the scene. Everyone quieted. One of the top generals—Dele, head of strategy—lay at a terrible angle along his lion's back, his foot firmly in the beast's jaws. The man held tightly onto the coarse fur. The lioness stared dumbly on, her eyes flicking in the light. She could have knocked the soldier off her and killed him quickly, but that wasn't her intent. Her jaw worked slowly, intermittently, to the soldier's slow whimpers.

The eran igbe eyed the Oba as he approached. She shifted

to the left and bit into the captured flesh. Dele wailed worse than before.

"All right, Nijla," Oba said, stroking the lion's fur. Nijla, quick as lightning, struck Oba's hand with her paw. Dele wailed from the sudden movement. The Oba winced and laid his other hand on her hide. "It's okay. You know who you are."

Out of the lion's sight, Niambe pulled his long sword out and crept forward. Oba raised his free, bloodied hand to pause the advance. The lion threw her head, tossed Dele forward and onto the ground like a ragdoll, and turned on Niambe.

The general tensed. Oba stilled his hand, clear in his command. Niambe closed his eyes and waited for death.

Nijla ran off. Niambe sucked in a deep breath and watched her leave.

"Note her gait, son."

Jalen already had his eye on it. The lioness didn't run with so much a limp as a lean. Her head tilted slightly toward the sky, and her tongue flapped lazily to the erratic beat of her stride.

"The spiritual burden here is heavier than I expected," the Oba said as he watched Nijla disappear into the night. Somewhere from beyond their sight she roared a roar that Jalen had never heard before. Something responded.

"Oba, your hand, it needs mending," the medic said.

"Then mend it," he said without looking. "But tend to Dele first. We will all need our energy. This is where we part with our eran igba."

His general looked shocked. "It is no burden for us to set up a stable for them. Once they have sleep and water—"

"This is not the behavior of thirst," Oba said. "They will be in no shape to return with us."

"Oba?"

"Do as I say."

The Uhuri unharnessed their paired lionesses. One warrior

did it as his companion stared at him, stone still, and Jalen wouldn't have been surprised if the beast ripped his neck open. Many of the pack—Jalen noticed they were all on the small side, juveniles if he had to guess-- immediately broke free and ran, nipping at each other's heels, through the forest. They let up the same cry as Nijla and the same response came from the night, this time thicker in number. The others lingered, confused and conflicted by their loyalty to the Oba and by whatever had possessed their siblings.

Niambe waved his hands and yelled at the lingering few. One of the felines nipped at his sword.

"Leave them be," Oba said.

"But you said—"

"I am aware of my words, as I am the one who spoke them. We should get going. The Citadel remains our goal."

The medic tended to Oba's hand while they walked.

Jalen thought of his words before he spoke them. "Is releasing our eran igbe into Osanobua's Garden part of the plan?"

To Jalen's surprise and slight delight, his Oba smiled. "Their spirits are strong. The ones that left did so because they do not trust themselves enough not to hurt us. Loyalty overrides instinct to stay."

"And of these?" Jalen said. "They stay with us."

"For as long as they can," Oba said.

"Are they a danger?"

"Yes," his father said, without hesitation. "But they are not *the* danger." They paused at the injured warrior, who swallowed his pain and sat tall at Oba's approach. "At ease. See here? See the damage? This is restraint. This is a conflicted spirit. The eran igbe that were born here will have no such motivation."

"They stay loyal to us in the trials."

"Through honor, not necessity. Do not conflate the two."

Darkness fell around them, and as Jalen took in his

surroundings he saw this was true. Instead of darkness deepening first in the east with twilight lingering in the west, the whole of the horizon darkened at once, paling uniformly as the sky curved overhead. Just above was purple.

"The eran igbe that tore apart that man in the trial…had the same thing come over it?"

"Yes. But there isn't anything that's come over the animals. It's more of what's lost."

"What do you mean?" Jalen said before he could catch himself. But his father didn't seem to take notice of the immediate response.

"The eran igbe are in a perfect balance. Their animal instinct to kill or maim us is balanced by our spiritual connection. Our trust. This relationship can unravel for two main reasons. One would be, as you suggested, a possession of sorts, an addition. I do not think that is the case. The other…"

"An absence."

"Yes. Something has broken our connection. In short, these animals are very unhappy with us."

"Is it because of the decisions you had to make?"

Oba nodded. That was all he gave. Jalen left it alone. For now.

"The land is soft here," Niambe said, jogging up from far enough away to not eavesdrop but to know when to interject.

"It would be needed for our collective graves. Don't slow. We are not far yet."

The sound started in Jalen's chest. A hum that, at first, he took as his own angst, welling up inside. Then the low vibration reached his ears. A buzzing noise, like what Jalen had once experienced the moments after a hornets' nest downed by the groundskeeper landed at his feet and before the cloud of fiery stings. It surrounded the Uhuri. They looked at each other, each man realizing in the other's eyes that this was no hallucination.

Branches snapped overhead. Treetops toppled into the brush.

Birds of all sizes and with tri-tipped wings that blot out the sun took flight.

The buzzing stopped. All other sound ceased to exist. The air emptied. Their party slowed.

Something unseen and unheard drew their collective gazes. Twirling vines tipped with blossoming white flowers wrapped around thick tree trunks curled apart as Nijla stepped out of the Garden's shadows. She was identifiable only by the harness still clipped in around her tattered neck. Half of her head was in ruin. The left eye and ear were completely missing. Her tongue sloughed out from its gaping cavity and lapped at loose bits of flesh.

Niambe readied his sword. The glistening metal trembled in his grip. Their Oba did not move to stop him.

There was no need. Nijla stumbled a step forward and fell in the dirt. She pawed at the ground. The Uhuri gasped. They all saw it at the same time. A hyena the size of a hippopotamus had emerged from the woods behind Nijla, quieter than what should be capable at that size. It growled a warning, bit into what remained of Nijla's head, and began to eat.

Another branch broke behind them. Air parted in front of them, then dissipated. Jalen felt himself move into his Oba, his father, expecting the stern leader to push him away, as there was no time to seek comfort. Instead, the Oba met him halfway.

"Set up a perimeter," Oba said to his mage.

"Here?" Tunde said.

"Here."

Tunde moved quickly for someone so advanced in years. He retrieved what looked like a rolled-up slab of meat from the carriage and unrolled it in the air. Jalen instinctively lunged to catch it, thinking it was a slip, but his father held him back. There wasn't meat in the roll at all, but candles. They fell upright to form a circle around them. The mage got into position and lifted his hands skyward.

He began to chant.

A crack in the sky cut both his spell and his life short. Lightning raced across the night, from star to star, and seemed to especially light up the old magi's face, which was already turned toward the heavens. Multiple strikes broke from the sky and came down to touch one of his hands, and then the other. Chains, sparkling in the lightshow, connected his wrists. His skin ripped open down his arms. His eyes burst in sprays of blood.

The thunder and lightning stopped. The sky cleared. The mage, his hands still raised, his mouth agape in shocked ululations, stood for another second or two and then fell to his side, stiff as a stone. He rolled onto his back. His eyes were gone from his sockets. A third shackle cuffed his neck.

"Tunde!" Niambe dropped down beside him. He yelled and retracted his hand from the shackles, as if they still held electricity. "Tunde!" He gripped the metal and this time didn't let go. It sparked in his grip and glowed a bright orange. Niambe roared through the obvious pain of it. His Uhuri brothers pulled him away. His hands, black and red and textured, smoked and sizzled in the cool night air.

Around them, the Garden was in a frenzy. The spirits were alive. Agitated. Restless. Angry. Hungry. Jalen couldn't wrap his mind around what was happening. Omoba of the Uhuri Empire, future Oba, beloved only son of Ehengbua, Jalen had never seen such danger.

A wail cut through the noise. More animals—one couldn't be sure if they were birds—took flight. This broke whatever temporary trance had overcome their party.

"Run," their Oba commanded. They ran.

The forest tried to swallow them. The tree branches reached

across the path and braided into one another. Niambe cut through them with significant effort. A claw as wide as Jalen's chest reached out from the void. Jalen planted his feet in the ground, leaned backward, and fell onto his back. The claw barely missed him but found a target. The Uhuri warrior stabbed the fingers with his dagger. The claw squeezed. The warrior stiffened. Blood leaked through the beast's fingers and misted the air. Then the hand was gone, back into the bush.

Niambe ran sword-first into the hole created by the claw. Oba followed without hesitation, and the Uhuri all plunged in. Living vines tore at Jalen's arms and legs, the hot breath of the forest burned his skin, and Osanobua's sung warnings rang in his ears.

And then…they came out of the other side. They entered a clearing. The world stood still.

"There!"

The Citadel. Just ahead was the fortress that hosted the Trials. Its rounded stone walls rose into the sky. The trees surrounding it were thick and moss-covered.

A drawbridge lowered as they approached. Jalen's father urged his Uhuri inside. One warrior paused to look back. He drew his sword, screamed, and then was lifted into the air by a lumbering shadow. The shadow grazed Jalen as it passed. It chilled the air to a deep cold that ached Jalen's bones on one side of his body.

"Fortify this place," Oba ordered of Niambe.

"But Oba, Tunde—"

"Is dead! You know the magic. You know the words. I demand of you—"

His father let out an oomph as he fell forward onto the marble floor of the Citadel. For the first time in his life, Jalen saw fear etched in his father's face. Instead of turning to confront whatever had him, the Oba instead turned to Jalen. The Oba hardened in his resolve. He managed a smile even as his blood gushed where several of his front teeth had shattered.

"Lead," he said. And then, he was gone.

"Oba," Jalen whispered. "Father."

Jalen said a quick prayer, as he was trained to do, his mouth and hands both trembling. He meditated in the moment, short as it was, so that he could be fully in it, because it was too painful to turn to everyone else, to make it that much more a reality.

"Continue the fortification," Jalen said. The voice that he heard come out of himself was small and weak. But Niambe moved to it.

"Fortify this place," Niambe said to the remaining Uhuri. "Quickly."

The warriors, still in shock, placed themselves along the perimeter of the Citadel as Niambe mumbled incantations.

Jalen looked around. He had only been in the Citadel by way of spiritual projection, his physical body safely stationed back in the castle.

He floated across the floor to the defendants' quarters, where they spent the night before a trial, and closed the door. He fingered the loose fabric of the singular pillow on the cot. If there was a safe place in this Garden, this was it. Somehow this put fear aside and left only numb sorrow.

Jalen laid back. The knot at the base of his skull pressed up against the edge of the bed. No matter. He stared at the ceiling, feeling the foundation move under him. Niambe shouted something. A Uhuri screamed in defiance.

His father. His Oba. Gone so quickly. So definitively. Jalen had failed him as a warrior. As an Omoba. As a son.

Jalen was safe enough to drift in and out of something close to sleep. As his thoughts calmed, he began to walk into his own subconscious. His corporeal body expanded into the surface of the sea. He felt and smelled air not immediately around him, heard the agitated and near-lost eran igbe halt against Niambe's imperfect magical border, saw them circle and pant and scheme to find some way into the Citadel.

Jalen sat up. Oba?

No, there was no Oba. Not to him. Not in the way he knew. Had known his entire life. There was only himself.

Jalen got up and went to the window. He didn't know if he could trust the stars here in the Garden, but they were all he had. Based on the constellations, the night was halfway through. The commotion he'd dozed to had quieted. Soft snoring floated from the other sections of the cabin. Good. His father's soldiers needed their rest.

Outside, the night seemed to have other things in mind. Every portion of it was alive. Movements among the trees. Songs through the branches.

Was the beast they hunted resting? Did it rest? Jalen thought back to the sound of it, saw again the marks on the elephant blocking the road. He remembered the deep gashes in the elephant's skull the most. How powerful the inflicting jaws must have been.

Had his father—their Oba—brought them here for death?

His ears perked. He tapped into the spirit world, reached his senses out. The expanse was just as intense as before, only now, expected. He held his breath against the onslaught of senses, sharp even in the night's supposed quiet, and focused. There. His top generals (*were they truly his yet?*) were still awake, of course. They had likely taken one of Tunde's potions to stave off sleep, an advantage they'd pay for after, if they survived this.

"Our lives are in the hand of a boy." Dele's voice, small but decided. Though the warrior spoke many walls away, Jalen heard him perfectly.

"He is your Oba," Niambe said. The warrior sounded tired, but not beat.

"You give up on Ehengbua?"

"No. But until that hope is realized and Ehengbua is back with us, Jalen must lead."

"He is not ready."

"He will have to be. One day he will be our Oba. The day will come, if not today. He will remember how we treated him here. Wait."

Jalen's heart froze. Had they found him out?

"What is it, Niambe?"

"Nothing. I thought I heard something. Tell me, Dele, what do you remember of your Oba?"

"It is too painful to think of."

"And think of it, you will. Was he smart? Did he move with purpose?"

"Yes. All of those things."

"Did he ever act without wisdom?"

"Never."

"He brought Jalen here for a reason."

"Do you think this boy—I am sorry, this Oba—can fulfill it?" Dele said.

Silence. Jalen reeled in his senses and sat back on his bed. He surveyed his breath, his body, the blood going through him.

Then, Jalen rose. He stepped out of his room as night turned over to dawn. The men on guard were surprised to see him. They were the youngest, given the least coveted shift. Ochuko winced as he bowed; near-soaked bandages wrapped his shoulder.

"I must mourn my father," Jalen said.

"But Jalen—Oba—there is no proper place."

He and Ochuko had grown up together before their respective birthrights led them to different poles of the Uhuri army.

The three of them—Jacquin included—would pretend-war as kids throughout the castle grounds. Now the boy—as much of a man as Jalen—looked at him with eyes of an old friend.

"My father," Jalen said, returning the sentiment, "is dead. I must honor him. I may have no other chance. I will only go to the edge of the forest. Niambe's protection should keep me if I don't go far."

The young Uhuri looked at each other. Ochuko lowered the bridge and escorted him out.

"I'm sorry about Oba," he said.

"As am I," Jalen said. "Thank you. Wait here. I will not be long."

Ochuko nodded and stood at the edge of the bridge. Jalen headed for the forest. He needed only fresh soil and live roots to give his father a proper spiritual burial. Jalen stepped into the thick detritus rug of the forest floor and went just past Ochuko's line of sight. Mourning was a private affair, and they would respect that, to an extent. Eventually they would seek him out. By then he should be far enough away. He hoped that Niambe would take it easy on the young Uhuri. "Father, give me strength."

Jalen kneeled, said the prayers for his father, then ran his hand through the soil. Slightly damp. His aura leaked into the ground and tapped into the forest. He'd heard of the euphoria when connecting directly to the spirit world from the Garden, but this was far from it. What he felt was a deep illness in the land. His heart raced. Nausea came in slow waves. He focused through it. Jalen didn't know what he was looking for but was grateful for it when he found it. Nikia's scent. Jalen studied the foliage. There, a little ahead, the branches were bent, a break in the green. She'd marked her territory so that he could find her.

Jalen followed Nikia's path. Forest vines thickened to where he spent more time climbing than on solid ground. They wrapped and unwrapped him, as if sensing his royal blood and considering if it was worth spilling.

Finally, the woods thinned. Soon a soft, steady thrum in the land he felt in his feet grew to the unmistakable thunder of crashing waves. Ever since Niambe took him to their beaches as a kid, Jalen had found comfort in a violent ocean.

A harrowing smell barely preceded Jalen's view of the shore. He leaned against the trunk of a thick fern and peaked out to the ocean. A massive whale carcass hosted a feast for many eran igbe—lions, apes, hippos, gators. Flies the size of small birds lifted and descended in hungry swarms.

Jalen, mesmerized by the spectacle, lost his balance and fell in the sand. The air stilled. The eran igbe paused the tearing of flesh and collectively looked up. Opportunistic flies landed on the whale's grayed and bloated hull. The beasts' pale eyes were dead blue pools in their sockets. Jalen's fall had surely drawn their collective attention, yet they seemed not to look at or through him, but…beside him?

Jalen heard the movement only a moment before a paw as big as his head pounded into his chest. An animal with more strength in one limb than Jalen possessed in his entire body held him firm. A lioness. Nikia. Before Jalen could fully register the reunion, she took his neck in her jaws. Hot pain shot up into his skull. He felt himself leak into the surrounding sand.

The other animals, all once sworn spirit brothers and sisters of the Uhuri kingdom, abandoned the carcass to circle this sacrifice. They let out low hoots of hunger for his blood and his spirit. But it wasn't only hunger. With the senses awarded to him by Osanobua, the gift and the punishment for entering his Garden, Jalen felt the rage. Experienced it. His spirit brethren hated him like only family could.

Nikia bit deeper. Blood drained from his neck and wet the

sand in an expanding tide. Jalen thought of Niambe and Dele, sending up the alarm, coming out to find him, and seeing their Oba in a pathetic pond of his own royal blood.

Jalen reached up for some help, some assistance. Osanobua, perhaps, or his father. Even the stars could provide some comfort. His fingers found Nikia's fur, stiff in her tension, but comforting all the same.

They had been born together. And maybe now they would enter into the afterlife together as well.

———————————

Jalen woke to the sound of clanging metal. Sharp, fresh pain jettisoned from the wound in his neck to bounce around his skull. Nikia tossed him onto the ground. Jalen struggled to stop the flow of new blood as her fangs unplugged from their deep gashes. Nikia pinned him with a strong paw and leaned down for what Jalen feared was the killing blow. Instead, she licked where she had opened him. A singular, long stroke with her muscular tongue.

His skin tightened in painful healing. Air passed through his mouth and into his lungs. He coughed up a ball of congealed blood.

Jalen looked around. Nikia sat on her haunches, half turned away from him.

She'd brought him to a white beach, different from the carcass-infested one before. The waves here were soft echoes against the sand. Docked not a league down shore was the largest ship Jalen had ever seen. The links in the chain attached to the anchor were individually the size of men. Gray water dripped from the moss-covered wood. The flags hung torn and tattered. Some crewmen, their gait erratic and stilted, moved about the deck. They threw familiar silhouettes overboard. Bodies.

Jalen's gaze fell from the ship. Cages lined the shore. They housed incongruent pairings of eran igbe. Gazelle with hyenas. Giraffes with baboons. Lions with hippos. The still-living feasted on the dead.

And then, finally, Jalen saw what must have been there all along. The beast, built like a man but twice as tall and wide, moved from entrapment to entrapment. The beast opened them with a key around its neck to reach in and feast on the still-alive eran igbe. It pulled a maimed gazelle from its cage, lifting it whole. The gazelle mewled—all the fight it had. The beast bit its head off and tossed the rest of the body into the sea.

Jalen struggled. Nikia kept him pinned, firm, as if commanding him to watch. The beast filled its belly with another eran igbe head, tossed the remains to the waves, and then began to load the ship. It slung two cages at a time over its back as if they were sacks of grain and boarded the vessel using the anchor's chain as a ladder.

Jalen failed at suppressing another scream as Nikia dragged him forward. He thought she planned to chuck him toward one of the cages, not caring if his body broke against the bars. Instead, she stopped short of one and released him into the dirt. She licked the back of his head, rough but with a hint of encouragement that only a loyal eran igbe could have. Jalen lifted his head.

He didn't know what he was looking at. Rabid meerkats feasted on a tiger, its belly spilling into the sand. Beyond, in the corner, a man sat crossed-legged, hunched over. Jalen recognized the Uhuri dress and the royal markings along the seams. Red blood from the man's eyes —nearly black in the poor light—streaked down dark brown skin.

"Oba!" Jalen's wail came out a harsh whisper. With strength he shouldn't have had, he scrambled up and against the metal cage. The enclosures were meant to hold beasts and Jalen—who was still much thinner in his youth than his father—slipped easily between the bars. He went to his father's side. "Oba. I thought I'd lost you."

The Oba didn't initially respond. He was alive still—his chest rose in shallow gurgles—but his hands were cold, his garments soaked. Up close, Jalen confirmed that his father's eyes had been removed.

"Come, Oba, Nikia will heal you." The eran igbe, restless outside the cage, did not leave them. The beast would be back soon.

But his father wouldn't move. Jalen could not budge him. Though Jalen would technically be a man soon—was likely already a man in the Uhuri's eyes if he survived this—his father was still twice his own size.

Jalen broke away and went to the dead tiger. One of the meerkats sensed his approach and growled a bloody warning. Jalen didn't think; he just did. He pushed into the frenzy and dipped his hands full into the tiger's warm belly. Two of the feasting animals turned their fervor toward him. Fire stung his cheek, his shoulder, down his back.

He pulled away, hands still cupped, and scrambled back in the sand. He lifted the fallen animal's blood to his father's face, across his lips, and into his eye sockets, which felt like dead wounds against Jalen's fingers.

His Oba gasped awake. He looked around like a man with new sight, though his eyes were still gone. Jalen seized the opportunity and urged his father to his feet and toward the cage where Nikia paced. The lioness licked his face through the bars and then dragged him through.

"Jalen, come," his father said, reaching back for him. The Oba's sclerae were returning. His face pleaded, commanded. Jalen did not go.

"This intruder will keep attacking our eran igbe. As Oba, I must protect them like I would protect my own men. You taught me that, father. Nikia, take him back to the Citadel."

Nikia needed no second order. She and Jalen's father disappeared into the forest. Jalen sat and waited.

The beast continued its quick work of loading the ship. Soon the shore was an empty mess of blood, feces, and indiscernible parts. Jalen feared the beast knew of the special cargo and that was why he'd saved their cage for last. But he hoisted them up just the same; Jalen clung to the bars to keep from slipping through. His mouth cracked against the metal; blood coated his tongue.

Once onboard, the beast tossed the cage beside the rest of them and hoisted the anchor from the shallows. The ship slid into the sea. Jalen left the confines of the cage and stayed in the shadows as the beast worked the ship. He checked the cages and threw overboard whatever eran igbe had died in transit. To starboard, another ship approached from the opposite direction, toward shore. The beast went to receive it. It readied itself to board the other. Jalen knew he had little time.

Remembering his father, remembering Tunde and Nikia, remembering the spirit that had kept him warm and safe since his infancy, Jalen lunged from the shadows.

The demon man, one leg steady on the side of the ship, turned quickly at Jalen's approach. He grabbed Jalen's wrist. The skin there burned. He cupped the side of Jalen's head and brought his face close to his own. Jalen almost gagged. It wasn't just the smell; it was that, and everything. The vibration of him. The beast traumatized every sense imaginable, and the ones Jalen had yet to know.

Jalen let his aura expand and wrap around the beast. He was exposing his spirit for collection but also tapping into that of the other. The beast, realizing his intention, began to resist. It tried to chuck Jalen into the ocean but could not. Jalen clung to him like a newborn to its mother, a tick to its bloodmeal.

Jalen saw it all. This beast was no beast, but a man. Jalen saw his crimes. The trial. The sentencing. The man's crimes. The trade to the Portuguese, his Oba overseeing it all. Jalen nearly lost his hold on reality and fell into the abyss; he was shaken so. Once a warrior, the man was stripped of all titles and belongings. He was stripped of his name and status. He was pressed against the flesh of other nameless captors and laid facedown, shackled from wrist to wrist to heel to heel, on the wet, moldy wood of a ship. Halfway across the ocean he became sick with fever, was bled, and then thrown overboard for dead. The man stared into the dead eyes of another captured warrior turned slave as he drowned. Aquatic scavengers tore at him as he descended to the deep. His Uhuri kingdom—sworn to an eternal spiritual bond—had abandoned him.

"We are sorry," Jalen said. "We will make this right. Just let them go."

The beast seemed to consider. Finally, it brought Jalen into its chest and leapt overboard, into the sea.

The Uhuri warriors found him wandering, naked, in the Mad Lands. As it was told to Jalen later, his generals tracked Jalen into the woods and to the land's edge. Seeing the slave ships, they thought Jalen had been taken out to sea, never to return. They decided it was best to get Oba back to their city so that he could heal and found Jalen along the way.

Once he had confirmation that his Oba was alive and recovering, Jalen slept most of the way back to the kingdom. He dreamed of eran igbe, ships, and chessboards.

Days later, Jalen paused outside his room. Like the last moment he stood here—which now felt a lifetime ago—he wanted rest. But he knew that wouldn't come. He knew who awaited him inside his chamber. More importantly, he now also knew who she was. He entered.

Jacquin sat at a prepared chessboard. Her hands trembled. Dado was nowhere in sight.

"How is father?" Jacquin said.

"He will live. I was just with him. He doesn't like the healing tea, but it's helping. He won't be the same, but our father lives."

"Praise Osanobua," she said.

They began to play without further words. They took each other's pieces with haste. There was little strategy, only onslaught. Each sacrificed to harm the other.

Finally, Jalen captured Jacquin's Omoba, sat back, and stared at his sister. She hadn't slept since he'd last seen her, judging from the pull of her eyes. She didn't return his gaze.

"What awaited you in the Garden?" Jacquin said.

"The consequence of human trade. Our father made a deal with the Portuguese, and it almost destroyed our relationship with the eran igbe."

Jacquin nodded. "Is it finished?"

"For now."

Jalen studied his sister's face. She seemed relieved.

"It makes sense to me why the eran igbe would be tormented over our actions. It also makes sense why the beast—the man—that hunted them would seek revenge on us." Jalen leaned forward. "But what I saw was no normal apparition. Someone made a dark deal with the gods."

Jacquin's hands moved away from the few pieces she had left as she considered this. "Who do you suspect?"

"The beast bit the head of its victims. You've always been fascinated with the gods who deal in souls."

His sister paused, her fingers still on her chess piece. He saw the lie began to formulate. Then, she smiled.

"You are more observant than I thought, brother. Have you told father?"

"No. I wouldn't want to break his heart."

"Checkmate," Jacquin said. Her hands still trembling, she lifted Jalen's Oba, bit its head, and then left it toppled on the board.

Jalen rose to leave. When he was halfway out the door, his sister called for him. He turned one eye back to her.

"I never meant for father to be hurt."

Jalen nodded and left. In the hall, Ochuko and Dele awaited him. Jalen hadn't decided what to do with his sister but found relief in knowing a decision would be quickly forced from him.

"My father rests well," Jalen said. "Gather the Council tomorrow. I have something grave to discuss."

His generals stood oddly firm. Then, without warning, they grabbed him by the arms.

"What is this?" Jalen said, feeling betrayed by his own boyhood fears.

"The Council convenes now. They demand you."

"For?"

"For the murder of Oba. He's been found dead in his bed. Poisoned."

"Brother?" Jacquin had come to the chamber door. The beginning of tears leaked from her eyes. "Brother, what have you done? What have you done?"

Jalen just looked at his sister as Ochuko—still so young, maybe only slightly senior to Jalen—and Dele dragged him away. The last he saw of his sister, her grimace curled into the beginnings of a smile. Her finger crawled down her face, done with her fake tears, and rested on her lips. She bit the tip of her index.

And then, she was gone. Jalen had only his uncertain fate to look toward.

The Shadow From the Vaults

Charles R. Rutledge

To Harald Sigurdsson, it seemed he had barely kicked off his boots and fallen onto his bed before someone was pounding on the door of his quarters. He grimaced as he pulled himself from sleep and glanced over at the open window. Still full dark.

"Captain!" a voice shouted through the door, followed by more pounding.

Harald crossed the room and pulled the door open. Haldor Snorre, his second in command, stood there, looking just as pleased to be awake as Harald felt.

"It is the Orphanotrophos," Haldor said. "He awaits in the entrance hall."

"What would the emperor's brother want with us in the middle of the night?" Harald said. "Nothing good, I'll wager. Tell him I'm coming."

Harald pulled on his boots and buckled on his sword belt. He would have to meet with John the Orphanotrophos in last night's tunic. Pushing his long hair from his face, he left his quarters and hurried to the front room of the barracks of the Life-Guard of Emperor Michael IV.

John, also known as John the Eunuch, stood glowering near the front door, a heavyset man with curly, dark hair and cruel eyes. As soon as he saw Harald he said, "Captain, gather five of your best men and come with me immediately."

"What has happened?" said Harald.

"Nothing I can speak of here. Now hurry."

For a moment, Harald considered telling the man the Varangians, even the city Varangians, didn't take orders from John, but he reminded himself that John was in many ways the power behind his ailing brother's throne. Since Harald had no way of knowing which way the political winds would blow on Michael's inevitable death, it was probably best not to antagonize the eunuch.

"Haldor, go and bring Ulf, Snorri, Kharrn, and Bjorn. Tell them to arm themselves. Speak to no one else and answer no questions." When Haldor left, Harald turned back to John. "Can you tell me nothing of what has occurred?"

John shook his head. "No other ears must hear this. You will see soon enough once we reach the royal chambers."

So it was something to do with Michael himself, and it required six warriors. Harold found himself intrigued. He knew the emperor's health was very poor. Though somehow he had roused himself for the campaign against the Bulgars, Michael had rarely been seen in public since the victory parade where he had marched his defeated enemies through the streets, many of them minus their eyes and noses. Even then, the emperor's fingers had been so swollen they looked like sausages.

Haldor returned with the other four Varangians. Three of them were Harald's countrymen, and he had known them for many years. No one knew where the giant, Kharrn, came from, but he had been with the Varangian Guard when Harald had arrived in Miklagard and was well known to many of the Norsemen there.

Kharrn had proven himself invaluable in Michael's campaigns in Sicily, Bulgaria, and Jerusalem. He was easily worth any three men in a fight, and like all the men in Harald's close circle, he could keep his mouth shut, an important attribute in the volatile court of Constantinople.

Harald and his men followed John out of the barracks and across a mosaic-tiled courtyard. The night winds whispered around them and sent leaves fluttering. The group made their way to one of the may interior entrances to the Great Palace, where two of Harald's men acknowledged their captain and allowed them to enter.

Harald had learned the hard way the palace was really made up of many small palaces that had been built and rebuilt, expanded and connected, over the years. The place was a veritable maze, yet John led them surely through the corridors to the outskirts of the living chambers of the emperor.

John paused by the door to an anteroom and said, "Look in here, and you will see why I came for you myself rather than sending a servant."

Harald stepped up to the door. A single torch lit the room, throwing wavering shadows across a scene of carnage. It was hard to tell how many dead men were in the room because their bodies had been torn apart. Limbs and torsos were scattered around the chamber. The torchlight reflected off the eyes of a severed head which sat upright in one corner. The floor, walls, and even the ceiling were slick with blood.

"That's Halfdan Andersson," said Haldor, pointing at the bodiless head.

Harald didn't answer. He felt bile in his throat. He had fought in his first battle at age fifteen, and he had seen many bloody sights since, but this? His men had been butchered like cattle within the walls of the imperial palace. Behind him he could hear the shocked reactions of his companions.

Harald took a moment to make sure his voice was steady. "How did this happen?"

"No one knows," John said. "Four of your Varangians guard

this corridor, which leads to the emperor's bed chambers. A servant heard screaming from this room and rushed here to find it as you see it."

Kharrn said, "We need more light."

Harald nodded. "Ulf, you and Bjorn find more torches. Quickly!" The two men hurried off, and Harald turned to John. "I need to speak to the servant who found my men."

John said, "I have had him removed."

"Then go and have someone bring him back."

John's face was unreadable. He said, "None return from where he's gone."

Of course. John couldn't have anyone talking of this. Harald would remember that.

Harald said, "What did he tell you?"

"Just what I said. He heard screams from this direction and came to see what was happening. He found the room like this and hurried to his overseer. That man came and found me."

Harald wondered if the overseer had met the same fate as the servant. He said, "So he came directly here after hearing the screams. That means whoever did this did it very quickly. It doesn't seem possible."

Kharrn said, "Here's something else that's impossible, Captain: there are no tracks leading from this chamber. With this much blood, there should be some trace."

"Is there another way out of this room?" Harald said.

John shook his head. "It is a waiting room for visitors. It has only the one entrance."

Ulf and Bjorn returned with the torches. Kharrn snatched one of the brands and leaned into the antechamber without crossing the threshold. Harald sometimes bristled a bit at the big man's habit of acting without orders, but he had learned you couldn't have men who could think for themselves and expect them to be blindly obedient.

"No footprints here either," said Kharrn.

Kharrn stepped into the chamber. Harald took the other torch and followed him in. He gritted his teeth as he surveyed the damage wrought on the Varangians. They had literally been torn limb from limb, and now that he was closer, Harald could see what looked like the marks of claws on one of the torsos. Had an animal done this thing?

Kharrn said, "There are only three men in the room."

"Someone escaped, you think?"

Kharrn said, "Not through the door. Also, there is an extra forearm. Whoever isn't here didn't leave whole."

Kharrn walked around the room, his feet squelching in the thickening blood. He played the light from the torch along the floor. As always, Harald was amazed by the big man. He was a walking contradiction. At seven feet tall, with his scarred countenance, anyone would think Kharrn a simple brute, but Harald had seen the intelligence that lived behind the man's cold blue eyes.

And he had heard strange tales. One of the older men, who was getting ready to depart Miklagard when Harald arrived almost nine years earlier, had told him his father had gone raiding with a man named Kharrn, who was also a giant with a scarred face. But that had been decades past. Kharrn couldn't be more than thirty.

"Here," Kharrn said. "A body was dragged to this wall. And the marks go under it."

Harald crouched and looked at the floor. There were indeed signs that something had been dragged through the blood. There was a bloody handprint on the floor as well. He straightened and turned to John, who stood in the doorway. "Could there be a secret door in here?"

"Not that I am aware of," said John.

"And you would be aware," said Harald.

John said, "No one knows every secret of this place. It has been rebuilt so many times, and some of those secrets died with the builders."

"It's the only thing that makes sense," Harald said. "If no one left through the door, there has to be another way out."

John said, "I can tell you for certain that under this palace lies a warren of tunnels, cisterns, passages, and tombs. Some are known and some are lost. There are vast vaults below us that hold many things. Rumors persist that Emperor Theodosius had many tunnels built under the city in centuries past, but I have never seen evidence of them."

"There's a seam here," Kharrn said, running one huge hand along the wall. "Hidden by this piece of molding."

Kharrn placed his torch on the floor, where it hissed in the thin layer of blood. He unsheathed his sword and used it to break the strip of molding away from the wall. Harald noted Kharrn had taken the time to grab the big, double-bladed axe that was his preferred weapon and sling it across his back. Both the sword and the axe were of an unfamiliar design, and both seemed to be made of the same metal or alloy.

Kharrn put the sword's point into the seam and pushed it in. Then he used the heavy blade like a pry bar, pulling it toward him.

"You'll break your sword, man," Harold said.

"Not this sword. Still, it's obvious there's a sliding panel here, but it doesn't want to move."

"Probably bolted from within," John said. "We'll have to..."

Kharrn stepped back and sheathed his sword. He unslung the axe from his back and, grasping the handle in both hands, swung the weapon overhead and struck the wall. Wood shattered, and splinters flew as a great rent was torn in the panel.

The giant struck twice more, and the hidden door collapsed.

Harald began to cough as a thick, horrible stench flowed out of the opening.

"Fuck!" Harald said, stepping back. "It stinks like a thousand open graves in there."

Kharrn said nothing. He picked up his torch and held it inside the opening. "There's a trail of blood leading to the left."

"In we go then," said Harald. "Bjorn, grab that last torch and bring up the rear."

Kharrn stepped through the shattered panel and into the dark. Harald followed. He noted the giant man's shoulders were almost as wide as the tunnel, and he had to bend forward slightly so as not to brush his head on the ceiling.

The tunnel walls were lined with bricks, and Harald saw the floor was worn smooth from the passage of many feet. This tunnel had been well-used at some point. Perhaps it still was.

They followed the trail of blood for several hundred yards. Then Kharrn paused for a moment before stepping over something on the floor. When he was out of the way, Harald saw the still form of one of his men, Sigurd Erlingsson. His left forearm had been severed near the bicep. Blood had pooled around him.

Harald knelt beside Sigurd and was surprised to see the man's eyes open.

"Captain..." Sigurd said in a faint voice.

"Who did this to you, Sigurd?" Harald said. He could see the man didn't have long.

"Shadow...a shadow. We saw figures in the hall. Followed... them to ... anteroom. They were going through the wall." His eyes closed and for a moment. Harald thought the man dead, but then Sigurd said, "We challenged them and then...the shadow appeared. Ripped off my arm and cast me aside as the others attacked. I tried to follow through the wall. I tried..."

And then the man truly was dead. Harald said, "He's with Odin now. And the bastards that killed him went down this stinking tunnel."

"What did he mean about a shadow, do you think?" said Haldor.

"The ravings of a dying man. Now let's go. We'll find the whoresons who did this and gut them all."

Kharrn hefted his axe and led the way down the tunnel. Harald thought the floor began to slant downward, as if they were going deeper into the bowels of the palace. In all the times his duties had brought him within the great palace, Harald had never imagined what lay beneath.

Without warning, the tunnel opened up and they were in a large chamber. They fanned out, their torches revealing the room was a great circle. The ceiling was too high for the torchlight to reach. On the opposite side from where they entered, a great arched doorway led off into deeper darkness. The charnel house reek seemed stronger here.

Their footfalls echoed as they made their way to the center of the chamber. Here they found a small, round table and a wide stone altar. There was no mistaking the sinister purpose of iron rings set into either end of the altar, nor the blood groove carved into the stone. The table held several knives of various sizes. All looked sharp and held traces of blood.

"Over here," Kharrn said. "The origin of that awful stench."

Harald walked over to the big man and saw that Kharrn stood at the edge of a round opening in the floor. Harald looked into the pit. It was filled with human remains. Some of the corpses were whole, but most had been dismembered in some way.

Harald said, "Helvete! What have we walked into, Kharrn?"

"Sacrifices," said Kharrn. "Sacrifices to a dark god."

The giant stepped away from the pit to an alcove in the curved wall. He held his torch aloft, and the guttering light played upon a huge effigy carved in green stone. The entity portrayed had not the vaguest relation to a human being. It was an amorphous blob with many eyes and mouths. Swarms of tentacles sprouted from varying spots on the thing's misshapen body. The surface of the statue was caked with dried blood.

"What is it?" Harald whispered. It hurt his eyes to stare at the thing for too long.

Kharrn said, "It is Nsnigoth. One of the Outer Ones. A god of entropy and chaos."

"I've never heard of such gods."

"Few have in these days. The Outer Ones were gods in the distant past, and Nsnigoth was the worst of the lot. He was known as the devourer and the destroyer. We have found a cult of his worshippers, it seems."

"Captain!" Bjorn called. He came walking up to them and held out a purple cloak. "The clasp on this cloak has the seal of the emperor. I found it near the altar."

Harald said, "A token for a sorcerer's malice. This may explain the emperor's worsening condition. This cult has cursed him."

Kharrn said, "That doesn't seem…"

The big man was cut off by the appearance of three figures from the great arch at the far side of the room. The men were tall and clad in emerald, hooded robes. They walked in perfect unison, one just ahead of the other two, forming a triangle as they crossed the chamber. The lead figure carried a carved staff with a large red jewel embedded in its tip.

Harald held up his sword. "Come no closer. Are you the bastards who killed my men?"

None of the three figures answered. They did begin to speak though, chanting something in a language Harald didn't recognize.

Harald said, "Stop your chattering and answer me, or I'll gut you where you stand."

The lead figure held the staff up, and the jewel began to glow with an eldritch light. Harald felt the hairs on his arms stir. Without warning a bolt of crimson fire erupted from the jewel and flew across the room. It struck Bjorn Larsson and blasted a large hole in his chest. Blood and entrails sizzled as they rained on the floor.

"Thor's death!" Harald said, taking a step back. His heart was hammering in his chest, not just from the immediate danger, but from the sudden and undeniable truth of the reality of dark sorcery.

A second bolt hurtled forward, striking Snorri in the face. The man couldn't even scream as his skull exploded. Harald felt a hot spray of blood on his shoulder.

"Odin protect us," Harald said.

Kharrn began to stalk toward the trio. The lead figure turned toward the big man and lifted the staff again. The robed men continued their chant, and Harald waited for Kharrn's inevitable destruction.

The chamber was again lit by the coruscating red fire. It leaped toward the giant man, who raised his great axe. The fire struck the blades and flared for a moment before vanishing.

That gave the robed men a moment's pause, and in that pause, Kharrn surged forward and brought the axe down on the head of the lead figure. Even as the first man toppled, Kharrn jerked the blade free and swung the axe into the torso of a second figure. This elicited a satisfyingly human scream.

Harald rushed upon the last man and drove his sword deep into his chest. He whipped the blade free as the man fell.

"Gods, Kharrn," Harald said. "That was quick thinking, though I don't know how your axe stopped that mage's spell."

The big man said nothing, so Harald turned to the fallen

figures. He knelt and pulled back the hood from the closest of them. He didn't recognize the revealed face, but there was nothing unusual about it. The man could have been any citizen of Miklagard.

"There have to be far more than these three involved in this," Harald said. "We need to get back to the Orphanotrophos so he can warn the emperor of this plot against him."

"What of Bjorn and Snorri?" Haldor said.

Harald said, "We cannot take the time to take care of them now. They and Sigurd will be honored as they deserve, but now we must hurry out of this devil-spawned pit."

They had been six and now they were four. They had lost two of the torches, so now they hurried up the narrow tunnel with only the brand Kharrn carried to light their way. Harald took rear guard. If anything followed them up out of the dark, it would have to pass him to kill any more of his men.

It seemed an eternity before they saw faint radiance seeping through the hole in the wall. Harald breathed a sigh of relief when he and his companions were all out of the tunnel and back in the anteroom. John was still there, looking even less pleasant than usual.

"We have an urgent message for you to carry to your brother," Harald said, without preamble.

John said, "You may give it to him yourself. He gave me instructions to bring you to him immediately, if and when you returned."

"Then take us to him," Harald said.

They left the chamber and went down the corridor to a smaller receiving room just outside the royal quarters. Harald knew the emperor met with friends here, or had in better days.

They found Emperor Michael looking even worse than the last time Harald had seen him. He reclined on a lounge, clad in a heavy robe. His face and hands were so swollen it seemed to Harald the skin could barely contain what lay beneath. His dark hair was lank, his eyes weak, and his mouth slack.

"Tell me, Captain," Michael said in a raspy voice. "What did you find behind the walls of my palace?"

Harald said, "We followed a long tunnel to a chamber cut into the living stone, your highness. There we fought vile sorcery and found evidence of a plot against your royal person. Sacrifices had been performed there to a statue of the dark god Nsnigoth."

Michael started at the name. "What do you know of Nsnigoth?"

"Only what my soldier, Kharrn there, tells me. He has traveled in many lands and knows many strange things."

Michael's gaze traveled to Kharrn. "You know of the Outer Ones, outlander?"

Kharrn said, "Aye. Of Nsnigoth, Heng, Sethanis, and the others."

Harald said, "We found a cloak we think belonged to you, Highness. Perhaps a token used to afflict you with your current malady."

"Ah, yes," Michael said. "I was wondering where I left that."

All traces of weakness were gone from Michael's voice. He sat up with surprising agility and glared at them with eyes no longer weak or swollen.

"Brother!" John said.

"Yes, you great fool. I am still your brother, but now also an acolyte of my savior Nsnigoth."

"Wha-what do you mean?" John said.

"Nsnigoth's followers didn't curse me. They offered me salvation after our own god had failed me."

"Blasphemy!" John said.

Michael said, "Blasphemy? I traveled to the shrine in Thessalonica. I built churches to your god. I gave money and gifts to every priest and monk in my cursed empire and prayed night and day to your worthless god. And what did I receive in return? Nothing. My sickness worsened."

Michael was standing now, and Harald's stomach roiled as he realized the emperor's feet weren't touching the ground. The air in the room felt wrong, charged like the moments before a thunderstorm.

"Then a priest of Nsnigoth came to me," Michael continued. "They have long maintained a temple beneath our very feet. He offered me an end to my suffering. How else do you think I rose from my sickbed and led my armies against the Bulgars?"

"You are an unclean thing," John said. "A servant of Satan."

Michael said, "There is no Satan, you miserable wretch. And no god in heaven. Your religion is a lie. You pray to nothing and receive nothing. But enough. I am not ready for my plans to be revealed. All of you must be dealt with, as I dealt with those Varangians who discovered my priests."

As Harald watched in fascinated horror, Michael's form became more swollen, and he began to grow larger. His robe ripped open, and his flesh began to flow. Eyes and mouths opened across his expanding body. Writhing tentacles sprouted from his voluminous mass as all traces of humanity were lost and Michael became the image of the hideous god he worshipped.

Harald tried to will himself to flee, but his legs wouldn't respond. The huge, quivering mass that had been Michael surged forward, falling on Ulf Knutsen like a wave of foulness. Ulf screamed, and then the monster's tentacles tore him apart. Blood splattered and fell all around. This, then, was the shadow that had butchered the other Varangians. Haldor turned and fled, but the mass of writhing flesh flowed after him.

"Captain!" Kharrn shouted. Harald broke his paralysis and looked toward the giant. Kharrn held up his sword and then tossed it hilt first. "Your sword won't harm that thing, but this will."

As Harald caught the weapon, he saw Kharrn heft his great axe and run toward the creature. He reached it just as its tentacles wrapped around Haldor. Kharrn swung the axe in a glittering arc and cut a huge tear in the monster's flesh. A hundred fanged mouths screeched in pain and fury. The assault didn't help the unfortunate Haldor. His head went spinning away as a tentacle closed around his neck.

Then the monster turned its attention to Kharrn. Questing tentacles whipped out, and Kharrn severed them as they reached him. One managed to twist around his leg, but he cut through it before it could pull the limb off. As the tentacle fell away, Harald saw Kharrn's breeks had been shredded and there were deep lacerations on his thigh. Now he could see the undersides of the monster's appendages held wicked thorns.

Harald ran toward the monster, and following Kharrn's example, he cut at any of the writhing arms that sought to grasp him. He slashed into the thing's body, sending brackish fluid flying. Kharrn's sword was a marvel. It seemed very light, but it cut like a much heavier blade.

The thing that had been the emperor rolled over, seeking to trap the two men with its bulk. Kharrn slipped aside and cut another great gash in the creature's side. Pale, steaming innards spattered on the tiled floor, and there were tiny things crawling in them.

A flailing knot of tentacles lashed out, striking Kharrn and sending him tumbling. The wounded monster lurched after the big man, with multiple mouths snapping open and closed. Harald reversed the grip on the sword and drove it, point first, deep into the thing's body.

The monster shrieked and spasmed, jerking away from the pain and tearing the sword hilt from Harald's grasp. Kharrn was on his feet again, and he bulled his way past the waving feelers and made three deep cuts, causing the quivering form to burst open and more obscene entrails to flow out. The creature gave a great shudder and stopped moving.

But Kharrn wasn't done. He caught up a torch from a sconce on one wall and tossed it onto the fallen horror. The thing erupted in flames as if it had been coated in oil. A few of the wriggling creatures from within it tried to pull themselves across the floor, but Kharrn stomped them under his boots.

"This isn't possible," John the Orphanotrophos said from behind a heavy chest where he had sought shelter. "How could this be? God wouldn't allow this."

Harald glared at John. "Is that all you can say? Your brother just turned into a fucking obscenity and killed my men."

John didn't answer. He was wandering around the room looking at the carnage. "Michael is dead. How will I explain this?" His eyes were wide with something close to madness.

"If you're thinking of blaming the Varangians, I would think again," said Kharrn.

John said, "Have care how you speak to me, outlander. My reach is still long."

Kharrn said, "So is mine, and there's an axe at the end of it." He let that sink in. "The wisest course would be to tell your inner circle that Michael killed himself in despair and you burned his body to save him the shame."

John said, "Yes. Yes, I can do that. And we'll tell the citizens that Michael took the tonsure. It had long been his stated intention. A few months hence we can announce he died in the service of God. And we'll need a new emperor. Theodora favors her nephew, but we will see about that."

Courtiers, Harald thought. John had grieved for his brother for mere moments before turning his mind to scheming. "See that what remains of my men are gathered for burial."

Harald caught Kharrn's eye and inclined his head toward the door. They left John the Eunuch to his plotting. Behind them, the bloated servant of a dark god was consumed in flame.

The sun was edging the horizon as the two men crossed the courtyard on the way back to the barracks. Harald said, "I think my days in Miklagard grow short, friend Kharrn. Despite your warning to John, I believe an evil time may soon fall on the Varangians under my command."

"I've little doubt of that, Captain," said Kharrn.

"Will you return with me then to Norway? I would value your aide and friendship."

"Let me think on it," Kharrn said.

"Aye, we both have much to think upon. I have learned of darker things than any I have ever dreamed of. How does a man go on, knowing such things exist?"

Kharrn said nothing. Perhaps there was nothing to say.

The God of Rot

James A. Moore

Croaguagh. Toad men was what most people called them, because of the color and texture of their skin, mottled gray and sagging into folds of finely scaled flesh. That and the bulging black eyes of their people.

They were not a pretty species, but they made up for that fact by being brutal in combat. Currently most of the ones he could see were asleep, and Berek thought that was a fine idea. Let them sleep until his blade could offer eternal slumber.

Three days earlier, the toads had attacked a caravan and killed everyone they encountered, taking horses and supplies and a few of the wagons themselves. The bodies they left behind, less the parts they took with them to eat, as some of their kind found humans savory.

Somewhere along the way, they cut off Aluvar Hurst's hands. Berek resented that almost as much as he loathed the bastards for killing his friend in the first place. Aluvar was a weaponsmith and trader. He made good swords, but he traded in specialized weapons and high-end swords—or at least he had until the Croaguagh came along and killed him. He'd been a friend in earlier days and damned near a brother in later years, and Berek intended to see him avenged.

They'd been meeting because Aluvar had a special weapon for Valen. Whatever weapon it might have been, it was stolen along with the rest.

There were a dozen soldiers out looking for the toad men,

but he had been lucky enough to find them first. Berek would make them pay for their actions. He'd see them sent to whatever hell they could find.

The night air was hot and sticky, and though it was not raining, there was a threat of a pending storm. Heavy clouds hid away the stars and the moon alike and gave birth to a strong breeze. Dark smoke tainted the air. Humid as it was, warm as it was, the toad men had four great blazes going to make it even warmer. Berek flicked the long hair away from his broad, angular face as he considered the campfires. Just behind him, Valen looked on wordlessly, following his lead. Aluvar was going to sell Valen a sword worthy of royalty. Valen's cousin was a king and wanted a worthy sword. Valen was to procure it.

It only took Berek a few seconds to tie his hair back with a strip of leather. Loose hair could be caught too easily in combat.

His weapon of choice was a very large dagger, capable of carving through flesh easily. He did not hesitate to use it.

The blade punched through meat and bone and the heavyset guard died quietly, which was exactly what Berek wanted. There were enough of the damned things to fight without announcing themselves. Better to act quickly and quietly while they could. Any silence was unlikely to last very long.

Valen moved as silently as a shadow, a rarity to be sure, and slit a toad's throat with one harsh slash of his blade. The Cro-aguagh shuddered and bled, but never made a sound louder than a wet gasp.

Up ahead of them in the caravan, the leader of this particular group held his swollen arm against his bloated belly and uttered several curses. What was wrong with his arm Berek could not say, but it was wrapped in several layers of thin cloth that had already gone damp with blood.

The toad men cried out in their own tongue, one unfamiliar to

Berek, and he did his best to ignore them, save for any possible cries of alarm. So far there were none.

Valen actually listened to the chatter between the toads as if he could understand it. Maybe he could. He was a man with many talents.

Valen spoke softly and said, "They plan to sell the swords they took."

Berek nodded. "Of course they do. I plan to get them back."

Two of the amphibians turned their way and attacked with unexpected savagery, and both men kept their tongues as they defended themselves. The Croaguagh looked clumsy and use-less, but they were able fighters. Berek defended himself against the powerful attack, blocking a dagger thrust with effort, and pushing his own blade slowly toward the toad man's throat. In the meantime, Valen drove his heels into his enemy's ribcage and did his best to crush the air from the Croaguagh's chest.

The toad man let out a wheezing grunt as Valen got the better of him, and boot heels kicked and strained until bones bent painfully and the ribs beneath them snapped. If the damned thing could have cried out, he surely would have, but instead heit wheezed and then let out a soft squawk as Valen pushed his blade up into his head from below.

Berek hacked into the side of his enemy's neck, very nearly beheading him. That would do the job, he hoped, as they were still on the wrong side of the numbers, and things were already dangerously noisy. Sooner or later, someone would see the damage they'd done and come looking for revenge.

By the time that happened Berek longed to be elsewhere by the time that happened.

Some things, however, are simply not meant to be. The Croaguagh with the swollen arm started screaming in his own language. Great round eyes rolled madly in that bastard's head as he sounded the alarm, and he winced as he moved his swollen arm against his chest, shrieking away to catch the attention of the other toad men.

Berek lunged forward, fully aware that he was too late, and kicked the damned fool in the side of his head hard enough to knock him into a stupor.

"Enough of this, Berek. We're outnumbered,." Valen said.

"Not for long." Berek shook the words away. They made sense, of course. Valen was sensible. Berek was not. He wanted revenge. He wanted the stolen weapons. He wanted blood. He intended to have all three before he was done.

The toads came for them then, six all told, bearing swords that seemed too small for their clumsy hands. They were forged with humans in mind, and that made a difference. The Croaguagh were not much larger than humans, but they were built differently. The short swords seemed more like daggers in their wide hands, with their impossibly long arms.

Valen didn't appear to care. Berek's friend had been raised in the courts of Moridar, trained as a swordsman since his youth. He was very good with the weapons at his disposal, which was doubly a blessing under the circumstances. The first of the toad men nearly impaled himself on Valen's sword as the fighting began.

Valen helped the second of his enemies follow the first one's lead.

Berek stifled a battle cry as the first of his enemies came for him with a deep, resonating bellow. The Croaguagh surged in close, hissing sibilant words, and Berek used his free hand to punch the toad in his face, even as he blocked a blow meant to carve his own face away from his skull.

A moment later, all attempts at swordplay failed, and the two were pummeling each other with several brutal punches. Exactly where things went wrong was uncertain. Berek just knew his blade was gone, and the damned toad was trying to beat him to death.

He reached for one of the stolen swords and was fortunate enough to capture his prize by the hilt. In seconds he was cutting into his enemy, bleeding the toad man even as it tried to return the favor.

Chaos. Madness. Berek fought on and Valen fought beside him, and then, abruptly, the fighting was done. The Croaguagh were dead, and Valen was gasping for breath, even as Berek tried to make sense of what had just happened.

The toads were dead or dying. It had to be enough.

Except the one with the wrapped, wet arm.

He spoke again, invoking a name. "Crumshlicht."

Berek shook his head. He knew that name from somewhere. One of the stories he'd heard as a child. Back when he was younger, his mother had shared tales of many creatures and gods, and Crumshlicht was one of them. A dark member of a dark pantheon, a god among the monsters.

He closed his eyes a moment, trusting in Valen to watch over him as he sorted his memories for the reference.

Most eloquently called the Knight of Decay, it was a dark thing capable of killing with a single touch.

Berek's eyes flew wide. "We must leave here. Now!"

The toad man let out a loud laugh and nodded his head as he looked directly at Berek.

Valen frowned, shook his head, and said, "Where are we going?"

"The toads always call down curses when they lose. This one, he might be a wizard or a priest, but he calls with true power. I can feel it in the air."

"What does he call?" Valen's voice was almost yelling.

Berek looked around with wild eyes, feeling the air pressure around them shift and roil. His skin crawled as he considered the stories. The Knight of Decay sounded like a proper title for a noble beast, and perhaps it was to the toads, but he knew the monster by another name and had seen it once at a distance in his youth—and witnessed what happened to those it touched.

"My mother. She warned us against the toads. They have their own gods, their own rules. We need to be gone, Valen. Before that damned thing is summoned here." The heat of the night paled against the cold he felt pulling at his guts.

"What thing are you talking about? You're acting like we're doomed."

"The toads have several gods, each worse than the one before, but the god they call on for vengeance is the God of Rot, and it lives up to its name."

Berek shook his head, remembering the dark presence from his childhood, the pestilent nightmare he had seen once before, and the trail of dead men it left in its wake. Each man it touched died horribly, rotting away before him even as they cried out for mercy. His uncle, a man called Korien, had let out a scream that became a sigh as his flesh blackened and collapsed in on itself, melting away like snow under a steady downpour of rain and leaving a latticework of bones behind to mark its passing.

There was a reason he hated the toad men. They were hateful, vile things that reveled in the deaths of their enemies.

The bloated toad man with his swollen arm let out a hiss of pain and rolled sideways in his seat, doing his best to sit up despite his obvious discomfort.

Berek, fed up with the Croaguagh and their damnable curses, stabbed out with his new blade and skewered the toad, offering up a quick death.

"Where do we go, Berek?"

"Back to our horses and away from here."

Valen nodded and listened. In most cases, Valen was in charge. He paid Berek for his sword arm and his protection, but there were always exceptions, and this was one of them. Though Valen did not brag or make claims, he was royalty. He had wealth, he had political clout if he chose to use it, and he had a bodyguard, even if said guard was also one of his closest friends.

Berek was to keep the man safe. He was paid handsomely enough to do so.

When Berek told him to move, Valen almost always obeyed. Today was no exception.

How many deaths did it take to summon a death god? Who could possibly say? Long before they saw anything, they felt the gaze of a deity upon them. Berek could not have explained what he sensed any more than a rabbit might explain the jaws of a hungry wolf. All he knew is that he'd been noticed, and he suspected that was enough to make the toad man happy, though the bastard was already dead.

When he was a child, his mother told her tales and warned him and his sisters to beware the swamps and the creatures that dwelled there. Berek had been raised in the mountains of Koldath, where the snows of winter crushed the oppressive heat and drove the vile insects of the marshlands into retreat.

He preferred the cold. The winter winds were honest and clean, even when they were brutal.

The God of Rot spoke, the voice as foul as stagnant waters.

The words meant nothing to him, and Berek shook his head as if he might cast those uttered phrases into the winds.

Valen took the time to actually listen, and then to translate.

"I see no one, but I hear the speech. We are warned away from here."

"Of course we are. The God of Rot is coming."

"Must you say that? It sounds very final." Valen's round face grew pinched.

Berek chose not to answer. He felt the hairs on his body rise like the hackles on a dog and did his best not to cringe.

The darkness chose that moment to show itself. The fires of the toad men, the bodies of the same, everything stood out in stark relief as the shadows seemed to exhale and grow.

"What have you done, Berek?"

Berek ignored the question and pushed back the way they'd come, ready to be as far from where he was as possible.

Valen did not repeat himself, but moved faster now, visibly shaken by the change in atmosphere.

The darkness rose from the heat of the campfires, black smoke sweeping upward to swallow the blazes of the toad men. They did not care. They were dead. Bright fires dulled but did not die as the creature came forth.

Berek, very much alive in that moment, would have preferred to keep the light from the fires. He wanted to see what he faced.

Valen cursed under his breath and drew his sword from its scabbard.

Not far away, the men seeking the Croaguagh moved along in their own caravan, and Berek rode toward them, hoping for strength in numbers, perhaps, or even just for something to distract the god that had been summoned.

"Run, you damned fool. We face a god!" Berek hissed the words as he moved forward.

Valen shook his head. "I don't want to face a god. I want an ale."

"If we get away from the god, I'll buy you three ales. Just move."

Valen followed after him, looking around, seeing nothing but feeling the darkness like a stormfront blowing in hard.

Somehow, they managed to get on their horses and ride hard away from that growing sense of dread. They rode north and west, toward distant Ulluriah and the prospect of safety. They rode into the night without thought, save to get away from the growing, towering darkness of a manifesting god.

Crumshlicht was not a human deity. It was worshiped by toad men, and the toads were direct in what they did and how they did it. The god was meant as a punishment to those who offended the Croaguagh, and the remains they left behind after a slaughter were the offerings they made to that god. The stories Berek had heard were blunt. The god liked his offerings. And they'd killed the followers who gifted the god with many sacrifices.

Several of the men who'd come looking for the toads saw them coming and tried to call out. Perhaps they offered warnings, or they wanted to simply know what drove Berek and Valen to ride so hard, but whatever the case, Berek had no time for them. Instead of conversing, he simply called out, "Run! It follows us!"

To their credit, several of the men listened. They called to others and prepared to retreat as best they could from whatever was coming on the horizon.

Lightning marred the skies to the south and showed them their first glimpse of Crumshlicht. A towering column of darkness. Berek didn't know what he's expected to see, really. Perhaps a toad man in plate mail armor with a great helm, but what he got was a bent, lean shape, crouching, long limbs and a lowered head, looking down, with what seemed to be one burning eye where a face might be. If it was an eye he saw, it was not human in shape or design, but something else entirely, that glowed the same dull red as molten steel cooling on a blacksmith's tongs.

Whatever the case, Berek felt the malignant glare and feared it hunted for him personally.

In truth perhaps it did, but he and Valen were both on the run, and the men and horses between him and the God of Rot seemed distraction enough for the moment. Though he could not risk the time, he did so just the same, and looked over his shoulder to see a few of those very men caught by Crumshlicht and punished for whatever sins he'd committed against the deity of the Croaguagh.

What the god touched, the god destroyed. Armor blackened as if it had not been tended to in years. Spots of rust spread, and in some cases the metal itself ruptured. Flesh withered and ran, great fissures split open healthy meat, and blackened blood coagulated as it fell from new wounds. Muscles atrophied in seconds, leaving behind the rotting bones beneath them, and throughout the process those affected uttered wails of sorrow and damnation as they rotted away in seconds.

Berek thought he remembered how the men he'd witnessed in the past had died, but this? This brought home all the horrors his mind had faded over time, a kindness for a small child. They died now, fear boiling behind their eyes, mingling with panic and pain.

Valen rode close behind him and lashed out with his sword in an effort to stop the god's approach. His sword held well enough; it was a fine sword, after all, and meant to last. But the metal still darkened as if with decades of neglect, and though the blade struck true it caused no damage to the flesh it struck.

It was not mortal flesh. It was the skin of a god. Might as well strike a stone wall for all the damage done.

The god grew like shadows stretched at sunset, reaching with impossible arms until Berek felt certain they would all die. What possible hope could they have if swords did no harm? That single hateful eye glared in his direction.

Still, he had no choice but to defend himself, and so Berek turned as the shadowy grip of Crumshlicht touched his mount and the horse screamed out in agony.

Berek fell as the animal collapsed. The same atrophy that killed men worked as well on beasts, and equine flesh gave way to decay. Flesh blackened and rotted as the horse died in shrieking horror, eyes rolling madly as meat and bone alike melted into putrescence.

The ground beat at him as Berek rolled and smashed into rocks and soil alike. The skin on his left cheek scraped against sandstone and lost the battle, bruising and bleeding. Through sheer desperation, he held onto his sword as he spun and crashed again and again.

Valen came away from his horse more gracefully, somehow managing to keep his footing even as he dismounted the moving animal. Berek's own horse died in a horrid wave, but Valen's ran on, escaping the god in a mad dash.

And Valen attacked the god again, his eyes wild, his face a mask of fear as his sword hacked at the outstretched arm reaching for Berek. No damage was done, but the sword stopped the god from touching Berek as he struggled to his feet.

There was no time to think, only to react. Instinct drove Berek forward and brought his sword into a hard strike against the malformed hand of the god. No one was more surprised than Berek himself when his sword sliced into flesh and drew blood.

It was not a massive wound, but it was there, and noticeable, and it bled. The blood of a god dripped from his blade and hit the ground with an audible hiss. The soil blackened and bubbled where the wound bled down into it. Crumshlicht made a noise then, not a word, but a grunt of surprise. It stared at the wound as if insulted, that baleful single eye glaring hatred at the offending mark as if infuriated by the very notion of flesh daring to let itself be injured.

Berek lashed out again, stepping into the strike as he'd been trained to long ago, and felt metal meet flesh, then felt flesh open with minimal resistance. Blood flowed, and this time around he felt the blade scrape against bone before he pulled back.

Valen struck again, his sword bouncing uselessly off of the same arm Berek had just bled twice.

And Crumshlicht lashed out, sending Valen through the air and bouncing across the ground, stunned and battered if not actually broken.

The two of them attacked a god, like toddlers facing off against a dragon. Valen's best blows did nothing; Berek's strikes drew blood, though he had no idea why. All he knew was that he had to take advantage of the situation while he could, and so he lurched forward and struck again, his sword tip driving into the palm of the toad god's hand. Meat and flesh parted, and blood flowed again, and the god made a fist and captured the weapon.

Berek felt the god's strength, the impossible power of a deity reaching out and crushing down on his weapon, and had the good sense to release the hilt before it was too late.

There seemed nothing remarkable about the blade. It was well balanced, yes. The weapon was not overly ornate, but the blade was good and easy to hold. Berek hadn't had much time to consider anything beyond those facts. He'd been too busy running and fighting for anything else to matter.

Yet for reasons he could not hope to understand, the weapon had cut Crumshlicht when Valen's own excellent weapon had managed not even one scratch.

The darkness that was the god reached out and pulled the blade from its wounded hand before casting it aside.

A few feet away, Valen did his best to recover from the blow a god had delivered, crawling to his hands and knees and groaning, the side of his face reddened and starting to bruise already.

The God of Rot reached for Berek, but the hillsman danced aside, knowing full well he would rot and die like all the rest if the god decided to wither him.

Had he not seen the end results? The foul smelling liquid

remains of several men and horses stank in the air around them. What few bones had not completely rotted away lay festering in the darkness, while to the east it looked as if dawn would soon come their way.

Crumshlicht reached for him again, and Berek retreated, looking around for any possible weapon and settling once more on the sword the god had dropped.

Berek saw the other men who'd hunted for the toads alongside he and Valen. They did not seem at all eager to involve themselves in his situation, and he did not blame them. Like him, they'd seen what the god's touch could do, and they wanted to survive that madness.

Crumshlicht spoke then in its vile language. The words echoed painfully in Berek's ears and rang through his head like a great bell, the noise powerful enough to stagger him. "Come to me, Berek, son of Huldar," he said. How he knew Berek's name was a mystery. The only answer was simply that he was a god and knew things mortals could only guess at. "I shall repay your caresses with my own."

If he could reach the sword, there was a chance, however small, that they could get away. The only obstacle was a god who could kill with a single touch.

But didn't always. He'd touched the men and they had rotted. He'd touched the animals and they decayed, but he'd struck Valen and knocked him half senseless instead of corrupting his flesh. Perhaps it chose whether or not a person died quickly. Perhaps it wanted Berek and Valen to suffer more than one blow before they died. They had deprived Crumshlicht of its followers, after all.

Valen seemed to come from nowhere once again, his sword flashing in the pale firelight of the now distant toad men's fires and the growing light of dawn. The fine blade crashed against the god, and the metal sparked and scraped as it came around four times in hard slashes that surely bruised Valen's palms with each strike. Metal met god and dented again and again, and then Crumshlicht was upon the man, pulling Berek's best friend in close to look at him with his dull, burning eye.

Valen's voice groaned as the god held him in both hands and shook him like a disobedient child.

And Berek did the only thing he could in that moment and lunged for the sword the god had cast aside, the only weapon he'd seen do anything at all to cause the God of Rot any discomfort.

Had he thought the weapon well-balanced? Perhaps it had been, but Crumshlicht's grip had taken that good blade and bent it out of shape as easily as a hammer and anvil on molten steel.

Still, it had an edge and a point, and it would have to do.

Valen grunted and gasped as the god pushed one thumb into his shoulder and broke skin easily, drawing blood.

Berek stepped closer and considered where to strike, knowing he would be lucky to wound the god one last time before surely dying for his efforts.

Valen's grunt became a scream of pain, and Crumshlicht let out a noise as well, that might have been the start of a laugh.

And then Berek stepped forward and jumped, planting his foot on the god's leg as he swung his ruined sword and drove the bent tip of the blade into the one glaring, hateful eye of the God of Rot.

Crumshlicht's head snapped back as he sought to escape the sudden pain of metal on soft flesh. The eye resisted, of course, and perhaps against Valen's sword that would have been enough, but the weapon Berek used was a different story, mangled or not. The tip pushed against that resistance and slid into the new wound it made. The sword sheathed itself in that ruptured eye socket even as glowing red ichor bled from the wound.

Valen was released as the god reached for its wounded eye.

Barely seen even in the surprising rush of burning blood, the god's inhuman features twisted into a carved expression of agony, and Berek had enough time to feel a dull flare of satisfaction before he was knocked aside.

In his life he had been thrown by horses, kicked by a mule, punched by at least a hundred men, and once even pummeled by an ogre. Nothing came close to being struck by a god, even if it were a glancing blow.

The world spun, and Berek closed his eyes, the impact catching him completely by surprise. The whole right side of him seemed to bend in toward the center of his mass, and he was thrown a dozen feet or more before once more smashing into the ground with bone-shaking force.

Crumshlicht staggered back, both hands clawing at the pain where its eye had been. The Knight of Decay, a god in an inhuman pantheon, turned and roared and bled, desperate to escape the pain that surely had to be overwhelming.

Berek looked in that direction and prayed to his own gods that Crumshlicht would leave, would act the part of a beast and try to flee the agony it surely endured.

Glowing red embers bled down that monstrous visage, and the God of Rot turned and staggered aside.

And then Crumshlicht vanished, a scattering of dark clouds in a hurricane breeze. A great wind blew from the area and sent men and horses staggering, cast aside what few tents had been raised by the men, and extinguished the great blazes of the toad men.

In the east, the sun painted the world in shades of red and brought angry color to a dark, dull night.

In the skies, the stars faded away, lost to daybreak, and a calm settled over everything as the last roars of Crumshlicht echoed in the distance.

"Why aren't we dead?" Valen asked as he helped Berek struggle to his feet. Every part of his body hurt, and his ears rang with a high, clear note.

Berek shook his head and thought for several heartbeats before answering, "Because we are luckier than we have any right to be."

"We should definitely be dead." Considering the ruined corpses around them, Berek could not disagree.

Wayfaring Stranger

Steven L. Shrewsbury

A Rogan story

---

*"Once the sword was drawn there was no going
back; for blood called for blood, and vengeance
followed swift on the heels of atrocity."*
-- ROBERT E. HOWARD

"Rogan, look," the youth clad in buckskin clothes whispered.
He pointed at the huge man standing by the stallion. "The
Wayfaring Stranger is going to leave before your father and
the warriors return from the fight."

Rogan, dressed like the other youth who peered from behind
the blacksmith's shop, pulled his arm away. "Don't call him
that, Baden."

Desperation hung in the auburn haired boy's voice as he
hissed, "He showed up to help your father make weapons on
that giant horse. He has to be the Wayfaring Stranger."

"God incarnate? C'mon." Rogan's face wore a sour expression
as he looked at the man atop the horse and then at the distant
mountains of Caucasia. "Ya believe all the tales they tell us
Kelts around the campfire? The Wayfaring Stranger who visits,

tells a chosen smith how to make weapons better, and endows them with spirits?"

Baden asked, "Then who is he?"

Smoky breath emitting from his mouth, Rogan replied, "Maybe his name is Erik, Bjorn, or some common crap. I dunno. Dad said he knows his craft, though."

"But he's taking off this morning before the men return." Baden near to hopped up and down. "With most of the warriors gone on the great hunt around the sea, we are easy pickin's."

To that, Rogan nodded. "That prick up north, Garl, who leads the Hattians, prolly his time to gather up those tribes by him and raid us."

"But why?" Baden wondered.

Rogan shot him a sideways glance. "Settle down. You know the stories and what time of year this is for us all."

"Vernal equinox." Baden swallowed hard. "Near to planting, they need sacrifices for their god, Telipinu, to bless the crops."

Rogan snorted. "Glad we Kelts only do a few deer for that and not people."

"Yeah," Baden agreed.

"Good eatin' after, too. They are damn savages, the Hattians," Rogan named them and spat to his right. "All this for sacrifices to some damn god who isn't real? Piss on Telipinu and his dragon. Wodan curse them all."

The tall man on horseback adjusted his hood and turned his mount about, locking his gaze to Rogan.

Baden, though, pointed away from them and into the open field to the north. "Look! They are on the way back!"

Shaking off Baden's grip again, Rogan did look to see the group of warriors his father had led out against those encroaching on their village. Both boys started to walk from their hiding place, but Rogan alone looked again to the man on horseback. The Stranger was gone.

Once the men from their village had neared the smithy, many climbed off their horses, but Rogan witnessed his father fall off his. Though the big man went quick to his boots, Rogan saw his father, Jarek, sported a crude dressing on his left thigh. Blood seeped out of the bandage. Other warriors, though, dragged a man with them from their mounts and deposited him near the porch of the blacksmith's shop.

This man, bearded and hulking, much like Rogan's sire, rose to all fours, but Jarek jumped on him, like two youths wrestling in a field. As Jarek grasped the man's scalp and punched him in the back of his head, he soon planted a knee in his spine. Rogan understood their struggle as no jape.

Though blood rose from the bandages on Jarek's thigh, he still pinned the outlander commander down.

"How many of you are there?" Jarek demanded, his knee digging into the back of the hulking warrior who also bled from his leg. "I'm bright enough to tell the difference between pickets and an advance patrol."

Rogan watched his father and several warriors of his tribe abusing the soldier they'd captured in that morning's skirmish. He looked north to the edge of the forest, beyond which the battle had taken place, as if he could see more Hattians at the tree line. He couldn't.

"Hundreds," the man choked out under the pressure of Jarek as the huge man struck the back of his head again, then nodded at his fellow tribesman from the Zalpa Sea. Rogan recognized Alder, the leader of their fighters, securing a strap to the left wrist of the pinned man, while another secured a line on the man's right hand.

"Bullshit," Jarek snapped at him and punched the Hattian in his leg wound, causing him to cry out louder. "Your fathers can't screw that well. How many?"

"Five hundred," the man gasped.

Other youths near to Rogan's age moved up behind him to watch as the beating went on.

"Three hundred," the suffering man said as two more of Rogan's tribesman arrived on horseback.

Jarek looked up at them. "Three hundred?"

One of them shook his head. "He's lying."

Again, Jarek dug his knee in deeper and squeezed the bloody wound. "We can do this all day."

The Hattian half laughed. "No you can't. Garl will overrun you by noon."

After Jarek's balled up fist connected with the back of the man's head yet again, he looked up at Rogan.

The youth said nothing and betrayed no emotion to the bearded face of his father.

A half-dozen women in hooded cloaks bound at the waist drew to the scene from around Jarek's blacksmith shop. At the edge of the village of log domiciles, the women had arrived with poultices for the men injured from the morning's fight.

"Near to a hundred," the man choked as those on horseback took up the straps attached to his wrists from opposite directions.

Jarek arose off him and staggered back, unable to stand. One of the women allowed the huge man to use her as a crutch. Not a small woman, Rogan recognized her as the one Jarek had taken for his partner: Truda. Although not his mother, Rogan had known no other than her growing up. The other women his father produced offspring with were not important, to him or his father, or Truda.

"This world will end soon," the Hattian grunted. "The gods will drown us all. It is written on the wind."

Jarek sighed and replied, "I've heard tell the gods will piss on us and drown the world. Sometimes, I wish they'd hurry up."

Jarek raised his meaty arm, cried out, and the horsemen

pulled back at the same time. The Hattian, heaved up to his boots, screamed as the riders bolted and the straps straightened. The young ones gasped as one of the Hattian's arms ripped from the socket and still stretched. A few hid their eyes as the arm elongated, but Rogan stared at the scene. His father glared at him watching and grinned. As one arm came loose, a few of the boys turned and even a few left, but Rogan did not. Flesh rent off and the other horseman proceeded to drag the man away. They could hear his screams for a long time.

Breathing heavy, Jarek waved to the women, saying, "Bring stools and bind us down, form a cripple wall for the berserkers."

Rogan understood what that meant. Those injured this morning would form a defensive wall if the invaders got by the forces Jarek sent against them. Who were the berserkers? His father was about to become one.

Adler said to Jarek, "Shoulda hit him a few more times. I'd rather face fifty than a hundred." All shared a laugh at the jest as the women brought out weapons from the smithy.

"You will lead well," Jarek assured Adler, cursing his bloody leg that Truda wrapped again to try and restrict his blood loss.

"Stay still," she groused at him, slapping his rump hard.

"Bitch, bitch, bitch," Jarek replied as she yanked the tourniquet tighter, causing him to groan and glower at her. He then looked to those assembling for the fight. "Only a dozen warriors and these young'uns?"

Adler nodded. "I like our odds against a hundred of those bastards."

The women in the cloaks undid the waist belts and dropped their coverings. All wore chainmail and armor head to toe. They each took up a spear and a small shield, including Truda.

More boys and girls returned to take up slings, bows, knives and small shields. Rogan went to his father and reached out to touch the massive broadsword his parent held.

Jarek reached behind him and handed him a sledgehammer. Rogan took up the weapon with both hands and grinned. Jarek half smiled. "Handle it well."

"I will."

His father then let go of his weapon and gripped Rogan by the shoulders. Leering into his eyes, the intense face of Jarek near to frozen, then said, "You saw the Wayfaring Stranger, and all you little ones tell his tale?"

"Yes sir."

"Shut your ass," said Jarek, his grip on him tightening. "Wodan in human form, visiting to put spirits into the weapons to make them stronger?"

Rogan blinked, not speaking.

Jarek went on to say, "What if I told you that was all manure, and that was Karl the Large from three tribes over, owing me a favor?"

Again, Rogan remained silent.

Jarek winked at him, but remained intense. "I create these weapons, but it is you I send out to fight. You are the hammer I made, not the weapon you hold." His grip trembled as Jarek instructed, "Be the hammer, not the nail. Strike. You are the armament I forged. I made you in flesh, stronger than the rest. Strike. Show them on the battlefield what Jarek can make that didn't come from a forge. Strike. If you die, go unto the gates of Valhalla and write my name in blood with the prick of that sonofabitch, Garl. Tell Wodan I shall be along presently."

He then released Rogan, pushing him away so hard he almost turned him around.

Rogan didn't turn back in full, as he'd been whipped for not listening to the edict to never do so. However, out of the corner of his eye he saw Jarek recline on the stool, his injured leg out, and take up his sword again. He also saw Truda step near to him, spear in hand, and their eyes meet.

Jarek said, "Come back to me."

Truda looked away and said, "Bitch, bitch, bitch."

Adler led the forces from the village. A striking figure like Jarek, Adler showed no fear in his face or manner.

Baden walked near to Rogan and two dozen others near their age. He said to him, "Adler is a great warrior."

"Yeah," Rogan agreed, looking at the tree line that separated them from the clang of forces on the broad field beyond.

"I'd feel better if your father were leading," one of the girls near Rogan said.

Rogan felt the same way, but said, "Heta, that coward bastard, Garl, attacks when he knows most of the fighters are away from the village."

Baden spoke up to say, "They say Garl has three balls."

Most of the youths looked at Baden, but a few shrugged. They'd heard that, too.

One of the boys laughed and then said, "Not much of a coward with that many balls."

Rogan replied, "That won't help him fight."

Heta quipped, "Might make riding a horse a bother."

As the youths all shared a laugh, they all received scowls from the women and men on horseback. With a slight pause, they went through the tree line and into the open field.

Out of the gap in the forest beyond assembled a prodigious force on horseback. Rogan tried to count them and wagered that the number of a hundred rang close enough to the truth. His hands gripped his sledge as he glanced along their lines. A dozen boys near his age stood shoulder to shoulder with just as many girls, all armed and ready to fight. A few wore pained expressions, but most wouldn't give an inch to the savages from the north. None of the village's dozen women looked afraid, either. Rogan knew each could punch through a wall and kick like a mule.

The distance ran far enough between their opponents, but Rogan could hear laughter. The hilarity from the invaders increased as Truda gave out a guttural roar and the children all ran forward at once.

Laughing still, the hundred on horseback didn't even advance as the children drew closer. The sniggering stopped when twenty five Keltos warriors erupted from the tree line, all armed and shouting for aide from their god.

The breach closed fast as Adler led the men toward the aggressors and the gaggle of children between them. Nearly on top of the Hattians, the children stopped and took a knee. Each girl unslung and drew back a bow, quickly notching and releasing an arrow, then another and another. The boys all pulled out their bolos and threw them the short distance, either tangling a horse's legs or enwrapping a warrior's face.

Into this confusion went Adler's men, striking like madmen with their long lances, knocking many interlopers off their mounts. The Kelts dropped the lances as they passed through the first lines and pulled swords, striking at more Hattian men as they went.

As the girls kept raining arrows on the invaders, the boys moved in, striking targets with their small axes. Rogan joined with his hammer. The horses took it hard as the boys knew to get the animals down so the men would have to fall or fight.

Chaos soon reigned an imposing number on horseback quickly halved and their lines broke.

Several of the Keltos horsemen died after the initial strike, but they did their job. Many abandoned their mounts to cripple the Hattian's horses, knocking them to the unplowed field.

One of these men, a bald brute with a bushy red beard, rolled on the ground near Rogan. Without hesitation, Rogan reared back and dropped the hammer to the man's head. Mouth wide and full of grim teeth, the invader saw it coming as Rogan brained him. The man's skull made a loud pop that made Rogan's joints shiver. His father once joked with his brethren that one gets used to such sounds.

"Not yet today," Rogan said to no one as he waded into the fray, striking and swinging the hammer about. The hammer touched flesh at every turn. *It's hard to miss*, he thought.

The spears of the women struck low on the horse's bellies and often into the men that fell from their saddles. Rogan didn't take much notice to how they fought as he figured they knew what they were doing. By the cries of the trespassers, his theory proved correct.

The child in him wanted to see Adler fight, as the big man had always been so good at it. He did see Adler cut through the warriors, moving toward the man in the rear.

Rogan saw this figure back farther than the rest. He sat atop a great black stallion with a cloak that draped down to the ground. Behind this man, in the forest, stood a thin figure. Around that skinny fellow surged a green light. When that man turned, Rogan swore he sported antlers.

Adler's lance had long since dropped as he rode to confront the one sure to be the Hattian leader, Garl. A bloody sword brought to the ready, Adler rode right at Garl like the proud champion his skills had made him.

As the fight thinned out, Rogan watched and felt panic in his chest.

"It's wrong," the youth hissed as Baden drew near to him.

Adler thundered in and drew back to strike.

Garl's cloak parted and a long cudgel swung up, connecting with Adler's elbow.

Baden and Rogan winced as one when they saw the great swordsman's arm break, bend at an impossible angle, and the sword fall harmlessly to the earth beside Garl's horse. Adler went on past Garl, but his left arm reined in his mount. Adler looked at his broken arm, but turned to face the man in the woods. The boys advanced but stopped as they drew a clearer image of that thin individual.

The emerald glow throbbed brighter behind the reedy man, head truly adorned with two antlers. Rogan's keen eyes thought he saw movement from the man, but had no time to process it as Adler's horse suddenly reared up on two legs and spun. Adler fell from the saddle, landing on his ruined right sword arm. As he cried out, Garl turned his horse about and swung the cudgel once more.

The boys couldn't see it, but they heard the sickening sound that told them Adler's head had been smashed.

Rogan and the boys held back as Adler passed wind. Looking in the woods, Rogan raised his hammer, causing the band of boys hold up from approaching the edge of the forest. They saw the man sporting deer antlers holding a branch up. They could hear him chant.

"Screw him," Rogan barked at the boys, loud enough for Garl on horseback to hear and face him. "I'm not fightin' a wizard."

As Rogan stepped forward, Baden yelped, "But he just killed Adler."

"With me!" Rogan shouted at them, before bellowing, "WODAN!"

From within the helmet, surrounded by a heavy beard, Rogan saw Garl smile. When Rogan ran up to the man on horseback and ducked the swing of the cudgel, Garl no longer smiled. Rogan thought he heard him curse, but the blood pounding in his ears shut all that out as he swung and smashed the horse's front knee with his hammer.

The great horse drew back, up on his hindlegs, bellowing out as the others threw their bolos. His rear legs bound, the horse stumbled as it went back down to all fours, but the damaged leg gave out and the animal pitched over, slamming to the earth.

Garl flew from the back of the horse and swung his cudgel up in defense. More bolos wrapped the weapon, one binding it to his wrist, but that didn't stop Garl from swing out, keeping the boys back.

"Baden!" Rogan barked at his friend and swiped the air with his hammer.

Baden reached to his belt, pulled up his tomahawk, and reared back.

Garl's grin returned as Rogan charged him.

Baden let the tomahawk fly, but the cudgel came up to block it. Rogan went in low and swung at Garl's legs. He planned to ruin Garl's knee, like he'd done to his horse, but the big man had been in battle before. Garl bent away and Rogan missed, swinging through the strike. Rogan oscillated so hard he tumbled at Garl's boots. The warrior gripped the cudgel and raised it up to bring the butt down on Rogan's head. The other boys threw knives and tomahawks, most of which bounced off Garl's leathery armor, but they disturbed his aim. The cudgel dropped, and Rogan felt the weapon slide past his cheek to the earth.

"Damn boy," Garl cursed him.

Rogan curled his legs around the cudgel in the earth and swayed about it, bringing up the hammer to strike. However, Garl's huge fist gripped the head of the hammer. Garl chuckled as he stopped Rogan's attempt, but his humor ceased when Rogan's balled up fist punched him in the crotch.

Garl's body hunched a bit, and he released the hammer's head.

Both hands back on the sledge, Rogan brought it up, slamming it into the beard of the stooped over man, then swinging the handle up on the follow through and hitting Garl's crotch again.

Growling, Garl reached out with one hand at Rogan, while his other tried to grip his groin. He had ahold of Rogan's hair as the youth swung again, this time connecting with Garl's left knee, but only smashing into the metal legging guard. Three of the boys jumped on Garl and made him release Rogan's hair. Garl threw the kids off, but he stumbled, now holding his groin.

Rogan advanced with the hammer, but Garl's right hand came up from his crotch and backhanded the youth's face. Blood spurted from Rogan's nose, and he dropped the hammer. Their eyes met for a moment as Rogan dived at Garl's left leg. Both hands on the metal guard, Rogan wrenched the armor piece free. Garl grabbed Rogan's head again with both hands, but he didn't have time to do much before Rogan drove the metal plate into the exposed flesh of Garl's knee. The big man howled and released him as Rogan twisted the knee guard, blood gouting out. More boys climbed on Garl as he fell at last.

Rogan drew back and then kicked the plate still lodged in Garl's leg.

The big man yelled as the boys surrounded him, all holding a weapon of some sort.

Rogan picked up the sledge and wiped the blood across his face. He then looked at the scarlet fluid on his hand.

Garl grunted, "Kill me."

Baden grinned at Rogan, then reached out to touch the blood on his face. "It looks great."

Laughing, Rogan looked at Garl.

"Kill me!" Garl shouted. "Kill me, you little pukes."

Rogan stood out of arm's reach, holding the hammer with bloody hands. "You're gonna wish we did."

The boys then all started to kick the big man, who reached out and tried to strike them.

Rogan danced about, chose his spot, and nailed Garl in the head with the sledge.

Garl's head wobbled, and he went back down flat, laying still.

The women jogged up, all bearing bloody spears.

Truda smirked at Rogan, but for only a moment. She handed him her spear and picked up one of Garl's legs. Another of the women picked up the other by the boot as the boys and women went to the body of Adler.

Rogan walked with the dragging body of Garl, ready to jab him in the head if he stirred. He glanced back at the forest where the old one they thought a wizard had stood. He could see no one in the woods, but an eerie green glow washed out from amongst the trees.

Rogan watched Truda and Hilde drag Garl by his boots across the harvested plain. The rumpled sod showed the Hattian no kindness as his head smashed into divots time after time.

Baden giggled to Rogan, "They wrapped up the knee you ruined, real good."

"They don't want him to bleed out before they get him back to father."

"Yeah." His face turning ashen, Baden looked back at Garl again and then forward to the smithy, where the chained-down men were being released from their spikes. "He's gonna wish he died."

Although a few of the other women changed places with Hilde in dragging Garl, Rogan's mother soldiered on in her labors the entire trip. When they stopped at last by the men free from their berserker positions, the two women dropped Garl's legs. Rogan half expected Garl to jump up and run, but nothing in him held that ability. Garl made a move to grasp his injured knee, but then his hands clutched his head.

Truda's hands shook, but she balled her fingers into fists. Rogan saw it, but doubted anyone else did. She walked over to his father, who reclined on a small stool, his own injured leg splayed out.

"I think the deer on the spit is ready," he said, a wine skin in his hand.

She snatched the wine skin and put it to her bloody lips. When Truda upended the skin, all those in the area gave out a grunt of approval. She handed the vessel back to him. The left side of his bearded face jerked in a smirk. He licked the blood from the opening and drank as well.

As two of the men helped Rogan's father up to balance on his right leg, one of the women handed him her spear and he used it like a cane. Hopping on his right foot, he waved to the men as they began to lift Garl. Face to face, Garl struggled to keep his eyes open.

"Take him inside and wake him up," Rogan heard his father say as he turned away and struggled to the smithy, though he needed no help to get to the porch.

As the men carried Garl in after him, Rogan followed along, but stopped by the entranceway. Over by the stables, Rogan saw a huge draft horse and the man climbing off.

"Wodan," he whispered as his mouth ran dry. "The Wayfaring Stranger." Rogan nearly grabbed the flask of wine his father had sat on the porch bench, but his fear propelled him within the smithy. His mind raced over why the Stranger had returned. Rogan wanted to tell his father, but once he journeyed through the shop into the large area past the bellows in back, he kept his mouth shut.

Garl sat on the floor, awake and talking. His right arm extended out fully, but lay strapped by cords to Rogan's father's anvil.

"What is it you want to know?" Garl growled.

His father limped past him, waving at a few people to turn up the lanterns to increase the light. Jarek turned around to face Garl and said, "Nothing." As a few figures entered the smithy from the rear door, Garl shouted, "Then what is it you want?"

"For you to die," were the words from Rogan's father, as

he held up a claw hammer in his left hand. However, he held it out and a cloaked figure stepped up to take it from his grip.

"Who is she?" Garl wondered, half laughing at the woman with reddish hair.

"Her? That is Mya, the wife of Adler."

"Who?"

"The big bastard you slew out on the edge of the forest."

Mya walked over to the end of the anvil. She held the claw hammer with two hands, raised it over her head to nearly hit the ceiling, and dropped it down. The flat of the hammer struck Garl's fingers and smashed two at the middle knuckles. He cried out as she held the hammer high again and brought it down. Again, the sound of bones breaking echoed in the room. The men and women encircling the scene tittered.

A smaller version of Mya stepped from the group.

Rogan heard his father say, "That is Syna, the eldest daughter of Adler."

The girl, several years older than Rogan, took the hammer from her mother and repeated the actions. After two shots, screams, and a broken wrist, another girl emerged from the group. This one was a few inches shorter than Syna, but also sported red hair. Rogan knew her and learned to scale fish with her years ago. She took to her task like a champ, hitting Garl more than once.

Rogan turned away and started to leave the area, as he knew Adler had several daughters. He did turn and look back before he left and saw Syna holding up her brother, barely a toddler, to help with a strike.

Rogan and a few of the other young ones left the smithy as the howls continued. A couple of the girls and boys outright ran toward the village while a few lingered. Rogan stepped no farther from the porch of the smithy, eyes closed tight, jumping a little as each blow fell and another scream emitted from the huge Hattian leader. He paused, opening his eyes when his friend ran into him from behind.

Baden looked both ways and stopped in his rushing motion. "I wasn't running away."

"Me either," Rogan muttered.

"Wanna go hunting?"

"Yeah," he told Baden as his eyes focused on the horse a tad larger than the other mounts tethered near the stable. "Go get our stuff."

A gleeful look on his face, Baden jogged toward the village.

Rogan blinked, and a towering figure stood by him. He hadn't noticed the man walk around the smithy. His heart thudded as he recognized the one they had nicknamed the Wayfaring Stranger.

"Your friend was glad to leave." The voice fell out from the hood of the tall man, seeming to come from the depths of a well.

Rogan jumped again as the next howl from within the shop rang out. He looked straight ahead and nodded.

"No shame in going away from such a thing."

Again, Rogan squeezed his eyes shut as another scream bellowed out. His eyes opened, and the Hattian yelled again.

The Wayfaring Stranger still stood near him.

"How long..." Rogan said, words drifting away.

"How long will it go on?" the Stranger asked, also looking off at the pines in the distance.

"No, how long can a man scream like that?"

"As long as it hurts," the Wayfaring Stranger stated.

Rogan peered up at him again. "Why did you come back?"

"I returned for what was mine." From out of the fold of the Stranger's long cloak appeared the sledgehammer Rogan had used in battle. Blood still coated the implement. "Your father doesn't need this hammer. After all, he has you."

Rogan swallowed hard, staring up into the hood, seeing the cragged face and long, ivory-colored beard, but little else.

"Why did they come?" Rogan asked the man. "They came to raid us for sacrifices for their god at harvest? At the behest of that wizard in the woods? To get our weapons? Why?"

"What man could ever know what pleases God? They fall drunk on their own council and desire, so who can say? We can only react and fight, using what our fathers and mothers taught us. What else is life but that?"

"One big assed struggle?"

"I wish I could tell you it was one long trip to the whore-house, but it isn't."

The Wayfaring Stranger walked to his mount and climbed atop him.

Rogan's heart continued to jump as he pondered the fact that the Stranger wasn't there when his father made that speech about him being the hammer. "Perhaps they talked about that before," Rogan said aloud as the Stranger wheeled his great mount about.

As the horse turned, Rogan swore the beast had more than four legs, as many as eight, but the illusion soon faded. He rubbed his eyes as the Stranger gazed back at him, and from within that shrouded cowl Rogan beheld a light glisten, like when one sees a wolf in the night.

However, there were not two eyes that looked down on Rogan, but just a single light.

Rogan turned away and saw one of the wine skins discarded by the warriors. He grabbed it, upended it, and sucked down the last mouthful in the skin. He turned again to look for the figure on the draft horse, but the Wayfaring Stranger had gone.

Tiger Claws and Crocodile Jaws

Rena Mason

Lek ran. Whistling closed in behind her. She darted behind a thick tree and waited, breathing so hard the back of her head struck bark in rhythmic thumps. She gripped a dagger's hilt at her waist. Its owner, Thong Di, flashed before her eyes.

"Go," he mouthed.

After a moment, she recognized the harsh, cadenced shrills as breaths blasting over her dry lips. Nothing left to vomit, bile foam rose and clung to the side of her mouth. Lek hunched over and retched, anticipating pieces of throat and lungs splattering to the ground. Thankfully, they did not.

Maybe in night's dark, under forest cover, she'd pass for a woman and not an army soldier. Lek tore at her bloody uniform and then reworked it on to fit more like a halter and sarong, ignoring miserably the biting slashes across her arms, legs, and face from trees and grasses with blades for leaves. Patches of grated flesh where bark had taken her skin stung on contact with her sweat and touch.

Because she knew how much it would hurt, Lek never slowed her shrill respirations and started off right into the same breakneck speed she'd stopped at. If not, she wouldn't make it home, and she had many days ahead to get back to Rayong. The soldiers chasing her would catch up and apprehend her. Decapitation awaited, or worse, having her body torn apart by the king's elephants. The punishment would amplify a thousandfold when they discovered she wasn't a man—one of them. Fear of humiliation and torment for her family made her push more, go faster, breathe harder, everything inflicting an inhuman intensity to the intolerable physical agony she'd already endured.

But if anyone could outrun the Thai army, Lek could. Her mother had raised her to be strong.

Unfortunately, her mother had also taught her to kowtow—especially if it might improve the family's status. So when word of an opportunity came for Lek to find a good soldier husband in the north near her cousin Kra Tàay's village, her mother encouraged Lek to go.

At a young age, Lek had wanted to join the army. Sent away at ten to learn Lakhon Nai, she became conflicted by her mother's lessons. With Burma always attacking and killing loved ones, Lek wanted to do more than story dancing, even though she loved it. After watching two soldiers perform a match at a local market and seeing the similarities between dancing and fighting, she taught herself the art of the eight limbs some called muay boran and then how to use weapons like a krabi and a kris instead of a krabong because she was too small to hold a sword. Lek would practice all the moves together with a stick and the long, curved knife. She'd even sneak out of dance school, pretending to be a boy, just to fight and hone her skills. After several years, her techniques and even her disguise became near perfect.

A noisy rush of air came at Lek, and she dived off the footpath opposite the sound into a thick cluster of naat. Stuck in the middle of the bushes like a bird in flight, she waited for a soldier's ngao to whiz past, visualizing the bladed staff missing her by mere inches before striking soft ground with a dull clang. A shiver raced over her bones at the thought. The chill wrestled with the burning and aching within her chest, her heart battering away at them both. She knew the current numbness in her legs would soon wake to tingling and then fierce pain. Fleeing barefoot through miles of forest for hours, she struggled to slow it all down and focus on the immediate surroundings.

Sticky leaves scraped against wounds and fresh bare skin, pricking and stinging her from forehead to ankles. Oh, no! Her toes. She moved them freely. The soldiers would come upon a thick bush with feet poking out, obviously unnatural with her soles glowing in the moonlight.

Naat's strong medicinal smell flared her nostrils and irritated her raw throat. Perhaps its healing properties might benefit her injuries. Thousands of needles surrounded the leaves, jabbing her to prevent infection. Her aunties had told her ghosts supposedly didn't like naat either, but it was the fear of capture that led her inside the bush, not spirits. Lek had soldiered long enough to know herself capable of fighting just about anything, even the supernatural if she had to.

Lek stifled a cough as a soft rustle sounded overhead. Hard as she strained her neck and squinted her eyes, the bush's foliage was too dense to make out what had moved there. She prayed it wasn't a python. Everyone knew stories of unfortunate villagers gone missing, maybe even a few bigger in stature than her, being later found dead inside a slow-moving snake with a large bulge in its belly. After all, her nickname meant small, and she'd always taken it to signify she was little enough to be crushed underfoot or swallowed whole.

Maybe fighting came naturally for that reason, but so did the ability to hide. Living alongside men, she needed obscurity to keep her secret. So she kept quiet and worked low jobs under the army's weapons masters: gathering, cleaning, and sharpening. She was happy on occasion to spar when asked.

They'd even used her to train some of the soldiers to fight against smaller targets.

A light tap on her scalp halted her revelry. Then it came again. Rain could aid her current situation but not a downpour, not a monsoon rain. The wet season had barely started. No wind moved through the trees that she could hear or feel, and the moisture accumulating on her head had a strange warmth and thicker consistency than water.

"You guys hear that?" a man's voice shouted nearby.

Lek drew in a slow breath and held it, biting down on her bottom lip, concentrating on shrinking her body even smaller.

"I swear we're being followed," another man said. "Doesn't Nang Mai haunt these woods?"

"Will you two stop it with your nonsense and superstitions? We need to be serious about this mission. The king wants revenge for Thong Di's sword breaking. We could've lost the battle because of those idiots maintaining our weapons."

"No way we would've lost. Thong Di's too good a fighter."

"They're calling him Triumphant Overlord of the Broken Sword now. He's a hero."

Lek considered untangling herself to outrun the three by sprinting away from the footpath and through the forest. She'd double back, split them up, and then take them on one at a time. Escaping a few close calls had given her confidence, but she worried about it being false.

The dripping on her head gathered and rolled through her hair, onto her face, and into her mouth. Well before decamping, she knew the taste of human blood.

A loud thud sounded just to her left. The soldiers ran toward it. Toward her.

"You hear that this time?" a soldier said.

"I doubt anyone got this far," the other soldier said. "We've caught most of them."

"We should at least question the nearby villagers to be sure," the leader said.

"Hey! What's that over there?" the first soldier said.

"Is that a woman's leg?"

Lek closed her eyes and prayed, imagining her feet growing smaller and disappearing.

"Where did it—" the leader said.

"Look. Up there!" the first soldier shouted.

A long scream cut through the air. Lek had never heard a man howl like that before. It sounded like the second soldier but was difficult to tell. Loud continuous thumps shook everything around her. Lek's body sunk deeper into the naat, cutting up her skin. More men's screams reverberated between the ground pounding and moist whacks. Then quiet returned. It was more silent now than before the soldiers came.

Terror replaced the fear of capture and decapitation. Lek struggled, freeing her arms and legs from the naat. Wriggling and shifting limbs this way and that, she lowered her feet to the ground and then stood, forcing the prickly leaves to scrape her up even worse. But short as she was, Lek's head and body remained in the bush. A woman's hand appeared through thinning leaves, reaching toward Lek. Lek instinctively grabbed hold of it. Two gold bangles hung off the wrist and caught the moon's light. She recognized the baubles. They belonged to her cousin, Kra Tàay! Her nickname meant rabbit, and a rabbit lives in the moon, so it was a good sign and just like her cousin to come to the rescue. As Lek pulled Kra Tàay's dainty fingers toward her, nothing resisted Lek's pull. Her cousin's hand didn't stop. It took Lek a moment to understand Kra Tàay's hand was no longer attached to an arm. Lek cried out, remembering the still-damp blood at the corner of her mouth.

Holding onto Kra Tàay's cooling flesh, Lek stepped out of the naat and straight onto pulp that hadn't been there before.

As she cried and whispered a prayer, Lek released her cousin's hand, letting it fall away. It seemed from afar, Lek heard the dull tinkle of Kra Tàay's jewelry. Lek swiped her cousin's blood from the side of her mouth and wondered where the men had gone. Her soles squelched atop the forest floor as she cautiously circled and scanned the area. All their screaming had come to a sudden stop, but what had happened? Lek needed to know they wouldn't give chase before resuming her escape.

Dark pools and shallow mounds too low to be a person struck her as odd and new. They didn't match up to tree shadows. Maybe it had rained after all. Her eyes followed the nearest one up to her toes. She wiggled them in goo, and her next breath stuck at her throat as if she'd swallowed a lychee whole. A wind gust tickled her nose with pungent odors, a stink she knew gathering weapons from the dead after battle. The caught breath erupted from her mouth in a spray of bile foam.

Glossy bone shards came into focus near her feet. She stepped back, making what had taken place somewhat clear. The soldiers. They'd been crushed, almost pulverized. It made little sense. Who had done this? No. No man or even several men were capable of this slaughter. What had done this, then? Up until the time of their demise, filled with screams, she'd heard nothing else but their voices. Moments ago, living, breathing men stood here, fighters she may have known and had interacted with, and now she could scarcely tell they'd ever been men at all.

The soldiers' blood and remains covered the trail, spilling down its sides. Dazed and trembling, Lek staggered over the gore until she could see through the trees and up at the night sky to get her bearings. Deep sorrow squeezed her heart. Staying in her cousin's village no longer a wise idea, she'd have to take the southerly route she dreaded and pray that whatever had killed Kra Tàay and the soldiers had gone.

It was time to run again, but what was once men coated her feet. The soldiers' fear, their screams, and violent deaths might seep inside, stain her soul. Her emotions rose far beyond the disrespect of walking on deceased men. Lek had to wash them off. Now. The horror of her feet never feeling clean again too overwhelming to imagine, panic took over and jolted her to act.

At first Lek tiptoed and then skipped her way out of the carnage, splattering it.

"Don't think of it," she whispered. So she thought of Thong Di's *Go*. Lek kept her line of sight straight ahead and then started off into a jog over the muck, glancing down now and then to avoid the thicker masses that might shoot bone slivers through her soles.

Fleeing once more into the night, her mind worked hard not to think of what stuck to her feet. Her mother's warning about making decisions came to mind. *You should be careful not to escape from a tiger's claws only to step right into the jaws of a crocodile.*

It was a mistake staying close to the path. She knew it now. Her chances would improve if she followed the Salwen River south to the Ping and then onto the Chao Phraya, but of all the cautionary truths and tales her mother had told, the ones about water stuck most, instilling a deep-rooted fear Lek could not purge. Falling into water scared her more than any capture, torture, or death.

After the king had given his orders, Thong Di had sent her a message.

Go.

He'd written just the word on a cloth wound around the small dagger she'd once complimented him on to avoid having to say much else. She patted the kris he'd given her, its wavy blade looked just like moving water, confirming the route choice he might've suggested with the parting gift but avoided writing down.

Lek had met him long before he became a triumphant over-lord of a broken sword and held in the king's highest esteem. They'd first met when he'd requested to spar with her. He'd said he'd wanted to improve his skills on taking down a smaller adversary. Man or woman, her nickname always remained Lek. More soldiers came for similar training after that, and she'd always wondered if Thong Di had initiated his interest to bring her more into the camaraderie of the other soldiers.

A few hours left until sunrise, Lek climbed down the bank of the Salwen, staying close to the edge but wetting her feet. Dirt now encrusted the sticky gore she knew she had to wash, but the thought of a vengeful, pregnant ghost pulling her into the water remained at the forefront of her mind.

Holding her arms out for balance, Lek waded out across flattened rocks, moving her feet across them to scrub grit from her soles. The current ran slower than usual. She disregarded the anomaly with reasoning that the rainy season hadn't yet truly begun. Lek avoided looking down into the dark water, marveling instead at the silver ripples where the current moved past her body and caught stones in the moonlight. Upriver, Lek watched a massive area of shimmer move from one bank to the other before disappearing as if something had submerged. She then rushed at cleansing her body and face, keeping her eyes open for new, sparkly disturbances on the river's surface while holding her breath and squeezing her lips tight.

"Why don't you take your clothes off?" a man said.

Lek squawked, lost her footing, and slipped underwater for a moment. Forcing herself not to think of the taste in her mouth and what it was, she hurried to the safety of the shore.

"Show yourself," she said. "Where are you?"

The man laughed. "Close enough to see you are a beautiful woman," he said.

"Go away and clean your eyes," she shouted in a deep voice. "I don't want to hurt you, but I will if I must."

"Those are big words coming from someone so little."

Lek shook water from her hair, readjusted her clothing, and then headed up the bank. She wanted to put a little distance between her, the river, and the big thing slinking through it. Should the man mocking her be waiting to ambush her, she'd make quick work of him with the dagger.

Standing on the embankment, Lek scoured the water and surrounding area for the man.

Thwack! An explosion of light struck the side of her head. She reached up and winced. Her skin and scalp were mangled. Hot blood ran down her fingers. Before she could scream another blow came. White stars filled her vision. Lek swooned, blinked, and then righted her stance.

"Keep still," the man said.

"What?" Lek's head tilted back as she swayed again, and that's when she saw him. "Krahang!" She dropped into a crouch and kept her eyes on the sky.

"Dammit, you made me miss again. I thought I told you to stop moving."

"Stay away from me you...you, evil..." Lek knew from tales he was a sorcerer, but saying it aloud might make him more powerful.

"You look so much like the woman I killed earlier this evening." He flew past in a blur. This close she heard the flapping of the woven baskets he used for wings. The pestle he rode extended further than a broom. Its bulbous end appeared to be moist. Pink and red meat matted with dark hair clung to it.

"I took my time with her," he said. "Plucked her from a small village near Chiang Mai and then defiled her and tore her to pieces. The king's soldiers couldn't even stop me, although I was surprised they'd come for the nobodies I've taken there. I smashed them to nothingness."

Lek gasped. He'd killed her cousin and the soldiers.

Krahang laughed again and nosedived. She grabbed a piece of broken branch off the ground, pulled the dagger from her waist, and readied herself.

The sorcerer aimed the pestle between his legs at her head. Lek lunged to the side and whipped the branch around, striking his back.

He yowled.

"Only one time, lucky!" he shouted. Then he came around even faster.

As she readjusted her grip on the stick, he accelerated. Lek didn't move fast enough, and the bloody pestle smacked her shoulder, knocking her on her rear. The sorcerer circled with lightning speed and hit the dagger from her hand. It launched through the night sky toward the river below. A splash sounded.

Lek got up and tossed the stick. She'd use the art of the eight limbs and bash his face in, but she needed him closer and on the ground. The pestle came at her legs. Lek push kicked it away, sending Krahang into a midair wobble.

"Almost!" he shouted, straightening his course, and then he flew out of sight.

Two soldiers came from the forest and approached her on the ridge. The tall one pointed at her and yelled, "Don't move!"

"You won't get away with what you've done," the shorter one said. "We found what's left of our comrades back there. At least we think that's them."

"I didn't do that," Lek said. "Haven't you seen who I've been fighting here? Get ready before he attacks again."

"What are you talking about?" the tall soldier said.

The men stood inches away now, eyeing her up and down,

moving in close to inspect the head injuries. "At least our guys didn't go down without a fight."

"You think they did this me?" Lek said. She stood still but continued searching above.

The soldiers scrutinized the surroundings, looking over her head and into the darkness behind her. "I don't see anyone else here. Do you, Yai?"

The tall one shook his head then poked at the fabric wound around her hips. "This looks like a soldier's uniform you're wearing as a sarong."

"You playing tricks?" the shorter soldier said. "It's illegal to steal our uniforms and even more insulting to see it used this way."

"That's right," Yai said. "We should take her in, Khem. Even if she didn't kill the men."

"Good idea," Khem said. "Better than returning empty-handed. I doubt we'll find anymore traitors. No one's that fast or has that kind of stamina. I doubt Thong Di could—"

"Shut up," Lek said. She wanted to pick up on any flapping sounds and didn't care to hear anyone slander the only man who'd ever helped her.

Yai grabbed Lek's arms and Khem bound them together at the wrists with rope while she struggled with them and strained her neck for a clear view of the night sky.

"Listen," she said.

"Enough," Khem said. Then he shot straight up and disappeared.

A faint scream carried away and then cut out.

"Khem!" Yai shouted up into the air.

"I told you," Lek said. "It's Krahang. Now untie me before he comes back."

"But—"

"Do it," she said, struggling against and then slipping free of the untightened bonds. "He killed my cousin and those soldiers on the footpath."

Lek wrapped the rope tight around her forearm and then flexed at the knees, readying her stance.

"If you tune in, you can hear baskets rustling. Try and knock him off the pestle," she said.

Krahang came at them in a whir. Lek push kicked Yai out of the way.

"Wake up, you idiot!" Lek shouted. "You want to die next? He pounded your friends into paste. You want that to hap—"

The pestle rammed her back and knocked her clear to the edge of the embankment. She heard the river below, rolled over, and couldn't believe what she saw.

Krahang was down! Yai stood over him with his fist bloodied and resting at his side.

Lek groaned and got up on her elbows, rolling again to get onto her knees. As she stood up, the pestle flew toward the sorcerer. He jumped onto it, and off they went.

"Stop him!" Lek shouted as she ran to Yai.

Hunched over in front of him to catch her breath and alleviate some of the pain radiating from her back, she noticed Yai frozen and in a daze.

"Oh no, he's put you in some kind of spell." She snapped her fingers in front of his face. "Come out of it. Please."

She heard rustling and spun around but saw nothing.

Then a loud thud, cracking, and popping filled the air as Krahang's pestle dropped directly above Yai, squashing the soldier from the head down. His torso dropped to his ankles, and everything in between splashed out onto Lek and the ground. The pestle struck again and again, pounding Yai into pulp. Lek prayed he felt nothing in his bewitched state.

Blood-soaked and deflated, a sob escaped her lips in a spray of crimson. Not like this, she thought. Then she spat on the ground and stomped her foot.

"Come on then," she shouted to the sky.

Lek got into a low stance and readied her legs and arms. Death before defilement. She refused to be taken alive and without a good fight.

Krahang flew at her with his arms out to grab her, and she countered, clocking his approach. Lek set up her move, locked her eye on the target, and then spun, using her arm in a punch for counterbalance and for added strength. She threw a kick so powered by rage and revenge that when her foot made contact with his ribs, the sorcerer's body sailed through the air. The pestle turned to retrieve its master, but before reaching him, a gilded horn shot up from the river and pierced his back. Krahang shrieked. He shook his fists, kicked his legs, and then called out a spell.

Lek ran to the edge of the embankment.

A Naga, water cascading over, around, and down golden scales of its head, protruded from the dark liquid below. Mesmerized by cinnabar-colored rivulets streaming through shimmering water, Lek's eyes followed the red to something she recognized jutting from the sacred creature's neck.

The kris's hilt.

She gasped for fear she'd injured the snake dragon. Then the pestle whipped around and whacked the back of the Naga's head. Krahang's body shot off the horn and glided through the air upriver. The pestle continued batting the Naga.

"No," Lek shouted. She ran to the other side of the hill, accelerating as she circled back toward the river. Pushing her feet off the edge, Lek dove toward the Naga, aiming for the kris.

As her body smacked against the Naga, she stretched her arm, screaming to make it go farther, kicking her way up as razor-sharp scales sliced her shins. Her fingers reached for and then clutched the hilt of the kris. She pulled herself toward it, lessening her body weight, so she could climb the scales without injury.

The Naga roared and then shook its head to dodge the pestle. Lek went airborne into the night. The dagger's blade came loose of the snake dragon's neck, but she kept a firm grip on its hilt. She heard music as she flew through the air, and so she bowed to her teachers, the Naga, and even Krahang, and then she danced like she had so many times before a match but with Thong Di's kris hard against her palm. All the sensations so unparalleled, she knew it was a good fight. This death would be an honorable one, canceling any fears she'd ever had of disappointing her mother and aunties, or the water and what awaited her there.

Krahang advanced, and as she raised her leg and turned, she outstretched her arm, pointing the dagger toward him. The wavy blade sank into his neck, freeing his head from his body. Lek watched both pieces drop from the sky.

The Naga rose up and opened its maw, catching the sorcerer. The snake dragon then closed its mouth and breathed white fire into itself, making its nostrils and lips glow.

The light so bright, Lek hadn't noticed she'd fallen into the river and looked up from below. She kicked until the surface broke and then took in a deep breath. Thong Di's kris still in her hand, Lek stared at the night sky until it came down and took her.

Warm water rushed over her feet as if nature itself cleaned them in its way of reverence. Lek woke on a familiar riverbank, the sky the color of grapefruit before the sun pierced it, her mother's home a short walk away. Vines and leaves covered her naked body. Both hands were empty.

The Scorpion and the Crow

Aaron Conaway

It is an age of wonder.

Monsters and magic run as commonplace as swords and shields, and the coin of the realm is adventure.

But superstition is its lifeblood.

A babe born into this world imperfect was often cast out as impure, as touched by evil, demonic. Left to the providence of the elements, or, for the immoral, money-minded parents, sold to those with dark intentions.

Such was the fate of the denizens of Tangleknot Cave.

"Orynthesca is bitter today," Tess mumbled, taking care not to nick herself as her pale, nimble fingers sliced blue fungus loose from the cavern wall. A small crow tattoo lived on her left hand, on the web of flesh between her finger and thumb.

Collecting the fungus as well, Mu'dai gave a noncommittal nod. As this was the young girl's typical response, Tess didn't even bother looking for confirmation in the torchlight the two shared.

"Mu'dai…do you ever think about leaving? What you'll do once your days are your own?" Tess wondered to her friend, her sister, without looking up from her work.

Mu'dai paused, holding the blue fungus she'd freed from the wall above their basket, and stared up at Tess. The girl was a mirror image of Mu'dai. Pale-skinned where Mu'dai was dark, sure, and Mu'dai's similarly placed tattoo was a scorpion, not a crow, but it went beyond this. Orynthesca had collected Tess for being born blind in her right eye. Mu'dai wasn't blind, but she had a dark patch of skin—a birthmark in the shape of a handprint—that covered her left eye and ran up her scalp, turning her raven hair stark white in four distinctive streaks. Having only vague recollections of their families before Tangleknot Cave, the two would sometimes pretend to be twins, split at birth.

One soul in two bodies.

Truth be told, Mu'dai never thought about leaving Tangleknot Cave beyond the necessary hunting for food and collection of winter provisions for the cave. This was her life, and she was adept at living it. But, of course, Spyders—what Orynthesca referred to her reclaimed children as—did leave. They aged beyond what the witch found useful and eventually went to make their way into the world.

"Never mind, sister," Tess said, misunderstanding Mu'dai's silence. "I was just—"

"Winky, Mud Eye, snap to," a deep voice bellowed from outside their cavern. "It's showtime. Best not keep the mistress waiting."

A twisted soul hidden under layers of fat, Dorner was Orynthesca's right-hand man and the only other adult to walk the caverns of Tangleknot. He was her eyes and ears outside of the cave, as Orynthesca only left on the rare occasion to collect another Spyder.

Tess gathered up the basket, placing her slender blade inside, while Mu'dai removed their torch from the rocks, and both girls began the trip back to Orynthesca in the Great Hall of the main cavern. They walked past Dorner with their eyes down, as dutiful Spyders learned to do.

"Wait now," Dorner barked, grabbing ahold of Tess's arm. "I must say, Winky, you're growing into quite a looker. Ya know, so long as you keep that freakish eye toward the wall. Hey, now, why don't you hang back?"

Tess's eyes went wide and unfocused yet remained down-turned.

"Only for a few minutes!" Dorner sneered what he seemingly thought was a reassuring smile. The oil from his thin mustache reflected the torchlight. He ran his hand down her arm to the edge of her sheer, dirty dress, pulling at it. "Mistress won't mind. I have something I want to show you."

Mu'dai, who had taken three steps more as Dorner stopped Tess, now turned around.

"Eh, what?" Dorner grunted, sensing Mu'dai's presence and half-turning to look at her behind him. "No, carry on, Mud Eye. You're all spindly arms and legs, next to no curves. Built like a boy, really, wearing trousers and all. You wouldn't appreciate what I've got for our Winky here."

Mu'dai had the torch in one hand and her own slender blade in the other. Opting at that moment for the former, Mu'dai took one step toward Dorner and reached out with the torch.

Smoke began to rise toward the top of the tunnel from where she had lit Dorner on fire.

"Ow!" Dorner spun away from Tess, batting at his shoulder where his singed cloak had begun to flame. "Mule-headed ass!" He swung a free fist toward Mu'dai, who easily dodged. He didn't notice the blade in her other hand as she deftly spun it, prepared to strike. In the chaos, Tess snapped out of her trance.

"When the Widow summons, her Spyders obey," Tess half-shrieked as she grabbed Mu'dai, pushing the pair down the tunnel away from the smoking fat man. Mu'dai initially fought

against her momentum but quickly allowed Tess to take the lead, tucking the small blade into her belt.

"Time's up, girlies! Just ye wait! Once your fates find ye, what ol' Dorner's offerin' won't seem so bad!" Both girls could hear Dorner yelling down the cavern as they quickly made their way through multiple slender, rocky tunnels. Tess suddenly grabbed the torch from Mu'dai and flung it down a separate shaft before leading the two down another.

"What were you thinking?" Tess hissed, pulling them down to a crouch in the pitch black tunnel. "You were going to kill him—I saw it!"

Mu'dai stiffened at the sound of their approaching pursuer, but the dimwitted Dorner fell for Tess's ruse and chased down the shaft housing their forgotten torch. Mu'dai returned to a standing position, jerking free from Tess as she did so.

"I'll thank you not to read my fate, *sister*," Mu'dai huffed before continuing down the darkened cavern.

"You know I don't have that kind of control," Tess said, then lowered her voice. "I can't help that—"

To my sanctum, at once!

The voice itched, echoing in the minds of both girls in a harsh cacophony of intelligible whispers—its message stretching beyond the capacity of either girl's senses to perceive anything else.

When the Widow of Tangleknot Cave summoned, her Spyders obeyed.

An acrid scent carried within faint wisps of smoke began to emerge, as if fog from the rock walls, as the Spyders filed through the tunnels toward the central cavern of Tangleknot. The smell haunted them, only growing worse—the stench more pungent and the smoke denser—as they neared their mistress.

Mu'dai and Tess saw they were the last to arrive as they entered the gigantic cavern serving as the Great Hall of Tangleknot. Oil-filled braziers burned along the walls, lighting the scene in heat and flame. Orynthesca stood on a small dais carved from a massive stone in the hall's center. Her tall, thin frame stood nude but for her amaranthine orb, ever-present around her neck, and the gilding done by the hands of young children surrounding her. A half-dozen of the younger Spyders, the Hatchlings, covered the witch's body with ornate symbols and patterns as the youngest Spyders, Foundlings, sat in a circle around the dais chanting in hivemind Orynthesca's words.

Brought forth on cosmic winds,

The yawning abyss does near

To claim the cask of darkness,

And banish those who dwell

In the False Lord's light

A slight shiver ran up Mu'dai's back at the sound of the small children, mere toddlers, chanting Chigauroth's prayer. Being part of the hivemind was always harsher for Mu'dai than it had been for the other children when she was their age. All Spyders shared the same childhood—tattooed with various animals as Foundlings, taught to paint the correct symbols as Hatchlings—but unlike the others, Mu'dai's wits always remained during the intonement, as though Mu'dai wandered lost in a dream behind the words, separating herself from her mistress's mind.

Orynthesca never warmed to this fact.

"You Who Are Less stand judged before Chigauroth and found wanting," the witch said, her booming voice echoing throughout the cavern. The Hatchlings, having completed placing the necessary symbols on Orythnesca's body, sat on the cavern floor next to the Foundlings as the toddlers continued to chant quietly. Finally, she turned a tilted head toward Mu'dai and Tess. *Crow. Scorpion. To your places.*

The itchy-brain feeling overcame both girls again as their mistress silently spoke to them directly. As the eldest Spyders, Tess and Mu'dai had places of prestige in the Great Hall during a calling ritual. Essentially, they were to stand upon their prepared sigils at opposite ends of the hall to better channel Orynthesca's power as the witch called upon Chigauroth for enlightenment.

Tonight would be the third time she and Tess stood in the prestigious spaces, and, as far as Mu'dai knew, Chigauroth had never shown enlightenment to their mistress on the other occasions.

In unison born of repeated performances, both girls climbed the stone steps that marked the narrow path up to their positions. Mu'dai's eyes began to wet from the scent and smoke that filled the cavern as she climbed, one heavy foot in front of the other until she reached her mark, the sigil of a scorpion carved into the rock. Then, turning, she found herself still in concert with Tess, with the girls now facing each other. Once everyone was in position, the ceremony began as it always did. The Hatchlings joined the Foundlings' hivemind, chanting:

Brought forth on cosmic winds,

The yawning abyss does near

To claim the cask of darkness,

And banish those who dwell

In the False Lord's light

Then, at a certain point—at the exact moment in every ceremony—Orynthesca screamed, a bloodcurdling shriek echoing along the walls amidst the smoke and stench.

Something was different this time, Mu'dai noticed. There were voices within the echoes of the witch's scream, buried at its edges. Whispered secrets of bloodletting and flesh consumed by moldy time. Mu'dai saw then—painted in the hushed murmurs—visions of discarded Spyders, mere husks, their meat gone bad through holes in the bodies, dashed skulls, and broken bones, all dumped unceremoniously within a secret cavern in Tangleknot.

Not freed upon a wide world at a certain age, but fed to a dark, lonesome cave.

Then this was not a call for enlightenment to some lost elder god across the cosmos, Mu'dai realized, but a dinner bell to feed something ancient closer to home.

And with that realization came a voice she recognized, deep within the cacophony of dark muttering.

Something wrong is going to happen! Tess's voice yelled just behind Mu'dai's consciousness, causing her to jump. **We've got to stop her!**

Mu'dai attempted to shake off the smoke's effects as best she could, but it was hard to do, as high as she was in the cavern. She knelt, gasping for cleaner air. Then, shaking her head free of the horrifying vision, Mu'dai began to crawl down the steps from her stony plinth. Though the thickening smoke made it increasingly difficult, she could see the outline of Tess across the cavern, still standing at her perch.

I ca—move—legs. Tess's voice raced across Mu'dai's brain in broken jumbles, lost amidst the sea of other angrier whispers. The smoke seeping from the cavern walls grew thicker as Mu'dai continued crawling down the stone stairs. The accompanying sour scent became ever stronger. Finally, she tumbled down the last few and stood shakily, untrusting of her own legs.

"Tess?" Mu'dai managed to croak, her throat growing raw from breathing the accursed air. A dark wind kicked up, swirling the thick smoke. She made her way toward her sister, stumbling through the maelstrom as though one blind as the chanting ebbed and flowed in volume over the dark-spirited whispers and bleak portents.

Brought forth on cosmic winds,

The yawning abyss does near

To claim the cask of darkness,

And banish those who dwell

In the False Lord's light

Mu'dai crossed the length of the hall toward Tess's raised position, but as she grew closer to Orynthesca's shrine, her sibling Spyders' chants growing louder in the dark, the witch's arm shot out from the smoke and pulled Mu'dai up off the ground and toward her nightmarish visage. The flesh of Orynthesca's face swirled as one with the smoke whirling around the hall, its features dancing as maiden, mother, and crone in turn. Her eye bulged and sagged with age as her lips pouted pink and beautiful, then jagged slashes wiped the work away as though the details were but done in charcoal on a child's parchment and begun anew.

You, the witch's voice screeched around and through Mu'dai's mind.

Mu'dai flinched, pulling back against Orynthesca's hold, but gained no ground. Then the young girl grasped the knife at her belt and quickly slashed the hand that held her, causing the Widow of Tangleknot Cave to drop her prey. Mu'dai took in then, standing stark against the grimness of the cave, the monstrous new form—or maybe it was her actual shape, Mu'dai quickly wondered—of Orynthesca. Beneath her painted upper torso, with its transforming face and customary arms and hands, was attached the translucent body of a cavern crayfish. Mu'dai nearly met her end as the crayfish's pincers click-clacked at her face, snapping her out of her astonished stare.

"Dorner!" the witch turned her head and yelled, the orb

glowing a deep purple at her neck. "Finish the ritual! We must nourish our Lord!"

Mu'dai slunk into the smoke as the wind and the chanting grew ever louder, sneaking behind a thick stalagmite toward Tess. Her mind's voice was the only clarity Mu'dai could find as she crept.

Tess? she thought, nearly picturing each letter in the name individually for emphasis.

I can't seem...it. Tess's voice was dimming under the madness of the cavern hall. Then, ever so faintly, **Something has me, Mu'dai**.

"No!" Mu'dai stood, and it saved her life as the crayfish claw smashed into the stalagmite she'd been hiding behind, obliterating the stony deposits.

You Who Are Less stand judged before Chigauroth, and I'll drag you to our Lord's stomach myself! The creature that had been Orynthesca bellowed with a force that seemed to shake Mu'dai's brain.

Mu'dai rolled away from the second claw attack, narrowly dodging a seated Spyder— she could no longer tell Foundling from Hatchling as all of the smaller children's eyes had gone white as they continued chanting over the smokey storm.

Brought forth on cosmic winds,
The yawning abyss does near
To claim the cask of darkness,
And banish those who dwell
In the False Lord's light

Sister...hurry, came Tess, her voice now a whisper in Mu'dai's mind.

Mu'dai dove through the smoke, her small knife still in hand, toward where she thought the path to Tess was, feeling the rush of Orynthesca's movements behind her. Luckily, the first stone step was before her. She started the climb, walking sideways with her blade drawn in her right hand—toward Orynthesca's direction—though aware that Dorner, too, might be in the direction she was heading. Mu'dai stepped lightly but quickly up the stone steps, one by one, as they became visible in front of her.

Mu'dai heard a clicking even over the din of the roaring wind within Tangleknot. She thought at first as she made her way forward that it was Orynthesca's crayfish form making its way up the stairs behind her, but the sound came from in front of her.

A deep rumbling belched throughout the cavern as the stone staircase began to tremble underneath Mu'dai. Stumbling about to keep her balance, she knelt, nearly crawling, and continued up the stairs. She placed her small dagger in her mouth to free up both hands, skittering up the carved rock on the tips of her fingers and toes.

Luckily, Mu'dai dared a look back in time to see Orynthesca, unable in her new form to navigate the path after Mu'dai, snap a stalagmite from the ground and fling it up after her prey. Mu'dai rolled, dangling off the edge of the stairs as solid rock shot over where she'd been but a heart's beat before.

Orynthesca roared in frustration as Mu'dai, pulling herself upright, continued after Tess up the stairs. The air grew increasingly thicker with smoke and stench, causing Mu'dai to cough and retch as her stomach heaved. Soon the steps in front of her were no longer visible, yet higher she climbed, dagger back in hand.

"I should have reached Tess by now," Mu'dai noticed.

She cried out with her thoughts again, yet the sound of the wind was the only response. Then, finally, Mu'dai came to Tess's sigil, a crow. It glowed blue-white in the darkening cavern, yet Tess was not there.

"Tess!" she screamed.

Ever so briefly, the smoke parted enough that Mu'dai could make out a space in the wall beyond. An emptiness that had never been there; she would have seen it before. Yet, somehow, a passageway had formed. Mu'dai approached it warily, her dagger pointed into the darkness. At its archway, she met a slimy membrane, thick yet transparent, that gave a subtle resistance before her blade sliced through it. Fresh air rushed past her face as though the tunnel had exhaled. Mu'dai paused to breathe it in, trying not to cough, then wiped tears from her smoke-filled eyes and continued down the tunnel.

"It's a damn shame, is what it is," Dorner huffed as he lit the candles around the altar where Tess's catatonic body lay. After lighting the last candle—it had to be nine to keep her under—the flabby man paused to stare at Tess. His hand slid under his trousers to adjust himself.

"Well, now," he snickered. "Nothing saying she's got to be dressed for the ritual."

Dorner moved closer to Tess's upper body, his belly plopping onto her bare arm as he made to pull her dress down. He slid the worn fabric off each of the sleeping girl's shoulders, changed his mind, then grabbed the large dagger from his belt to cut the dress from her.

"Move away, or I will kill you," Mu'dai's voice came from the darkness behind him.

Dorner slowly turned toward the thin girl, still armed with his dagger. He eyed hers as she stepped into the light.

"You gonna kill me, eh? That's a laugh, that is. What, with that pig sticker?"

"Yes," Mu'dai said, stalking forward.

Dorner paused, licking his lips, and wiped the sweat from his brow with his empty hand.

"Mistress is going to be upset that you're botching the ceremony," he said, licking his lips again.

"Orynthesca isn't here," Mu'dai spoke quietly, yet forcefully. "Move away."

Dorner felt a flash of rage at the insolence of this welp and dove at her, slashing his blade. Mu'dai pivoted out of his reach with ease, expecting such an apparent attack. She responded with two quick slashes, one at his dagger hand and its sister at his face. Dorner's dagger dropped to the ground as he put both hands on the gash on his cheek.

He pulled his hand away, covered in blood.

Bellowing, mad with hatred, Dorner made to tackle Mu'dai but gained no ground as she rolled under his arms. The fat man couldn't stop his formidable girth in time, knocking over two of the candles in his wake.

Mu'dai took the opportunity to check if Tess was alive.

Tess? she thought. **Tess, please wake up.**

Mu'dai looked up just in time to slide out of another one of Dorner's tackles, slashing him across the armpit as he flew by. Three more candles fell.

And then it seemed as though the entire world began to shake.

The quake knocked Mu'dai to the ground, and she lost her dagger. Somehow, Dorner was upon her in the chaos. He pinned her shoulders with his massive, meaty hands and slid them to her neck. His fat tongue shot about his mouth as though trying to escape from the exertion of strangling her.

"Kill you, kill you, kill—"

Suddenly, Dorner's eyes began to cross as his tongue turned thinner. And silver. Blood poured from his mouth, covering Mu'dai in gore as Tess removed his dagger from the back of his head.

"I'm sorry!" Tess squealed as Mu'dai crawled out from under the dead Dorner.

"Don't worry about—" Mu'dai had started to say before Tangleknot shook again, this time deeper and longer.

"Let's get out of here," both girls said, getting to their feet.

Their way was dark and full of screams.

All the braziers had gone out in the Great Hall as Mu'dai led Tess back down the stairs from the hidden altar room. Each girl was armed with a blade, though neither could see it in their hand. Mu'dai didn't know if the wind had died down or if the screams were just that much louder.

Once the girls hit the bottom of the stairs, the rocky cavern floor began to squelch with each step they took.

"This—what is happening?" Tess yelled.

I don't know, Mu'dai thought to her. **But it's getting stickier.**

Then came the familiar click-clack, directionless, from somewhere in the abyss around them.

Before Mu'dai could inform Tess that Orthynesca, the Widow of Tangleknot Cave, was now some sort of hybrid monstrosity, the Great Hall filled with intense light as every brazier exploded with ten-foot flame.

And the source of the screaming then became evident.

Orynthesca haphazardly danced around in her crayfish form, pouncing upon Spyders as she caught them two, three at a time. She was pinning them to the floor and, with the orb pendant held above her head, morphing their flesh into the cavern, spreading them like jelly over toast into individual meat rugs.

"Our Lord must feed," *eat his fill of the unworthy*! she kept on, vacillating between screaming aloud and doing so psychically, all to sounds of children—no longer in hivemind—yet still crying in anguished chorus.

Stop!

For an instant, everyone in the Great Hall froze. It took Mu'dai a moment to realize that Tess had been the cause, and just as she did, another massive quake began to hit.

Tess ran toward the monster that was Orynthesca just as the crayfish Widow lunged toward her, then the entirety of Tangleknot upended.

Mu'dai, along with a handful of other Spyders, slid down the floor—as it turned into a wall—dodging stalagmites the best she could as she fell. Eventually, her hip clipped painfully into a large stone, spinning Mu'dai down and further away from where Tess was grappling Orynthesca but allowing her body to rest in the curve of another stone.

"Our Lord has feasted this day!" Orynthesca screamed in Tess's face as the two played tug-of-war with the purple orb. "And HE HAS RISEN!"

Tess said nothing as she fought for the necklace, her face grim with determination. She'd lost her dagger in the turmoil of the cavern *waking*, so all she could do was claw at the witch's eyes with her free hand as the two danced upon the plinth, pivoting in time with the cavern's rotation. The crayfish's pincers snapped for her legs but only caught Tess's dress's hem for its efforts. Tess noticed the orb briefly as they fought, realizing it had a crayfish inside that matched the tattoo on Orynthesca's hand.

In Tess's lapse in attention, Orynthesca's teeth found her fingers. Tess let out a howl as she lost two, the pinky and ring finger of her left hand, to the Widow's maw.

Mu'dai climbed as fast as she could toward the pair, hurried by her sister's cry.

Foolish girl, Orynthesca's voice snarled in and out of Tess's mind. "I am the Widow of Tangleknot," *possessor of the spherule!* "All will cower when I'm by my Lord Chigauroth's side!"

"It's more like his ribcage!" Mu'dai shouted, diving from behind the pair as they wrestled, landing on Orynthesca's back. She carved her small blade into the wrist of the witch, nearly hacking it off in one go. Tess took the opportunity to wrench the orb free from the Widow's ruined hand.

Upon losing the orb, Orynthesca's face began to sink into itself. Her crayfish form slowly turned into ash.

"M-m-ma-mu" she mouthed as her lower jaw folded into her mouth, her eyes wide in panic.

Mu'dai and Tess each kicked her and watched as her tattered form fell into the depths of her god.

More of the stone cavern turned to flesh as their surroundings shook. Tess held the orb up as she'd seen Orynthesca do. Mu'dai watched as the crayfish inside transformed into the crow tattoo on Tess' mangled hand.

"You're not going to turn into a big crow now that you've got that thing, are you?" Mu'dai worried.

"Gods, I hope not," Tess replied. She was focused hard on something else, though.

"Tess, we've got to get out of here," Mu'dai pleaded.

Tess looked at her sister, her eyes welling with tears. "You're right. Let's go!"

They climbed down, hopping from stalagmite to rocky mound when they could control their exit, sliding at stretches when they couldn't. Finally, Mu'dai saw the light from outside of Tangleknot. She took Tess's hand, and the two slid-fell down what had once been the ceiling to the cave's entrance. Mu'dai looked out at ground that had replaced a horizon.

"We're really inside a standing god," Mu'dai remarked, gobsmacked. "I don't recognize anything about this landscape."

"Chigauroth is teleporting all over the planet," Tess explained. "Until he sleeps, it won't stop."

"It's not far to the ground, though," Mu'dai said, ignoring her. "The fall won't hurt. Much. And we'll figure out where we are. I can hunt anywhere, or we can find work. If there's a city nearby."

Mu'dai, Tess spoke quietly in her mind.

Mu'dai turned, her adrenaline spike growing sour in her veins as she looked into Tess's eyes.

"I can't go," Tess looked down, unable to keep eye contact. "I can put Chigauroth back to sleep with the spherule, but I have to remain here to do so."

Mu'dai reached for the pendant. "Then let me do it. You only got the orb because I carved it from the witch's hand. It should be me."

Tess held the spherule away, looking back to Mu'dai with sad eyes. "It wouldn't work for you. It needs psychic abilities to function, and you've only a bond with mine."

"Then I'm staying, too!" Mu'dai shouted.

"Oh, how I wish you could, sister," Tess cried. She pointed toward the encroaching wave of flesh along the cavern. "But, until he sleeps again, Chigauroth will consume everything that is Tangleknot, inside and out. Everything but the bearer of the spherule. I am the new Widow of Tangleknot Cave."

"I don't care, I—" Mu'dai began, but Tess kicked her square in the chest, knocking her out of the cave entrance some fifteen feet to the ground below. With no air in her lungs, Mu'dai could do naught but cry, gasping, as she looked up into her sister's own tear-strewn face.

People talked for years afterward about the day the mountain range that housed Tangleknot Cave just appeared, towering over the landscape. Its rocky exterior seemed overrun with tattered flesh, and it almost began to walk. Then, with a twitch here and wrinkle there, the entire mountain began to fold in on itself, eating away until it was gone completely.

Mu'dai felt the loss of Tess immediately. She lay in that unknown field for hours after Tangleknot Cave had disappeared, looking into that foreign sky until the stars came out to prove what she knew to be true. Then, she got up and moved forward. Mu'dai replayed her sister's goodbye message in her memory whenever she felt really low until the end of her days.

This is not forever, Mu'dai. Forever does not start until we are together again, however long that might be. I'll survive with your borrowed strength as you will with mine. I don't know where I'll end up or what you'll go through to find that place, but I know we'll be together again. Scorpion and Crow: the sisters who thwarted a rapist, a witch, and a god, all in one day. With naught but daggers.

Wrench and Sorcery

Joe R. Lansdale

When the demon pushed back the garage door with its gooey tentacle, I said to Olo, "Hand me that wrench, the big motherfucker."

They used to call a thing like that a monkey wrench, but all I could think of in the moment was to just call it the big motherfucker. And big it is, and painted blood red. It was hard for Olo to handle. His knees nearly buckled. Course, he was already so low to the ground if he took off his pants his nutsack might drag in the dirt.

Olo gave me the wrench, stepped back as the demon whirled at me, spitting goo and blowing across the floor like a snot wad shot from a cannon.

I said, "Ajax," and the wrench glowed a little, and before I had time to be sure it was all het up with red light and magic, the snot wad came within reach, tentacles writhing. I hit it a good one.

Ajax was het up enough, and frankly I might not have needed its magic. I can still do the basic business with the basic tools, though a bit of magic never hurts, if it's better magic than the magic messing with you.

The cables and hinges in my arm moved with a slight twang of tension. The demon took the hit and glowed and splashed to the concrete floor and melted like a slug in a microwave.

"You ain't lost no Ps and Qs," Olo said. "That was same as the old days, though I think you might have ripped your shirt there. Bicep flex and all."

I laid Ajax on the worktable. "Yep, ripped. I liked this one." And I did. It had my name stitched over the pocket. GREASY ROBERT.

I went ahead and tore the right sleeve off the shirt and tossed it into the barrel stove, let the flames lick it.

I finished up working on the transmission that was set out on the tool table, waiting for Old Bill to show up, way he always did when something odd happened. A snot demon, like the one I wrenched, meant some serious-ass business was coming down, that a deliberate crack in the universe had been opened, right here where I was holed up: Old Earth, 1971. That little demon was like a calling card. Old Bill would want to put me to work, because I owed him either the labor or my soul. It was that way as long as I had the spell on me. And that was my fault.

Anyway, that was just Old Bill sending bad magic to warm me up to the idea, as if I had any choice.

Olo knew how it worked. Short little guy with gyrating apparatus in his head, visible only through his eyes and ears. Had a real heart, though, and it was as big and beautiful as the outdoors. Except when he was helping me kill something. He seemed a little less altruistic then.

About fifteen minutes later, I heard the expected humming of Old Bill's automobile coming up the street. I went and slid the aluminum door wider. It was already cracked where the demon had come in. I only kept it partially open in cold weather so the barrel stove could warm me up, and the dark smoke that leaked from it wouldn't make us miserable, would flow out through the opening like it was coughing up a chimney.

Old Bill's car was a nineteen-twenty-five Rolls Royce Phantom, red as a baboon's ass, now and then belching a black cloud that smelled like dog doo. The clouds it puffed from its tailpipe hung in the air just behind it, flashed a bit of lightning, rumbled some dropped dish thunder, then puffed away.

Olo came outside and stood beside me at the edge of the street.

"This guy always makes me nervous," he said, just before the Rolls stopped in front of the shop.

"He should."

"He make you nervous?"

"Not that I'd admit."

Old Bill stopped a bit abruptly, as he wasn't the universe's best driver. The right-side door opened (British got their left and right mixed up when it comes to roadways), and Old Bill got out, and got out, and got out. He was tall enough to be in two time zones.

He walked around to our side, clicking his hooves, and leaned on his car. He was red-headed with small bronze-colored horns on his noggin. His skin was white as a brand-new Kleenex and he had a thin-lipped mouth with silver and gold grill-work teeth. In his eyes, I could see shiny machinery, gears whirling and tiny pistons pumping. Smoke burped from his ears.

He had something in his hand, and when he un-wadded it, I saw it was a red sweater hat with a white cotton ball on the top. He slipped it on. He had some decorative gold chains around his neck, resting on a bare chest. They sparkled in the morning light. The only top he was wearing was a blood-red vest. He had on a silver cod piece as usual, a large one, and the closest thing he had to pants were super-hairy legs.

"Damn, I forget how cold it is here in February," he said. He opened the car door and pulled out a dark leather duster and flipped it on.

He left the door open, and that's when Motor Dog oozed out, all slippery-wet metal with revolving teeth.

"How are you two?" Old Bill said.

"I was doing all right until you showed up," I said.

"Were you now? Olo, what about you?"

"I'm cool. Hard and happy."

"No need to always send me a little present like that snot demon to let me know you're coming," I said. "Just come on over and save us both some energy."

"Tradition. See you got an empty stall there, Greasy. Be all right I drove my car inside, and we close it up? Maybe you have coffee here."

When he had his car inside, I pulled the sliding aluminum door almost shut, leaving it slightly cracked.

I put some scoops of coffee in the pot, some water, set it on the hot plate. He watched me do this with his grill-work showing. Olo pulled some almost-clean cups out of the cabinet, dumped a dead bug out of one, claimed it for himself. The cup and the bug. He popped the bug into his mouth like a peanut.

Motor Dog lay on the floor with his eyes closed, dreaming of sucking blood and chewing bones.

Old Bill said, "In the future, they'll have these little coffee pods, and they're very nice. Far future, androids will piss coffee in your cup, wheeze cookie turds onto your plate."

"On that future, I can wait," I said.

I poured him some coffee, handed him the cup. He sipped, made a scrunch face. "Damn, man. You aren't supposed to leave your worn underwear in the pot."

"Tell me," I said. "What do you want?"

The machinery in his eyes really began to motivate then. There were pops and crackles and the grillwork on his teeth sparkled bright as a toothpaste commercial.

"You know you owe me, so you can keep your soul intact," he said.

"Worst trade I ever made."

"But you are forever in love with Brighton," he said. "Just what you asked for."

This was true. I pined for her nights, craved her during the day. I saw her face in motor oil, and in my eggs, sunny side up. I saw her everywhere. I could almost taste her when the morning air was sharp, could smell her when flowers bled their smells. All this came Special Delivery, via Old Bill's spells.

"Not exactly what I asked for, and you know it. I am, but she's not. You didn't exactly explain that end of the deal."

"In all fairness, you didn't ask. Had you been trading for horses you'd have gotten a dead one with a transmissible disease."

"Just get on with it."

"You'll like this," Old Bill said, snapping his fingers on fire and licked the flames dead. "Brighton needs rescuing, just like in an old fairy tale. She's way up in a tower, dry of oil and thin of purpose. She merely lies there waiting under glass, like a pastry.

"And how did that happen?"

"Woman like that, machine like that, whoopie ki yay, there's always someone wants to take her away, or imprison or enshrine her. And if you can control her, you might control her magic. That's a big might, but there you have it. Thing is, they got her up for sale. The auction is tomorrow. All them that plan to throw a bid are there with her in a tower so as to watch one another, make sure no one takes away the gal in the night."

"You tell me this now, with so little time to do something about it?"

"Been busy, got others to manipulate."

"You did this," I said. "You set up this auction—if there is one. I know you, you smoke-wheezing asshole. When there's a rift in the dimensions, it's mostly you that tears it. The whole thing is you want my soul, and that's it. You want it because I've scrambled a few plans of yours."

"A few? Don't be so disingenuous. But yeah, I want your soul, and until I get it, I like having you under my thumb, all wrapped up in a pussy-whipped spell."

"But you give me too much credit. I'm not as all-knowing as some might think. I didn't know anything about it until this morning. I was fucking Motor Dog—" Motor Dog lifted his sleepy head and barked "—and a minion rolled in, said, 'They done snapped up Brighton.'"

Then he gave me some details.

"I'll tell you how bad things are at home. The fires burn low in the pit, and the minions sometimes appear before me with flat tires. Who does that, right? Course, that messenger got his shiny ass sent to the crusher. I've lost some clout, Greasy. Among my minions, I think, secretly, underneath all the metal and plastic, four-ply tires, there's an insurgence afoot. Bottom line is as you suspect, though. I like the idea of sending you in at the last moment, wishing you luck, and hoping you have none. Your little oily soul I'd like to have. But you got to die for me to get that. You'd look good fixed up with a motor with tires. I could have you in two or three times a day, depending on my diet, to wipe my ass with scented sandpaper. And little Olo: Greasy loses, so do you. He gets to wipe my ass, but you, you get to lick it."

"That's not very nice," Olo said.

Old Bill eyed Ajax on the bench. "You lose, I not only get your soul, I get Ajax to do my bidding, and of course, I re-collect Brighton to happy up my long and bored nights. Motor Dog is all right, but he's got sharp edges."

Motor Dog barked.

"I don't intend to lose," I said.

"If intentions were a certainty, you wouldn't be in your

current condition, lovesick and low-down and never happy. I send you to rescue her, and if you don't, you get a condo in the smoking pit with a yard full of flames. You do win, then she won't care. You have a kind of dynamite love for her, but she couldn't be bothered to piss on you if you were on fire and stuffed with money."

"Don't fill the smoky condo with broken furniture just yet," I said. "Pack your shit, Olo, we'll be traveling."

We got a travel bag apiece and locked up the garage. From the carport at home, I drove us into the light of the world in a shiny blue and white '57 Chevrolet. It was full of gas and sass, fresh with maintenance, gorged with high performance.

With Olo beside me, little sword strapped to his hip, Ajax the Monkey Wrench between us, coiled ropes and grapples on the back seat with our travel bags, away we went.

Hi-ho.

Shifting into eighth gear, a special set-up for my '57 Chevy, the car clicked and groaned. I could see the horizon melt. I could feel the highway dissolve. There was a sudden gathering of stars, like a mass of sparkling bees. We were spinning like a top, and then an explosion of green light, a looseness in the bowels that required concentration not to loosen too much, then a sensation like my nuts were falling off, and we were there.

"I always hate that part," Olo said.

It was a world of rising silver skyscrapers and golden strip-malls. Cars bright as sunlight, little androids running North, South, East and West, shopping for I knew not what. Motor oil, maybe.

"We been here before," Olo said.

"Several times."

"Oh yeah, this is the place we fought the Jersey Devil, and

you didn't even use that magic wrench. Knocked him ass over teakettle with your fists and an attitude, that's for sure. Later, they found one of his hooves in a ditch."

"I had a good breakfast that morning."

On past the silver towers and the golden mall, we came to a sign that said, IT ALL ENDS HERE.

I drove us out to where the hills eventually swelled into mountains and piled to the clouds, dark and puffy and full of rain.

"You know where you're going, right?" Olo said.

"Mostly. Old Bill gave me directions. He wants me to get there quick so I can get killed quick, then he'll have my soul down there in the fire pit, and Brighton, well, he doesn't care what happens to her. But he will take her magic as always. She owes him with deals of her own."

"I never understood any of this," Olo said.

"Here's the pocket size version. I fell in love with Brighton, a sorceress, and she seemed in love with me. But wasn't. Not for long, if ever. She actually took up with Old Bill. Spells didn't make her do that. Thirst for power did."

"Ouch."

"Yep. After the spell, in the dreams that Old Bill sent me, I could hear them go at it for hours, her hot flesh and his hot machinery at work. It made me sick, which was the idea. I had always been able to steer clear of him. I did what I did freelance, but for the greater good. 'Howdy there, you got a demon in your pantry, got a monster on the porch, got an alligator in the yard? I can take care of that for a small fee.'

"But Brighton ate at me. I was lovesick-bonkers, and you know what? She didn't care that much for me. Greased my rod, had a laugh, and went her way. Comes right down to it, she's mean as a snake. But I couldn't let her go. Not in my head, anyway. Old Bill wanted my soul for years, could never have it. But in a moment, when I was lower than the dirt beneath my feet, he comes to me, driving out of the mist in that red Rolls, me on my front porch sipping coffee, and says through an open window, 'Hey there, buddy. Have I got a deal for you!'"

"He promised eternal love for you and Brighton."

"Nope. He said, 'I can make it so you love Brighton forever, and a true love it will be.' He failed to mention the part where the spell doesn't affect her. I love her, but she doesn't love me, and my love is insane, a runaway train. Reason she's under glass is probably a lie, but it's her, and I got to go. I'm like the organ grinder's monkey, long as it has to do with her. I'm bound to Old Bill, and silly as it is, knowing I'm walking into a simple trap, I can't not do it, because—"

"You have this eternal love thing."

"Yep. Thinking of her my heart beats faster. My common sense wanes. And if I lose at my mission, die, I'm a gone son-of-a-bitch. Sorry Mom, you were alright. But that's how it is."

Up we rolled into the heights of the mountains. When we reached the fog on the slopes, the road narrowed enough to be only three inches wider than the width of our tires. Even with the lights full blast, it was tough going, near impossible. But the impossible is my business. I say this to encourage myself from time to time.

We rose out of the fog to a higher peak, and on that peak rose a tall, white, stone tower with a conical red roof. Within that tower, Brighton, the Bitch-Witch, lay asleep. She should stay there forever, truth be told, because you see, when she wasn't fucking over folk like me, she was messing with the world. Spitting in the cosmic machinery you might say. Rescuing her wouldn't put me in good steads with anyone, not even her.

The land by the tower got wide enough I could park the car. I took hold of my wrench. We got out. Olo with the coiled ropes and grapples around each shoulder. His little sword hung from his scabbard, looked about as effective as a drinking straw against a two-by-four. But I knew Olo's skill with that thing.

We stood beneath the tower, the ground littered with broken blue and white stones, and looked up at the open window. The tower was some distance from where we stood, and there was a bit of distance from the window to the top of the tower.

Before we climbed, though, we surveyed.

We walked around and around the tower. No doors. One more window, higher up than the first, and with a closed shutter.

"It's never easy, is it?" Olo said.

"Nope."

Back beneath the open window. Original plan. Olo handed me a rope and grapple. I won't lie to you, I had to toss that goddamn grapple half a dozen times before it hooked in the window, but as soon as I tried to pull it tight, it popped loose. Four more casts, and I hung it good.

Olo stood with his coiled rope and grapples still on his shoulder, waiting for me to do what I did.

Up I went, hand over hand. Only a monkey could have done it better. I got to the window, threw one leg inside, and took a peek. It was dark in there. I looked down at Olo, and motioned him up.

He took hold of the rope and made the climb better than me. I'd have to give him a raise.

When we were both inside, standing in the dark, I said softly to Ajax, "Light up," and it did. The wrench gave off a red beam that threw light down a long corridor paved with dark stone. The walls bordering it were solid and gray. The air smelled rotten with decay.

Olo said, "I would be alright going back to nineteen seventy-one, finishing up that transmission."

"You can. I can't. You know my score."

Olo didn't bail on me. We went on down the corridor, the stench becoming strong enough to dance with us.

Soon there were baubles in the walls, emeralds, rubies, diamonds, and heads of creatures carved from stone. Olo paused, used the tip of his grapple to snap one of the small rubies free, and dropped it into the bag tied around his waist.

"Look," I said, moving Ajax toward the wall. The spot where the ruby had been was bleeding.

"One more," Olo said.

"No. Move on."

Finally, the corridor widened into a room, and I could see a wide, shadowy hole in the center of the floor, a narrow, slick, stone slab trail built around it. On the far side were stairs that climbed to a higher portion of the tower. From the pit came a stench more powerful than before, strong enough to not only dance with us, but it could call us baby. In the glow from Ajax, I could see fumes wavering in the air like the beginnings of a desert mirage.

Easing around the hole, toward the stairs, there was a rumbling, and then a crackling sound, like something had awakened in a nest of glass.

The smell intensified—to put it mildly. And then, before we could make it to the staircase, a dark form rose from the pit.

Squirm-a-mighty, a snake as thick as twenty men tied together rose out of that pit. It had fangs that made Olo's sword look like a pocketknife. The fangs dripped pea-green poison.

And it struck. Olo jumped. I dodged. The fangs took a chunk out of the stone path, stuck right through it like a dinner knife through bread. When it lifted its head from the strike, a stone slab was stuck through the fangs, and it hung there tight.

In the light of Ajax, I saw the true horror of the thing. Its body was not only thick, it was made up of squirming men and women. Children and assorted sheep and cattle, a dog or two, a cat or four, made up its writing skin. They were all greenly colored, plumped up and tucked full of poison, but alive of sorts. They were like the great snake's scales. When it huffed in and out, they went out and in.

It struck again. I didn't move, even though I was its singular target. I swung the wrench. Let me tell you of the wonder and excitement of Ajax splitting the air, supersonic with a sound barrier boom.

I hit the snake so hard one would expect its ancient ancestors that still had legs to roll over and look for religion. My blow even knocked the slab stuck in its fangs loose. The slab fell silently into the pit.

But that enormous and incredible blow from Ajax didn't stop the snake.

It moved quick. The thing's coils wrapped around me in such a way that Ajax was pinned to my side, me not able to swing it.

The coils tightened. My body knotted. The puss-filled humans in the scales reached out and touched me. One grabbed my ankle. Their hands were as icy as an ice tray in an igloo. Poison dripped from them like a leaky catheter.

The head of the great snake, possibly the Worm Ouroboros itself, dipped down and looked at me. And I kid thee not, I could see the cosmos in those golden reptilian eyes, and the cosmos spun and vibrated, black holes opened and closed, and something unidentifiable moved out of the dark at the back of its eyes and eased toward me. It looked like the Old Bill, minus coat and snow hat.

The mouth opened. It was as if I was looking down a subway tunnel. Goodbye and so long, I thought, and then something struck one of the snake's eyes, and get this, the snake screamed.

It was so loud the human bodies twitched. I could feel the vibration all the way down to the dark bottom of the pit. My dick practically tied itself in a knot.

Olo, that smooth little booger, had tossed the grapple, hung it in the edge of the great snake's eye. And boy, was Ye Ole Reptile mad.

I looked down. Olo yelled a mighty yell and swung on the rope, right past the writing body of the snake, the weight of him pulling at the hooked eye. Olo swung right across the pit to the other side.

The eyes had lost their passenger. Old Bill was no longer visible. The damaged eye was oozing out of the snake's head like hot honey. It dripped along its horrid jaws.

The coils loosened, and I fell.

Having seen too many movies, perhaps, Tarzan on a vine, maybe Robin Hood on a rope, Olo swung back across the pit and grabbed me as I fell.

He was a strong little guy to carry a weight like mine with one arm, considering he could barely lift the wrench. Maybe he just had the right grip and momentum on his side. The swing back was wild, dippy, and up, because the snake was writhing in its death throes.

We made the other side as the snake dropped, and Olo let go of the rope.

I whirled, wrench in hand. I could feel Ajax throb against my palm.

Olo said, "I wee-ed myself a little."

I held the glowing wrench over the pit for light. The snake dropped and dropped, trailing the rope, until it was out of sight. We waited for the sound of contact.

But then, as if powered by a rocket in its ass, it shot back up, one-eyed and pissed off. It screamed again. Its mouth opened wide enough to accommodate a couple of city buses running side by side, and then it struck.

This time I swung Ajax up, catching the snake under its lower, slime-dripping jaw. Hit it so hard a couple of rock slabs slipped off the trail and skidded into the hole. Bodies of humans and a handful of sheep fell loose of the snake. One of its fangs dropped with a clank on the stones between me and Olo.

I hit it again, on the side of the head this time. The wrench sizzled red and blue smoke hissed in the air. The heat from it toasted my eyebrows.

To add to the snake's less than satisfying experience, Olo leaned forward and poked his sword into it, just below its throat—wait, does a snake have a throat?

Whatever the case, the snake did a tight wiggle, and down that reptilian bastard went, shedding poisoned humans and critters as it fell. It was big enough that even though its fall was a great one, way down deep in the Earth, we heard it do a satisfying Jell-O splat at the bottom of the pit.

Olo made with our war cry. Hi-ho!

Up the stairs we went. The snot demons were all along our path, between lit torches stuck in the walls. The stairway had a heartbeat, like a concert of tom-toms.

I smacked about a half dozen snotties with the wrench. Olo stabbed a few.

They weren't up for much. Died easy, died quick were soon gone.

At the top of the stairs was a great round, torchlit room. A variety of massive, precious stones were fixed into the circular wall and glimmered like Christmas lights. There was a window on one side of the room, the shuttered one we had seen from below.

In the center of the room was a dais, and placed over it was a rectangular glass cover. Under the glass was Brighton, a specimen of rare design. She looked ethereal, not quite earthly.

I stood frozen in my tracks. Her beauty, even from that distance stood out. Dark curled hair, her black skin shiny as wet coal, features so divine. She was long and lean and asleep.

Okay, what was the rub? Was the snake and the snotties all there was to it? Break the glass, grab the dame, escape with her before she turned mean?

Not likely.

"Where are the auction folk?" Olo said.

"They never were," I said. "Hitch up your drawers and be ready, Olo."

"I was born ready. Except when I'm sleeping. Sometimes on the toilet or in the act of passionate sex with a plastic love doll I'm not ready, but other than that I'm as alert as a fucking fox."

"Okay," I said. I didn't want to send him further down that path of thought.

We walked all the way to the glass cover, the tower breathing under our feet. Nothing jumped out at us. No one said boo.

Leaning over the glass, I stared, enraptured, at her face. Past memories, soft and loving, warm and sweet, and ultimately false, surged through me. She was my passion, my curse, my soul on ice. She made my knees buckle a bit. I started to cry a little.

"Well, hell," Olo said.

I tapped the glass gently with Ajax. There was an eruption of glass shards that clattered on the floor and rested on Brighton. One stuck into her cheek and made it bleed.

I reached down and tenderly removed the shard.

Brighton's eyes snapped open. So dark, like bottomless pits where snakes like the one we had just slain might dwell.

Brighton's hand grabbed my wrist and twisted Ajax from me. It clanked to the floor, and then, without obvious movement, she was standing up and pushing me back.

She bent down for the wrench and picked it up effortlessly. It might as well have been a walking cane way she handled it; weren't many who could do that. I needed to take it from her, but I knew to do that I would have to kill her. I couldn't do that. The spell had hold of me. But if she hit me with Ajax killed me, my soul was long gone, warm and toasty in a pit of fire.

As suspected, that was what it was about all along. Lure me in so she might take the wrench. That way, Old Bill got soul and wrench and kept Brighton too. He could play with my soul daily like it was a toy. Wind me up, watch me dance.

I backed to the wall, slid along it, slowly stalked by Brighton's gorgeous, almost apparition-like presence. She became more and more solid as she stalked.

I came to the shuttered window, and now she smiled. She knew my situation. I was a like an insect pinned to a board, helpless.

As she came to the window, her smile widened. I waited for a tooth shattering kiss from Ajax. She cocked the wrench. She was so beautiful, desirable. Still, I could sense what she was beneath my love-binding spell. Pure evil with a side of mean. The hair on the back of my neck stood up.

And then a short burst of something small and low to the ground jetted across the room palms extended, hit Brighton, and drove her against the shutter, which snapped open and off like a China plate.

The light leapt in, slightly orange as the sun fell down behind the mountain, and out she went, the wrench flying up in the air.

She just had time to say, "Well, shit."

Ajax clattered to the floor.

Me and Olo looked out the window.

Magic hadn't helped her on the way down. It had happened too quick. She had landed on her cranium and her neck was torqued, her head dangling off of it like a dying sunflower.

She came up on her hands and knees with considerable determination. Her head swung loose.

Olo had recovered Ajax and rested the business end of it on the floor. He leaned on it, grabbed my hand, pulled it to the wrench.

When I touched Ajax, it glowed. Olo leaned out the open window, hoisted the wrench with grunting effort, and dropped it.

Bingo.

There was a puff of blue-white mushroom cloud, a sound like God farting after a good breakfast.

We looked out the window. The mushroom cloud was clearing, and we could see what was left of Brighton.

The wrench had hit her in her twisted head and driven her skull into the dirt. Ajax stood straight up, as the heavy end had stuck into the ground. Around Ajax there were little fragments of busted flesh that vibrated like they were being touched by a hot electric wire. The stony earth became covered in a dark sludge that oozed out of the pieces and dissolved between the flagstones. Little wheels and gears were spread about like robot parade confetti.

Olo looked at me. "Don't kill me, Greasy. I know you love her on account of the spell. But she had to go."

"Shit, spell's over. Killing her...I couldn't do it, but you did it nicely. Me, I feel right as rain now. Feel whole. I could practically dance. Juju love for that bitch was killing me."

And I did feel remarkable. It was like my ass had been uncorked so I could crap her out of me. I felt lighter and brighter.

Before we left, we pried a large number of valuable stones

from the wall. It was more than we could carry. We tossed them out the window with the plan to pick them up from the ground and carry them to the car.

We tossed them, but before we could make the stairs, the tower rumbled.

Then gushes of blood shot from the gaps where the stones had been, flooding the room as if shot from fire hoses.

I grabbed Olo's rope and grapple off his shoulder so hard his arm snapped out and back. I hooked the grapple on the window, grabbed him, and swung out.

Great gouts of blood from the jewels flooded out the window and washed me off the rope. When we hit at the bottom of the tower, the blood was deep, a kind of wet cushion. The fall hurt, but it didn't break us.

We stood up as the blood washed down the hill, carrying the jewels with it. They no longer seemed worth the hassle. We waded around to the other side of the tower.

Blood washed under and against my car, on down and out of sight. The tower trembled and rumbled, and then, like a limp dick, it collapsed. Stones slapped the earth, slid along and over the sides of the hill, some up against the Chevy. There was something else there as well: the tower's red stone heart, and it was still pulsing. A moment later it wasn't. It was, well, as still as stone.

The car was fine. Only had to move a few slabs of rock out of the way so it could go. We grabbed our travel bags, changed clothes, and tossed the blood-soaked ones away. We roared out of there, down from the mountain, through the glowing city with its shiny inhabitants.

I shifted to that eighth gear smooth as a goose shits, and we jumped.

Yellow mist. The Chevy spinning about. A solid road. 1971, rolling on home.

Old Bill was parked at my house, in front of the carport in such a way we couldn't pull my car inside. Old Bill was leaning on the Phantom. Motor Dog was with him, crouched on his haunches, close to his feet.

We got out. I had Ajax clutched tight.

Motor Dog growled.

"Oh, shut up," I said.

Motor Dog closed his eyes and wished me away.

"I never thought about your little bastard killing Brighton," Old Bill said. "I thought she'd have you easy, spell you're under. Thought she'd kill you, give me the wrench, and give me herself, as usual."

"And I thought you thought that," I said.

"Damn, word travels fast," Olo said.

"Magic time," Old Bill said. "Till next time, Greasy."

"There is no next time," I said. "I'm free of your spell, thanks to Olo."

Olo bowed.

"Figured all this guy was, was someone to hold your pecker while you peed."

"He's far more than that. He's a brave and loyal friend."

Olo smiled.

"I'm a do-gooder now, all the way," I said. "No deeds left to fulfill for you, just the ones I want to do. I know how Hercules must have felt when he finished the last of his labors and asked for a beer, maybe a ham sandwich, cut the mustard."

"All right, then." Old Bill's face was lemon-bite sour. He and Motor Dog (one last growl) climbed into the Phantom and were out of there, belching dog-turd clouds, the tires whispering against the driveway as if telling secrets, the sky wadding up around them, and then they were gone, and within a few minutes, the air smelled sweet.

Olo reached in the small bag around his waist pulled out the first ruby he had scratched from the wall. He held it up and smiled, said, "Hi-ho!"

About the Authors

Wile E. Young

Wile E. Young is an author who not only has a price on his head but also specializes in southern themed horror stories, both terrifying and bizarre. His novels include Catfish in the *Cradle* (2019), *The Perfectly Fine House* (2020), and the *Magpie Coffin* (2020). His short stories have been featured in various anthologies including the *Clickers Forever* (2018), *Behind the Mask- Tales From the Id* (2018), *Corporate Cthulhu* (2018) and *And Hell Followed* (2019).

Brian Keene

Brian Keene writes novels, comic books, short stories, and nonfiction. He is the author of over fifty books, mostly in the horror, crime, fantasy, and non-fiction genres. They have been translated into over a dozen different languages and have won numerous awards. The father of two sons and the stepfather to one daughter, Keene lives in rural Pennsylvania with his wife, author Mary SanGiovanni.

Glenn Parris

Glenn Parris writes in the genres of sci-fi, fantasy, and medical mystery. Considered by some an expert in Afrofuturism, he is a self-described lifelong sci-fi nerd. His interest in the topic began as a tween before the term Afrofuturism was even coined.

Josh Roberts

Josh Roberts is a writer who loves comic books, science fiction & fantasy, werewolves, and good bourbon. He will tell you he was raised by wolves, but he actually grew up in Missouri, so same difference, really. He is also essentially a scientist.

Jonathan Maberry

Jonathan Maberry is a New York Times best-seller, five-time Bram Stoker Award-winner, anthology editor, comic book writer, executive producer, magazine feature writer, playwright, and writing teacher/lecturer. He is the editor of *Weird Tales Magazine* and president of the International Association of Media Tie-in Writers. He is the recipient of the Inkpot Award, three Scribe Awards, and was named one of the Today's Top Ten Horror Writers. His books have been sold to more than thirty countries. He writes in several genres including thriller, horror, science fiction, epic fantasy, and mystery; and he writes for adults, middle grade, and young adult.

Hailey Piper

Hailey Piper is the Bram Stoker Award-winning author of several horror books, including *Queen of Teeth, The Worm and His Kings*, and *No Gods for Drowning* which shares its world with her *Swords in the Shadows* story. Her short fiction appears in *Vastarien, Pseudopod, Cosmic Horror Monthly*, and dozens of other publications. She lives with her wife in Maryland, where their occult rituals are secret. Find Hailey at www.haileypiper.com.

Heath Amodio

Heath Amodio is the co-creator and co-writer of *The Heathens* (Aftershock) and the *Croatoan* with Cullen Bunn. He founded the TV and Film production company Hustle & Heart Films with Cullen in 2018, where they've developed and sold three shows so far.

Allison Pang

Allison is the author of the Abby Sinclair UF series, the steampunk fantasy *IronHeart Chronicles* and the graphic novel/webcomic *Fox & Willow*. She has also published several short stories that range from horror to humor to tragically melancholy and she particularly enjoys twisting fairy tales for her own dark purposes. She likes elves, LEGO and LEGO elves. And bacon.

Jonathan Janz

Jonathan Janz is a novelist, screenwriter, and film teacher. His ghost story *The Siren and the Specter* was selected as a Goodreads Choice nominee for Best Horror. Additionally, his novels *Children of the Dark* and *The Dark Game* were chosen by Booklist and Library Journal as Top Ten Horror Books of the Year.

Mary SanGiovanni

Mary SanGiovanni is an award-winning American horror and thriller writer of over a dozen novels, including *The Hollower* trilogy, *Thrall*, *Chaos*, *The Kathy Ryan* series, and others, as well as numerous novellas, short stories, comics, and non-fiction. Her work has been translated internationally. She has a Masters degree in Writing Popular Fiction from Seton Hill University, Pittsburgh, and is currently a member of The Authors Guild, The International Thriller Writers, and Penn Writers. She was a co-host on the popular podcast The Horror Show with Brian Keene and her own podcast-turned-blog on cosmic horror, Cosmic Shenanigans, and is currently a cohost of The Ghost Writers Podcast. She has the distinction of being one of the first women to speak about writing at the CIA Headquarters in Langley, VA, and offers talks and workshops on writing around the country. Born and raised in New Jersey, she currently resides in Pennsylvania.

L.C. Mortimer

L.C. Mortimer loves ghosts, zombies, and monsters. Her work features diverse characters who explore unexpected places and find monsters they didn't plan to meet. Mortimer especially loves any type of horror story that has a mysterious twist. Her latest series, Stay Dead, features the zombie apocalypse and a group of cruise ship survivors. Mortimer lives in Kansas with her family.

Scott Schmidt

Scott Schmidt is a creator of comic books, writer of pulp fiction, reader of westerns, player of retro games and drinker of good beer.

Mike Oliveri

Mike Oliveri is the Bram Stoker Award-winning author of several short stories, novellas, and comics, and he penned the novels *Winter Kill* and *Lie with the Dead*, both part of his The Pack series. His book *Restore from Backup* (co-written with the late J.F. Gonzalez) and its related short, "*Algorithms of the Heart*," were partially inspired by his full-time gig in IT. He opened his own karate dojo in central Illinois in 2019, he enjoys weight lifting, bourbon, and cigars, and he finally got his motorcycle working again.

Stephen Graham Jones

Stephen Graham Jones is the NYT bestselling author of some thirty novels and collections, and there's novellas and comic books in there as well. Most recent are *The Babysitter Lives* and *Earthdivers* and *Don't Fear the Reaper*. Soon are the third *Indian Lake* novel and *I Was a Teenage Slasher*. Stephen lives and teaches in Boulder, Colorado.

James A. Moore

JAMES A. MOORE is a best-selling fantasy and horror author. He has been nominated for the Bram Stoker award four times and won the Shirley Jackson Award with Christopher Golden, for editing The Twisted Book of Shadows anthology. He has written novels for the Aliens franchise, Buffy The Vampire Slayer, and Predator, in addition to writing extensively for the award winning World of Darkness role-playing games and for Marvel Comics. His original fiction includes the *Blood Red* series of vampire novels, the *Serenity Falls Trilogy* with his recurring anti-hero the immortal Jonathan Crowley, the critically acclaimed *Seven Forges* series of fantasy novels and the grimdark *Tides of War* trilogy and, with Charles R. Rutledge, the *Griffin & Price* series of crime-horror novels.

JimmyZ Johnston

JimmyZ Johnston is the writer of comic books such as *Warlock 5*, *The Tick*, and *The Micronauts*. He is also a game designer.

Steven L. Shrewsbury

Award winning author STEVEN L. SHREWSBURY lives and works in Central Illinois. He writes hardcore sword & sorcery, horror and western novels. Twenty of his novels have been published, including *KILLER OF GIANTS, BEYOND NIGHT, BORN OF SWORDS, WITHIN, OVERKILL, PHILISTINE, HELL BILLY, THRALL, HAWG, GODFORSAKEN* and soon, *RECKONING DAY*. His horror/western series includes *LAST MAN SCREAMING, MOJO HAND* and *ALONG COME EVENING*. He has collaborated with Brian Keene on the *BASTARDS S&S* series. A big fan of books, football, history, religion and sports, he tries to seek out brightness in the world, wherever it may hide. He also fights down rumors he is Robert E. Howard reincarnated.

Rena Mason

Rena Mason is an American horror and dark speculative fiction author of Thai-Chinese descent and a three-time winner of the Bram Stoker Award. Her co-written screenplay *RIPPERS* was a 2014 Stage 32 /The Blood List Presents®: The Search for New Blood Screenwriting Contest Quarter-Finalist. She is a member of the Horror Writers Association, Mystery Writers of America, International Thriller Writers, The International Screenwriters Association, Science Fiction & Fantasy Writers of America, and the Public Safety Writers Association. She is a retired operating room RN and currently resides in the Great Lakes State of Michigan.

Aaron Conaway

Aaron Conaway was born and raised in Southwest Missouri, weaving stories out of the dark woods, rolling fields, and lonely country roads to entertain family and friends. Living in Kansas City, Missouri now, Aaron makes up stories more than he eats, eats more than he sleeps, and has been given to frequent a Ferris wheel when occasion permits. Aaron authors urban fantasy in *The Timberhaven Chronicles*, horror in *The Michael Gideon Collection*, and is the creator of *Jan the Vagabond*, a comic book destined for his Wandering Wizard Comics imprint. He is also the co-founder of New Vision Comics Collective, where he writes the *Harrowed Earth* novella series and the anthology comic book *Vision Tales*, drawn by NVCC's co-founder Daniel Moler.

Charles R. Rutledge

Charles R. Rutledge is the author of Dracula's Return, and co-author of three novels in the *Griffin and Price* supernatural suspense series, written with James A. Moore. His short stories have appeared in over thirty anthologies. He owns entirely too many editions of the novel *Dracula*, keeps actual soil from Transylvania on his desk, and is seldom seen in daylight.

Justin C. Key

Justin C. Key is a speculative fiction writer and psychiatrist. His short stories have appeared in *The Magazine of Fantasy & Science Fiction*, *Strange Horizons*, and *Crossed Genres*. He graduated from Clarion West in 2015 and earned his MD from the Icahn School of Medicine at Mount Sinai two years later.

Joe R. Lansdale

Champion Mojo Storyteller Joe R. Lansdale has written novels and stories in many genres, including western, horror, science fiction, mystery, and suspense. He has also written for comics as well as *"Batman: The Animated Series."* As of 2020, he has written 50 novels and published more than 30 short-story collections (maybe 40 by now?!) along with many chapbooks and comic-book adaptations. His stories have won ten Bram Stoker Awards, a British Fantasy Award, an Edgar Award, a World Horror Convention Grand Master Award, a Sugarprize, a Grinzane Cavour Prize for Literature, a Spur Award, and a Raymond Chandler Lifetime Achievement Award. He has been inducted into The Texas Literary Hall of Fame, and several of his novels have been adapted to film.